EMPRESS OF NYTE

With blood comes the memories,
the transformation, and the destruction.

BOOK THREE *of the* NYTE SERIES

ALEXANDRIA CAINLOCKE

Empress of Nyte

With blood comes the memories,
the transformation, and the destruction.

BOOK THREE *of the* NYTE SERIES

This book is a work of fiction. Names, characters, places, and incidents are the product of the author's imagination or are used fictitiously. Any resemblance to actual events, locales, or persons, living or dead, is coincidental.

Copyright © 2025 by Alexandria Cainlocke

Cover Design: Enchanted Ink Publishing
Book Design and Typesetting: Enchanted Ink Publishing

ISBN: 978-1-7352704-6-3 (E-book)
ISBN: 978-1-7352704-7-0 (Paperback)
ISBN: 978-1-7352704-8-7 (Hardcover)

Thank you for your support of the author's rights.

WWW.ALEXANDRIACAINLOCKE.COM

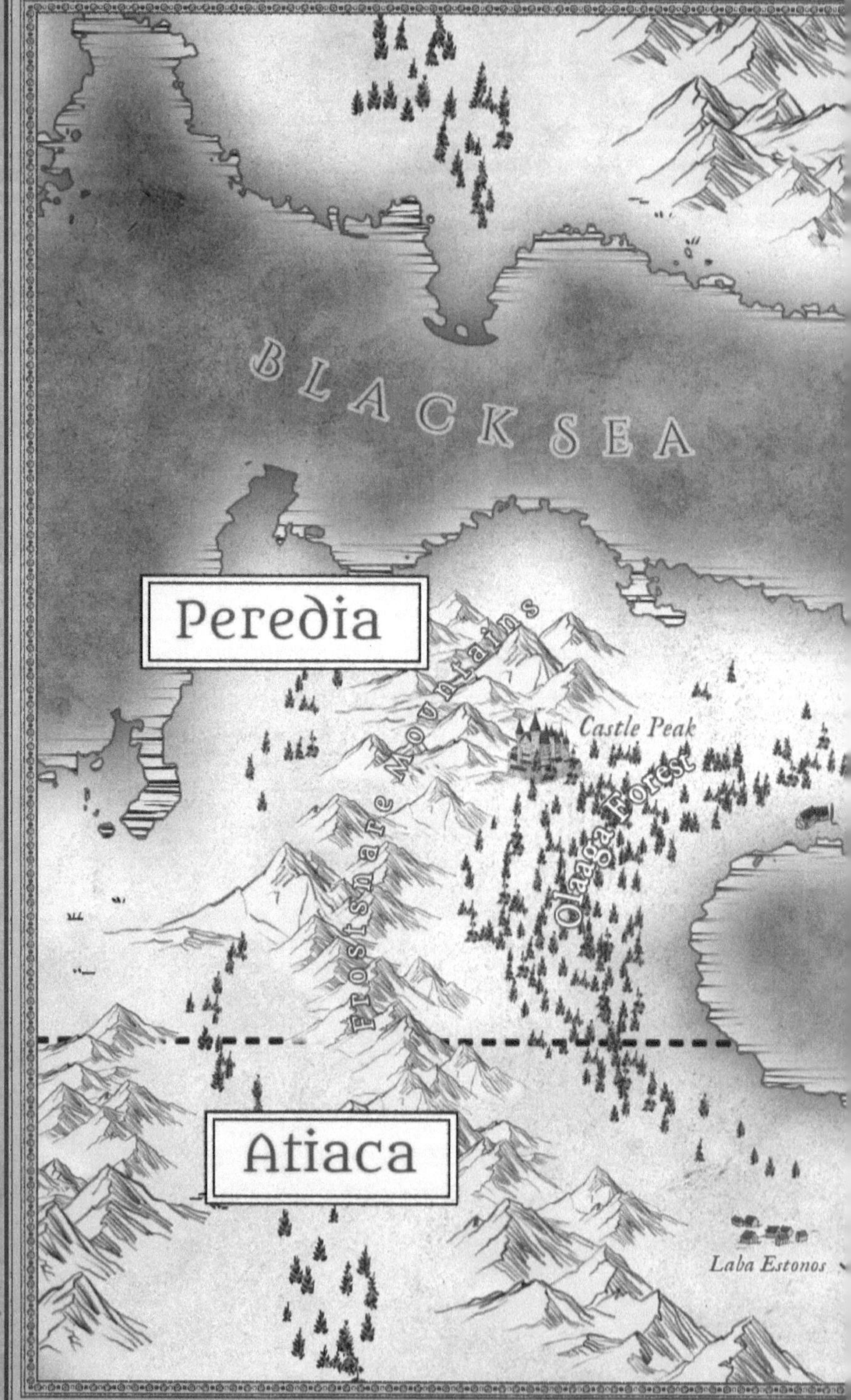

BLACK SEA
Peredia
Atiaca
Frostspare Mountains
Castle Peak
Olaaga Forest
Laba Estonos

Sundise Mouche
Ostin Lon
ARAJI SEA
Kazuumar

PART I

TRIALS AND TRIBULATIONS

CHAPTER 1

Evangeline stared down her prey, its black beady eyes like two polished stones glinting in the pale moonlight. Like the rabbit Evangeline currently stalked, they both faced a death sentence.

Crisp air rolled through the long stalks of grass brushing her bare feet, and the smell of turned soil and blood hit the back of her throat. Winter was shaking off the last of its cold snap, giving way to a bearably cool spring. Here, in the Atiacan empire, spring was like a cloudy summer day in Peredia. But it still didn't chip away the frozen fear that had gripped her for the past two days since arriving here in Barto's family's territory, Laba Estonos, the flattened plains.

In the upcoming days, she'd either be a free woman or on the run again.

Soft cotton rubbed her bare arms and legs as she pressed closer to the moist ground. Her thin shorts and shirt were loose and comfortable but didn't cover nearly as much as the

nightgowns she wore back in Peredia, but she preferred it this way. The rabbit's whiskers twitched, its small gray form tensing to leave. Evangeline inched forward with silent feet, the movement becoming more practiced every time she left Barto's home—dome, as they referred to it here—to hunt. If anyone discovered what she really did on her nightly outings, she would be the one hunted.

Evangeline crouched a decent distance away from the dome to avoid detection from Barto's family—and Ceven, who thought she only went out to clear her mind—but close enough that the boisterous laughs and chatter still carried faintly on the wind. Their carefree nature was wholly foreign to her. Ryker and herself never exchanged laughs, or smiles for that matter. Lani, may she finally be at peace wherever she was, hadn't laughed since Evangeline was adopted by the king's advisor, her smiles as rare as a halfing. Meanwhile, Ceven had acclimated quickly, while Evangeline felt like an outsider.

A whisper shuffled through the trees, and she stilled. The ghost of fingertips grazed the nape of her neck, her heart pounding loudly against the quiet hush of nightfall. She jerked her focus to the shadows at the edge of the grassy opening. She didn't see anything but felt it.

Someone was watching her.

Is it someone from Barto's village? She crouched lower, as if the tall grass could shield her from their eyes. Time crawled until the prickles on the back of her neck lessened, her heart calmed. The feeling of being watched never fully dissipated, but she couldn't afford to linger. She needed to secure her kill and get out of there.

The stalks brushed her calves, her tongue roving over the sharpened canines she had grown more accustomed to, as the rabbit neared. Closer and closer until the rabbit pounced, but she was faster. Its warm blood coated the back of her throat, eyes closing in bliss as it pooled down her insides, filling the hole that had been growing hungrier with each passing day. Her limbs hummed with power, craving to run, jump, spring into action. The shadows that danced across the grassy plains, in the crevices of overarching trees, cast by the moon overhead, zoomed into focus, revealing the nocturnal creatures that scurried in the pockets of darkness. Wet-soaked soil, spilled blood, and the briefest aroma of smoked meat from someone's earlier dinner sharpened her unsated hunger.

The beast that now co-existed—or maybe it had always been there, sleeping silently—roared to life, wanting more, *demanding* more, but she kept her grip on its neck firm, wrapping mental chains around its meaty paws and sharp incisors. Now that she indulged in its hunger for blood, it was stronger than ever before. She wouldn't be defenseless ever again, she wouldn't let it refuse her call like it had back in the throne room of the castle, but she also wouldn't lose control of it like she had in those woods. Blood controlled it, thus controlled her, and she would find that balance. Would learn as much as she could before facing what was to come in the capital city.

Evangeline carried the rabbit's carcass farther away from the dome, burying it in the marshy soil by the creek created from the heavy rains the evening before. Shame pricked her cheeks, as it did after every hunt when the initial euphoric rush of feeding subsided. She told herself these night excur-

sions weren't only to fill the hunger in her belly, but to find answers about who she was, *what* she was, blood being the quickest tool to unlock flashes of her past memories—what Avana had told her they were when these strange hallucinations were first discussed.

Her gaze occasionally strayed to the edges of the trees, the uncomfortable feeling from earlier growing as she made quick work of rinsing her hands and face in the creek, the clear water running red. She was getting better at hiding the evidence.

Droplets ran down her chin, dampening the front of her shirt and cooling her skin. While the air here was thicker than Peredia, the breeze was cool in the evenings and in the shade of the wide palms during the day, her exposed legs prickling at the change in temperature. She didn't care if it meant she could be alone with her thoughts and the crickets that rang throughout night. Nobody to tell her what to do, how to act. No scowls, glares, or pinches. No meetings with Ryker to extort information out of her she didn't have. This was the closest she'd ever had to freedom. What she had always read about in novels, experienced in her daydreams, yearned for.

She would do anything to keep it.

The blood had washed away with the current, the again-clear water lapping at the sides, skimming over varying colors and sizes of pebbles when the familiar scent of old blood and crushed leaves jolted her upright. It wasn't Ceven or anyone she could think of, so why did it make her heart race? The clearing was empty of any Nytes or humans, and the strange scent had vanished as quickly as it had come. Did she imagine it? Was it the stranger she swore she felt watching her?

She turned to flee, her senses on high alert, when blood skated past her feet, the water running red once more, but not from her. Her mind shuttered to a halt. *No, please not another vision.* But when she glanced up, she wished it had been.

A man lay naked farther upstream, the water trailing around his battered body. His marked body. A gut-twisting set of familiar Castanian symbols lined his skin from head to toe, matching the same one that branded Evangeline's right hand. He was clear of any other wounds except his head, which was scabbed with old blood and—Evangeline turned away, swallowing tonight's meal that crawled back up her throat.

I must get closer. I have to make sure it's real.

Evangeline knew the man was dead before she felt for a pulse. The overwhelming smell of blood made her mouth water even as the gruesome sight made her want to vomit at the same time. Dark Castanian marks slithered over the human's gray skin, wringing the life from him like all the other humans that had been kidnapped and marked in the castle's west wing. Like Lani.

She fisted the air and glared at her own mark accusingly—the three triangles, encompassed in a bold circle with indecipherable runes in its center. Raiythlen had told her the truth behind these markings, what they did. How they drained the energy from those branded and channeled it to another. Evangeline still didn't know how she was connected or why this was happening, not that it mattered to the Atiacan empress, who demanded she face trial for crimes she didn't commit. Evangeline no longer denied she was a monster, but she'd sooner kill herself then inflict the same type of suffering Lani had endured on others.

Well, except maybe those who deserved it.

Evangeline left the body where it was, hoping no animals got to it before she alerted the others. Then she paused. It would look suspicious if she was the one to find the body when no one else was around late at night. She was guilty enough as it was. Clenching her jaw, she returned to the broken man and buried him next to the rabbit she'd killed earlier. Sweat beaded her brow as she washed herself again in the stream.

Katya, one of Barto's younger sisters, had showed Evangeline the surrounding patches of wildflowers when she had first arrived here. They grew in wild abandon around the community's domes, sprinkled throughout the patch of grassy plains amidst the overlapping fronds and thick bushes. Evangeline plucked the fragrant flowers hastily, creating a small bouquet of purples, yellows, and oranges. She made a habit of giving the bouquet to Grace, Barto's mother, whenever she returned from these nightly hunts. It gave her an excuse for why she went out in the first place and also helped cover the stench of blood from a Rathan's sensitive nose.

She was just full of secrets nowadays.

The laughter and chatter had quieted, the orange glow of lit candles that had illuminated the windows replaced by dying embers still smoking from the dome's chimney as Evangeline retraced her steps back to Barto's community. Vines slithered from the thicket nearby, climbing across the mud-packed house that resembled more of a handcrafted cave dug out of the ground. Like the rest of the domes that saddled near Barto's family's, only the front door and the flapping curtains covering the make-shift windows—no glass but netted—gave any indication that someone lived here. The rest of the house blended into the ground.

The dome was quiet aside from a few rattling snores as she glided across the clay-packed ground, placing the stack of flowers in the pot of water next to her previous batch. It was odd to have the natural ground be part of a home, unlike the marble floors of Peredia's castle, but it wasn't dirty. It was firm and smooth and muted her steps into her and Ceven's shared room. The wooden door didn't do much to block out Barto and his family's chattering in the morning, but at least it gave them some privacy. More than the other five rooms in the odd-shaped home. Beads or blankets were the closest thing to a door the rest of the house had, which made her believe Barto's family had crafted this wood door specifically for her and Ceven's guest room before their arrival.

The bed indented more on the right side where Ceven usually slept, stray blue and gold feathers sticking to the fabric. He'd mentioned earlier that day he, Barto, and Tarry would camp out farther away from the community to check if anyone had followed them into Atiaca.

She lay down on Ceven's side of the bed, taking in his scent, her fingers teasing the silky smoothness of one of his stray feathers. Even though it was much easier to escape in the night without him here, she missed him dearly.

If Ceven ever found out the truth, found out she wasn't the innocent human girl he'd fallen in love with as a kid, he'd leave her in a heartbeat. Not that she planned on telling him. Ever.

CHAPTER 2

CEVEN

Ceven was happy to fully unfurl his wings, the blue and gold feathers wavering in the crisp breeze. Cramped up in the dome with everyone forced him to keep them closely tucked to his side, the muscles aching to let loose. Tarry must have felt the same, his blue and gray wings outstretched, brushing against the foliage that Barto prowled through silently, unlike them.

Ceven rolled up the sleeves of his brown, hand-spun shirt that hung loose over black trousers tucked into black boots. Barto was equipped much the same, except he kept his feet bare, the black fur clumped around his ankles and the top of his feet as they skated across the forest floor. Tarry wasn't happy with his new set of armor, shifting and readjusting the brown leather tunic with metal plates strapped to his arms, breast, and legs. It was obvious the old Aerian missed his Royal Guard attire, but it had needed too much repair after he escaped the castle battle.

Barto paused in front of them, and Ceven instinctually settled a palm on the padded hilt of his sword. His friend unsheathed his claws and pounced up a tree heavy with swaying leaves and unpicked fruit.

"Look out below!" Barto shook its trunk, and a clump of orange and green fruit fell at his feet. "Told you I'd find us breakfast," he said, jumping down and cutting open the mangos with his claws. Ceven took several, but Tarry refused, his lip curling. Who knew the hardened former mercenary didn't like mangos?

"The first trap should be a few paces to the right ahead." Barto shoved the rest of the fruit in his mouth and pointed. Ceven squinted through the tall grass and thick fronds. A wire was cinched discretely across the pathway, through stretches of trees. Knives dangled in the trees, ready to fly at the unknown attackers when triggered.

"Looks sturdy," he said, glancing up cautiously at the dangling blades.

Hunters for the community didn't go out this far, and even if they did, Barto had warned them about the twenty traps he and Ceven had placed around the area.

"Your Highness," Tarry said, despite Ceven telling him to drop the title. Not only was he a bastard prince, but now a wanted one for the murder of King Calais. Even if the kingdom found out it was their other prince, Sehn LuRogue, who did the deed, they would still vouch for Ceven's death. The bloodthirsty Nytes of his home city never liked him much after Queen Beatrix's betrayal of the king.

"What is it?" He gathered by the spot Tarry bent at. There, the teethed spring trap clasped a bit off the trunk of a log. But it wasn't the casual falling of a tree branch. All eight traps were triggered. Someone had been here.

"Do you think one of the hunters had gotten too close?" he asked Barto, who was crouched next to the trap.

"Unlikely. They don't trek this far, and it's a ways from the beaten path. Either a lone animal, or something that doesn't bode well for us."

Tarry un-hooked one of the axes from his belt. Ceven kept his sword sheathed but pulled out the knife from the leather holster strapped to his thigh. With the cluster of trees around them, the forearm-length knife would suit better for close combat.

Barto waved at them, and they followed. The sun was still just starting to rise, and dew wiped across their clothes as the ventured farther into the forest. Unlike the capital, Kazuumar, that lay farther south, Laba Estonos territory carried the cool winds from the Frostsnare Mountains, and it rose the hairs on his tanned arms. His boots cracked branches, and he cursed. Maybe he should learn to go barefoot like Barto. Or maybe he'd just end up with scarred feet.

As if he read his thoughts, Barto held up his hand. "I'll go ahead and ride the trees. You two are louder than a bear after a meal."

Tarry didn't look pleased. Not because his face moved from its usual stoic expression, but because his neck muscles shifted to show the subtle clench of his jaw, proving his displeasure. Ceven had learned on his first trip to Atiaca that he was far out of his element, but he had grown used to it. Maybe it was because it was only Tarry now left to protect Ceven—not that he couldn't take care of himself—ever since Xilo, his former partner and Ceven's former bodyguard, had betrayed them.

Barto sprinted ahead, taking to the trees, his leather-clad figure darting between the branches. Ceven looked on enviously, following a few paces behind him.

"You can take to the skies if you feel it necessary, Tarry," Ceven said, keeping his tone neutral. Although it still pained him to have such beautiful, useless wings, the pain was now a dull thud. There but endurable.

"I will stay here," was all he said.

When the Rathan was fully out of sight, something rustled through the grass in front of them. Too late.

With a snap, a flurry of arrows rained down on them. Tarry slammed into Ceven, taking them both to the ground as the sound of whizzing arrows echoed in the quiet forest above. They rolled together, Tarry lifting his arm to block the pointed heads with his metal braces. Ceven's aim had to be more precise, using the flat of his blade to deflect the arrows. One scraped his arm, another his right calf. He curled his wings in time, but roughly a dozen had snagged Tarry's. Blood dripped onto the forest floor, but Tarry still didn't show any sign he was in pain. His brown gaze flicked across the trees, across the knee-length grass. Ceven's followed his, hoping that was the only trap they had sprung.

Tarry spoke Ceven's thoughts aloud. "It seems we aren't the only ones with traps."

"But is it Peredian assassins, or soldiers from another territory?" Ceven knew there was the occasional strife between communities across the territories. Although they were minor enough to be classified as banditry, and not big enough to hint at a possible rebellion—not that anyone would cross the empress or, more importantly, her dangerous brigade of warriors forged from the wild tropics of Atiaca—there was the occasional turf war. Clusters of warriors who fought, for many different reasons. Some for power, some for resources or food, and others because they could.

"Take to the skies," Ceven said again, but this time a demand. Tarry had once said that he followed Ceven, not because of his oath to the crown, but because he believed he was meant for something greater. That he served as the ex-merc's personal moral compass. Whatever it was, Ceven hoped he would listen.

To his credit, Tarry agreed, if slightly reluctant. His wings extended and lifted in a gust that had leaves, trees, and grass dancing back. Ceven prowled farther, his eyes flicking to the grass that parted at his feet and the branches that swayed in the consistent wind.

All was quiet except the snapping of twigs, the whistle of the wind, and birds chattering in the canopy. He cursed his clumsy footing, wishing he had listened to Barto more when he had trained with him for two years in these same woods. He had been cocky enough to believe the Royal Guard was all the training he needed. That the elite Aerian soldiers that underwent heaps of training, even in the cold winter months, would be the path to invincibility. Or close to it. He figured he didn't need stealth if he had raw strength to fight any enemy thrown his way, but after stumbling through the west wing in the dark, being attacked and surrounded by the

Peredian army at his execution, he was starting to hear the words Tarry and Xilo always scolded him with. *Strength alone will only get you so far. You'll need everything at your disposal to not only win, but survive.*

Stealth was another tool, another piece to be played in strategizing the field. Not a coward's way of fighting, like he always secretly believed Barto and his crew to be when they employed it. When they told Ceven to keep quiet as they rounded behind the bandits that trapped them and ambushed them from the leaves instead of facing them head-on. That had been last year, not too far from this spot, actually.

Something whizzed by his left ear, and he flicked out his wings, propelling him backwards, dodging the log that had been aimed for his head with a sword tied to its trunk, the size of Ceven's torso. He crouched and remained still. Listening. He didn't have the superb hearing of a Rathan, but he practiced blindfolded—as per the course of his training—listening for the shifts in movements, the slicing of air. And for a moment he closed his eyes, cueing into the ambience.

The wind rolled through, shifting the grass that swatted his knees. Birds still chirped overhead. *Chirp chirp.* Pause. *Chirp, chirp.* Pause. Ceven frowned and then strained his ears further. It wasn't birds talking but Nytes—or humans. Two people were communicating with one another among the trees, the distinct pauses and lilts, intentional.

He had to tell Tarry and Barto, but he couldn't see them. The steady flapping of wings came from above, heartier with longer gusts in between to indicate it was his bodyguard, but he was too far. He couldn't shout without alerting whoever was here to his presence. Though it was likely they already knew where he was.

Sunlight slithered through patches in the canopy, skimming branches that could host a body, if nimble enough. But Ceven saw no one.

Something flickered to his right. Above. He twirled, avoiding the arrow, throwing an oath when another one skimmed his shoulder, notching a second mark where the other arrow had sliced him earlier. He was so busy dodging the metal arrow heads that he didn't see the direction that the enemy went. Or where they were hiding.

Crouching in the grass, his arm and leg bleeding through the cut fabric of his clothes, he searched the floor. There, next to the slight clearing of grass, where the roots curved into a collapsing heart. Underneath the purposefully placed leaves was a trigger. A thin cord attached to another that would activate his own trap. If anything, maybe the noise would alert his two friends.

He crept closer to the thick trunk, its frame large enough to carry the entire canopy surrounding him for several lengths. Then, with his knife, he snapped the taut cord and tumbled into the crevice of roots and tall thicket. The whooshing of thirty small darts skated across the trees and the ground. The pointed tips doused in poison. Vell root, found in the mossy rocks by the stream. It had been Tor, Barto's father's, idea. After all, he had been the Empress's former poison taster, testing her foods and drinks for a variety of different poisons. The king had food tasters as well, but rather than being thoroughly versed in poisons and herbal remedies as those employed by the Empress, they only determined whether the prepared meals were safe to eat. It would be nothing to the former king of Peredia if another human died under his reign.

For several pounding moments, Ceven thought the trap hadn't worked. But then a thud resounded by him as someone toppled from the trees above. Ceven lurched from his spot, sword drawn. Before he could see the attacker, a flurry of green and dark eyes rushed him, their cutlass aimed for Ceven's leg. Ceven cut low, parrying his blade and elbowing the attacker's side. He sucked in a fit of air, and the enemy was already behind him, their dagger aimed for his neck. To kill.

Ceven collapsed his legs, and the dagger stabbed at air. Focusing on the strength of his limbs, he spun on the heels of his feet, forcing himself to be fast. Faster than the enemy as he grabbed their wrist, the blade falling from their hands. Ceven didn't make another move when the green hooded figure collapsed. A poison dart must have found them, working through their system in minutes.

The mysterious attacker didn't have wings, but when Ceven pulled back the cloak, he saw the fur-lined cheeks and a jaw covered in a trimmed, brown beard. His ears were human, but his hands had nails as sharp as Barto's and had a speed that matched his Rathan friend. Both human and Rathan—a halfling.

"Your Highness!" Ceven turned when Tarry landed with a graceful touch of his toes across from the dead assassin. "You're hurt."

"And so are you." He glanced at his bodyguard's red, matted feathers. Tarry had already ripped out the arrows, the flexible muscle healing. At least they weren't poisoned. Maybe these assassins had planned to take them alive? Or his brother Sehn had hired amateurs, which seemed more unlikely.

I'm telling you the truth. Sehn is Council member Aimee—and no, don't ask me how I know that. You won't like the answer, Evangeline had told him. And he guessed where that bit of knowledge came from, a smug blue-eyed Caster popping into his head, and it was true he wasn't pleased. But still, Ceven didn't believe it. He had spoken to Sehn, watched him carve a knife into his forearm and his own for their shared blood promise, a mark he was grateful had vanished after the king had collapsed on the throne room floor. There was no way the brother he grew up with was now this Council member. He couldn't believe the king and the rest of the royal court could have been so easily fooled.

That he had been so easily fooled.

"Where's Barto?" As soon as Ceven said it, the Rathan slunk from the branches above. His thick black hair curled around leaves and branches that stuck to it. His black, pointed ears flicked at the bugs that swarmed him.

The usual sloppy grin he had worn this morning was gone. "I lost the other one." He crouched next to the assassin. "There were multiple. I counted two, but there could be more."

Tarry palmed both axes that appeared deceivingly lax at his sides. "I couldn't see much from above, but judging by the moving trees, they headed north. There was also movement headed east."

"Is he Peredian?" Ceven bowed next to his friend. He glistened with sweat, and the damp dirt and crushed leaves of the forest couldn't hide the smell of burnt bread and leather that clung to him. More prominent now that they were back in his home territory.

Barto's nostrils twitched. "I can't be sure. His scent alludes me. His clothes"—he slid the dull green fabric through his hands, and it wasn't as flexible as he imagined cloth to be— "bear the cactus hide of our neighboring territory. But underneath, he smells like stale water. Like he'd been underground for a long period of time, but it's mixed with blood and fire."

Ceven was still amazed at how perceptive Barto's nose was. How all Rathan noses were. But Barto, like Rasha and Quan— Barto's former bodyguards that had traveled ahead to report to the empress—had learned to hone his abilities. Trained to hunt down those who opposed the empress or her ideals. His official title while in the kingdom had been as an emissary, but he was much more than that.

"Either way, they don't look like they're from the castle." Then again, with Ceven's woven shirt and beaded neckline of crushed shells—a popular design amongst Barto's tribe—and Tarry's brown warrior leather, he amended, "Well, at least I don't think so. King Calais didn't accept halflings into his army, at least not knowingly, unless Sehn has recently been more proactive in the Peredian military's recruitment as the new king." Ceven knew the former king's prejudice ran deep, extending beyond humans, to anyone who wasn't pure or seemed weak. "If they were warriors from another tribe or community, they would have no need to attack us, though I guess it is a possibility. And bandits wouldn't waste laying traps in the wild where nobody travels except animals."

"Either way, this spells trouble for us and the others." Barto cut off a piece of the assassin's hood to hunt later. "The others are still out there, and they know we're now aware of their presence."

Ceven grimaced. "And if they're not Peredian assassins, then that means we have more than one enemy to deal with."

CHAPTER 3

ᔆ EVANGELINE ᔆ

"Good, you're awake!" A girl bombarded Evangeline before she fully stepped out of the bedroom. Her black and brown furred ears flicked between her curls. "We need an outsider's opinion." She pointed at the wood table, where three of Barto's sisters bickered and popped dried apricots into their mouths. "Who do you think is prettier, me or Katya?"

Evangeline's cheeks warmed. Her eyes flitted from the small Rathan in front of her who—if she remembered correctly—was named Hanna, to Katya and the two other girls, Orianne and Lavake. They then drifted to the gray-haired Rathan, Tor, and Grace hovering over the brick fireplace fixated at the back end of the circular home, stirring something in a brass pot that came up to their waists. Evangeline didn't spot any familiar faces to help her. Barto and Ceven must still be out.

Hanna's brown eyes widened, her pupils shrinking into narrow slits. She leaned on her toes, bringing her height up to

Evangeline's chest, to poke Evangeline's cheeks. "Wow, your face is so red!"

Evangeline reared back, rubbing her face. She knew the girl was no older than Evangeline when Lord Ryker had adopted her—eleven years old—but she was never any good around people, let alone children. And most human children weren't as energetic as Hanna. Any happiness or childlike wonder, beaten out of them at far too young an age like Evangeline's had been.

"You're both pretty," Evangeline said, rolling the unfamiliar syllables around in her mouth. She understood Atiacan, but her speech could have used a couple more tutoring sessions from Lord Ryker. Ceven had done most of the talking since they arrived, the language falling effortlessly from his lips. After all, he had lived here for two years before returning to Peredia. Before Evangeline had worked with a Caster in killing her former father and dragging Ceven into being a wanted murderer. Maybe it would've been best if Ceven had never returned to Peredia at all.

Or better yet, if he had never met her.

Those familiar doubts chased Evangeline as she walked past Hanna. She hadn't waited for the child's reply, making a quick escape to the only other human in the room.

As she skirted by the table, whose edges were as organic as the curves of the house, smoked meat and vegetables rose from the pot and punched her right in the gut. Normal food no longer satisfied the hunger in her, thus her new habit of evening hunts.

"The sun embraces you." Grace's small hands rubbed Evangeline's shoulder before giving it a light squeeze.

Evangeline stilled at the touch. She still wasn't used to how freely these people touched one another, especially her, a stranger. And a wanted one at that. "And you," Evangeline said, butchering the beautiful Atiacan greeting.

Tor peeked from beside Grace's blue linen pants. "Your heart-mate and Barto are still out checking the surrounding traps, but they should return shortly."

Evangeline nodded. Although she and Ceven weren't married in the traditional Atiacan way like Grace and Tor—binding each other with a yellow cord (a symbol of the Goddess's blessing) and holding a seven-day celebration (the amount of time it took for the Goddess to give birth to her child, the first Nyte to walk the land) from what she was told—Barto's family already saw them as such. It seemed Barto had told them a lot of things, to Evangeline's growing frustration.

"I hope they find no trouble," Evangeline said.

"Take these to the girls, will you?" Grace didn't wait for her reply, handing over sliced cheese and bread. "And make sure to save some for yourself. If you're going to stay in this dome, you need to learn to be quicker." When she smiled, her teeth were refreshingly dull. Unlike the sharp pointers everyone else had around her.

Evangeline balanced the bread and cheese platter on her arms. Before she even set it down on the table, a fit of limbs flew at her, snatching and fingering the bits of food. Despite Grace's words, Evangeline waited before grabbing a few slices of cheese and bread. Her stomach revolted at the measly two squares of cheese and torn loaf of bread as she took a bite.

"Decided to finally join us?"

Evangeline's first instinct was to put her head down. Instead, she forced her chin up, even rolling back her shoulders. She shoved another mouthful of bread as Sadia strolled in, her red and orange pants flowing like the wildflowers in front of the dome. Unlike the rest of Barto's sisters, Sadia's sharp, brown face was crowned by a curly puff of hair. It bounced with each graceful step as she slid into the bench—as far away from Evangeline as possible.

Evangeline held her tongue. Sadia's distaste towards her didn't bother her as much as the Rathan probably would've liked. She was used to Nytes and humans hating her. Sadia was no different.

"With your evening walks and then how much you lay in bed all day, I almost wonder if you're avoiding us." Sadia snatched the last piece of cheese right from Katya's hands, whose angry retort slid away upon seeing her older sister's expression. "Almost as if you're guilty for dragging my family into your own problems. Who knows, maybe we'll all be put on trial for housing a criminal."

I'm not a criminal. Evangeline bit down on the bread again. But wasn't she? She had killed not one, but two Nytes now. She had planned to kill the king too, committing whatever crime it was to save her friends, but despite her many faults, what Sadia and the rest of the Atiacan empire was accusing Evangeline of, this wasn't one of them.

And just because Evangeline was used to the glares and mean comments all her life didn't mean she had to put up with them now.

"Thank you for the food," Evangeline said to no one in particular. She stood and grabbed her long brown coat off the hook, still faintly smelling of blood and water from last night, before storming out the front door.

Evangeline immediately steeled herself against a cluster of Rathan children that laughed and ran past her. "Slay the beast, slay the beast!" one of them shouted at the other children to join, splashing buckets of water Rathan men and woman were dipping swaths of colorful cloths into. A curse was hurled their way, but the children didn't care, flying past Evangeline's frozen form in front of the dome.

Her coat flirted around her bare ankles and feet, and she braced herself for the small rocks and prickly weeds. She wasn't going back inside.

"Don't get comfortable, Eve," she muttered to herself. "You won't be staying here long." She tore her gaze from the domes, the children, the Rathans hugging, talking, and performing duties that she'd only seen humans do in the castle, to the woods around her. She needed to be alone.

Sadia's hatred didn't bother Evangeline, but her words did leave a mark. When Evangeline had first arrived here, her only thought was of survival. The idea that Barto's family could be tried as potential accomplices for letting her stay didn't even cross her mind. Sadia's suspicious behavior was almost normal. Expected, in comparison to the rest of Barto's family.

Morning dew dampened her coat and thin shorts, the shade of the wide palm fronds and clustered canopy of trees shielding her from the relentless Atiacan sun. Birds chirped and flitted from branch to branch as she followed the sounds of rushing water, in the opposite direction of where she had hunted last night. She stopped when her feet brushed water.

Something rustled behind her, and she reached into the pocket of the coat, gripping the handle of a knife, her muscles tense.

A crown of sandy hair and flowing turquoise pants and blouse pulled from the thicket behind her. "Grace," Evangeline sighed. Her stuttering heart skipped several beats before finding a semi-normal tempo once more. She'd been jumpy before, but these past few weeks, Evangeline had reached a whole new level of paranoia. Last night hadn't helped either.

"Eve." Grace's thick brows reached her hairline. "I was hoping you'd have gone this way. Come to collect stones as well?" She had a woven basket in hand.

Eve peered down at the pebbles around her feet, picking up the first one that caught her eye. "Didn't plan on it, but here I am."

Grace admired the small rock that shimmered blue to green in the sunlight. "You got a pretty one. Would make a lovely piece for a necklace. Would you like me to make you one?"

She blinked. "That's nice of you, but—"

Grace waved her hand dismissively. "I'd love to do it, and it'd be my way of apologizing for Sadia. She's always been more distant and serious, but never rude. Something must be on her mind."

Whatever it was, it'd been on her mind since Evangeline had arrived, and she'd assumed Barto's family would follow suit and it would be no different than living in the castle, but they surprised her. Especially Grace. "It's fine."

"No, it's not. It's disrespectful. I'll have a talk with her later, since I know her father won't."

Evangeline glanced at the older woman, her chin-length brown hair tucked behind her ears, the only signs of age being the smile lines around her eyes and cheeks. Evangeline had only been with Barto's family for a few days now, but this woman touched Evangeline's heart in a way the others hadn't. She looked nothing like Lani, and yet, Grace reminded her so much of her dear friend.

Tears pricked the backs of her eyes, and she turned her head away. "How did you do it?" Evangeline asked, more so to distract herself. "You're human, but they treat you like family. Like a mother." She'd learned that Tor's former wife and the mother of Barto and his siblings had passed shortly after the youngest had been born. A common seasonal illness had gripped her, but she hadn't been able to fight it in her weakened state after giving birth.

"It wasn't always so. Although we have more rights here than your home country, there are a lot of Nytes who are still prejudiced. Mostly in the territories more isolated from outsiders, farther from the borders and the capital." She put down her basket, getting on her knees. Her fingers tussled the pebbles back and forth. "But this community, I've never seen anything like it, especially not back at the capital, in Kazuumar. And Tor. . ." She smiled. "Tor is a wonderful heart-mate."

Evangeline joined her, tossing her stone into the basket. The stones were cold and slippery and shined in the sunlight. "Really? This isn't normal?" The image of the empress living in a large, multilayered earthen dome with children running around wavered in her mind.

Grace laughed. "Goddess, no. Not in the capital or anywhere near it—oh, a nice one." The stone was the size of her hand and was a dusty pink with gold specks. "I wasn't the first human to pass through Tor's community, but I was the first to join them. Everyone was so kind, and so curious. They never experienced a lot of humans this far out in the wild. But I quickly felt like I was at home, more so than I ever felt at the palace."

Evangeline hoped to find more pretty rocks, but Grace had a better eye for this than she did. "So, if this place is so far away, how did you two meet?"

Grace's face melted into a beautiful smile. "We used to live in the capital, before moving here in Tor's home village. Before I quit and Tor retired, I was a servant for the empress and he was one of her advisors. I spilled coffee on him during a very important meeting one morning. I expected to be hit, fired, or punished in some way. Anybody else in there would have, but Tor, he . . ." She chuckled. "He smiled and said he didn't care for this shirt anyways—and took it off and remained bare-chested the remainder of the meeting."

Evangeline thought of Barto, a smile grazing her own lips. "Sounds like something Barto would do too."

She flinched when Grace's cold, wet fingers touched hers. "I know it's a lot to get used to. But I want you to feel as welcomed as I did when I first came here. I want this place to feel like home."

Warmth unfurled inside her, like a warm embrace. She could see herself living here (ideally in her own dome), collecting stones with Grace, helping her make jewelry. Laughing with Barto and his sisters and enjoying more of Ceven's kisses . . . Her chest tightened. The warmth evaporated, and the air became restricting. Suffocating. This place would never be home, because like Sadia had said, she was a guilty outsider, and in a few days she would stand trial.

They both returned awhile later to the dome, and Evangeline helped Grace cut the stones into shapes and bead them onto the strings on a soft patch of grass out front. Evangeline's thoughts turned to the dead man last night. The gruesome reality of what she'd seen conflicted with the peaceful, not-so-quiet community that chattered, ran, and whirled around her. She was still thinking about it when she then went inside and helped Tor and Barto's sisters with lunch while avoiding Sadia's stony glares. Should she tell them about the body after all? Would they find her suspicious? Probably more so, since she waited so long to say anything. What was a dead, marked body doing so close to Barto's community in the first place?

Ceven, Tarry, and Barto swung through the front door. Barto swept the room with a wide smile. "Miss me?" To his credit, his sisters piled on him, much like they did when he first walked through the door. Before she realized they were hugging one another, Evangeline had thought they were being attacked.

Evangeline softened, her shoulders dropping—until they reached Ceven's. To anyone else, with his smile and crossed arms, it seemed nothing was amiss. But she wasn't anyone else and noted the stiffness in his shoulders, the strain in his eyes. There were also tears in his clothes . . . and the smell of blood was unmistakable.

Grace followed behind them, touching Ceven's shoulder. "I'm glad you two are back. How were the traps?"

"As good as we left them. No problem here," Ceven said, the lie ringing loud in Evangeline's ears.

They all crowded around the table. Tarry stood by the door, his wings wrapped close to him. His hand rested on his axes, always alert and ready even though he was no longer a Royal Guard and they were no longer in Peredia. *Old habits die hard*, she guessed. Barto hugged his youngest sisters around their shoulders, Ceven beside him as Evangeline approached. He caught her staring at him and misunderstood.

"Miss me, too?" he teased, the green and gold within his eyes fighting for the spotlight in the afternoon sun streaming through the windows.

She covered her worry with a smile, and he leaned down to kiss her. Her face heated, and she turned her head in time for him to peck her cheek. He chuckled and whispered in her ear, "I'm starting to think you don't like me anymore."

Thank the Gods everyone else was distracted by Barto, waving his hands as he told one of his lengthy stories of their adventures. Well, everyone except Sadia, whose scowl deepened from across the table.

Evangeline poked Ceven in the ribs. "I told you, not in front of everyone," she hissed. Then her face wrinkled. "You lied. To Grace."

His smile vanished, and he clenched his jaw. "Later," was all he said.

They all gathered around the table. Tor and Grace served stew in brown bowls, painted with red and yellow wildflowers on the side (who knew Sadia was an artist in her spare time when she wasn't casting snide remarks?). Ceven reached for a tuft of bread gathered in the center of the table—that was also a mess of reaching hands—his rolled-up sleeves displaying the cuts lining his arm. They were pink, not yet fully healed, and certainly not there a day ago.

Evangeline feigned a stretch, leaning back in the bench seat and over Ceven's frame. Tarry still leaned against the wall closest to the entrance as if waiting for something. Evangeline wouldn't have found it odd, except he had finally caved and joined them for afternoon feast, abandoning his post by the door two days prior. If he was too cautious to let his guard down again today, then something bigger than she first imagined had happened. Even if the traps were triggered, she didn't think that would be enough to cause cuts on Ceven's arms. Who attacked them?

Barto wrapped up his story—thank the Gods—and Tor cut in. "The trial starts in two days. Are you prepared, Eve?" The conversation dimmed to scraping bowls and hesitant slurps.

Evangeline recoiled and rescinded her earlier mental comment. She wished Barto had kept rambling the entire night. Since no one was grabbing the bread, she opted to pull off a large chunk, cramming her mouth. Maybe if she kept shoving bread in her mouth, she'd have an excuse not to talk the rest of the night. Unlikely, as she swallowed the chunk and Tor was still staring at her expectantly. She briefly considered keeping silent, pretending to not have heard him, but relented, "Of course I'm not prepared." The truth slipped out before she could stop it. "I don't know what to expect. I could become a free woman or be sentenced to death." It seemed her life was spiraling into that small window of whether she was going to live to see next season. The next day, even.

But Evangeline was no longer defenseless, the beast prowling underneath her skin waiting to be set free. She'd die fighting before hanging for a crime she didn't commit, but she didn't dare speak that aloud. Especially not with Ceven present.

"I told you you're not going to—" Tor's hand interrupted Barto. A hand that was smooth and untarnished; Tor had chosen a different path in life from his son.

"Barto," he said, cutting him a sharp look, "should have told you how our country deals with its people. Its criminals and traitors."

The words clattered in her brain. Criminal. Traitor. She didn't feel like one, but she had murdered Ryker Ardonis, the king's advisor, and Vane Jarr, an officer of the Peredian army. Even if one had been trickery and the other pure self-defense, it didn't matter, especially for a human—although that label didn't quite suit Evangeline anymore. She was a criminal in a Nyte's eyes.

"She'll be fine," Barto retorted, and his younger sisters reared back, suddenly really interested in their empty bowls.

Grace noticed, shooting a disappointed look at Tor. As if she were also unsettled by the swift change in topic. "Girls, would you please play outside for a moment?" They didn't hesitate, bounding from the table. Sadia stayed, rolling her shoulders back as if Grace would fight her. She didn't.

"If she was fine, she wouldn't have the brand of a criminal." Sadia's gold eyes pinned hers.

Evangeline stared right back. "And how would you know that for certain? Have you seen the markings with your own eyes?" *Seen it writhe and suck the soul out of someone. Soak up their skin, their life, their very being leaving behind a husk of a human,* she didn't say.

"I see the marking, bold and true on your hand. What more is there to see?" Her calm expression wavered, and it looked like she wanted to reach across the table and wring her throat. Surprisingly, Evangeline wanted her to, her skin itching to fight.

Ceven shifted next to her, the soft feathers on his wings brushing her back through the thin fabric, but the hard lines on his face were anything but soft. "Hold your tongue, Sadi. Don't talk about things you know nothing about."

The Rathan bristled. Her lip pulled back in a full sneer, and there wasn't any doubt that if the others weren't here, she would've killed Evangeline on the spot. Or tried to, at least. Was she so convinced that Evangeline was the culprit behind all the missing people, both in the kingdom and the Atiacan empire? That she'd played a hand in murdering potentially thousands of innocents? No, there had to be something else at play.

"I know that she's wanted by the empress, by the whole empire and Peredia. Why are we treating her like a guest when she should be tied up!"

Barto and Tor growled a warning, and Grace continued to stare at Sadia. Grace didn't say anything but kept her eyes fixed on Sadia's.

Evangeline plastered on a wide, saccharine smile and flipped her wrists at the Rathan. "Then please, by all means, tie me up if it makes you feel better. Since you feel so *threatened*." She didn't know what possessed her to say that, or why, but her skin still crawled, her hands flexing. Maybe it wasn't Sadia she was angry at, but she was the one to spark it.

Sadia shot her feet. Her dark brown ears flicked back, poking through the curls of her hair, her thin tail held rigidly still. Her pupils had expanded, eclipsing the gold irises, and her sharp nails had extended. Barto stood with her, a hand already on her shoulder. *Digging* into her shoulder. "Maybe you should go for a walk?" It was phrased as a question, but everyone knew it wasn't.

Evangeline disengaged from the table, flicking back her hair. "No," she drawled, "because I'll be leaving." Again.

Barto protested, but Evangeline didn't care, already out the door. Her face bunched at the sun, and children continued to laugh and run around the domes, but this time Evangeline didn't linger. She marched back towards the woods, in the direction she had been earlier.

Fronds and branches smacked at her skin as she stormed through the foliage rather than with gentle curiosity. A light drizzle tickled her arms and legs. She'd forgotten her coat.

Heavy footsteps echoed behind her, and Ceven caught up with her in a few paces—holding her coat.

"Care for a partner?" He kept his tone light, even though his posture spoke otherwise.

He handed her the coat, and she gratefully put it on. "As long as it's not Sadia, sure."

His fingers wove through hers. "Come, I know a spot."

CHAPTER 4

~ EVANGELINE ~

They traveled a few paces away from the community when Ceven pulled aside a patch of leaves. Yawning trunks stretched from the crystal-clear waters to the sky. Streaks of sun played across the water's flat, still surface. It almost appeared as if there wasn't any water at all, that waving weeds at its bottom and different colored rocks weren't fully submerged. Tempted, she poked at the water and gasped. "It's *cold!*"

Ceven chuckled behind her, guiding her through the padded thicket, signs that others had been here before. Two fallen trees hankered near the water, and Ceven sat on one, but she didn't want to sit, her fingers still playing at the water's edge, mesmerized by the sheer clearness of it. She'd never seen anything like it.

"I've never seen a spring before," she guessed. At least that was what it was called in her books. She pointed at the stream of bubbles trickling up to the surface. "What's that?"

"It's clean water coming up from beneath these lands. It's purified. When it's warmer, the community will come here and go swimming."

Evangeline imagined diving in, exploring the depths, splashing with Hanna and Katya, and everyone *but* Sadia. Too bad she didn't know how to swim. Too bad tomorrow she would never see this place again. *Just enjoy this moment. Don't dwell on things that haven't happened yet,* she chided herself.

Ceven mistook her frown. "I could teach you how to swim." A sly smile spread across his face. "It would give me an excuse to touch you all over. In public."

She scooped up the water and chucked it his way. He yelped as the cold droplets splashed across his face, but his smile didn't dissipate. Evangeline smiled too, despite the rising heat in her cheeks. She was blessed to have such cold water at hand to cool off. It was odd to be so open with Ceven now, to have that part freed between the two of them. It made her body sing and fill with heat even on the coldest, bleakest day. It also scared the being out of her. That he could leave at any moment. Find out her secret and turn his back on her and everything they had shared. Or leave her permanently, like Lani had, and for her to be truly and utterly alone.

She thought back to the body she'd seen, the writhing black marks, the bleeding skull. And now Ceven's fresh cuts on his arms and legs. Why . . . why did trouble have to follow them here? To such a peaceful place? All she wanted was a life where she could be free, away from harm and trouble. Away from the life she had at the castle.

"So, what really happened while you were out?" She kept her gaze on the water and saw the skin furrow between his brows in its reflection.

"We have it under control."

She bit her inner cheek. As much as he made her thoughts fly and tangle whenever he merely touched her, he also managed to ignite her temper with so few words. "Then I guess what I saw last night is no big deal either."

The crevice in his face deepened. "What do you mean?"

She turned and curled up her own brow. "You first."

His fingers ensnared in his hair, mussing the hazelnut strands. Evangeline couldn't help but smirk. It was his telltale sign that he was frustrated—most of the time, it was because of her.

"I see the peaceful Atiacan atmosphere hasn't changed you much."

"Nor you," she countered. "I can plainly see the wounds on your arms and legs, Ceven. And don't try to tell me it was from the leaves and branches."

He closed his mouth, probably because he was going to say just that. Finally, he sighed. "We may have encountered a few people on our travels."

She scooped up another handful of water, but when she went to chuck it at the Aerian, he dodged and, in a gust of movement, had both her hands pinned to the ground. Her chest echoed the swelling of Ceven's, his face inches above hers.

Her stomach tightened, but it wasn't from anger. "Don't dance around the subject. I spent enough time with Ryker to have lost my patience for that years ago."

His eyes darkened, and he frowned. As if he realized his mistake in getting this close—or maybe that was part of his plan. To distract her. "What did you see, Eve?"

"Who were these 'people'?" She wasn't going to give in, even if his lips were right there. Even if her hands itched to rearrange the messy brown wisps of his hair. To slide her legs so she was touching his. So she was that much closer to him.

They both stared at one another, refusing to give in.

Ceven dipped his head, his lips grazing hers, but pulled back. "They were Rathans. Probably assassins. Your turn."

Evangeline's toes curled at the faint touch, but she smothered it with a cool, neutral expression. He was playing dirty. "How did you get hurt?"

He dipped again, his lashes fluttering halfway. "Your turn," he repeated.

Blast it, she hated herself for heating up, the fire settling in her cheeks like always. She ignored it and raised a brow, trying to hold on to that disinterested look, even if she knew Ceven would see through it. "I saw a body. A marked body."

She saw the hitch in his breath, even if his eyes never left hers. "Where?"

"By the stream in the opposite direction from here when I went out for a walk." She didn't tell him it was because that she was hunting, how the taste of the rabbit's blood made her feel more alive than the sweet rolls she loved so much back at the castle. "I left him there. I didn't want the others to worry." Or think she was guilty of it.

"Are you sure it wasn't a . . . hallucination?" His pause told her he didn't want to upset her, and it still made her uncomfortable that he knew. It was a secret only she and Ryker shared, that she'd carried close to her for so long that it made her feel vulnerable. And he knew that.

"At first I thought it was too," she admitted. "But then I checked his pulse. He had been dead for some time. I'm sure an animal has probably gotten to him by now." She wriggled her hands, which were still trapped beneath Ceven's palms. He instantly let up.

She sat up at the same time Ceven leaned back on his calves. They still hovered close to one another.

"Your turn," she tossed back.

He grimaced. "At first, we found some of the traps had been triggered. Then we were attacked with arrows. Tarry took the brunt of it."

Her fingers traced the raised scars between the fabric of his ripped shirt. Bumps rose along his skin, but he didn't move, and she felt the weight of his hazel gaze settle on her burning cheeks. "I'm glad you weren't too badly hurt." Her thumb rubbed the skin gently, as if she could erase them. This close, she heard his breathing shift, rapid.

He tucked a strand of her hair behind her ear. She hadn't thrown it in a usual braid but left it wild all morning. It wasn't going to be fun to brush later.

"I wonder if the two are connected somehow," he said. "We'll have a talk with Tor and Grace later, to make sure the community stays safe. But I don't want you leaving the grounds without me. Not now."

She snorted. "Not that it matters. Tomorrow I'll be escorted to the capital to stand trial." She traced the pink lines that ran across firm muscle with her eyes. It rippled, sensing her gaze.

Calloused fingers propped her chin up. His lips were thin, his eyes alight with something more than desire. "Whatever happens, Eve, I'll protect you. I won't let them throw you in jail or kill you."

So why don't we just run away now? You can protect me easier without a swarm of guards. But she knew why. He trusted Barto, especially after he had gone back and saved Ceven in the battle that had broken out in the throne room. Ceven wanted to trust in Barto and his family. Believe them when they said this was the best route. To run away would scream her guilt, before she even had a chance to fight for her innocence. Leaving now would guarantee that she would always be on the run, and if she were captured and brought to trial, she wouldn't be facing the possibility of death but its certainty.

Her last resort was releasing her beast from its mental shackles, but Ceven didn't need to know that.

"As long as you don't get yourself in trouble with me." She still felt guilty for getting him in this mess in the first place. If she hadn't been tricked into killing Ryker, Ceven wouldn't have taken the fall. Both of them wouldn't have been on the run, and Ceven could've had a chance to make a difference in the kingdom. He wouldn't be a traitor to his own lands.

"I recognize that look. Stop blaming yourself for all of this. I can make my own decisions, Eve. I know what I'm doing, what risks I chose to take."

She looked up at him. "Do you? Because you seem to act first and worry about the consequences later," she said. "I still can't believe you planned to murder the king and almost got yourself killed because of it."

His brows bounced, a hollow chuckle rumbling his chest. "Oh really? Because I can't get over that you worked with a Caster assassin and poisoned Ryker. Not to mention went into the west wing alone—"

"I wasn't alone."

"I found you and Lani close to death. Alone."

At the mention of Lani, the familiar sting was back in her eyes, her heart. She turned her head, and Ceven swore. "I'm sorry, Eve."

She pushed to her feet, swallowing down feelings she didn't want to re-open. She had cried enough, even if her body felt otherwise. Nothing was going to bring her friend back. "It's in the past now. And who knows, maybe I'll be seeing her sooner than expected."

"That's not funny, Evangeline."

She shrugged. "Wasn't meant to be. I'm just being realistic."

He gathered to his feet, shaking his feathers where stray droplets settled from the spring. "No, it's being cynical. You're too young for that. No matter what, Barto and I will make sure you're safe."

She didn't share his optimism but didn't voice it, lest it lead to a fight. "Oh? And you, being a whole year older, are so much wiser than me?"

She tried to keep her intimidating expression, but when he took two steps to stand beside her, she was eclipsed in his shadow. It was hard to look intimidating when her neck was completely arched up at the sky. Why was he so spitting tall?

He was so much better at the intimidating look, even if it made her insides melt in a whole different reaction than

he probably expected. "Wise enough to know there's more to life you've yet to experience. More to learn." Something shifted in his expression, and his lips curled into a knowing smile. She swatted at him playfully, though her breathing hitched in anticipation.

Ceven was right, though. There was more to life she had yet to experience. She still wanted her adventure, to see the Atiacan jungles and the eastern plains. To visit the capital's markets and admire the wares from all over the empire, taste the sugary and fried foods she'd only imagined through Barto's stories. She even wanted to see Sundise Mouche, the country where magic resided alongside technology. Where Ryker had described ships that flew and buildings arching to the sky.

But wanting didn't make it happen, and it didn't change the fact that she was a human (or at least looked the part) in a Nyte's world. But she ignored that. Ignored the warring hope alongside the growing horror for what tomorrow brought. Instead, she focused on the rising desire in the pit of her stomach climbing all the way up to her chest. She rose to the toes of her bare feet at the same time Ceven bent down and met her lips.

She breathed him in, the spice, the tang of sweat, mixed with pine as her mouth melted to his. His fingers curved around her waist and drew her closer to his pounding heart.

"You're too good at that," she whispered, breaking from the kiss.

She expected a cocky smirk, a haughty raised brow, but he surprised her by cupping her cheeks. "Whatever happens at the capital, I want you to trust me. I don't want you thinking this is the end. It's the start. The start of a new life."

Her cheeks rubbed his textured palms. "The start of a new life," she repeated.

His lips found hers again, and they sank to the grassy bank, locked in an embrace.

CHAPTER 5

Evangeline hadn't slept a wink, even if she was wrapped in Ceven's arms all night. Even if Barto's family had been unusually quiet for the remainder of the night when they returned from the spring. As if the discussion at lunch had invited a tension that had yet to leave. It followed into the morning, when a soft mist of rain pattered against the closed curtains, stirring her awake. A crown of messy hair fell across dark eyes that blinked groggily at hers. Ceven hadn't slept well either.

Dressed in neutral green pants that flowed around her ankles with a beaded white shirt tied around her waist, Evangeline met everyone aside from Barto's sisters by the crackling fire in the main space. Barto smiled at her, but it was pinched. Like Ceven and Tarry behind her, he wore the brown leather molding across their athletic frames, their forearms, breasts, and legs wrapped in steel plates.

"The sun embraces you," Grace said, meeting everyone's eyes.

They all murmured "And you."

She then turned to Evangeline, motioning for her to spin around. Frowning, she did as she was told and felt something smooth and cool caress her neck. Reaching for her collar, Evangeline brushed over the stone she'd found the other night, shimmering a bright turquoise in the sun. The finger-sized stone was carved into a sharp point, like a fang.

"It represents strength," Grace murmured as Evangeline continued to admire the coral, gray, and purple stones around it. "May the Goddess shine down on the path before you."

"Thank you," she whispered into the too-quiet room. "It's beautiful."

A large purple shirt draped across Tor's lean frame, and the unattractive combination with the off-green pants made her think of Barto and where he got his questionable fashion tastes. He had agreed to escort them to the capital, a large brown pack slung over his shoulders as well as the others. Swords, axes, and knives also hung at their sides and backs. Evangeline kept two daggers for herself, one strapped to her thigh, the pocket of her pants open for her to reach and grab it at any time. The other was in the padded brown boots that were laced up mid-calf.

Nothing but the soft splat of rain and boots shuffling out the door filled the overwhelming silence. Evangeline bowed one last time at Grace, mentioning how grateful she was to her and Tor for sheltering them and feeding them these past couple days. Her heart squeezed when Grace tugged her into a fierce hug. It reminded her so much of her and Lani's last embrace before she . . . Evangeline abruptly pulled away, dabbing at her eyes with her sleeve.

Three gray manes and one brown horse kicked at the ground in front of the dome. Others in the community had gathered outside, their thin attired soaking up the skies. Yet, they all stayed and watched her, some bowing their heads, others splaying their fingers wide around their faces, a gesture to represent the Goddess. A blessing—Barto told her.

It was odd that these strangers didn't hold any malice toward her but in fact wished her luck. Odd but not unwelcomed, even if she didn't understand why anyone would trust a wanted criminal. She couldn't help but think that maybe Barto's community wasn't very smart and that one day their naivete would be the end of them.

She flushed at the horrible thought. *You're truly despicable for thinking that, after everything they've done for you.* But reality was often horrible.

"Eve, Eve, Eve!" Her head swiveled to see that Barto's sisters had joined them, and judging by their soaked white threaded shirts, they'd been waiting outside in the rain holding flowers. Even Sadia, though she didn't look happy about it.

Evangeline forced a smile and bent by the three girls. The red and yellow wildflowers turned out to be a string, and each hung the flower necklaces around her neck. Before she knew what they were doing, they kissed her cheeks and hugged her. For a frozen moment she was taken back but then forced herself to return their embraces and smiles. Back to her feet, Evangeline swung to Sadia, who passed her. Much to her surprise, she placed her flower necklace around Ceven's shoulder, who looked as surprised as she had. He bowed his head stiffly, and Sadia's hands lingered, sliding down his torso and forcing

Ceven to take a step back to break the connection. It all made sense now.

Sadia wasn't upset that Evangeline was a criminal, or at least that wasn't the source of it. She was *jealous*. Of her. The idea seemed so ridiculous. That the tall, beautiful Rathan could be jealous of *her*. A human—or, more accurately, a monster in disguise.

Evangeline swallowed that revelation as Ceven helped her onto the gray mare. Sadia's face soured, and Evangeline felt a warm trickle in her chest. Even if the Rathan hated her, it meant that Evangeline had something she didn't. That, despite all her flaws, she had something a Nyte didn't, and it made her feel oddly powerful. She truly was turning out to be despicable.

Barto, Tarry, and Tor gathered on the remaining horses as Ceven saddled behind her, taking the reins. Everyone waved, and more fingers came up to splay the smiling faces around them. Evangeline nodded, cherishing the moment.

Knowing she would soon face her own potential death sentence, her teeth and claws were ready to be unsheathed.

They trekked through the tall grass and stretches of canopy that blended into sparse plains and back into thick wood over the next few days. All the while, her grip was knuckled on the saddle, the skin taut and white as it had been for most of the journey as the sun strolled across the sky and fell behind the hills, only for it to start all over the next day. They rested only as needed, riding for long stretches of time in between. Her

legs and rump ached, and the constant jostling was making her alarmingly nauseous. She'd ridden horseback with Ceven before, but never for so long, or with as much weight perched on her shoulders. It was hard to face her potential death when she couldn't even *move*. Not even Barto's jokes or Ceven's reassuring murmurs were enough to shake away the dread that gripped her since they'd left.

When the shroud of night took over again, they set up camp within the cover of trees. Evangeline helped Ceven roll out their bedding several paces away from the others behind a smattering of bushes. Close enough for safety, but far enough away for privacy, or at least the illusion of it.

The flower necklaces the girls had gifted Evangeline had withered a couple days ago, but as soon as they were far enough away from the village, Evangeline had pulled Sadia's from around Ceven's neck and discarded it in the woods. He'd raised a brow at her, and she ignored him.

"You're not still upset about Sadia, are you?" Ceven asked, keeping his voice lowered as he lay down beside her. She rolled away from him, more so he wouldn't see the flare of jealousy in her face.

"Of course not," she lied.

His arm snaked around her waist, pulling her closer to him, and despite herself, she relaxed and melted into his embrace. "You're the only one for me, Eve."

She bit her lip. She was being ridiculous, but she couldn't ignore the dark thoughts that had haunted her since they were kids. How she and Ceven were so different. That the only reason they became friends was because of his mother's affair making him an outcast like her. But what if Queen Beatrix's affair had never been discovered? Or if the nobility had turned a blind eye and accepted him with open arms? Ceven had always been leagues above her, while she only succeeded in dragging him into her own problems.

The temperature had dropped, cooling her sweat-stained clothes while Ceven's warmth radiated up her back and across her belly, where she wove her fingers with his. "What if we ran away tonight?" she whispered.

He stiffened, and her heart sank, knowing his answer before he said it. "You know that's a terrible idea, Eve."

She matched his rigidness, pulling away. He sighed, his breath brushing her neck.

"Despite what you believe, you're not going to die. Barto said he'll win your freedom, and I trust him. Besides, no matter what happens, I'll protect you."

That's the problem, she didn't say. The last thing she wanted was for Ceven to endanger himself because of her. Then again, if they ran away, he would be considered an accomplice. She would be turning him against his friends. "Forget I said anything."

His hold tightened, his lips caressing the slope of her neck, and she shivered at the light touch. "Everything will be fine."

She closed her eyes, wanting to believe him. But she didn't.

When Ceven's breathing slowed to a steady pace and the murmurs and rustling of the others dissipated into the low hum of crickets, shuddering leaves, and the hoot of a nearby owl, Evangeline carefully crawled out of their bedroll. Her steps were practiced, her limbs light as she carried herself across the labyrinth of roots, grasses, and leaves highlighted through the patches of moonlight through the canopy. Tonight, Barto stood watch with his back pressed to a tree as he carved chunks off a branch with his knife. It hadn't been her first time sneaking away from camp, her nightly hunts since arriving in Atiaca granting her far more grace to escape the Nytes' keen senses than back in the kingdom, but she kept them few and far between, not wanting to arouse any suspicions.

The few times Ceven had caught her moving, she'd lied and said it was to relieve herself. She stuck to her usual prey of small rodents, burying her kills far away from camp, and when the breeze would carry the scent away in the opposite direction. Tonight was no exception, but when she returned, her gaze lingered on the horses tied to the trunks surrounding camp. Her fingers itched to unravel the rope and ride off into the night. She would be leaving Ceven behind, the life they could potentially have together if everything did turn out fine like he promised. She would be on the run, chased, hunted, but she would be free.

And alone.

Something shifted to her right, and she yanked out her dagger as Barto's puff of black hair and pointed ears peered from between the trees. Instead of his usual carefree smile, his lips were thin, brows furrowed. Evangeline's pulse picked up, and she wondered if she looked as guilty as she felt. She was ready to hurl out an excuse for why she was standing there in the middle of the night, staring at the horses, when the Rathan whispered, "We're being watched. Wake Ceven and gather your things. Slowly. We don't want to alert them that we're aware of their presence."

She shoved down the spike of panic and nodded. She woke up Ceven and methodically packed up camp alongside the others. No one said anything, using the slivers of moonlight to light their way. It had been too risky to start a fire here, not that it mattered now.

They mounted their horses, starting at a steady pace. Barto and Tor led the pack up front and looked none the wiser—except Barto hadn't uttered a word, unlike his usual travel banter, and Tor had one hand on his lap, closer to where his crossbow was strapped to his side. Grace had said he was one of the empress's retired advisors, but despite the lines in his face and gray strands in his small bun, he didn't look retired at all.

Tarry's horse banked Ceven and hers, his usual stoic expression giving nothing away. Evangeline shifted so she had better access to the dagger strapped to her side, if needed. The night had fallen silent at one point, the call of birds and chirping insects quieting as awareness tinged the back of Evangeline's neck. Ceven tensed behind her, his grip tightening on the reins.

A whoosh of air came from the left, and Evangeline turned at the same time Barto shouted, "Archers!"

A snap of blue and gold wings shielded her as Ceven spurred the horse forward, jerking them at a breakneck speed. More arrows whizzed out from the passing trees as the sound of hooves pounded into the dirt, air rushing past her ears. Ceven grunted behind her, and the smell of blood hit her like a punch in the gut. Red stained the blue feathers on her left, an arrow poking through, inches from her face.

"Ceven, you're hurt!" she shouted, terror and rage gripping at her. How dare someone attack them, how dare someone hurt Ceven. If he died now . . . Her dagger was in her hand, not realizing she had reached for it at some point, the beast snarling for retribution in the back of her mind.

Barto shouted something up ahead, but Evangeline couldn't hear over the rushing air and the howling in her head as another arrow shot past her—Ceven veering them to the right just in time.

Unbarred moonlight illuminated the plains stretching ahead of them as they escaped the pocket of woods. Masked figures emerged from the trees behind them on horseback, four to their left and three on the right—now only two on the right as Tor's crossbolt picked one of them clean off their saddle, the horse galloping away.

Ceven sped up beside Barto. "Take her! I'll hold them off."

"Don't you dare!" Evangeline slapped at Ceven's hands, but he ignored her as he thrust her towards Barto's outstretched arms. She howled at the Rathan, but he didn't let go as Ceven dispatched from the group, his wing still bleeding.

"We have to go back! What are you doing!" Both her legs hung over the side of the horse, her hand clenching her dagger. She didn't want to hurt Barto, but if he didn't let her off this horse, she would do whatever she had to do.

"He can handle it. Now stop bucking or else we won't—"

The horse whinnied loudly beneath them before crashing into the ground. She slammed into her side, the breath shooting out of her lungs. Rocks and grass pegged her face as she rolled. Shouts and the smell of blood and metal split the quiet plains around her as she lurched back to her feet, ignoring how the world spun.

Her gaze fixed on a hooded figure on horseback, their sword inches from decapitating her. She ducked, narrowly dodging the blade, and fumbled for the dagger in her boot—the other had flown from her hands in the fall. The attacker circled back, and her heart pounded in her chest, adrenaline racing in her veins. The beast clawed at her insides, demanding release, the chains snapping one by one.

She didn't have time to check on Barto or the others as the attacker fast approached her. Could she lash out in time to deflect his blade? Should she dodge last minute? Or should she aim for the horse to dismount them? She clenched her dagger, her knees bent to leap out of the way when a cross-bolt whizzed by her shoulder. It missed the attacker as they leaned heavily to the right, but it was enough to unbalance them, losing grip on their horse.

Evangeline moved, instinct taking over. She shifted the dagger in her grip and focused on the hooded figure. They were already back on their feet and rushing her, but when their gazes met, their eyes widened a fraction.

The scent of fear hit her nostrils, and she grinned.

Her fingers worked the hilt of her blade with a practiced deftness. Before she could strike at their jugular, a bolt jutted from their skull, and they collapsed to the ground. She fell at their feet, the overwhelming smell of blood tugging at her insides, the beast roaring loudly alongside the beat of hooves as Tor approached her.

"Evangeline! Are you alright?"

Her lips peeled back in a snarl, her knuckles bleeding white around where she gripped the dirt. The attacker was a Caster, their hood pulled back to reveal horns. Blood flowed from their pierced eye, luring her closer until her hands felt the warmth of their life essence. She was vaguely aware of Barto joining Tor, the voices distant over the siren call from the red liquid that encompassed her senses. Somewhere in the back of her mind, she knew she had to get control of herself. She couldn't lose it here. Not with the others so close by. Not when Ceven would find out the truth.

Someone gripped her shoulder, pulling her back. Barto's gaze met hers, and he flinched, dropping his hand. She blinked, the world coming back into focus around her, making it easier to ignore the blood.

"I'm fine," she croaked, her voice sounding lower than usual.

Barto stared, as if unsure of who he was looking at. Evangeline sometimes felt the same way when she looked at herself in the mirror. She ignored him and glanced around, finding Ceven and Tarry riding towards them in the distance, the remaining attackers either having fled or been killed. She sighed in relief.

Barto's horse had been shot, but they were able to steal one of the attacker's mounts. Ceven had immediately wrapped Evangeline in his arms, checking her for any wounds even as his wing continued to drip blood. It took both her and everyone else barking at him to sit down before he listened and let Barto patch up him up. It was confirmed by their scent, weapons, and clothing that the attackers were assassins sent from Peredia. Except this time, they had a missive on them, validating what everyone already suspected.

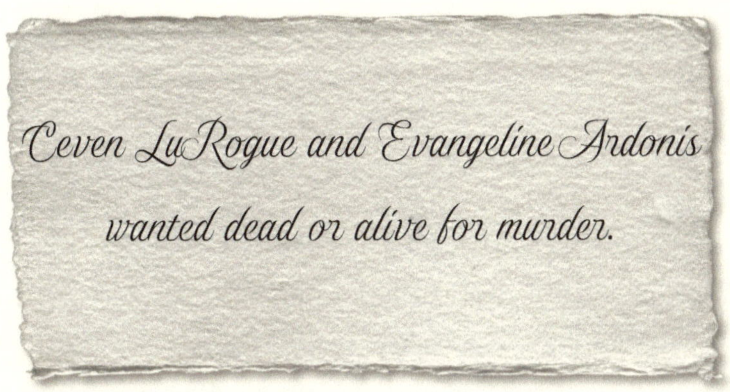

Evangeline met Ceven's gaze, the unspoken words hanging in the air. They would speak on this later, but first they needed to get to the capital.

Night merged into dawn as everyone nursed their wounds and scouted for any other assassins lying in wait. Barto shot Evangeline a few wary glances that squeezed at her heart. She had lost control for a split second and Barto had witnessed it, but would he tell Ceven? Or use it against her in the trial? She needed to figure out how to control it before another incident happened. If she survived the trial, maybe she could find a library or someone in the capital to help her research her symptoms, see if there had been anyone else like her in the past—preferably someone who was currently alive.

Evangeline excused herself from the group with the need to wash up. When she felt she was far enough away, she licked the blood clean from her hands, hating herself for how she reveled in the taste of it.

CHAPTER 6

Stale water and cool passageways were all Avana had come to know the past few days. The cave was massive in size and length, tunnels spanning in all directions. But the man who'd claimed these caves wasn't without taste.

Rugs, both plain and ornate, treaded the paths, with couches as green as the fake palms that had lined her apartment in Sundise Mouche. Which he had as well, the ferns fanning over knee-high tables that often were littered with maps, papers, and books of all languages, some she didn't even recognize. All of it illuminated by glass light fixtures like the ones back in her city, though where he was getting electricity in this forsaken place—wherever this was, she still didn't know—was beyond her.

She sat on the cleaner couch, one that wasn't piled with books and papers, her thumbnail prodding the pad of her index finger, a permanent mark from where she constantly poked it to bleed. To write out her spells and create her potions and tonics.

Just where *was* he? She'd been waiting for more than an hour, and he said this "errand" would only take a few minutes. Funny how she'd spent her life searching for a man like him, like Evangeline, had spent endless hours, years waiting for a moment like this. And now that she was here and given the opportunity to explore that, to *prove* herself, she was stuck waiting. Again.

Her gaze slid over the tome's bindings. History, languages, war strategies, and more she couldn't decipher. Whoever this man was, Jaden, he called himself, he consumed books like the Aerians consumed their alcohol. The cave was spilling with them, and she was still left wondering just how he had gotten all of them, all of these thing in this . . . cave.

The air intensified, the breath sucked from her lungs for a split second. Then it released, and from the corner of the room, Jaden stepped out from the rippling rock wall. The decorations used to resemble a normal abode was a laughable attempt to cover the fact that this man lived in a cave, but the man himself was anything but laughable.

"Avana." His smile was slow and confident, as if he hadn't made her wait for over an hour. Black silk straddled his legs and arms. The only color on him was his eyes, which were an unsettling green, set into a olive-skinned face with features she couldn't identify the origin of. For a cave-dweller, he was clean and smelled like crushed leaves in autumn and the tang of old blood.

She stood, smoothing her black dress. She hadn't intended to match him; she just preferred the color black. It was simple and practical and hid the stains when she made her alchemic solutions. "I had hoped you'd return sooner." And she hoped she kept the bite away from her tone. Even if this man, Jaden, shared the same mark on his hand like Evangeline, he was not her. He looked young, maybe a year or so older than her, in his early twenties, but his eyes told her that he was ancient. That he had lived many more lives than Avana or anyone she knew had.

And that he would kill her if he so chose.

As if reading her thoughts, he pulled a blade from the belt hidden at his waist. The ring of metal echoed in the room, and he plopped down on the couch across from her, taking a rag off the floor to wipe the blade clean. It was slick with blood, but she didn't dare ask whose. Like her relationship—former relationship—with Ryker Ardonis, she didn't ask questions, simply observed. Watched his mannerisms, the deft way he cleaned the blade as if he'd done it a thousand times. How his eyes concentrated on his nimble fingers, but she was sure he was observing her as well. Evangeline had still been a child, lost and in need of a helping hand, one she could easily lend and manipulate. But this man . . . he was a warrior. A soldier. A fighter. And a killer. If she pushed, he would push back ten times harder.

"I apologize for the delay," he said at last, making her wait. Yet again. Then his lips curled into a satisfactory grin, one she hadn't seen before. "I've found Evangeline."

Her spine straightened and her nose twitched in remembrance of the time Evangeline had broken it. Ignorant girl.

"And?" Avana shifted on her feet, crossing her arms. She was temporarily taller than Jaden while he sat, but she mostly remained on her feet around him to give her a semblance of control. Or the illusion of it.

"There is a trial. Being held tomorrow in the capital of Atiaca. I want you to go there and watch. Don't do anything. Just watch." He cocked his head, the blade shining, like his eyes. "Depending on the outcome, I will give you orders. From there you will capture Evangeline and bring her here."

Avana flicked her hair over her shoulder, smoothing her expression lest Jaden see her annoyance. Ever since this man had invaded her room at the castle, he'd been more obsessed with the blonde-haired woman than she had. He'd given her bits of information of why he wanted Avana's help, luring her with the promise of giving her all the answers she sought and the proof she desperately wanted. The proof to show the Council, to show everyone who had ever doubted her, that she wasn't crazy. That her family wasn't crazy and that her grandmother, Anali, wasn't a traitor but a powerful *genius*.

"Why can't you retrieve her yourself?"

Jaden didn't respond right away, and the pregnant silence weighed on her shoulders. Eventually he said, "I don't want her to see me yet."

As usual, Avana didn't ask questions, nor did she ask how she would travel to the Atiacan capital. Much like how she got here, it would be through the forgotten Shadow Doors.

"I'll lay out everything for you when the time comes." He rolled his shoulder, pushing aside the torso-length black hair, before pinning her with his gaze. She refused to cower beneath it. "Do not intervene, no matter what, and wait for my command. Maybe things will work in my favor, like they usually do." It was an arrogant statement, but there was no cockiness in his tone. Just fact, and Avana noted that in her mental journal. Whoever Jaden was or had been, it seemed he always got what he wanted.

CHAPTER 7

The remainder of the trip went by without any more trouble. They reached a long bank of rushing water that flowed off into the foggy distance, the setting sun hiding behind thick clouds of rain that misted them on and off through their journey. Houses, not domes, settled on stilts, and the thatched roofs came into view as the hooves of their group stamped into the muddy path through the small village.

"This settlement is often plagued by bandits because of the ferries that pass through its docks," Ceven said, watching her face. "I've been through here once in my two years in the empire. Still as unpleasant as last time."

"Why doesn't the empress help them?" she asked.

"I'm sure she'd love to, but the reality is that there are a bunch of villages much like this one that survive off the river and its goods and people," Tor said over the stampede of hooves. "Too many to help, not when most of the empire's resources are clustered at the capital and main ports. It's up to us to protect and produce our own goods this far away." Despite his words, he smiled. "But at the same time, the rules of the empire fall through the cracks the farther we are from the capital." His brown gaze stayed on hers, and Evangeline didn't miss his double meaning.

They took the ferry down the calm, winding river toward the capital. Ceven stood next to her at the railing the entire ride, taking in the passing marshes, the sun beating overhead, and the consistent wheel of churning water propelling them down the river. Evangeline tried to take it all in but found it hard when Ceven would touch her lower back, brush her arm, or tuck a stray hair behind her ear, sending her spine tingling and her face sprinkling with color. She remarked she wasn't going to plummet overboard—he didn't need to stand guard next to her. He simply smirked at her glare, his eyes softening when she sighed and twined her fingers with his. Some of the tension left her shoulders. Barto hadn't said anything to him about her losing it after the attack, but maybe the Rathan was waiting until they had a moment alone—or hopefully he would ignore it altogether.

"What's on your mind?" Ceven leaned closer to her ear.

She stared at the swirling water. "What do you think?"

He squeezed her fingers in their interlocked hands. "Something else has been eating away at you. Since the attack."

She swallowed, avoiding his gaze, knowing he'd see right through her. "I don't want to talk about it. There's already enough going on right now."

"Is it about the assassins? We'll be safe once we're in the capital. They wouldn't dare attack there."

It was more than that, but while he brought it up . . . "We have to do something, Ceven. We—you—can't live like this." Regardless of what happened to her at the trial, knowing Ceven would forever be hunted made her break out in a cold sweat. "We have to clear your name somehow."

He shook his head, the sun glinting off the ruby-red earring that had belonged to his mother. "I have something in mind. I plan to speak to the empress after the trial."

She frowned. That was the first she'd heard of this. If she decided to release the beast as a last effort to save herself, she would ruin Ceven's chances of any peaceful talks with the empress. "You can't talk to her before?"

He arched a brow. "You have something planned for the trial I don't know about?"

Her frown deepened. "Other than plead my innocence and try not to die? Of course not."

"Liar." His tone was playful, but his eyes turned serious. "You better not risk yourself, Eve."

More than I already am? She didn't say. Knowing Ceven wouldn't drop it now that he knew she was up to something, she turned and pressed her chest to his. His gaze darkened, making her wish they were back at the spring where Ceven's body slid with hers and it was only the two of them. "We'll get through this," she murmured before reaching up and snatching his lips in a fierce kiss.

Bodies swarmed as soon as they all stepped onto the stone docks on the outskirts of the capital city. The beast stirred restlessly, and Evangeline kept a mental grip on its muzzle. *I will not lose control. I will not lose control. I will not lose control.*

They squeezed through the dense pockets of people around the docks, the stench of sweat, fish, and an odd mix of sugar following them as they maneuvered through the dirt trodden streets. Homes were built from large slabs of concrete or brick, or whatever was available. Sometimes the roof wasn't even solid, taking the form of a haphazard tarp or cloth that sheltered all different colors of ears, tails, and furred Rathans. Humans were sprinkled in the mix, and even though some irrational part of her expected to see the black and purple uniform like the slaves in Peredia wore, these people, like the Rathans, adorned flowing silks and diaphanous fabrics, revealing much more than Evangeline wanted to see. A couple of Rathans even ran past them—an elbow ramming into her side—naked. *Naked.*

Fortunately, Ceven and the others remained close, Ceven plastered to her side, his wings branching farther than their usual tucked position, giving her room to breathe. Despite the soreness she still felt from being in a saddle, she missed riding in the open countryside away from so many Nytes. The capital here felt just as suffocating as Castle Peak, perhaps more so.

"What. . . what is this madness?" she exclaimed over the shouts, bustle, and stampede of feet and—was that a carriage? It was striding through the dirt street, heaps of people lunging out of the way, flicking only a brief aggravated glance, but nothing that screamed it was unordinary. This place was chaos.

Barto grinned at her. "Never been to the slums, dear? Not exactly like the posh, pristine streets of Castle Peak."

No, it wasn't. And though it wasn't as impoverished as the

sorry state of Lani's former room and slave quarters, it was filled with hundreds more people. And twice the size.

"How do people live like this?" Though she didn't need an answer. It was the same way the slaves in Peredia lived. They survived by any means necessary, and the Rathans surrounding her were already at more of advantage then they were. She shouldn't feel bad at the hovering bodies surrounding pockets of fire, or the naked children running in the streets. They were Nytes, and if they so chose, they could create a better life for themselves, unlike humans. They were damned the day they were born.

Tor and Barto led the way as Tarry and Ceven battered crowds with their wings and muscle at her sides. Soon, gates approached them, as well as guards. Unlike the plated silver or black mesh that armed soldiers wore in Peredia, these men—and women, much to Evangeline's surprise—were fastened in breathable leather dyed a shade darker than Ceven, Barto, and Terry's with metal bracers and plates across their legs and chests.

The broad-shouldered guard didn't pull the scimitar from his belt but laid a palm on it—matching the other five guards in front of the towering black gate. Evangeline couldn't tell if it was made from pure stone or another mineral, their faces and the swarm of bodies behind them glinting off its smooth surface.

Recognition flashed across the guard's face. "Advisor Nu'yuen?"

"*Former* Advisor." Tor's expression didn't change, the lines in his face rigid. Not at all relaxed like it had been prior to their trip.

Barto stepped forward, and the guards swiveled to him, giving him a salute. "Captain Nu'yuen. The Goddess is happy to have you back."

Captain? I thought he was only an emissary? Evangeline thought.

In his usual flare of charm, Barto beamed a sharp-toothed smile. "It's good to be back. Peredia's too cold for my liking." He squinted at the tallest Rathan to the left with a sandy-furred tail thick and curved down. "Serah? What are you doing guarding the front?"

Serah's blue eyes didn't shift from the moving crowd. "Guarding, sir."

Barto's brow bounced. "Yes, I see that. Your training isn't done. I'm reassigning you."

Red bloomed in the girl's freckled cheeks, and for once Evangeline was grateful someone else's cheeks revealed as much emotion. "Captain, I can—"

"Open the gates," he said, a pinch in his face.

Thick, silver rope stabbed into two holes at both sides of the thick slab. The ground shuddered, and the ropes moved, descending in a downward motion till a swirling city fell before them. One Evangeline had originally imagined the capital to look like.

Barto looked at her. "Welcome to Kazuumar, the capital of the empire."

They passed through, the doors thundering closed behind them. Evangeline gaped at the white, purple, and orange buildings clustered around them. Rectangles and squares resting atop one another in no particular order, blocks of stone and stairs sloping up in the distance to meld with curling blue spirals and what appeared to be a castle, even if it didn't look anything like the one she grew up with.

The stone path was wider than the dirt streets behind them, but just as many bodies ambled through, as well as wagons and carriages. Ceven and Tarry still pressed close to her as she looked in all directions. Rathans, Aerians, and humans hummed around a circular plaza, people shouting from different stands to buy their wares. Rugs, jewelry, and patterned fabrics dangled in the salty breeze, gulls fighting to be heard over the din of the crowd. It reminded Evangeline of the plaza back in Castle Peak, except here there were fewer reservations, more excitement—and no executioner's poles with nooses dangling ominously in the distance.

One distinct scent rose above the others, stirring that familiar deep well of emotions inside her she could only scratch the surface of. Her beast stirred immediately, and she tightened its reins, whipping toward the smell of crushed leaves and stale blood. She imagined clashing with a pair of green eyes and the faint hint of a smile in the crowd even as she met with only strangers. Gods, she yearned to see that smile, even if she didn't know why.

"Everything alright?" Ceven had lowered his head, his words grazing her earlobe. Heat rushed her cheeks. Ceven's crooked smile and gentle touch were all she needed in her life. Besides, her mystery man was surely long dead, or worse, didn't exist.

"It's nothing," she lied.

Evangeline lurched forward as they came to an abrupt stop. More guards clattered in front of them, the people around them giving a wide berth. These Rathans didn't look as friendly.

Scars painted their faces and the knuckles of their hands, which were resting on matching scimitars and cutlasses. Evangeline was more fascinated by the bronze collar and arm bands that settled tightly against patchy, furred skin.

"Sun Warriors, an elite squad of solders in the empress's military," Ceven said, for her benefit.

All their eyes fell on her, and she squirmed.

"At the empress's behest, we will escort the criminal from here to the palace."

Criminal. Though the guards didn't raise their voices, heads swung their way, and the curious stares turned into something else. Hate. And she couldn't help but laugh. Here she was in a strange city, in a whole new country, and the only sense of familiarity she felt was the mutual hatred of the crowd around her. The sneers and judgmental glares weren't anything new to her. In fact, they could learn a thing or two from the nobles back at the castle.

Ceven tensed, her hand in his. She craned her neck up at him, sending silent prayers in her eyes that he wouldn't try to fight or make a scene. She didn't care about the disgusted looks and curses aimed at her, but she didn't want them directed at Ceven.

He didn't look at her, but a sigh slipped out, his shoulders dropping, as if he realized there wasn't much he could do without causing more trouble. Tor stepped beside him, looking up slightly at Ceven. He nodded and then cast her a heartwarming smile. "It's time, my dear."

Her stomach plummeted.

The guards surrounded them, and Evangeline clenched at her pants, the fabric wrinkling. She turned to Ceven, and seeing her face, he tugged her close to him. The light kiss of his wings grazed her arms, and for a moment she was wrapped up in blue and gold and a face that was currently her rock in a riptide of emotion.

"No matter what, I'll make sure you're safe. You'll get through this alive and well, even if I have to knock some heads." He smiled, but she knew him too well. He was just as nervous as she was.

She cupped his cheek, which was rough with the beginnings of a beard. "Please, no knocking heads for my sake." She returned his smile. "Whatever happens, I'll be fine, so don't get yourself into any trouble."

One of the guards cleared their throat, and Ceven dipped his head, molding his lips to hers for a brief, blissful moment before releasing her.

At least she wasn't alone. Ceven and Tarry were forced to stay behind, as Tor and Barto trailed at her side. Even as they ventured farther into the city, she could still see Ceven's head from the sea of hats, scarves, and ears of different shapes and sizes.

Chains weren't attached to her neck and wrists, but she already felt the weight of them. "Am I going to die?" She had whispered the words, as if the sentence itself was too much too say out loud, but Barto's squeeze on her shoulder told her he heard. It was the first time he'd touched her since they'd been attacked by assassins.

Evangeline thought she had come to terms with her death. Had envisioned it during her endless nights of sleep when she'd first arrived here. Had accepted it long ago when she was beaten and malnourished in her early years as a slave for King

Calais and the other Nytes in the castle. When she faced the Wretched and when she murdered her foster father. But unlike improving her writing skill, or learning another language over time, she hadn't gotten better at dealing with the turbulent emotions that came with facing her own demise.

And before, she hadn't had to wrestle with a temperamental beast inside of her.

"You'll be fine," Barto said. "You're more of an asset alive, and Empress Zelene is a smart woman. She'll see that too. And with me by your side, you'll have nothing to worry about."

"What do you mean?" His confidence had a way of bolstering her spirits in the past, but this time, it felt too good to be true.

Tor scowled. "You should have explained everything to her, Barto."

Barto waved off his father's words with a flick of a ringed hand. "She'll find out soon enough. Don't worry, I'll be beside you the entire trial, and since I'm a familiar, respected face, we'll be sure to win your freedom." Barto smiled, and blast it, she wanted to believe in him. That she'd make it out of this alive. "Before the trial, we'll have time to talk privately. I'll explain how things work, and the plan. Until then, trust in me, and I'll make sure you're a free woman, Eve."

Evangeline caught the slight waver in his smile. Either he was lying about the outcome or he was as wary of her as the rest of his country seemed to be. *He's Ceven's friend, but is he mine too?*

The castle, or palace, as the guards had called it, was nothing like the rest of its city. It was made up of five rounded domes, the crystal blue ceiling glinting back the afternoon sun. Evangeline's feet ached as they clambered the stony stairs, hiking up to the blue spirals and span of other guards, these without the silver bracelets and necklaces. She was exhausted; sleeping on the ground out in the wilderness the past week hadn't been kind to her. Then again, she'd barely slept a wink since arriving in the empire.

Evangeline squeezed at Barto's arm, his black fur soft beneath her fingers. If he wasn't next to her, she was sure she would've been felled by the two-hundred-something steps. She should've been used to it, trekking between the castle and Lani's slave quarters for most of her life. And those stairs had been even steeper and more winding as they'd climbed into the side of a mountain.

But they never made it to the top when their surrounding guard led them in a different direction. Another dome branched out on the side of the palace, but it looked to be made up entirely of stone and settled closer to the ground, reminding her almost of a melted mushroom top.

"This is where we part." Barto detached his arm from hers, and panic flooded in. "But we'll meet again soon."

Tor put a hand on her shoulder, giving her a smile that couldn't warm her cold insides. "You'll be fine. Barto, I'll meet with you later before returning home. Grace would flay me alive if I didn't bring back gifts from the capital." Tor turned to her. "I hope you'll visit us again in the future, Evangeline. Don't worry, with Barto on your side, you can't lose."

No, don't leave me! She wanted to shout, to plead as the beast thrashed against her mental restraints, demanding she rip out the guards' throats and run as far away as she could. She bit her tongue. Hard. The familiar taste of iron hit the back of her

throat, and she focused on the pain as a distraction.

Tor waved goodbye, and Barto gave her one more reassuring squeeze before striding up the remaining stairs toward the blue domes. Evangeline and her personal escort of guards met another set of stairs—descending downwards.

Muted gray rock surrounded her head to toe, light coming through occasional openings in the ceiling, marking a bright beam in the shape of a square on the ground every few paces. The crash of waves echoed between their footsteps, and she imagined that on the other side of these stone walls stood the Araji Sea. At the end of the stairway was a hall with bronze doors fixed on both sides between the spaces of the square filter of light in the ceiling only a few heads above her. They entered the second door on her left.

"Sit," one of the four guards barked. She had short black hair that curled around black and gray furred, pointed ears prodding lower along the sides of her sharp face. Her hands were covered in pink flesh. She had been in a fight recently.

The other three guards settled at the corners of the room, which was small to begin with but now squeezed even tighter. A brusque hand shoved her into one of the two metal chairs in the room, and the Rathan loomed over her. Her eyes were a pale green, and there was no hate in them. Her lips didn't pull back into a sneer. Her jaw was tight, and instead what Evangeline felt was power. If she didn't do exactly what she was told, she wouldn't doubt this Rathan would smack her with a firm hand or pull out the curved blade from her side.

"I'm going to ask you some questions. And you're going to answer. Honestly. Every. Single. One."

Evangeline tensed. It wouldn't be the first time she was

questioned, but if they pressed her for the truth behind her mark, what it meant, and told them everything, would she be doomed to die anyway? Would she be able to lie with a straight face? She clenched and unclenched her hands, sweat beading down her back. Like Barto, would they catch a glimpse of the monster lurking beneath? Was she prepared to fight her way out?

She reluctantly bobbed her head, swallowing.

The Rathan guard folded her arms across her chest, her metal bracelets shining in the dimmed sunlight from the domed roof. "Then let's begin."

CHAPTER 8

⁓ CEVEN ⁓

The liquid burned down Ceven's throat, but it was welcomed. It helped to clear the knot building in his stomach. He set his glass down with a thunk on the slick, wood counter, sliding it toward the floppy red-eared Rathan behind the bar. "Another. Please," he added. Now that he was back in Atiaca, he wasn't a prince anymore. Not that he had been much of one to begin with, especially now. He didn't need to demand things or keep his mask on. It was nice to settle into the bustling crown of the tavern without the whispers, the looks, or the false bows.

"Keep this up and you won't be able to walk to your room."

Ceven didn't look at Tarry, who still wore his leather armor while Ceven had ditched it in favor for a loose knit shirt and pants. He sword remained at his side.

The Rathan filled his cup, and Ceven placed a gold coin on the counter, wings engraved on its surface.

"This is Peredian," the Rathan said, sliding it back.

This time he did look at Tarry sheepishly. The old Aerian shook his head, just enough for Ceven to catch, before reaching into his pocket and withdrawing several copper coins with five holes around their edges.

"Sit down, Tarry. You're making me nervous." Ceven embraced the hot liquid once more.

His voice lowered to a whisper, a soft rumble, almost like thunder. "You were almost assassinated mere days ago."

"We don't know if it was aimed for me, and they're leagues away now." But Ceven knew he was right; even if the alcohol danced in his brain, washing away those worries, he was still aware that anyone in this packed tavern could be ready to stick a knife in his back.

"The city is getting worse. They're letting too many people in. If anyone wanted to hurt you or Evangeline, it's easier now than ever."

Ceven grimaced. It was true, the streets were usually alive, at all hours of the day, from what he experienced during his two-year stay here, but as of late, the capital was filling up more and more.

"The attacks . . . they're getting more frequent," Barto said. The missing persons had turned into blatant attacks, whole villages being wiped out, leaving nothing behind but a trail of blood leading nowhere. And there had never been anyone left alive to tell who or what was going on. It was scaring everybody, having people flood to the cities and ports where better defenses were put in place. The empress may not want to turn away those in need, but it was going to get to a point where the capital was running out of room, and soon resources.

One of the females slinking throughout the tavern leaned over him, her painted nails delving across his unbuttoned chest. "Would you like some company?"

He gently grasped her wrist, removing it from his chest. He recognized the brown curls framing her red-brown skin. "No thank you, Lily." When Ceven had last visited this place, she and Quan had enjoyed each other's company the majority of the night. Granted, this time she was wearing more clothes and smelled more like burnt paper and musty water than fine wine and lavender.

Lily moved for Tarry, but he pinned her with a stony glare, and she scampered away.

"You know, it wouldn't hurt for you to relax." Ceven finished his glass. He was tempted to ask for another, but Tarry was right. He wanted to be able to walk to his room at least.

"It would. Xilo is no longer with us, and with you insistent on drinking away your problems, it's up to me to be your ears and eyes." At the mention of his former bodyguard, Ceven's head slunk down. His betrayal still slid over him like jagged glass. He'd known Xilo his whole life; Tarry even longer. Some small hope in him prayed that he made it out of the castle alive, but he knew the truth. Xilo was most likely executed, a loose end Sehn would certainly want cut.

Although Tarry's tone hadn't changed, Ceven sensed his disapproval and, frankly, Ceven agreed. He didn't want to admit it to the man, to anyone, how useless he felt. How much of a failed prince he was. He'd abandoned his kingdom and his soldiers when they needed him most. Let Sehn use him, throw him into muddy waters. Let him win and take his dignity as he fled. And tomorrow Evangeline would stand trial in front of the capital. He hadn't lied when he said he would protect her at all costs, but how he was going to do that, he didn't know. He trusted Barto, but did his friend really think that Evangeline wouldn't be sentenced to death? Ceven couldn't fight the empress and her entire brigade, and he was sure this time Barto wouldn't help him. Not against his own country.

He hated feeling so damned *useless*.

He asked for another drink.

Disapproval rolled off the Aerian in droves now. Ceven grumbled, "I wish Barto were here." The boisterous Rathan would've gladly joined him for drinks and then some. Ceven didn't know much about the Rathan anatomy, but he was sure Barto should've been Aerian, with how much alcohol he was able to store away in his slim figure.

A Rathan squeezed beside him, his hand waving for the bartender's attention. Ceven noted the ring on his finger, the asphite jewel shining pink in the dim fire lanterns. "You know, that ring you're wearing, it's told if you wear it every day, you will eventually find your true love." The Rathan turned, his cheeks flushed from previous drinks. He looked curious, and Ceven smiled, sinking into a story. Barto may not be there, but he would do his best impression of him.

Soon, a group of Nytes and humans hovered around Ceven as he told another story—this time of when he'd encountered a sandpit, stating this was why Aerians chose to fly. A horde of laughter erupted, and before he could delve into another tale, fingers curled around his bicep, and a sharp hiss hit his ears. "It's time to go."

Ceven scowled at Tarry but let him drag him away from the crowd. His footsteps fumbled a bit, but his bodyguard kept him upright to their room upstairs they had paid for earlier.

Tarry shut the door, sliding the lock into place as Ceven collapsed on the bed. Wool fought at the seams on the side, the wood planks it sat on groaning, but it was large enough for an Aerian of Ceven's size, which was why he gladly paid more for the master suite.

"Any one of those people could have killed you. Have you lost your head, Your Highness?" Tarry's words seemed harsher than his usual scoldings. Or maybe Ceven was too drunk to notice the difference.

"I'm not a prince anymore, Tarry. Drop that blasted title." He slung an arm over his head, grumbling at the old Aerian to snuff the lanterns.

Tarry didn't. He didn't move away from the door at all. There was only one window, the glass fogged from the heat inside the inn, but if anyone broke through it, they'd hear it. At least Tarry would; Ceven couldn't hear much from the buzzing in his ears in this state.

"What's the real problem?"

Ceven groaned. He didn't want to discuss his feelings with him. He wanted to keep them locked away. It was his problem and no one else's. "Nothing."

"You haven't been this reckless since you were a child."

Gods, the Aerian was relentless. Ceven just wanted to sleep, but anger surged in his toes, and his hands fisted around the pillow. "Let me have this, Tarry. I'm not a prince anymore; it doesn't matter what I do or how reckless I am. It's not like I can do anything anyway."

Tarry crossed his arms, the lantern light pitching across the wrinkles around his eyes and thinned lips. "We both know that's far from the truth."

Ceven raised his hand and stared at the rough callouses across his palms. He was far from useless, he knew that, but in this situation, he needed more than just brute strength. He hated to admit it, but he needed the charisma and silver tongue his brother possessed.

"No matter what happens, I'll always be here." Tarry's voice had dropped to a low whisper. Almost paternal.

Ceven let his arm fall to his side, the humming never fading. "Goodnight, Tarry."

First it was a pressure, like someone had sat on his chest, before his charmed necklace—an extra given to him by Tor when he lost his charmed jewelry back at the castle—heated against his chest, a fiery warning telling him magic was present. Ceven darted from bed, his eyes adjusting in the dark to see Tarry fighting with a shadowy figure. He grabbed for his sword, but it wasn't at his side. Instead, he pulled the knife from his boot, which he fortunately hadn't taken off before going to sleep.

The figure was fast, slipping through them, but Tarry blocked the door, his axes baring down, trying to get a solid hit on the shadow. Ceven ducked low, sweeping his leg out. The shadow slipped but landed on their hands, propelling themselves back up. It was then Ceven caught the black horns that curled inward around a shadowed face.

The figure pulled something from its cloak and threw it at Ceven. Tarry snapped to him as Ceven dodged, but the alcohol in his system made him sluggish, and wet liquid smacked into his right shoulder. Pins and needles prickled down his arm and into his fingers before his knife clattered to the floor, his right arm falling limply to his side.

"I'm fine." Ceven gritted his teeth, gesturing toward the door with the arm that still functioned.

Tarry spun, his axe pinning the edge of the attacker's cloak against the wall as they sped past. Light poured in from the inn's hallway as the figure swung open the door before bouncing back, their cloak firmly lodged beneath Tarry's blade. In the stream of lantern light, Ceven caught a glimpse of a snarl from beneath their hood. Ceven snatched his knife with his left arm, lunging for the Caster, when his legs locked in place. A blue substance coated the floor around his and Tarry's feet, preventing them from moving, as if their boots had been melded to the floorboards. He hadn't even seen the Caster drop anything.

The figure yanked at the edges of their trapped cloak when Tarry lashed out with his other axe, the blade notching itches from their face as the cloak tore free. They slipped out of the room at an unnatural speed. Ceven cursed, tugging against whatever concoction the Caster had trapped them in.

"Are you alright?" Tarry tugged against his own bindings, his eyes scanning Ceven for any sign of injuries.

"I'm fine," he repeated, embarrassment heating his cheeks. The liquid was already dry but left a green stain on Ceven's shirt. He tried bending his fingers on his right hand. It was slow, but after a moment of concentrating, they loosened and blood rushed back, reclaiming his muscles from the Caster's magic.

Tarry didn't bother giving him the 'I told you so' speech. Not that he ever had, but Ceven always saw it in his face. The raised brows and subtle, smug smile that grazed him, or maybe Ceven imagined it. But there was no time for that, as they needed to get themselves out of the Caster's trap.

He took his knife, carving his boots free from the glue-like material. "How'd they get in here?" Ceven cursed himself for drinking too much. Tarry was right; he had been reckless. If he'd been alone, he could've died or been easily maimed.

Tarry mirrored him pulling his own knife from his thigh and cutting away at the bottom of his boots. "I don't know. It was almost as if they had come out of the wall." A grimace slipped past his stoic features. "Caster magic." Ceven was sure the former Royal guard and ex-merc didn't like the idea that someone got the jump on him.

"Well, whoever it was, they didn't plan on killing either of us. It looked like they were just trying to escape." With Ceven dead asleep and Tarry unaware, it would've been easy for the Caster to make the first move. And that first move could've been lethal. "But why were they here in the first place?" he thought aloud.

Tarry looked at him. "To get information and to report back to someone else is a possibility."

That idea didn't sit well. That someone could slide in un-aware, watching him in the dark, made his stomach twist. "You're right," Ceven hated to admit. "I was being careless. From here on, I'll be on my guard." Because if he didn't, the next time he would no longer be a traitor prince, but a dead one.

CHAPTER 9

Questions hammered into Evangeline's skull, her legs and behind sore. Still, she didn't move or flinch, forcing her eyes to remain locked on the Rathan's slitted green ones. She was used to being interrogated by Ryker, twice a day, for most of her life, so answering the mundane questions was no problem. Only difference was that she'd sat on a much more comfortable couch, usually with food in front of her, in the past. The last time she had eaten had been on the ferry: dried jerky, nuts, and a few berries they'd foraged on their travels. She had quit her nightly hunts since the assassin attack. Everyone had been on high alert since, giving her no time to sneak off. The beast's displeasure rose every day, and she knew it was only a matter of time before she would have no choice but to indulge it one way or another.

At first the questions were simple. What was her name? Evangeline Ardonis. How old was she? Eighteen, she guessed. Where was she born? She was found in a ruin with no family to claim her. Why was she in the ruin? She didn't know, she was young. How young? She repeated that she didn't know, that she had no memory from her earlier life. It was assumed she was either four or five years old. Why did the king's advisor adopt you? There were rumors she looked like his daughter who died.

The Rathan leaned closer; her breath smelled of meat and metal. She repeated the questions, and Evangeline forced herself not to squirm. It reminded her of the first time she'd encountered Raiythlen, the Caster assassin she had regretted saving from the Peredian winter. One wrong move, and he would've killed her. And like him, it seemed this Rathan didn't believe her either.

Cold, furred hands gripped her wrist, pulling forward her marked hand. "You're telling me nobody knew how you got this mark? The advisor? The king?"

"No. They did tests on me, but they didn't know what it meant, or how I got it." Her grip tightened. Bone grinded, and Evangeline sucked in a pained gasp, blood rushing her ears, the beast clawing at her insides for release. "Ryker. . . I think Ryker knew. But I don't know how. He never told me anything."

"But you know what it means." Her grip didn't loosen, but it didn't tighten either, and it took all of Evangeline's effort not to snap at the Rathan's face. "Tell me. What does this mean? Why is it on our missing people?"

Evangeline hesitated, and pain flared again in her wrist as the Rathan squeezed. A growl bubbled up Evangeline's throat, and visions of her tearing into this warrior's neck danced in her mind. "I don't know why it's on your missing people. All I know is that it is Caster in origin, that it's draining the lives of others. I swear, I don't know why it's on me." Something else slithered in her thoughts. Raiythlen's threat.

If you ever tell anyone else about this, I'll make sure you and Lani die a slow, painful death.

She swallowed the hollow laugh in her throat. Lani had already died a slow, painful death without any of his help. And the Caster was no longer around to finish the job if he ever found out that she told this secret.

The Rathan didn't move, but her eyes narrowed. "What do you mean 'draining?'"

The secret was out now; Evangeline only hoped it wouldn't damn her when it came time for her trial. She kept her voice level as well as her eyes. "It means that whoever is putting these marks on people is draining them of their life. It's a slow, painful death. Worse than any disease." Lani's withered skin wrapped around her bones, the life ebbing away from her eyes. The pain in her wrist was nothing to the loss she felt in her chest.

It felt like hours, maybe longer, of questions. Not even Ryker had ever drilled her this long. Her tongue felt like lead, twisting and fumbling over words. They doubted her to the point she doubted herself. Why did she have this mark? Maybe she did somehow play a role in the disappearances of the missing people? She shook her head. Everything was blending together, and she just wanted their questions—no, their *demands*—to stop.

Eventually they did, and her shoulders slumped as hands gripped her, dragging her out of the cramped room. Cool air hit her face when the doors opened, and she was grateful for the space, to breathe more freely again, until they faced another door down the hallway to what she assumed would be her cell.

Shortly after the guards left her, Barto entered to her lying on the thin mattress shoved in the corner of the room, surrounded by the same gray stone. Sunlight streamed through the square opening in the ceiling.

"I think I'd take sharing a room with Sadia any day over that Rathan." Evangeline kept her eyes closed, a headache forming around her temples.

Barto shuffled closer, the door clicking shut behind him. "Sorry about Asmen. She does a fine job, but she's unrelenting and unwavering when it comes to her duty. I hope you still are mind enough to talk after all that."

Against the protest and exhaustion rolling in her muscles, Evangeline sat up and forced a smirk. "What do you mean? Asmen and I had a great chat. She even offered me tea and iced cakes. Though, we didn't have enough time to get to the part where we exchanged our most embarrassing secrets."

Barto chuckled, sitting on the mattress beside her. "At least you still have a sense of humor after that. Most people don't."

"Why are their metal bracelets around their wrists and neck?" She'd noticed that when she'd first encountered the Sun Warriors. They all wore them.

"They were once criminals. Given a second chance at life, only if they serve the empress. Those bracelets are fastened to their person, and the only way to remove it is by very, very careful means of melting the metal and breaking free. Or chopping off your hands and neck. Either way, not pleasant."

She thought of the Rathan woman with the scars. It was odd to think Asmen had been in Evangeline's place at one point. What had she done to get those bands?

"You should've told me. Prepared me for that."

Barto crossed a leg. "Nothing would've prepared you for that. It would've just made you more anxious."

A troubling, dark thought skittered in her mind. Did Barto not tell her on purpose? Did he think she was guilty and wanted to know the answers as well?

She turned her face away, pretending to scrutinize the carvings on the wall from the cell's previous tenants. "I'm not your enemy, Barto."

"Of course not. I wouldn't represent you if you were."

Evangeline turned, placing her full gaze on him, and he tensed. "That's not the full truth. You and I both know that."

His yellow eyes met hers for a silent moment before he let out a sigh, shifting the thick fur on his crossed arms. "There's something you're hiding. I won't pry," he said quickly when she opened her mouth, "it's clear you don't plan on talking about it. That being said, I can't figure out if it'll come back to bite me later." He pursed his lips when she remained quiet. "As captain, I do have an obligation to my empress and the people's protection first."

Evangeline wanted to confide in Barto, wanted to believe he would take her side, but how could she trust someone else with this secret, when she didn't even trust herself to stay in control? She wouldn't risk Ceven finding out and pushing her away. She wouldn't risk being branded a monster before she even had a chance to plead her innocence.

"Captain, not emissary," she said.

Barto frowned at the change in subject but shrugged. "These past couple years I've felt more like an emissary and tour guide than captain." Something in his tone suggested that he hadn't been too happy with that. "But at least the prince was pleasant enough to look upon." He winked as if they shared a secret, but it lacked its usual enthusiasm.

He clapped his hands together. "Now, for tomorrow, here's what I have planned . . ."

The more egregious criminal trials were held in a separate space away from the palace but spanned almost equally in size in a domed stadium that Evangeline, Barto, and their escort quickly approached. Hundreds of paces around, the Summoning Grounds (as Barto called it) rested within a massive sphere nestled on the coast of Kazuumar, the sun radiating off its roof like a giant turquoise jewel, with a full troop of warriors to guard its perimeter alongside a spiked iron wall tall enough to give any Rathan a hard time climbing and towers to hunt down any Aerians flying overhead.

It wasn't very far from the cells Evangeline had stayed in the night prior. A private path connected the two structures away from the public eye, giving her only a temporary reprieve from the roaring crowd warning her of the hundreds of faces she'd soon stare down.

They'll never take us as prisoners again. An echo of a memory riled up the beast, teeth bared. The promise of power within reach was so overwhelming, Evangeline had to inhale a deep breath of the salty air and let the sun overhead soak into her skin as her bare feet glided across the smoothed pavement. The beast continued to protest, but she drowned it out with the crashing waves coming from her left and the shouting of gulls overhead mixed with the cacophony of the crowd that gathered closer through the thicket of trees and bushes that sheltered their path to the side of the monstrous dome.

Barto, who kept stride next to her, stayed quiet like Asmen and their surrounding escort of guards, but he did give her arm a pat when she loosened a sharp breath of nerves. He looked handsome fitted in a silky amber shirt, the sleeves billowing and cuffing at his wrists with slits along the sides that did nothing to hide his athletic figure. His pants were of the same nature, but they blessedly matched—black silk with white stitching decorating the front.

He'd given her a slim pearl-white dress to wear this morning, her right leg almost completely exposed and the front dipping to her naval—nothing at all like the gowns the Aerians wore—but she didn't feel beautiful or delicate, as Barto suggested she act. Instead, the burning inside her tightened as her life unreeled before her. A human slave who had nothing but Lani's love, then Ryker's adopted daughter who had comforts she'd only dreamed of as a child, but at the cost of her friend and the hatred of other humans. She'd never had true freedom in this lifetime, and the suppressed rage, the yearning to be in charge of her own life was so overwhelming she nearly bolted right then and there. But it was too late to escape now. Not when it would scream her guilt and pit Ceven against the empress, who they needed on their side to survive the bounty on their heads.

Evangeline clutched her necklace from Grace, the stone cool between her fingers, as the thrum of people gathered closer like a hive of angry bees. Asmen and the other warriors hovered near Evangeline, shielding her from the crowd of Nytes and humans as they entered a side door into the Summoning Grounds. Heat immediately pressed at her cheeks, sweat beading at her temples while the crowd roared just beyond her makeshift shield of Nytes. Evangeline tried to keep her gaze straight ahead, but curiosity had her peering through the gaps of her armed escort.

Benches carved out of stone and covered with colorful cushions encircled the raised landing at the center of the dome. A gap was left between the rows of benches for a balcony that overlooked the landing. The size of the dome matched the length of the castle's courtyard, where Evangeline had secretly watched Ceven and other Aerians train, easily over hundred paces around. However, except for pockets of dirt and grass, like the courtyard back home, the ground was tiled with a sprinkle of yellow, white, and blue. Sunlight filtered through the transparent ceiling, making the floor shine and dim like receding waves and highlighting the two singular chairs on the landing. One red, the other white. Evangeline would've thought it all gorgeous and so different from the castle, if her thoughts hadn't been clouded by the steepness of the landing, if she would survive the fall if she leapt from it. Or if Ceven stood in the surrounding crowd with a plan ready for them if this all went horribly wrong—or if he would end up just as condemned as she was.

The beast howled in her ears, louder than the roar of the crowd, the shuffling of their feet as they climbed the landing, and Barto's soft words of encouragement. It promised her power, control, and respect. Her nostrils flared, and the stadium blurred to a sea of red, to a cluster of broken bodies and screams. Barto gripped her arm, keeping her upright and pulling her back to reality.

The landing and balcony hovered well above the crowd, held up by solid white stone splintering the Nytes and humans gathered around it, eager to witness the trial. The crowd either stood at the edge of the landing, necks craned up, or opted for the surrounding seating. They all wanted to catch a glimpse of the criminal, of *her*, the closest thing anyone in Atiaca had to the attacks, the missing people.

Asmen and the other guards peeled back, showcasing the white and red chair at the top of the landing, in view of hundreds of faces.

Barto gave a gentle push at the small of her back, toward the crowd. "It's showtime."

CHAPTER 10

The thundering roar of the crowd felt like stones pelting against Evangeline's chest. Her limbs locked in place, old habits digging their claws into her. Barto had told her to act weak and innocent, but she didn't have to act. In this moment, she felt like an ant. Like any moment she'd be crushed, whether from the crowd, the empress, or the guards lining the sides with sharp, curved swords. She didn't have time to catch any familiar faces in the crowd—not that she wanted to observe the faces that stared at her with a gut-wrenching amount of hate. No, it was much easier to keep her gaze contained to the floor.

At some point, the empress had walked onto the landing, holding the crowd's attention with a speech that didn't register in the chaos that clogged Evangeline's thoughts. Barto's description of Empress Zelene didn't do her justice. Up close, she was far more beautiful, with her purple dress accentuating the strong curves of her body up to her fierce eyes, the ends sliced in pink points like the pointed, furred ears prodding out her halo of brown curls. This Rathan had the power to sentence her to die. *No, that's not true,* she thought, taking in the crowd. Barto told her it was ultimately up to the people, and Gods, that made it so much worse.

The empress's words continued to calm and quiet the stadium, but Evangeline couldn't hear over the buzzing in her ears. Her insides burned, but she refused to vomit in front of hundreds of strangers. The empress waved a hand, each nail pointed and painted blue. The movement snagged Evangeline's attention, not on the empress but the two guards behind her. It was hard to tell in the shadowed overhang of the balcony, but she recognized Quan and Rasha. They stood still, their faces unchanging.

Quan had once tried to insult her, comparing her obstinance to Rasha. Unknowingly, she took it as a compliment, and right now it would give her strength.

Closing her eyes, she imagined the strong Rathan, the hard, unforgiving planes of her face that had the power to smile or make people squirm. The swiftness to which she wielded her blades and commanded herself. Evangeline sucked in a few deep breaths, and when she opened her eyes again, the buzzing had subsided, the heat dwindling. It was still there but bearable.

Barto urged her to take a seat in the red chair, the back standing taller than her and arched so that two wooden points framed her head. It was far from comfortable, and the scarlet cushion contrasted against her pale skin. Two other figures emerged onto the landing, coming up the stairs from the trapdoor behind them. It was a Rathan with orange ears that sagged on either side of a mop of brown hair, fringed with gray.

More hair gathered in clumps on his hands, which clenched a polished cane that made large thuds where it came down on the stone. Evangeline didn't know who the man was. He wasn't dressed as a guard, a blue and gold robe wrapping around his crescent figure, and he was far too old.

Behind him was—Evangeline's eyes widened. Even from twenty paces away, the smell of blood, metal, and crushed leaves danced around her, igniting all her senses. The familiar scent sparked a fire in her gut and raised her flesh, a reaction stronger than any memory could illicit, grabbing the beast's attention as if he had gripped its very neck and yanked it toward him. Between the rumbling of her inner monster and the heat rising rapidly up her feet to the pits behind her eyes, her vision blurred.

No . . . it can't be him. It's not possible.

The man behind the older Rathan wore the same attire, but the blue robes fitted a body that had more youth and power in it. Long black hair swept down his back, woven with three gold bands matching the trim of his sleeves, and he wore an expression that told others to keep their distance while luring Evangeline closer. She wanted to cradle his face, take all of him in, before clasping her fingers around his throat.

Jaden's emerald eyes locked with hers as he walked past to stand behind the white chair the old Rathan had sat in. Evangeline could breathe again, but she didn't look away, her eyes drawn to Jaden's hands bangled in bracelets. No symbols marred his skin.

"Today," an Aerian with powder-green wings bellowed. The empress had vanished, the shuffle of the white curtain from the raised balcony dismissing her presence. "We are presented with our two esteemed advisors, Ehmad Pervanste,"—the old Rathan waved, more so a swat of the hand than a formal one—"and Zindelis Mahem." The younger man bowed briefly at the hip. "Their combined wisdom and insight to these disappearances will hold a reasonable and logical attack against the accused, Evangeline Ardonis."

Evangeline pinched her brows together, her lips pressed into a thin line. Her eyes never left the dark-haired man whose presence rattled her with such force that beads of sweat formed along her skull.

The Aerian continued, "In defense of the accused is Barto Nu'yuen. Captain and son of former advisor, Tor Nu'yuen."

There were no cheers, or shouts, for either party. The Summoning Grounds had grown quiet and still. Serious. Attentive. Evangeline kept her head low and shoulders even lower. It was hard to pretend she was strong and weak at the same time. A war she had been fighting with herself for a long time.

"Let the trial begin."

Jaden, who currently called himself Zindelis—Evangeline found it hard to believe this wasn't the same man who occasionally haunted her dreams—helped the old Rathan, advisor Ehmad, stand up from the white chair that looked sturdier than this Nyte struggling to stand. Evangeline pitied him until he opened his mouth.

"This criminal does not even need this trial. Her guilt is already written on her for everyone"—he tried to sweep his arm but faltered back to his cane before he lost his balance—"to see. Why does she stand here, alive, when our loved ones are not? Why do these strange markings take from others but not from her?"

Evangeline prayed Advisor Ehmad would lose his balance and fall flat on his face.

I was born with this mark. It's not my fault! she wanted to shout, but she bit her tongue instead. She didn't want to ruin Barto's chances of defending her, choosing to trust him. For now.

Barto stepped forward. The usual smile that grazed his features was absent; in its place were narrowed eyes and a rigid set to his jaw. "These past few weeks, I have accompanied *Evangeline*," Barto stressed, "and do not find a criminal or someone of mischievous or sinister plans. Rather, she is a victim. As a human, she was sold into the labor force for the Aerian royalty at the age of four. She was forced to work day and night for years. As a child, she already had this mark. If this were a child and not a woman standing next to me, would you still find her guilty? Would you still think a child, a human child of Peredia, be held accountable for the hundreds of missing persons in Atiaca?" Barto pinned a look at the old Rathan, whose gaze remained fixed on the crowd. "I respect your position, advisor, and I have known you to be of the logical type. Even you must see the impossibility in this accusation."

Ehmad didn't speak, but his partner took a step closer. Evangeline swallowed a gasp as a surge of heat welled in her stomach, her jaw clenched as if it were she ready to pounce and not the beast inside her.

Jaden didn't look their way. In fact, his face was entirely bereft of any emotion, aside from the occasional twitch of his lips. As if he'd already won this case. Evangeline flared her nostrils, and her nails bit into her skin, as if claws would spring forward at any moment if she didn't stop herself.

Is this really the man who has haunted my dreams? Who I had loved in another life? Is that even possible? Emotion and thoughts whirled together, as if different parts of her were forming back into place, but she still couldn't quite see the bigger picture.

"What accusation, Captain Nu'yuen?" said Advisor Zindelis. "Our intent isn't to pin all these attacks and missing persons on this woman. Indeed, that would be improbable, though I wouldn't outright say impossible." A slight smile broke out, but it was far from kind. "No, we simply want to shed light on the fact that she is no more innocent than any other soldier on the field."

Take it. Take it. Take it all and leave nothing. The familiar phrase sang to her, forcing her to inhale deeply through clenched teeth. Gods, not now. She couldn't lose control, not when it would only confirm that she was a monster. A murderer. A criminal. It would seal her fate, and she would die here today. *Why not let it out? Prove to them all who's in power here, who is really in control. You've fought for your freedom before; don't give that all away now.* Evangeline couldn't be sure if it was her own voice compelling her or something else. She was too focused on not leaping from her chair and diving for Advisor Zindelis, which made her feel . . . well, she didn't know exactly what this feeling was.

"Child or not, she is involved in all of this," Zindelis—Jaden—continued. "That mark is the only evidence we have to what is happening in this empire. The only link."

This time their gazes met, and Evangeline was standing before she could stop herself. "You know that's not true!" Her eyes flitted to his hand, lacking the same marking damning her to this trial, but she knew it was there. Or had been.

His green stare flashed, as if daring her. "Oh? And how so?"

Eyes, *hundreds* of them, fell to her. The weight of them made her sag back into the seat, but it was too late. She'd already embarrassed herself, accusing one of the empress's esteemed advisors in front of everyone. If they didn't think her guilty, they would surely think her crazy. She gritted her teeth, boring holes in Zindelis's face and the blasted smirk pressing at his lips.

If this trial went up in flames, she would take him down with her.

Barto trained his face to remain indifferent, but he had to be wondering what she was doing. Why she had lost her calm like that. She questioned it too, when Jaden's mouth twitched again and the fury roared back. *I'm going to lose it.*

As if sensing it, Barto shifted closer, placing a firm hand on her shoulder. She didn't know if it was reassuring or confining, but his hand was warm, and the aroma of oranges and lemongrass wrapped around her, easing her nerves. "My time in Peredia proved that others, maybe more than those we've lost here, have fallen victim to these strange markings. And Evangeline wasn't at the center of them, but Ryker Ardonis himself, who the prince had killed on behalf of all the victims who had died from these runes. One of the victims being Evangeline's dear friend, Delani Thorp."

At the mention of Lani, even the beast within her paused, the fire in her gut reduced to a mere candle flame now. Evangeline could almost hear Lani's scolding, telling her to get a grip and to stop acting foolish. *Gods*, she missed her. She'd trade anything to see her, even if for a few stolen moments, to tell her how sorry she was for not getting them out sooner, for not protecting her like she'd promised. For letting her down.

"And yet, Evangeline lives, while the others have died. Why is that?" Advisor Zindelis's voice scraped along her skin, drawing her back to the present. To where she was—

a prisoner, held guilty by the bloodthirsty Nytes surrounding her. Their hatred rising and choking her along with the oppressive heat of everyone's eyes on her, bodies packed tightly and trapping her on the landing with no clear path to escape.

Evangeline clawed at the arms of her chair. Barto's hand on her shoulder tightened in warning, but she snapped, "How do you know for sure they're all dead? Have you seen them with your own eyes?" *Something you'd like to share, advisor?* she wanted to snark.

"Eve, what are you doing?" Barto hissed under his breath.

Advisor Ehmad spoke up, his voice rattling like a hornet's nest compared to the smooth cadence of his partner's. "You said it yourself, Captain Nu'yuen." He completely ignored her. "Ryker Ardonis was found guilty of marking and taking the lives of these victims. It's in her namesake. As Ryker Ardonis's adopted daughter, is she an accomplice or the mastermind behind it all? I wonder."

Jeers rose from the crowd, and sunlight streamed through the domed roof, reflecting off a sea of teeth and narrowed eyes all directed at her. What was worse: the Peredian tradition of being executed without trial? Or this Atiacan tradition of sitting and listening to pointless slandering and opinions before meeting her end? At least in Peredia when someone met the axe, or was about to be hanged, there was no false hope. No useless bickering.

Evangeline clenched her jaw shut to keep from shouting

profanities at the old puss-filled advisor, but what was the point in holding back? Clearly, they weren't winning. If the crowd already deemed her guilty, why not prove it? Release the beast and claw her own way to freedom. *But then what would happen to Ceven?* She clenched her eyes shut, imagining him thrown in chains as an accomplice for harboring a monster. The same hatred in his eyes like the crowd's as he saw her for what she truly was. A bloodthirsty beast.

"If you still wish to see her as a criminal, which she is far from, then let me appeal to your curious natures, advisors," Barto said, and the swarm of angry Nytes quieted, leaving only the shuffling of feet and remaining bickers echoing off the surrounding stone. "As you said, she is the only link. The only living proof anyone has of these strange markings and disappearances." Both Evangeline and Barto knew that wasn't the case—Peredian soldiers had the same markings as she did and looked to be doing fine, more than fine. "We can perform tests on her, if need be. Use her as an asset in this investigation. I know you're as eager as I to place the blame on someone, to direct this anger, but she is not the culprit. She is the key to finding them."

Barto's hand was still firm on Evangeline's shoulder, which she now assumed was less out of comfort and more to restrain her. As if she would make a scene—worse than she already had. As much as she abhorred everyone around her deciding her fate with barely a peep from her own mouth, she understood her words had only fallen on deaf ears and had stirred the crowd even more. Barto's suggestion that they use her as a tool didn't sit well with her—her skin crawled remembering the way Avana's magical vials had prickled and warmed her skin, the way Ryker's eyes felt on her as if she were a science experiment and not a living being every time another scholar came and pierced her with a needle—but she understood the captain's angle. If Barto made Evangeline useful, she might live to see another day.

And she wouldn't have to hurt anyone.

"Mayhap," the old, annoying Rathan droned, "but she is still unpredictable. If she's behind these disappearances or is working with someone connected to these attacks, she can also prove to be a liability. Letting the enemy sit idle to be rescued or to plan another attack is a risk."

"All strategic moves in war pose a risk. And what you're implying I still find deplorable and unreasonable." Barto arched a brow.

"All due respect, Captain Nu'yuen, she has worked with Casters and has a Caster mark. What I'm implying is very reasonable."

"Working with Casters doesn't automatically make you a criminal."

"On the contrary—"

"*Enough.*" Empress Zelene's voice snapped the old Rathan's mouth shut.

Evangeline jerked up to see the empress's pink painted eyes as she stepped out from behind the balcony curtain. She walked with deliberately slow steps, her bare feet sliding across the surface gracefully with nothing but the gold bracelets around her ankles chiming together into an oddly calming sound. Her hands curled around the railing, blue tinting the white stone from the sunlight seeping through the stained-glass roof.

"She indeed would be a useful asset, Barto Nu'yuen." Despite how much higher the balcony stood from where Evangeline was on the landing, the empress's soft words carried across the expansive stadium. "But I do agree she is unpredictable, and we still don't know what she is capable of."

The Summoning Grounds went silent. No one objected.

Then, the empress waved her hand, breaking the spell she had over the crowd. "It is time to adjourn."

Evangeline frowned, and Barto gave her a reassuring smile, though it was tight-lipped. Worry edged his eyes, which would have warranted a panicked "what's going to happen?" from Evangeline if Advisor Zindelis hadn't turned to her, his eyes fixating on hers at the same time she felt the overwhelming pressure of a nearby Shadow Door.

CHAPTER 11

The hooded figure tangled through the crowd. They would've been unnoticeable, blending in with the hundreds of bodies shoved together, if Ceven's eyes hadn't been concentrated on them this entire time. He bounced his right leg up and down on the sole of his foot, eager to shoot up from his seat and follow the mysterious figure. Sea watery hells, he'd love to be able to fly across the Summoning Grounds and confront the stranger himself, but with the surrounding warriors keeping one eye on the landing and the other on him, he was confined to his seat. The empress was compassionate but not a fool. Ceven and Tarry had been invited to hold witness to Evangeline's trial, but any interference would be met with deadly force. His lip curled; the empress had him and Evangeline right where she wanted.

Two weeks ago, Ceven and the others had crossed the border into the Atiacan empire through a series of underground supply tunnels and border checkpoints where soldiers had not yet been informed of Ceven's treason, allowing them to pass through without much trouble. While Ceven and Evangeline remained with Barto in his village, Rasha and Quan, along with others who had joined them in escaping the kingdom, continued ahead to the capital. While Barto may have exaggerated some truths on Ceven's behalf to the empress, Rasha and Quan would leave no details out—including that he was wanted for treason. That is, if his brother hadn't already informed the empress.

Ceven wanted the empress's protection for both himself and Evangeline, but what would it cost him?

"They're moving towards the balcony," Tarry murmured from beside him on the stone bench.

Ceven nodded, eyes tracing the figure through the occasional bobbing of heads and thrashing arms. The heat of the stadium made Ceven's cheeks burn, and it was miraculous the figure adorned completely head to toe in dark fabrics hadn't fainted of heat stroke.

What's their goal? Did they plan to assassinate the empress? Ceven snorted. They wouldn't make it out of here alive, if that was the case. Not only because of the warriors lining the perimeter, but the people would rip them to shreds for attacking their beloved empress.

Empress Zelene ducked behind the white curtain, and the Aerian announcer rang out today's trial. Ceven's vision danced between Evangeline, her face shielded by a halo of hair, and the moving stranger. Tarry's hand subtly brushed his side, his chin angled towards a nearby exit, one of four interspersed throughout the Summoning Grounds. Ceven hadn't explored them before but knew hallways had been dug out beneath the rows of seating to provide easier access around the Summoning Grounds. Impatience welled, and he surged to his feet, elbowing his way to the underground exit with Tarry close behind him.

Ceven made it to the hallway's opening, a pocket in the surrounding crowd where an overhang crested between the sections of seated Nytes and humans, before armed warriors blocked his path. The landing was still in clear view, but they hung below the swarm of Nytes and humans, the ceiling rumbling from stomping feet.

"Please return to your seat, Prince Ceven," the Rathan warrior said, her sharp nails already on the hilt of her scabbard.

"I will as soon as soon as you do something about that Caster." He kept his voice level.

Her forehead crinkled in confusion before it smoothed. "What Caster?"

"The one making for your empress's balcony." Ceven pointed in the direction he had last seen the Caster. "Brown cloak, glamoured their horns away. Don't you have any jewelry against magic? How can you not have noticed?" As if in response, Tarry's frostlite ring turned from its milky white neutral state to a light blue, indicating magic was in the vicinity. Ceven's charmed necklace hidden beneath his collared shirt was cool against his skin— they weren't in danger. Not yet, at least.

"We did." Ceven turned and faced Quan, who was walking towards him from the opposite side of the hallway, the overhead lanterns reflecting off the double-headed spear strapped to his back and knives at his belt. The two feline-like ears sprouting from his head and the graceful way he took his steps spoke of his Rathan background, but unlike others of his kind, his russet skin was bereft of fur or hair, showcasing the gold flecks within his brown irises, his pupils slitted like the wrinkles between his brows where he often scowled.

How did he get down here so fast? The furless feline sure was nimbler and more flexible than Ceven ever had been—not that would prevent him from winning if a fight broke out between the two of them here and now.

Barto's steel-tipped tone carried off the cream-colored stone with ease, muting the crowd. Ceven glanced briefly at the landing, at Evangeline, before steering his attention back to Quan. He would do whatever it took to protect her.

"We've noticed since they entered, and we have our eyes on them. But the empress isn't their target," the furless Rathan said.

Ceven frowned, thinking back to the intruder in their room. They hadn't aimed to kill them, but why were they there in the first place? And if they weren't here to assassinate the empress . . . "How do you know for certain?"

"Her eyes haven't left Evangeline since she entered."

"She?" Ceven's eyes darted to Evangeline—who looked far from the calm and collected woman he'd seen initially cross the landing—to where he'd last seen the Caster who had now disappeared. "Why Evangeline?"

"Her glamour is thick and decidedly female but not confirmed. We don't know any other changes that may have been made. The warriors in the east block have relayed she is carrying at least one knife on her right hip, and a slip of her hand showed tattoos. We're searching the grounds for any Caster symbols." As he said that, he motioned to the other Rathan that had first intersected him. She nodded and turned on her heel, the remaining two warriors following suit.

"Then what are you waiting for? You need to apprehend her now. Warn the empress." Tarry nodded in agreement, but Quan's expression didn't change. Ceven wondered if he still still held a grudge against him for ordering Xilo to take Evangeline to safety behind the warrior's back.

"I have. I'm good at my job, Ceven," Quan said, dismissing his title, and Ceven couldn't be sure if it was intentional or not. "I'm under orders, *by the empress*, to not attack but observe."

Gods, curse this. Of course, Ceven saw the reasoning behind it. To lure out the figure's intentions. But what if they caught on too late? What if waiting and observing got Evangeline killed? Or Barto? Or this whole stadium?

As if sensing it, Quan snatched his spear and whipped it at Ceven before Tarry rushed in front of him, the steel point a hair's length away from Tarry's palm. Like Ceven, he'd been smart enough to not draw his weapon, knowing the last thing they needed was to fight one of the empress's best warriors.

Quan *definitely* hadn't forgiven him.

Ceven flipped his hands up in universal sign of surrender. "Calm down. I don't plan on leaving, I'm just curious."

"Then go be curious back at your seat. We have this under control." Quan's spear didn't move.

Ceven raised a brow. "Is Barto aware of all this?" Quan didn't reply, but the twitch of his right ear told him all he needed to know.

Suddenly the air tightened, as if it had become a living thing expanding the room, sucking the oxygen from it. Ceven's feathers rustled, the energy prickling through them, making every hair on him stand on edge. He shared a look with Tarry before their eyes jerked across the dome for the Caster. This was the same sensation they'd felt back at the inn.

Quan followed their gazes, confusion etched into the lines of his forehead. He retracted his spear. "What's happening?"

As much as Ceven wanted to give the bastard a *you should've listened to me* smirk, he didn't want anyone to get hurt—or die. He told Quan everything that had happened to him and Tarry at the inn, including the same pressure they were experiencing now, in hopes the more info they had, the better their chances at preparing for the worst.

The crowd, from what he saw from their secluded dip in the side of the Summoning Grounds, were transfixed to the landing. Unaware of anything happening in the sidelines. Ceven continued to skim the heads until—there. The Caster ducked in and out of the rows of seats, faster and more obvious now, closest to the balcony. Heads turned towards her, and warriors trailed after her moving figure.

"You were attacked?" Quan said, but Ceven ignored him, focusing on the Caster, then at the landing. Quan was right. Their eyes did not seemed focus on the empress at all on the balcony but the trial itself. His vision wasn't as strong as a Rathan's, so he couldn't be sure if it was Evangeline they were staring at or the landing in general.

Another eruption of pressure shuddered through him, and this time he noticed a similar disturbance in the crowd. "Quan, I understand you have your orders, but we need to act now."

This time Quan didn't argue. "I'll inform the empress. To the right, down the hall behind you will take you to the far side of the dome. You'll be closer to the Caster from that angle."

A strong-jawed warrior came down from the rows of seats, murmuring something into Quan's ear. His eyes found Ceven's and narrowed. "But you're not allowed to leave. The empress wants a word with you, and if you leave these premises, it'll be your trial next."

Ceven and Tarry pedaled down the hallway, the air cooling the beads of sweat that had formed on his temple from the oppressive crowd above. The landing and the sea of people were hidden behind thick stone, but the pressure still hummed in the air, taut as if someone were slowly pulling back a bowstring. A stream of filtered sunlight rose ahead, signaling the stadium's eastern exit back into the crowd and closest to where the Caster had last been sighted, when a man stepped in their path.

Ceven immediately recognized him from where he had just stood on the landing.

"Prince Ceven." Advisor Zindelis's eyes flashed, the green irises shrinking briefly. "Leaving so soon?"

"I'm surprised to find you here, advisor. I was under the impression the trial hadn't yet ended." Ceven's voice was calm despite the sinking feeling in the pit of his stomach.

Advisor Zindelis flicked his hand, as if dismissing Ceven's statement, but his eyes narrowed on Ceven's fingers, which clasped his sword. Ceven hissed in pain as his necklace flared to life, searing his skin with an intensity he hadn't felt before. Over his shoulder, Tarry's ring had swirled a pitch black.

Ceven's narrowed gaze reined in the man head to toe. Advisor Zindelis had been present for the last trial Ceven had attended here two years ago. He remembered this advisor announcing the woman guilty, immune to the woman's pleas as she cried on the landing, begging for clemency. The lack of emotion the advisor had possessed at the time, and even now, unnerved Ceven. Not to mention he was the only human in the midst of advisors—in an empire that still viewed humans as second-class citizens in some territories. There was more to this advisor than what Ceven had originally thought. Just what kind of power did he possess?

"Advisor Ehmad is plenty capable to speak on my behalf. Besides, the empress has already made up her mind on what she wants from the girl. The illusion that the decision is in the people's hands is laughable. The empress always gets what she wants, whether or not anyone knows that." He tucked back his black hair, the air around his hand shimmering. Almost like a double vision before it dispersed—a glamour. Ceven's sword was drawn at the same time Tarry unhooked his axes.

The advisor didn't move, didn't even flinch as he continued, "But then, so do I." His smile didn't reach his eyes as he walked towards him. Ceven clenched his sword tighter as the advisor walked right past them, a whiff of burnt paper and stagnant water. Ceven's eyes widened, and when he spun to face Tarry, pain exploded in his chest.

CHAPTER 12

EVANGELINE

Evangeline was constrained to a room that reminded her of a cell, the exception being the walls were painted blue like the ceiling, and the speckled floor told her she was still somewhere in the Summoning Grounds. A few chairs crammed the space, but she chose to stand, pacing her confining quarters. At least the beast in her stomach had quieted, leaving behind a bone-deep exhaustion, but sleep was the farthest thing from her mind.

A Shadow Door. That presence, it was without a doubt a Shadow Door opening. And Advisor Zindelis, that had to have been Jaden, right? Or was she simply mad? The beast had responded so fiercely she was surprised she hadn't lost control right then and there. And those eyes, it was as if he was coaxing it out of her, wanting her to lose her grip on it. What the blazes was happening?

Evangeline coiled a string of hair tightly around her finger, her teeth pressing into her bottom lip. The door was locked—she had already tested it—and there was no window or translucent dome ceiling to tell her the time of day. It had been Asmen and two warriors to escort her to these rooms hidden beneath a trapdoor below the landing that held the trial. Barto followed Advisor Ehmad to a separate place while Advisor Zindelis had left to do Gods know what. She didn't have any time to warn Barto about the Shadow Door or Advisor Zindelis's true identity.

Voices echoed faintly down the hall, but Evangeline could make out the low timbre of who she assumed were two guards. She crouched by the stone door, not even a sliver of space to see beyond into the hallway, but when she closed her eyes and focused on their conversation over the beating of her own heart, she heard everything she needed to know.

"—sentences have been called," one said.

The other scoffed. "You think she deserves to live?"

"I don't know what to believe."

"Either way, she's not making it out alive. You saw that crowd."

There was a hum of agreement. "It's a death sentence for sure."

She bit down hard on her lip, drawing blood. Her nostrils flared as the walls closed in around her, stealing her breath. She was going to die.

No, I didn't come this far to die now.

A snarl escaped her throat before she could stop it, the beast leeching into her veins at the threat of their survival. She could launch herself at the next Nyte to open that door, but would she be able to wrestle back control? This wasn't a rabbit, or some small rodent she was attacking, but full-fledged, trained warriors. Even with the beast's help, there was no guarantee she'd make it out alive or unscathed.

Although the door was locked and there were no windows, the room itself wasn't stifling. There was air flow. Not cool, but enough to indicate there was circulation coming in from somewhere. The ceiling appeared smooth—no place for air to travel through—but along the base of the wall was a series of vertical openings, and when testing the space in front of it, fresh air pushed at her fingertips. She picked at the opening with her nails, testing its toughness. It didn't feel like stone, maybe hardened clay or its equivalent.

She peered around the room as if magically a sharp object would appear out of nowhere. She grasped at her necklace, the sharpened rock cool and firm in her hand. She kissed it. "Thank you, Grace." Unclasping the chain, she carved into the wall, expanding the vertical slits, but the process was painstakingly slow. Sweat beaded her brow, her heart racing as she waited for the door to slam open. For the Nyte warriors to drag her off to meet her doom.

This was taking too long; she needed to get of there *now*. She bit her lip, glancing at her dress and then her hands. She didn't have to release the beast, but maybe she could lean on its strength. Ripping off the ends of her dress, she wrapped her fists with the white fabric, cushioning her blow as she flew a fist into the weakened opening.

Pain shot up her arm, luring the beast closer to the surface. Its power crawled into her veins, fighting for control as her vision blackened around the edges. She shook her head, focusing on escaping, on finding Ceven and getting the blazes out of here. She hurled another punch at the wall. Then another and another.

The vertical slats crumbled.

Blood stained the white fabric around her knuckles as she pulled away the debris to reveal a hole that made her chest constrict. She would fit, but barely. What if the opening was wider than at its end? What if she got trapped?

Closing her eyes, she envisioned the noose that hung in the city plaza back in Castle Peak, feeling the rope tighten around her neck until she couldn't breathe. Then the terror that seized her when Raiythlen kneeled before his sister, Avana, wielding the king's executioner's axe. The sharp blade had been inches from slicing his head from his body, his life brutally severed.

Without looking back, she re-clasped Grace's necklace and crawled into the hole.

It was worse than she'd imagined. The hole wasn't smoothed, but made just wide enough for enough air to flow through. Jagged pieces scraped along her skin and dress, blood welling up in its place as she wiggled farther into the dark. A faint light emanated in the distance, closer than she expected but father than was comfortable. When she approached a series of branching paths, her eyes stung with sweat, and panic fought to take hold. Light shined from all directions. She decided on the safest, continuing straight while the others curved in directions she wouldn't be able to maneuver.

Her fists and stomach were clenched, her skin decorated in raw cuts, grime, and sweat when the makeshift tunnel dipped. Fear would have pegged her to the spot, if it wasn't for the low thrum of the crowd and light peering through vertical openings—her exit. It wasn't the greatest angle, but judging by the boots, sandals, and bare feet that shuffled past between her digs at the opening, she was near the public, close to ground level.

The exit vent was larger than the one she had crawled through initially, the tunnel walls around her giving her enough room to carve at the vertical slats, her muscles straining at the odd angle. Using the beast's strength and her own desperation, she yanked at the slats until she was free. Tears sprang to her eyes when she squirmed out, the hall temporarily cleared of any passing bodies. Her limbs ached, her skinned knees and scratched arms screaming in pain, but she was free—well, not entirely. She was still inside the Summoning Grounds in a hallway she had not entered through but looked to run below the stone benches that had surrounded her at the landing. Finding Ceven right now would be almost impossible, the arena too vast and crawling with warriors who would soon learn of her escape. She had to find the closest exit and hope she spotted him on the way or figure out a plan when she wasn't out in the open for anyone to see.

Slinking close to the wall, Evangeline hurried on bare feet, passing through intersecting gaps peering into the arena. Something wasn't right. The hallway was suspiciously lacking in guards, and the crowd above her was stirring but it wasn't with hate or slurs. Not even hoots or hollers danced across the stadium. An undertone of tension laced the air, matching the darkened Summoning Grounds that'd been previously lit by the afternoon sun and were now illuminated in flickering lanterns and burning torches. Shadows crawled across the speckled floor and stone walls, and faces blurred together.

Needles prickled across her skin, drawing a sharp gasp. A Shadow Door, but stronger. No, not stronger but . . . more than one. This pressure crawling across her skin, making her chest want to explode, she'd experienced this same feeling inside the castle's west wing back in Peredia.

"Ceven," she murmured. Strange faces and bodies bobbed around her, but she didn't catch sight of a pair of blue and gold wings. As if she had suddenly come back to life in this waking moment, the reality of her situation and how incredibly alone she felt crippled her. She paused at an intersection, unable to move, unable to see past the blood between the hurls of screams and pain that pinned her. A room, much narrower with stain glass windows, replayed in her mind, fog clotting the gold throne and the blood-drenched marble platform. So much blood. A burning pain licked up her legs, to her throat, where Vane had sunk his teeth into her and—

"Eve!"

Her gaze snapped to Barto and two unfamiliar warriors running at her from the opposite end of the hallway. His eyes were narrowed and determined. Determined to help her, or determined to capture her?

She clenched her hands into fists, not that it would do much good against these warriors' swords and claws. "I'm not going back. I'm not dying here today." Without waiting for his reply, she spun on her heel and ran.

Barto shouted something behind her, but it was lost in the pounding of her heart timed with her feet against the cool, hard ground. The tension from the collective Shadow Doors rose with a cloying thickness. A high-pitched whine rang in her ears; whether it came from the hum of surrounding Nytes and humans or her own frazzled state, she didn't know. *Ceven, where is Ceven!* The ringing grew louder and louder. Hotter and hotter. Evangeline stumbled and clutched her chest as if the air had been knocked from her, pausing at another intersection between the hallway and stadium with no exit in sight. The heat and buzzing grew, spiraling. Spiraling inside her with nowhere to go. Between the pressure of the Shadow Doors and the beast clawing inside her, she felt she would implode.

Then it did erupt, but not from her.

Black, green, and brown tendrils shot out of the crowd. The sinuous bundle crashed into the landing and then back into the sea of people like angry waves. Screams splintered the Summoning Grounds. In the span of a heartbeat, Wretched had infiltrated the stadium through what had to be dozens of Shadow Doors.

"No, no, no . . . " Evangeline chanted. It was the west wing all over again. The slimy tentacles sliding over her limbs and dragging her across the broken, crumbling wing of the castle. And this time she was on her own.

Barto dashed in front of her. "Get behind me!" He unsheathed his claws as tentacles and people poured into the hallway from the open stadium.

Evangeline snapped her chin up, gritting her teeth. She wasn't in the west wing and she wasn't alone. And she sure in blazes wasn't going to have survived all of that just to die here.

Cries for help split her eardrums. Nytes and humans slammed into her, crushing her against the wall. She shoved out her elbows to give herself room against the rising tide of people. A flurry of wide eyes, ripped clothing, and bloodied faces swarmed her. She knocked into Barto, who gripped her arm in time before the stampede took her.

Tentacles licked their way through the crowd. People tripped over themselves to avoid the onslaught only to be trampled. The familiar cold sliminess wrapped around Evangeline's ankles, and she stomped on the fleshy tentacle. It retreated, black ooze pouring from it, matching the dirt and grime on her exposed legs and feet. Barto kept his hold firm on her arm, her lifeline from being pounded beneath a hundred feet.

"We have to find an opening!" she shouted. The longer they stayed here, the higher the risk they'd be trampled. The hallway was too narrow for this amount of people. Barto nodded, and together they wormed through the crowd, toward the branching path back into the stadium. Toward danger, but it was the only opening to escape.

They burst from the flooded hallway back inside the stadium. Wretched and warriors were locked in a battle of life and death, the span of stone benches decorated in red and black blood. The stench of rotting flesh suffocated the air. The ring of metal and chaos an all-too-familiar melody to Evangeline.

The shadow of a massive Wretched overtook her before Barto darted past, his nails lacerating the front of the monster's torso. Black blood splattered across his amber shirt and coated Evangeline's arm. The Wretched screeched, shaking her very bones and slinking back, but there was at least a dozen more to take its place.

"I need a weapon, give me something!" Evangeline shouted as more tentacles latched onto them. One hammered into her back, knocking the air from her lungs. Another whipped against her left elbow and calf. Pain trickled in, raging in sync with the beast roaring to be released as each tentacle sliced at the air around her.

Take it. Take it. Take it all!

"Evangeline, catch!" Barto's voice cut through the beast's call. She caught the arm-length sword he tossed her way, slicing through her flesh-made shackles. Her fighting skill certainly lacked the poise and accuracy of the empress's warriors and the captain redirecting most of the Wretched's blows away from her, but she wasn't useless. She had grown up observing the Peredian soldiers fighting, honing her skill in private, then training with Ceven and Barto in the castle's underground storage rooms.

This isn't the west wing. I may not have magical daggers that always hit your opponent, but I've been training my whole life for this. No, that wasn't the whole truth. Deep inside herself, she'd always known how. Had felt the call.

I was born to fight.

Fire danced up her arms as she whirled the blade. Her world narrowed on the incoming tentacles. Left. Right. Dodge. Duck. Slice now. She jumped and sank her blade between the Wretched's filmy eyes, the gelatinous skin peeling away as it died. Her victory was short-lived when pain split into her cheek. Blood poured into her mouth where her teeth bit into it, a tentacle retracting for another blow. She yanked her blade in front of her just in time. The slimy flesh pummeled into her sword, shoving her backwards. Her blood-slicked feet scrambled for purchase against the smooth stone, the landing wall growing closer. Before being crushed between the slew of arms and the stone landing, Evangeline leapt to the right. Needles of fire radiated up her shoulder where she braced her fall before shooting back to her feet.

A screech from a nearby horde of dying Wretched bounced off the high domed ceilings. Distracted, Evangeline missed the mass of tentacles heading her way until their wet, cold, slimy arms curled around her legs and pulled. *Hard.* The stadium turned on its head as she slammed into the ground. The Wretched dragged her closer toward its gaping mouth in the center of its shapeless mass, the stone floor scraping against her exposed back. She howled and kicked her feet. Spinning the blade in her wrist, she severed her slimy restraints, hurtling herself away as two warriors leapt onto its back, grabbing its full attention.

She grappled for breath, her open wounds licking at her skin like wildfire as she ran a few paces away and leaned against the landing decorated in a morbid display of death. The Wretched had temporarily lost track of her—they were blind, and with the chaos, her sounds joined the cacophony of the stadium. The number of Wretched had dwindled, but so did the warriors still locked in battle. Barto fought paces to her left—thank the Gods he was still alive—and Evangeline recognized the tall, broad-shouldered Rathan, with two blades in hand beside him. Asmen. The shouts had dimmed, leaving behind only fighting and those that didn't make it out alive.

Fear pierced her heart. Where the blazes was Ceven?

Pressure bit into her back, and the lingering sensation of a Shadow Door opening behind her crawled across her skin. Two more Wretched emerged from the invisible portal, its presence only noted by the faint ripples in the air, separating the cracked, bloodied benches of the stadium to a place far beyond here.

Exhaustion hugged her body like a second skin, but she didn't have a choice. Evangeline raised her blade as the Wretched surrounded her.

Take it. Take it. Take it all, Evangeline.

Adrenaline riddled her limbs, the sword handle almost buckling beneath her grip. The smell of blood sharpened. Her stomach muscles tightened. Her mouth ached, and her tongue roved over sharpened teeth that hadn't been there prior. Release. To let loose. To feel the rush of the kill. The call was hauntingly sweet, and for one blissful moment, she tilted her head back.

And before she knew it, she lost herself.

Evangeline straightened into position. Smoke filled her nostrils, her lungs, but it was a familiar scent. Her eyes watered, but she ignored it as she ignored the screams and cries for help. For mercy. If they had wanted mercy, they shouldn't have condemned her people, forced them to live as tools to be used and discarded. Like Jaden always said, they were all at fault. They were all guilty.

So why did this all feel so wrong?

She squashed those feelings, those dark whispers in the back of her mind, and narrowed her eyes on the gray-tailed Rathan coming at her with a shovel. Not even a weapon. The whispers stirred in her mind. Anali's soft caresses, light gentle kisses and words of encouragement to do the right thing. She ignored them all, plunging her dagger into the Rathan's lower right ribcage. He crumpled like a tree that had lost its roots.

More bodies like his littered the ground, and she trampled over them along with the rest of her troops. No remorse, no regrets. That was what they were, what the Nytes expected of them. They took and took and took. Until there was nothing left. They were monsters, but it was all necessary, she told herself. In the end, it was either her or them, and she would do anything for her people. For Jaden.

Even destroy the world.

Reality sank back in with a crushing weight of sound and feeling. The translucent domed ceiling of the Summoning Grounds faced her, the stone floor biting into her back. She peeled her head off the ground, the world spinning. Fighting still echoed around her, but she now rested on the opposite side of the stadium from where she had been. Barto was nowhere to be seen, but Asmen and less than a dozen warriors wrecked through the remaining Wretched within shouting distance.

Evangeline shook away the vivid memory that still clung to her along with the taste of blood in her mouth, her nose, the air she breathed. When she struggled to stand, a face shrouded in the shadows of a large cowl crouched beside her and offered a hand. Evangeline jerked back but was too spent to do anything other than narrow her eyes. "Who are you?"

"The one who saved you. Remember that when I return." The voice was soft, feminine. And painstakingly familiar.

Save me from what? The Wretched or myself? Evangeline didn't have a chance to say when Asmen rushed her, the Rathan's large hands banding like steel around Evangeline's upper arms. The mysterious figure, whom Evangeline was sure had been Avana, disappeared entirely—or at least out of sight, knowing the Quincara siblings had a fondness for invisibility magic.

Evangeline's futile attempt to tug free from the warrior's grasp would have been laughable if she wasn't sitting in the middle of a massacre without her friends and missing a pocket of her memory of the last few moments. "Where are Barto and Ceven?"

"You will move," Asmen growled, immune to Evangeline's death glare—the only thing she was capable of at this point. Her muscles had turned to lead, her eyes fighting the eclipse of sleep as Asmen hauled her out of the Summoning Grounds.

CHAPTER 13

Avana retreated from the Shadow Door, its magic and pull dripping off her as she landed on the floor to her cavernous—now temporary—dwelling. Her black cloak hung off her in frayed edges, and her hands blistered where her fire spells had backfired, a known side effect when working her blaze and burn symbols, but the Wretched had left her no choice. She couldn't risk them killing Evangeline.

She breathed in stale air and the lingering smell of damp pages, an unexpected improvement from the Summoning Grounds crammed with bodies drenched in sweat from the sweltering heat. The cave was blessedly silent and empty, unlike her thoughts. Anger bubbled, warming her cheeks before logic stormed in, sweeping across her like a cool tidal wave. She would not lose her calm. She would not risk Jaden calling her crazy too. Even if she wanted to scream at him, demand that he tell her what had just happened.

But when he arrived later, still dressed in blue robes, his hair pinned back, the anger resurfaced. Avana inhaled through her nose, envisioning a pool of water, still and frozen. Cold and calm as she fixed her steady gaze on him.

He tugged at his cuffs, the tips coated in red blood. He looked up and raised a brow. "Your coat is ruined."

Avana gritted her teeth, the icy lake at the forefront of her mind wavering. Calm. Cool. Collected. She was logical and above emotion that changed people like the colors in her alchemic experiments.

When she felt all traces of emotion vanish, she said, "As is your coat. *Advisor.*"

He smiled but didn't contradict her. Nor did he proceed to explain what had happened. Did he seriously expect her to follow along with everything and not ask questions? When he turned and walked toward a black wardrobe shoved to the side of the rounded rock cavern, she realized he did.

"Why did you have me risk revealing my presence in front of them, if you were going to be there the entire time?" As an advisor, no less. With a horde of Wretched at his beck and call. With a seemingly endless supply of Shadow Doors at his disposal. This man and his intentions eluded her.

And it terrified her.

Jaden peeled off his robe, showcasing firm muscle and smooth skin. She didn't turn away, not that he was embarrassed. In fact, watching him change into the black slacks and navy top was more unsettling for her than him, but she wasn't going to give him any courtesy or respect. After all, he had given her none.

"It always pays to have a backup plan, Avana," he said, buttoning up the shirt. He strolled toward her, the same knowing smile in place. "And it paid off. To think Eve could barely defend herself. Control herself. She's fallen so far."

Avana fought the urge to frown. "I thought you wanted Evangeline alive. She almost died from this . . . plan." One she'd been left in the dark on.

Jaden cocked his head, the condescending gesture not lost on her. "She was never in any danger. I merely wanted to see her potential. What she remembered. Which isn't much, I'm afraid." He tapped his chin. "Or maybe that's a blessing." He chuckled, low and controlled, as if he stood amongst the royals on the upper floors of Peredia's castle or alongside the Council in their penthouse suites in the highest towers in Sundise Mouche, and not in a remote cave somewhere in Ostin Lon.

Potential for what? And remember what? She didn't ask, knowing he wouldn't give her any answers. Yet. But maybe she could piece some of the story together on her own. "What do you mean she wasn't in danger? She was surrounded by Wretched and a heartbeat from being their meal when I found her." Her chin was tight.

He hummed at her, walking to his desk, which looked to have been pulled from a royal's study, the dark wood curved at the edges and appearing heavier than both of them combined. He licked his finger before flipping through the neatly piled pages on its surface.

Some of her façade slipped. "I don't appreciate my time and efforts being wasted, Jaden. If you don't intend to give me the answers I seek, I'll get them elsewhere." They both knew she insinuated she'd get those answers from Evangeline herself.

Faster than she'd seen any Nyte move, Jaden appeared inches from her face, and she stumbled backwards. Power, like sizzling static, rolled off him. She stilled, like the frozen lake in her mind's eye that started to fracture.

"Avana," he murmured, almost comforting. "I'm hurt you wouldn't trust me."

Pain exploded in her legs, and she fell at his feet. It took a moment for her to realize he had kicked out the backs of her knees, but it was a blur. This man had moved so *fast*. Too fast. Impossibly fast.

The sharpened nail on her thumb reached to cut the pad of her index finger. Too slow. Jaden gripped her wrist and wrenched it above her head. They both remained still, Avana on her knees with her arm above her, breathing heavily. Jaden was calm, cool, and collected. Everything she was supposed to be. Had strived to be after years of being labeled as crazy or insane. She'd never felt so powerless.

"I admire you, Avana. I really do." His grip didn't loosen or tighten, and she refused to show her discomfort. "But I also won't stand to be threatened, demanded of, or undermined. I've experienced enough of that in my life, and my patience for it had vanished long ago." He released her, and she shoved to her feet, taking few paces back. "Don't sour my good intentions. You'll get your answers soon enough."

Avana stared, acutely aware in this moment she didn't know anything about this man. Jaden was unpredictable and dangerous, and far less easy to manipulate than Evangeline. Jaden held a wealth of knowledge, could give her answers, proof, and validation of what her grandmother had dedicated her life's work to, but she was playing by his rules in a game she didn't fully understand. She feared it wouldn't end well for her. Evangeline's innocence and naivety was obvious in comparison, but Avana could still mold that to her advantage.

But at least now, with Jaden's help, Avana knew exactly where Evangeline was. Now all Avana needed to do was devise a plan to get Jaden out of the way.

PART 2

Distant Lovers

CHAPTER 14

Ceven woke on a mattress that cradled his sides, Rasha standing beside him draped in rich purple fabric. It was rare seeing the fierce Rathan warrior in a dress, and even rarer to see the hardened lines of her face soften into genuine concern—more so since it was aimed at Ceven. No light streamed from the floor-to-ceiling windows framing both sides of the puddle of blankets and pillows he rested on, but lit lanterns hung on black hooks around the spacious room. The soft glow caught on blue and green glass dripping from the ceiling like trapped stars, reflecting off sage walls and fur rugs. Even if he couldn't hear the roaring waves, he'd know he lay in one of the palace's guest rooms, having stayed in a similar one upon his first arrival in Atiaca years ago.

He sat up and grunted. Bloodstained bandages wrapped around his bare chest, and his brow furrowed. The last thing he remembered was talking to Advisor Zindelis before his chest exploded in pain.

"You're lucky it wasn't your heart, but it was close," Rasha said, leaning over to peer at his pink-tinted bandages. The gold beads in her hair matched the golden embroidery of her dress—claws encased in a fiery sun. The empress's insignia. She checked his dressings, her hands quick and methodical as if she'd done this countless times before.

Ceven never asked nor thought much about Rasha's past, only knowing that she had been a warrior in the empress's brigade for a period before she was assigned as Barto's part-time bodyguard. From the little he did know—tidbits from his and Barto's drunken nights—she had been promoted to be part of the empress's personal guard before being reassigned. He wondered if something had happened, or if Rasha simply preferred Barto's company over that of Empress Zelene. Ceven stifled a chuckle at the thought. That was unlikely. Whatever the reason, it wasn't his business.

"What . . . happened?" Ceven asked, cringing at how his voice cracked. Rasha shoved a glass of water his way, and he finished it in two gulps.

"Tarry said a Wretched attacked you. A tentacle right through the chest. If he hadn't flown you to a healer in time, you would've bled out."

Ceven blinked. Wretched? Here in Atiaca? But how? And how come he didn't even see or hear the Wretched before he was attacked? Ceven whipped his feet over the side of the bed, but Rasha read his mind before he moved, blocking him with her arms crossed.

"You almost died, prince. Lie back down." Her tone left no room for debate.

"Where's Evangeline? Tarry? Barto? Are they safe?"

"They're fine." Her mouth twitched, and uneasiness settled in his injured chest.

He narrowed his eyes. "What is it?"

Rasha cocked her head, refusing to budge from her spot in front of him. She knew him well enough to know the moment she moved, he would rush to the door. "Barto is badly injured, but nothing he can't recover from," she said. "Two fractured ribs and a broken left arm. His tail isn't moving like it should, and the muscle might be strained. Evangeline . . . she's currently locked up. No injures, as far as Asmen informed me."

"Locked up? What was her sentence?" He cursed himself for not staying, for not looking after her like he'd promised. What if she had died? Gotten injured? He believed the Caster was the bigger threat, that stopping them would save everyone, but in the end he couldn't even save himself. Gods *blast* it.

"None, yet. The attack happened before anyone could vote." Rasha held up a glass vial of brown liquid. "Concentrated millow weed. If the pain comes back, place two drops on your tongue. But no more, or else you won't feel anything at all. I don't want to have to carry you out of here."

He gave her a mocking salute, and not an ounce of pain came from the movement. This stuff worked better than any of the healers' concoctions he'd been given back at the castle.

Rasha finally gave him space, her dress sashaying around her bare ankles. Ceven let his curiosity get the best of him. "Are you still Barto's assigned bodyguard?"

Her single, black-furred ear flicked, but her expression remained unchanged. "I'm honored to be the empress's

First-Warrior again. Her personal guard, spy, assassin, whatever she needs me to be." A sheepish smile graced her lips. "I'm certainly never bored."

His brows rose in response.

She waved her hand—whether to dismiss any more questions or to fan herself, Ceven didn't know. "Well, if you're insistent on getting up, then put this on." She tossed a cream silk top. "And when you're ready, the empress wants to meet you on the terrace."

Ceven left the guest room, passing two warriors stationed at his door. Although he wasn't behind bars, the empress didn't hide the fact he wasn't to leave without her permission. Not that he planned to. Not until he secured amnesty for himself and Eve.

Rasha led him through the tiled floors and ivy-spattered walls. It wasn't his first time in the palace, but it was his first time as a wanted criminal. As a possible enemy. She kept a slow pace even though Ceven didn't feel any pain. If anything, he felt numb, like he was walking on air. Sea watery hells, that medicine could easily get addicting.

The terrace was past two circular rooms combined by a wall of opened glass doors framed in thin white curtains swaying in the wind. Salt and the crashing waves carried on the incoming breeze, bringing the outside sea into the light blue space, its translucent dome illuminating the room in the moon's gray glow. Outside, the terrace itself was large enough to accommodate thirty people comfortably but half the size of the castle's balcony attached to the glass room. It was far more intimate.

Rasha paused at the glass doors. "Take a seat and try not to fall over the railing." Her smile disappeared as quickly as it had come. She meant well, but it didn't hide the fact that if Tarry had been the one injured, Ceven wouldn't have been able to fly him out to seek help in time. If their roles had been reversed, Tarry would've died.

His useless wings would always feel as heavy as the day the healers told him he would never be able to fly.

"No promises." Ceven laughed it off. Rasha nodded and left.

He didn't take a seat on the white chaises splayed in rugs and beaded pillows. Instead, he peered over the stone railing and gazed out at the sea, foamy waters cresting against the cliff-side the palace rested on. The moon hung in a curved sliver, the faint sprinkling of stars blanketing the sky. It was picturesque, and Ceven certainly didn't blame the empress for moving the new capital city here.

He imagined wisps of blonde hair tickling his shoulder, a wide smile and rosy cheeks staring up at him. Guilt gripped his throat. Evangeline should be beside him, not locked away. If he had brought her here only to condemn her to a life in a cell . . . No, he'd get her out. He wouldn't betray her like that, not after she finally started to trust him again.

"Prince Ceven LuRogue," the empress purred behind him. "It's barely been a season, and yet it feels like it's been a longer stretch of time since I last saw you."

Ceven turned and bowed. Gold bracelets cuffed Empress Zelene's wrists and neck—like the bronzed cuffs worn by her Sun Warriors—and thick brown fur gathered up her arms, shaven in swirling patterns. Chestnut curls rounded her heart-shaped face, the tips of pointed ears protruding lower than most Rathans', closer to her chin. Wisps of magenta flowed against her arms, across her belly and lower hips, held together by thin gold chains. The material was diaphanous and left nothing to the imagination, but Ceven kept his eyes firmly on the empress's brown ones, his chin angled down to do so.

"Still as beautiful as ever," Ceven said without pause.

"And a flatterer, much like your brother, whose words are as smooth as our steel." Her painted lips curled into a smile, and Ceven tensed. "We have much to discuss, Your Highness. A seat?" She waved her fingers to the chaises, a demand disguised as a question.

Ceven joined her, sitting at the edge of the white chaise, removing the pillows to make room for his wings, while the empress lounged across hers. The crash of waves stampeded to the beat of his heart. *Crash, crash, crash.* Contrary to the empress's words, Ceven was nothing like his brother. He wasn't good at talking on political matters such as the inevitable one about to unfold here. He wasn't good at playing the social prince, who carefully chose his words and pretended to enjoy others' company, at all. The empress knew this and would undoubtedly use that to her advantage. But he would stay on his guard and find a way to protect both Evangeline and himself. Not just from Sehn, his brother and the new King of Peredia, but from the empress herself.

Empress Zelene draped her legs across the thick cushion, propping her chin up with one hand, staring at him as if she were completely enthralled by his presence and not envisioning how to take him down with her words.

"You spoke with Sehn?" Ceven asked before she could start her onslaught. The empress's lips thinned, indicating he had made a wrong move.

"More or less. I received a letter detailing a great many things. Some that don't quite align with Barto Nu'yuen's story." She let those words hang in the air, but Ceven didn't take the bait. She eventually continued, "Tell me, prince: what is your purpose here? Why did you come to my lands?"

Ceven forced his hands to his side, his back straight. "I accompanied your captain, who informed me you required Evangeline's presence." It wasn't a lie. Though they both knew the real reason—if he'd stayed in Peredia, he wouldn't be alive right now, having this very conversation.

"*Accompanied.*" She laughed, and it was an unbecoming snort. At odds with the beautiful, charismatic empress, yet it made her more relatable, causing Ceven's stiff shoulders to ease a bit. "Yes, well, that is one way of putting it. I know you're a wanted Nyte, Ceven."

He smiled, and surprisingly, it wasn't forced. The truth was out in the open now, and it told Ceven everything he need to know about Empress Zelene's intentions. Zelene wanted something from him; otherwise he would've been locked up with a bow and sent back to his brother already.

"Oh? And on what account?" Ceven could pretend. He could play this game. But in no way did it make him like his brother or his former father, who was now dead. He ignored the small pang in his ribs, telling himself Calais had chosen his path—including placing his trust in his eldest son, who had betrayed him.

The empress leaned back, the soft material of her dress sliding across the chaise. Her eyes blazed despite the sun having set a while ago, matching the illuminated palace windows flickering behind her and the flaming dots of civilization even farther away, sprinkling the cliffside separating Kazuumar from the Araji sea. "Did you murder your father, Prince Ceven?"

His brows shot up. He hadn't been expecting the blunt question, but he appreciated the straightforwardness. "No. I wasn't behind King Calais's death."

"A likely answer from a traitor prince. Whether or not you speak the truth is another matter."

Ceven tried to mimic her feigned relaxed posture, loosening the muscles in his back and wings, lowering his shoulders but keeping his chin firm. Even sitting, he was a head taller than her, but he tried to appear less intimidating. It was a tactic that sometimes worked when he had been forced to negotiate with nobles and tradesmen for the former King of Peredia. To make it seem as if they were lifelong friends, helping one another, and not in a battle of wits.

The salty breeze teased the feathers on his wings, cooling the skin on the back of his neck. "Then why ask at all?"

"So I could figure out your tell, prince." A slender digit played with a curl hanging close to her face, a smirk tugging at her features. "Not only are you pretty to look at, you're also pretty easy to read."

Ceven's gut tightened, and he rose back to his full height instinctually. *She's an empress, protecting her country and her people. Her intentions are only for that. It's not to belittle you,* he reminded himself. *She's not Sehn or Calais.* "I can't quite say the same, Empress Zelene. I've never been able to figure you out."

Silence reigned for a few heartbeats. Only the two of them sat on the privacy of this terrace, waves sheltering them from eavesdroppers and the sliver of moonlight casting them both in shadows, concealing their silhouettes from potential onlookers with the arching balconies around them. The adjacent rooms he and Rasha had emerged from earlier were empty of visitors, or had the illusion of it at least. Ceven knew Rasha and other Sun Warriors lurked close enough to heed their empress's call in a moment's notice. Not that he'd dare put his hands on Empress Zelene, nor was she far from defenseless. She'd slaughtered her enemies and climbed over their corpses to grasp her throne with bloody claws, claiming it as hers decades past.

The ocean continued to roar relentlessly, but the empress didn't raise her voice. "No, you're nothing like your brother."

Ceven's toes curled in the soft leather shoes Rasha had provided him, his patience thinning like the fabric of Zelene's dress. If it could even be called that.

"But if you were," she continued, "you wouldn't be here, on my private terrace." She stood, her curls bouncing. "I despise war and what it does to my people, but I will also not bow to the whim of another. Not anymore."

Ceven frowned, not caring if she saw. What had Sehn written to the empress? And what was her plan? It certainly didn't bode well, but he kept his mouth shut. He'd let the empress answer these questions herself and see where he fit in. See what his leverage was.

She spread her arms, toes splayed and gripping the stone railing's edge as if rising to embrace the salt-laced breeze. "I want my people to feel as free as I do standing here. To do whatever they like, feel whatever they like, and be accepted no matter their circumstances."

His eyes went past her to the gaping sea. Admiration swirled, and . . . jealousy. He could've done something for Peredia. He could've saved those humans, made his country something worthy of admiration. Like he admired the empress and the empire she built, albeit with a few exceptions to how she ruled. Ceven knew freedom came at a cost, and that peace never prospered long enough before violence tainted it.

"I brought you here, prince, because I believe our goals align." She turned to him. "I do not want Sehn to be king. I do not want to agree to these 'new terms' he proposes. I will not have my people enslaved to a lying snake who conspires to turn against his own country. His own family." She raised a plucked brow at him, as if daring him to contradict her.

He nodded. "I do not believe Sehn has Peredia's best interest in mind," he admitted but sensed the empress wanted more. "And I agree that his methods are . . . far from honorable." The words felt heavy. It wasn't that long ago, Ceven had agreed to kill the king; even if he hadn't been able to follow through on it, he'd been no better than Sehn. He'd been far from honorable when he agreed to Sehn's blood promise, doing whatever it took to save Evangeline and what he believed was the right choice at the time.

The empress drew him from his thoughts. "You have earned Barto's trust, who I highly regard. You hold yourself as someone I believe would make a far better king than your brother."

The words inflated him, even though the compliment was aimed to make Ceven more pliable to the empress's actual request. He propped his leg across his knee and shifted on the chaise until he fully faced her and the glass doors leading to the terrace. Light from a multitude of lanterns inside illuminated the glass panels, humanoid shadows eclipsing the light periodically.

Ceven kept his face indifferent, but tension lined his shoulders and neck as if he were waiting for a troop of warriors to storm the terrace and accost him or an assassin to emerge from behind the large potted fern next to him as he said, "You want me to kill Sehn."

Her smile vanished, and Ceven hated how he felt as if he let her down.

"No, I'm simply wondering why you're here and not fighting for your own country."

He rose to his feet, stretching well above the empress. He kept several paces between them as to not appear threatening. "*My* country?" he scoffed, even though the words stirred his heart. Even though he'd had those same thoughts ever since he'd left Peredia, promising to Taryn, Ed, and the other soldiers of his return—a hollow promise he'd declared with too much enthusiasm at the time. "I'm a prince in title only. I don't hold the people's respect like you do, empress. And now I'm a traitor. A criminal."

She closed the distance between them, the moonlight creating a halo across the top of her curls making her appear almost ethereal. "You forget, Ceven, that I wasn't always an empress. And unlike you, I didn't have any claim to my throne."

Ceven hadn't forgotten, but he'd also never fully listened to the tale behind her coming to power. Just the bits he heard in songs, of a mighty warrior tearing through the land, claiming her army with words forged in fiery flames.

He crossed his arms, refusing to take a step back even as she crowded his space, as if challenging him. "I heard you overthrew the previous emperor eighty years ago." And with a Rathan's lifespan, the empress didn't look a day past forty, expecting to live another half a century—if she wasn't killed before then.

"And do you know why?" The lines of her face hardened, the faint signs of age framing her warm chocolate eyes, at odds with the cold expression only an empress molded from violence and war could muster.

When he shook his head, she continued, "Because, like you, I wanted to change things. To make a difference. But I did something about it." She splayed her hand, gesturing at the arching balconies and stone walls, up to the blue domed roof of the palace and down into the sloping roads and stacked houses of the city, alive with light and people singing, dancing, and chattering even in the dead of night.

Though the words were soft, Ceven bristled. "What do you expect from me? The moment I step back in Peredia, I'm dead. I don't have an army like you did." The few Peredian soldiers who would fight by his side—if there were any left—would not be enough to face the full force of the king's military.

The empress idly strolled back to the railing, a curl wrapped between her fingers, as if they were discussing different pottery and not the futures of both their countries. "It seems you don't know my full history, but that is a story for another time. One I think you would find enlightening given your current circumstance." Then she shrugged, as if none of this mattered, her eyes darting to the dancing shadows cast by the floating white drapes—or perhaps to the warriors lying in the darkness feet from where Ceven stood. "Maybe I was wrong to not turn you over to King Sehn. Maybe you won't be an asset like I originally thought."

He leaned back against the stone wall, feeling more prepared on his feet than he had been sitting. "Hard to contradict that, when you haven't exactly told me what it is you want." He knew what she wanted from him, but he needed her to confirm it. To say aloud that she needed his aid as much as he needed hers.

The empress directed her gaze back to his. "I can give you an army, Ceven, but only if you answer this one question, and answer it correctly."

Ceven arched a brow.

"What is it you really want out of all this?"

CHAPTER 15

Everything was a blur, from the whirl of people storming the docks from the Summoning Grounds to being dragged back to her underground cell prior to the trial. Evangeline didn't have any strength left to fight against Asmen's firm grip, nor the ability to shout for Ceven amidst the gruesome aftermath of blood and death. She couldn't even keep her eyes open when Asmen deposited her on the cool ground of her cell, an arm's length away from the single bed. She refused the encroaching call of sleep and desperately fought to lift her head, but her cheek stayed stubbornly against the cold floor.

"Ceven . . . please be safe . . ." she muttered into the quiet of her cell.

At some point, sleep had taken her, her dreams filled with screams and bloodied corpses digging at her open wounds. She cried out repeatedly for Ceven to the point her vocal chords strained, her cries turning into hoarse pleas. Clusters of arms and tentacles bit into her flesh, reeling her toward the snapping jaws of a beast larger than any monster she'd seen. Its eyes flashed brown, its face morphing into Vane—the sadistic torturer that haunted her, Lani, and the entire human population within Castle Peak. She thrashed against the restraints, tears streaking her cheeks, as she kicked out her feet.

My love . . .

Evangeline jerked at the gentle voice, staring into the inky blackness engulfing her. "Ceven?"

The beast at her back growled, the force of it radiating across her skin and sinking through her ribcage to hammer at her heart. The arms and tentacles rescinded, burrowing into the ground, and she used her freedom to claw at the dirt for a sharp blade, gripping its hilt. In a surge of courage, she lifted her chin. Instead of Vane's face, her own stared back at her with glowing irises fractured by hues of color settled on top of a snarling muzzle, snapping its arm-sized fangs at her.

Come back to me, my love . . .

The same voice whispered in the distance. A familiar melody that called to her through time and space. The beast—Evangeline herself—stalked closer, and a new fear coursed through her veins. One she couldn't face. Not yet. The beast pounced, and she raised her blade, stabbing its—her—heart. Blood, stark and sweet, knocked into her gut. It was everything. It was all-consuming.

Her eyes snapped open. A faint stream of sunlight slithered through the small barred window in the room's ceiling, splashing against muted stone on all sides, the smooth rock floor kissing her exposed skin through the gaps and tears of her bloodied white gown. Cold knifed at her back in contrast to the warmth dripping down her throat, pooling in her stomach, her tongue roving over salty flesh and blood the flavor of cinnamon and wine. The taste of it made the beast roar for more, this blood more promising than anything else she'd ever tasted.

Her gaze met a pair of emerald eyes with an expression and a face matching the jewel's refined exterior, from defined jawlines to a straight nose and sculpted lips. Arms of corded muscle cradled her head, pressing her mouth against a warm wrist, the scent of crushed leaves lingering in the aftertaste of blood.

Neither of them moved, locked in each other's gaze, his lifeblood continuing to spill into her, filling her with a strange tenderness that ran so deep that it left scars on her soul. Evangeline didn't care where she was or what had happened. She was just happy to be by his side again. A belonging, a contentedness that only went away in his presence.

Her fangs retracted from his wrist, her eyes still fixed to his. She raised her arm, the dark stubble on his cheeks rough against her fingertips as she cradled his face. "Jaden . . ." she murmured.

He stilled. His expression remained unreadable, but his lips parted.

Something wasn't right.

Her hand fell away, brows pinching together. Memories of soft caresses, passionate kisses, and unwavering devotion that had enveloped her upon first waking slowly unraveled as tears, desperate screams, and sharp fangs pierced the haze of confusion.

Jaden's fingers threaded through her hair, holding her tighter. Pain lanced across his features, swift but unmistakable.

"Not yet, please . . ." The words were barely a whisper, and Evangeline couldn't be sure she'd heard him correctly.

Images swirled inside her skull, both the past and the present clashing. Two worlds colliding and fighting for control. Her vision unfocused, her breath lodged in her throat as feelings of betrayal, guilt, and shame bubbled up in the pit of her belly, registering in her bones before her mind caught up.

She flung herself away from him, her heels scraping against the floor until her back hit the wall of the cell. "*You!*"

"Evangeline . . ." Her name on his lips almost sounded like a Caster spell, unfamiliar and full of power, one he knew he had and wielded well. His dark slacks and navy top were clear of any signs of blood or duress as well as his person, as if he'd left right before the Wretched attacked. His hand still lacked any markings.

Her mouth hung open, at a loss, expecting Advisor Zindelis—Jaden—to be the last person she'd find next to her upon waking, let alone have his blood filling her as he held her dangerously close. His life essence still lingered in her mouth as familiar as the mornings she woke with the taste of iron in the back of her throat, her head still foggy with surreal dreams.

It was, without a doubt, one and the same.

"What are you doing here?" she asked, finally conjuring the ability to speak. He didn't reply, standing up to his full height. She surged to her feet after him, legs shaking while she measured her distance to the cell door a few paces away. As if reading her mind, his strides matched hers like a lion cornering his prey until he blocked the exit. Sensing the shift, the unveiled danger, the beast reared its head. The blood had sated it, but it would never deny the opportunity for more.

Jaden remained silent. Blast it if it didn't put her more on edge then if he'd simply pulled out a blade. "Have you come to kill me?"

He cocked his head, and she swallowed. His eyes seemed to glow, an iridescent jade shining alongside gray rock. "I've thought about it, on more than one occasion."

"You wouldn't be the first."

He only smiled at that, and something about the expression warmed her, despite her building rage. This false advisor had vied for her death and had done nothing while the Summoning Grounds had turned its hatred on her. He called out to the beast inside her, to this storm of emotion, driving her mad, while he stood unaffected—as if he were above all of this. As if what had happened between them in the past wasn't now boiling to the surface.

Then again, this all felt fresh to her. It wasn't long ago, she thought Jaden was just a figment of her imagination. Who knew how long he had been carrying this baggage, the burden of their shared past that still hung in shattered clumps in her head while she had lived in blind ignorance. The way he looked at her, said her name . . .

Jaden may think he had her trapped, but she wouldn't let him leave until he told her everything.

He crept closer to her, halting a few steps away. His eyes were empty. Cold. Had she imagined the pain, the flash of vulnerability he'd shared with her moments earlier?

"Although you don't deserve it, I just saved your life. Avana claimed to have *saved* you without realizing she had condemned you."

The wall's smooth, cool edges brushed against her back as she slid to the left, edging around the cell's single cot and wood bucket. Nothing of use to fight with, nor did she have any weapons or sharp objects on her; Grace's necklace was absent from her neck, most likely crushed or swallowed by the slew of Wretched.

"What do you mean *saved* me?" Evangeline narrowed her eyes. The last name she expected to hear out of Jaden's mouth was Avana's. Then again, it made sense. The Caster had hunted Evangeline down for her mark and what she represented. While Jaden kept his concealed, Evangeline knew from memories past he had the same mark as her. Of course, Avana would somehow find a substitute to fulfill her scientific curiosities.

Jaden raised his wrist to his mouth, small beads of blood still welling up from where she'd bitten him. "Blood sustains and powers us. Without it, we're simply flames with dwindling oxygen, waiting to be snuffed out." His eyes never left hers as he licked the blood. "You lost control. You burned too brightly, too quickly, and before you could replenish yourself, sate the bloodlust, Avana had knocked you out and taken you from the pit of Wretched." He unrolled the sleeve of his shirt and rebuttoned the cuff of it, hiding the wound. "There was a time this knowledge was second nature to you, Eve."

Her nostrils flared at the casual way her name rolled across his tongue. It brought up visions past, her wrapped in his embrace underneath the pale moonlight, standing in the center of the gardens filled with roses and weeping willows. The steady trickle of a fountain dancing on the wind alongside blossoming jasmine as strong hands slid around her lower back. She remembered looking up into green eyes thinking she'd follow this man down any path. Would fight any war if he stayed by her side.

Evangeline crossed her arms—now lacking the cuts and bruises that had marred them before she passed out—and blocked out the memory to hold on to the fury creeping up her insides. "Why save me when you fought to have me killed? When I had betrayed you in the past?"

He stilled, and the breath evaporated from her lungs.

She took another hesitant step to the left, her eyes never straying from his as she put slightly more distance between them. He didn't move. The room fell silent, even the birds outside having fled, sensing the tension and violence in the air. Her heart ratcheted in her chest, pumping Jaden's blood through her limbs, her every breath soaking him in. She hated it.

Evangeline worked up the courage to continue, her voice sounding meek despite the rage uncoiling with every word. "Or maybe it was *you* who had betrayed *me*." Regardless of what Evangeline had done in the past, whatever love they had once shared for each other, after what happened at the Summoning Grounds, it was clear Jaden was now her enemy.

"Don't you *dare* say that . . ." His words were like static needling down the length of her spine. Like death itself had crept into the room, crowding it with its presence. "After everything . . ."

Pain shot through the back of her skull as she slammed into solid stone behind her. The room and Jaden's face blurred together. He'd been so spitting *fast*. One moment he stood a few paces away, then the next, he had had her pinned against the wall with his hand around her throat. She struggled to breathe as she imagined claws unfurling out of her fingers, hind legs stretching and expanding within the frame of her lower body.

"How weak—" He cut off when her foot caught his chest, faster than she expected, but still not as fast as him. It allowed her a few gulps of air before his forearm slammed against her throat, his body pressed tightly to hers as her nails sank into his sides, her knees driving up to buck him off her. Blood, rich like wine spiced with cinnamon, plowed into her, sharp pointers slicing into her tongue. She snarled, her mouth inches away from his face.

His eyes glowed brighter, his green irises battling against the growing white that housed flecks of colors. *Iridescent*, the word came to her again.

"Why?" He ground out, his voice raw with unshed emotion. He wasn't unaffected, like she'd originally thought; he was just better at hiding it. "You had everything. *We* had everything."

She heard his words, but they seemed muffled, her consciousness slipping away like it had in those woods, swallowed up by her grief and the smell of Lani's blood coagulating in the cold and the surrounding Casters, their blood fresh and warm as it coated her tongue. She snapped at his face, teeth grazing his cheek and drawing a thin scarlet line.

"Jaden," Evangeline growled. In the recesses of her mind, she clung to her sanity, the threads thinning faster than ever before. "You've always brought out the worst in me," she heard herself say but didn't know where those words came from.

Jaden jerked his head back, away from her snarling mouth, but his grip on her throat remained firm and unbreakable. "I was the *best* thing that ever happened to you. You forget, you'd be dead ten times over if it wasn't for me. It was you who changed, Eve. Now our kind, our people, are all dead because of you. I would have given you the world, and you destroyed me, *us*, so utterly that there's nothing left."

Footsteps echoed outside the cell door, farther down the hallway. Jaden's hold loosened, whether preparing to leave or kill her quickly, Evangeline didn't know. She threw her legs around his waist, gripping tightly. "If there was nothing left, then why are you still here, haunting me?"

He couldn't keep her pinned while trying to fend off her legs at the same time. "Release me, Evangeline."

"Tell me what happened, Jaden. What did I do?"

Now our kind, our people, are all dead because of you.

The thrum of boots against stone hovered at the door.

"Release. Me."

Shadows stretched beneath the crack of solid metal. Keys rattled.

"If you wanted me dead, why did you save my life?"

His hand clamped across her mouth. "Speak a word and I'll slit your prince's throat."

Evangeline went limp at the same time the metal door swung open, groaning from its weight. Asmen loomed in the frame, accompanied by two warriors brandishing the same arm bands and neck brace. Black and red tattoos painted their skin, but it wasn't the Caster symbols she'd seen on the soldiers back in Peredia who empowered themselves off human lives. The figures looked female and had their arms raised in worship to the sun; others were claws encased in a blazing sun. Beside them stood a sandy-haired and bushy-tailed Rathan whom

Evangeline remembered Barto talking to at the gate—Serah—who stood comically at half the height of Asmen.

Their gazes roved over the room, from the empty wooden bucket to the cot, past where Jaden had her pinned against the wall.

Asmen snapped to the other two warriors, "Alert the others: the criminal has escaped." The warriors spun, racing down the hall. Asmen turned to Serah. "The prince is staying in the palace's guest room. Check if the criminal is attempting to make contact."

Ceven, he's safe and in the palace, thank the Gods . . .

Serah bobbed her head and trailed after the warriors. Jaden's hand stayed latched to her mouth, the lingering smell of blood making her mouth water and her head spin. She swallowed, painfully aware of the movement as Asmen stepped into the room. The warrior's nose twitched, eyes circling the bare stone walls separated only by a handful of cracks and scratches from its previous tenants. The bed shoved in the corner sat on metal stilts and was still made up with its singular blanket and pillow, Evangeline having slept on the stone floor inches away from it throughout the night. Patches of dried blood from her old wounds still lay as evidence in the center of the room.

Jaden pressed closer. She could no longer see him, but the heat of his body seared through her shredded dress. Her instinct screamed to fight against his grip, while another part ached to bring him closer. Guilt struck her, her thoughts shifting to Ceven. How she wished she could be with him right now, far away from Asmen and the warriors. Away from Jaden, who took all her emotions and scrambled them so thoroughly she couldn't safely untangle them without unraveling her whole self.

Another step in, Asmen raised her chin. It wouldn't be long now before her stare caught on their blurred outlines, the space where they stood reflecting a warped cell. The dipped collar of Evangeline's dress was now damp and clung to her skin where Jaden had poured the Caster concoction over them both, turning them nearly invisible. Evangeline guessed it was one of Avana's, the smell of smoke and magic stinging her nostrils.

Evangeline tensed as Asmen drew even closer. The Rathan would either see the distortion or smell the magic in the air any moment now, if she didn't already.

Jaden's grip faltered on her mouth, the pressure loosening before it vanished altogether. In one breath, Asmen went from standing, hand gripping the hilt of her blade at her hip, to her knees hitting the floor, fingers clasping her shoulder. Iron suffocated the air before red droplets splattered the ground, adding to the stained floor. A snarl twisted the warrior's lips, her sword slamming into the ground as she leapt to her feet, head whipping toward the exit, away from Evangeline. With a roar, the Rathan darted from the room to chase after the invisible attacker.

Evangeline now stood alone with a belly full of warm blood, chasing away the old pain, stretching her muscles, Avana's magic still clinging to her skin. Her cell door hung open, light spilling in from the translucent domed hallway, touching the tips of her dirt-streaked feet.

She inhaled a sharp breath and ran.

CHAPTER 16

Evangeline squinted against pale skies shot through with pinks and golds as the sun stirred over curved roofs and trickled down past the palace gates into the rest of Kazuumar. In the chaos Jaden had ignited, and with Avana's magic still attached to her, Evangeline had sped past frantic shouting guards, the high ring of an alarm flagging her heels, spurring her faster. Asmen ran ahead of her, the smell of blood still clinging to the warrior, but Evangeline kept pace close enough to slip out the dungeon entrance behind her, where two more guards lay crumpled by the brassy door separating the dungeons from the palace grounds.

If it wasn't for the adrenaline chasing the chill away, the morning air would have made her shiver as the groomed patch of flowers brushed her ankles, decorating her skin in dew. She was careful to avoid the cloisters of rushing guards, keeping to the plant-strewn patches alongside the tiled paths until she broached the start of the palace steps. She knew this would likely be her only opportunity to escape, but she refused to leave without Ceven. Not when he could be a captive too.

Although they kept him in the palace guest room while you slept, filthy, in a dungeon cell . . .

She shook her head at the intrusive thought and danced up the stairs. There was also the matter of Advisor Zindelis—Jaden—and if the empress knew the truth. Evangeline wanted answers. *Needed* them if she was going to learn how to control the beast and figure out who she was. She wasn't leaving here until she sought him out and wrung the truth from him.

Evangeline kept her breaths controlled to avoid being heard. Several guards paused near her, their heads lifted to sniff the air, but fortunately the breeze worked in her favor, carrying her scent in the opposite direction. With the blood and dirt caked to her, though, if she stood still for too long they would discover her, especially since Asmen had shouted out warnings of Caster magic and invisible assailants.

The palace was unmistakable and just as massive as the castle back in Peredia she had resided in for most of her life. She slipped past blue and brass doors arching far higher than even the castle's, complete with polished sea glass tinting the entrance in a cascade of blues and greens. Stone blended into marble of all different shades of blue wherever sweeping glass windows weren't present, showcasing the raging sea behind the palace grounds.

Evangeline pressed to the walls, passing Nytes in loose garb, some almost entirely bare, and humans wearing blue silks. Judging by the fine attire and the lack of bags under their eyes, she couldn't tell if they were guests or servants. She padded through rooms. No halls, but clusters of open rooms.

Instead of chandeliers, gold-trimmed paintings, and textured wallpaper, there were pillows and low sitting tables, most occupied with Nytes playing cards or inhaling from pipes. Ivies and vines slithered across the walls and translucent dome ceiling. It reminded her of the castle's glass room. But instead of being completely sheer, it was enough to block the harsh light of the morning sun. If only she had arrived as a guest instead of a prisoner, she could have enjoyed it all more.

A flick of black braids run through with gold beads flashed in the corner of her eye. She turned and made direct eye contact with the warrior woman who had accompanied Barto back in Peredia and who had always regarded her with a careful eye.

"I can take you to Ceven, but you'll have to be quick," Rasha said and turned on her heel, not waiting for a response.

Evangeline had to be sure she was still invisible, glancing down at the shimmery space where her body should be. For all she knew, Rasha could have been speaking to someone else, though no one else hovered in their vicinity. Either way, it was the better option to follow Rasha than to trail around the armed palace until she was caught.

Keeping a steady pace, Evangeline trailed after the warrior, though she looked more the part of noble courtier than soldier, the edges of her yellow dress flowing behind her like the tail of a bird, matching the expensive-looking gold bangles at her hands and feet. Either by Rathan prowess or magic, Rasha's steps brushed against the tiled floor without a sound as she lithely passed down a set of hallways and two more rooms with an open layout and lingering Nytes lounging in leisure. She knocked on a seemingly ordinary paneled door and glanced over her shoulder at her, Evangeline's only indication Rasha had in fact been speaking to her. Maybe Rasha had picked up her scent and knew it was her? Why she decided to help, she still didn't know.

The warrior turned down the hall as the door opened, and Evangeline's heart stuttered. Tousled chestnut strands curled around a chiseled jaw with a few days of growth, and hazel eyes narrowed in suspicion. The skin beneath the brown and green orbs looked discolored, evidence of how stressful these past few days had been. The past few weeks. It was obvious he had been sleeping, even if a bit restfully, given his thin slacks, crumpled white shirt, and ruffled feathers.

Evangeline attempted to sneak past him, through the opening of the door, but his hand caught her hair, yanking her back.

She yelped and smacked his arm. "Blast it, Ceven, it's me, Eve! Now let me in." The Caster magic still stuck to her skin, but that didn't make her any less angry. He had yanked *hard*.

Ceven frowned but released her and shut the door gently behind him. The guest room of the palace certainly was a nicer abode than her cell, with windows overlooking the sea instead of stone gray walls and a bed designed to sleep four comfortably while she had spent the night on the floor.

"How did you—" Ceven started before shaking his head. "That doesn't matter. Sea watery hells, Eve, I was so worried." His eyes gazed up and down her shimmering form, as if he could faintly make out her silhouette. "Rasha told me what happened at the Summoning Grounds with the Wretched. She told me you were safe but they had put you back in the dungeons."

Evangeline rubbed her scalp, which still throbbed. "Yes, I had quite a night while you were resting peacefully here."

His face crumpled, and her insides immediately twisted in guilt.

"You know I would never leave you like that, Eve." He stepped forward, eyes still searching for hers. "I . . . I got injured. When I woke up, the empress had already set me up here with a pair of guards. The medicine they gave me is stronger stuff than they have back in Peredia and knocked me out cold."

The guilt tore at her heart even harder, and she walked into his warmth, wrapping her arms around his torso. "I'm sorry, I didn't know."

His hands immediately came down and tugged her in closer. She sighed into his chest and breathed him in, chasing away her encounter with Jaden earlier, the Wretched attack, and their current situation. No matter what, she'd make sure they both made it out of this alive. "Tell me what happened."

Ceven told her about the mysterious figure he'd caught in the crowds during the trial, about how he felt the pressure of the Shadow Doors, and his encounter with Advisor Zindelis right before he was stabbed through the chest. Evangeline pulled back to look at him, but he squeezed her tighter as if she would disappear. Her fingers felt the bandages beneath his shirt, the smell of old blood faint but present.

"Advisor Zindelis was the one who attacked you?" she asked carefully. Jaden's threat right before she'd fled now hung tighter around her throat. If he so much as laid a finger on Ceven, she would hunt him down and make him regret it.

His hold loosened, but he didn't let her go. "Tarry said it was a Wretched, but it all happened so fast, we can't be sure. If it was the advisor, I don't know what his motive would be and if the empress is aware."

Oh, Evangeline would make sure the empress was aware. Regardless of whether he saved her life or not, Jaden had fought for her death. She was sure once she told the empress everything, Evangeline wouldn't be the only one seeking answers from this so-called advisor.

Ceven opened his mouth to say more but paused. Hesitating. She was about to press him further—it was clear he was hiding something—when he said, "Your turn."

Evangeline let it go for now and told him how she had escaped the holding cells after overhearing the guards discussing her death, only to find herself in the midst of the attack. Ceven's brow creased when she relayed how she'd fought off the Wretched with Barto, omitting the part where the beast inside her took over. She did mention Avana, then her encounter with Advisor Zindelis in the dungeons and that they were working together, which was how she had access to Caster magic and managed to escape. She left out how the advisor went by another name, Jaden, who was her past lover—if she could trust her memories. How the taste of his blood still lingered in the back of her throat and his very presence made her question everything about herself. She could barely admit this to herself, let alone Ceven, and she knew he would only become more overprotective. She would tell him when she was ready. Eventually.

Ceven's hands dug tighter into her flesh, digging through the gaps of her shredded dress and brushing skin. It didn't hurt but told her he felt as reassured about the situation as she did. "The empress needs to know. If there's a traitor in her midst . . ."

Evangeline hummed in agreement.

"Are you hurt?" He cursed under his breath. "I hate that I can't see you."

She clasped his hand, bringing his fingers to caress her cheeks. "I'm fine." *Completely healed thanks to Jaden's blood,* she couldn't say.

He dipped his head, his forehead meeting hers. His breath tickled the loose strands framing her face. "Can you please stop finding yourself alone with dangerous Nytes?"

The Caster magic veiled the smirk toying her lips. "Does that include you?"

Uncertainty flashed across his features, and Evangeline kicked herself for hurting him. Again. "I didn't mean—"

"I know." He swallowed, glancing away before his gaze settled on hers again, the mix of greens, browns, and gold drawing her in. "Eve . . . there's something I have to tell you, but not here. We'll get you out of here and—"

The door crashed open, revealing a bloodied Asmen, her brown slitted pupils narrowed and murderous. Rasha stood behind her, a head shorter and expression more neutral than her companion's. Feelings of betrayal sprouted in Evangeline's gut before she squelched them. Of course Rasha wouldn't just let them sneak out of here, especially knowing how distrustful the Rathan had been of Evangeline back in Peredia. Letting her see Ceven, even briefly, was surely her plan to get them together so she could call on the others and capture them both.

Asmen clenched the hilt of her blade, the blood from Jaden's earlier wound on her shoulder still fresh but dried enough it didn't drip on the tiled floor. "Don't move."

Ceven pulled her closer as Rasha stepped past Asmen, holding a bowl.

"It's to dispel the Caster magic," Rasha explained to Ceven as he stepped in front of her, shielding the Rathan from Evangeline. Ceven still didn't move, and Rasha shrugged, tossing the bowl in their direction. Evangeline gasped as the icy liquid splashed against her chest. Her body solidified, Avana's magic dripping away from her, and when she licked her lips, she tasted salt water.

Droplets fell from Ceven's strewn hair as his gaze widened at hers; she probably looked like death. Heat rushed her cheeks as all three Nytes stood and stared at her in a mixture of rage, curiosity, and concern.

"Attacking a warrior and escaping your confinement is grounds for execution." Asmen hadn't released her grip on her sword, but at least her lips were no longer pulled back in a snarl, her features carefully indifferent now.

They think I attacked Asmen? "That wasn't me—"

"Save it for the empress. Move it, *now*," Asmen snapped.

Ceven now completely blocked her from Asmen's view, as if waiting for the warrior to leap across the room and attack Evangeline. That thought probably wasn't too far off, but she wouldn't let him get involved, not if he still wanted that interview with the empress.

Evangeline patted Ceven's arm, stepping out from behind him. "It's alright. Besides, this will be a good time to tell her what I just told you."

Ceven stepped in front of her again, earning him a glare. "I'm going with," he said.

Stubborn prince.

Rasha rolled her eyes. "You're not in the position to make demands here, prince. She'll be fine for now. Rest up so your wound doesn't open again." She turned to Evangeline, taking in her knotted hair caked with black blood, her shredded dress, and her dirt-stained feet. "But first, let's get you cleaned up. Then we'll get this all sorted."

CHAPTER 17

Rasha's quarters was expectedly spacious, with a thick bed lying on a wood platform in front of expansive windows overlooking the sea and sky. The theme of blue carried to the walls, white tile and stonework made up the floor, the color matching the curtains blowing in twirling heaps from the opened windows. No paintings, no statues or gaudy rugs. Then again, the sweeping view of the sea was enough to capture anyone's attention.

Ceven had insisted on following them, despite Asmen's threats. With Rasha as mediator, an agreement was made that Ceven would accompany Evangeline until her meeting with Empress Zelene. To hide Evangeline's identity from curious eyes, a large cloak covered her from head to toe, courtesy of Rasha, as she and Asmen escorted them both to the empress's private healer, who had remarked Evangeline was "suspiciously unscathed." Ceven shot her a glare until the healer dropped the subject and turned her attention to Asmen's injured shoulder.

Thankfully, Asmen stayed behind as Rasha and another warrior escorted her to the residential section of the palace several floors high (Evangeline refused to take the lift, opting for the spiral stairs.)

If circumstances were different, it would have been comical watching Rasha shove the Aerian prince out of her bedroom, stating Evangeline needed privacy to get ready for the empress.

Ceven's lips twitched, and he flashed Evangeline a heated look. "I can help with that." Her face caught fire.

"Out!" Rasha shut the door on Ceven and turned her ire on Evangeline. "If you or the prince try anything, I'll kill you both."

Evangeline would've been cowed a few weeks ago, maybe even a few days ago, but she met the warrior head-on. "As if we can. Ceven's too injured, and I can hear the cluster of guards outside the door." In fact, she heard a great many things, far beyond the door and the crashing sea, to the multitude of footsteps, chatter, clinking of glasses in rooms beyond this one, and the inhales of someone smoking too much of their pipe. "Besides, I want to speak with the empress. I have something important to tell her."

Rasha raised a brow but said nothing as she sped past her to the white armoire, yanking open the knobs made of hollowed seashells. Evangeline grimaced at her haggard dress. Ironic that it had served to make her look more innocent during her trial but now told another story, with black and red blood staining the fabric in an array of splatters.

"What happened to Barto? Did they find out who was behind the attack?" Evangeline asked.

Rasha tossed a green dress on the bed. "I'll explain everything, but first we need to get you cleaned."

The adjacent bathing room was similar to the suites back at the castle, the exception being more natural stone taking up the floor and walls. Plants hung in the corners and on the shelves, to the point Evangeline wasn't sure if this was a bathing room or an outside jungle. A tub carved out of the stone floor lay filled with steaming water.

Rasha at least gave Evangeline the courtesy to wash herself, albeit she was rushed along with commands like "Hurry up" and "Don't make me drag you out." Smelling of eucalyptus and jasmine, Evangeline emerged feeling significantly better before Rasha corralled her to the bed, gesturing towards the dress.

Evangeline opened her mouth, but Rasha cut her off. "I'll talk, you get changed."

The pistachio-green fabric was thin and soft in Evangeline's hands, though she wouldn't call it a dress, at least not in comparison to the gowns she wore back at the castle. It was flimsy and had too many openings. "I'd love to, except I don't know how."

The Rathan narrowed her eyes, huffing. Rasha might have traded her leather armor for silk gowns, but her demeanor remained the same, her patience about as thin as Evangeline's. Or maybe Rasha's patience was *only* thin with Evangeline. And Ceven. And Barto, for that matter.

Rasha was rough as she peeled off Evangeline's temporary robe after her bath. Evangeline's cheeks warmed as she stood, completely bare, in front of the Rathan, until Rasha said, "Barto fractured two of his ribs and broke his arm and tail."

Evangeline's eyes widened before she clenched her teeth. *If I hadn't lost my spitting mind and almost died, maybe I could have helped him.* "And Ceven? Was it really a Wretched who attacked him?" She carefully watched Rasha's expression to see if she had any suspicions, but the Rathan was an expert at hiding her inner thoughts. Something Evangeline was envious of.

Rasha held up the dress to Evangeline's chest, tilting her head as if debating her next words. "That is what I've been told, but there was too much happening at the stadium to say for sure." Her eyes narrowed. "If you have something to say, then say it."

Evangeline's heart thudded. "Did he tell you he was talking to Advisor Zindelis before he was attacked?"

"If you're implying Advisor Zindelis, the empress's first advisor and longtime friend, attacked the empress's protected guest, think again. The empress won't take to kindly to those baseless accusations."

Evangeline schooled her face to be indifferent even as shock jolted through her. How old was Jaden? And how had he schemed his way into the empress's good graces? Convincing the empress of his duplicity would be even more difficult, but she had to try if it meant cornering Jaden and getting answers from him.

"So, Ceven's a protected guest while I'm a wanted criminal?" Rasha ignored her and held out the openings in the dress. Evangeline wanted to be stubborn for the sake of it but shoved her limbs through, eager to be covered even if it was only scraps of fabric. She'd been eating regularly—including her nightly blood excursions—since she got to Atiaca, her hip bones and ribs no longer prodding out but instead curving like Rasha's. Her once-concaved torso was now replaced with toned muscle.

"Your sentence was never officially voted on," Rasha said, wrenching Evangeline's arm through one of the many holes.

"But the empress decided to seize this opportunity to give everyone what they wanted."

Rasha finished tying up her back, and Evangeline was surprised to find it wasn't a dress but a sort of pantsuit that billowed out. The top was tied around her neck and off her shoulders. And although she didn't have much of a chest, she was still concerned about exposing herself with the all-too-thin straps that covered her breasts.

"And that is?" Evangeline asked, letting Rasha slip dainty silver chains around her ankles, leaving her feet bare. "Last I heard it was a death sentence."

Rasha gave her a once-over and nodded before tackling her hair. "If the people had voted, you would have been executed. But Empress Zelene thought you were more useful alive."

Executed. Evangeline grimaced, thinking back on Barto's empty reassurances. Had he lied to her? Or had they lied to him? Jaden as Advisor Zindelis popped into her head, his eyes like twin jade snakes ready to swallow her whole. Atiaca wasn't very different from Peredia. She still couldn't trust anyone.

Evangeline bit back a snarl when Rasha ripped through knots, impatience etched into every brush. "We weren't expecting this attack, but it did make a perfect opening to fake your death. The people got their vengeance and the empress got you."

Another rip and Evangeline snatched the brush out of her hands, taking over. "Nobody *has* me. I will speak to the empress because I choose to."

Rasha's slitted pupils dilated, her eyes nearly black. "If you so much as try to escape, or betray the empress's trust, you'll be killed immediately."

*If you only knew about the predator prowling beneath this flesh .
. .* Evangeline stared into those black depths. Let Rasha, the empress, all these Nytes think she was nothing but a weak human.

They'd one day regret underestimating her.

Silence settled between the two of them as Rasha painted Evangeline's face and then settled a matching headdress around her shoulders, to cover her hair and part of her face. Ceven stood outside the door, talking to one of the warriors beside him, when they emerged. His lips peeled open as he took her in. Before Rasha could yank her away, Ceven banded an arm around Evangeline's waist and pulled her close. Her surprised yelp was squelched as his hold on her tightened, his lips tasting hers as if it would be their last kiss.

"Please be safe. I'll be back for you," he whispered in her ear as Rasha's sharp nails bit into his shoulder, tugging him back.

Evangeline squeezed his hand one last time before following Rasha down a series of halls. They entered a room smaller and much cozier than the castle's dining room where Evangeline had been forced to attend alongside Ryker and King Calais. She was still mulling over what she would say to the empress about Jaden—especially after Rasha's admission—when she froze. Curved walls enclosed the space on all sides except the farthest wall, made entirely of glass, showcasing the sun glistening off foamy waves, no curtains in sight. A round mosaic table rested in its center with four chairs, its surface topped with fruits, meats, cheeses, and beverages.

At the table sat Empress Zelene—and Advisor Zindelis.

Empress Zelene crossed her legs, blue satin spilling across toned calves as she raised a steaming cup to her lips. Her curls were clipped back with two purple butterfly clips, revealing a

face a painter would love to memorialize in their work. "Evangeline Ardonis. Lovely for you to join us."

Rasha elbowed Evangeline, and she took a deep breath, reining herself and the beast back under control. "A pleasure, Empress Zelene." Evangeline swept her leg back into a short curtsy. She purposefully ignored Jaden, who still sported the same black slacks and blue collared shirt from this morning, looking both immaculate and bored.

Even if Jaden was here, it didn't change her goals.

Rasha sat across from the empress, forcing Evangeline to sit directly in front of Jaden. She avoided his inquisitive gaze, focusing on the matching cup and teapot laid out before her. Jaden's blood satiated her enough that the silver platters of honeyed ribs, cheeses, and assorted berries didn't tempt her. She loathed owing this man anything, especially her life, but she hated how she craved his blood even more. Thank the gods Ceven hadn't joined them. She didn't want him anywhere near this man, nor did she want Ceven to see what he made her feel.

"I heard you Peredians really enjoy your tea, so I had some brought for us today. Though, I'll be frank, I much prefer our roasted beans." The empress tapped the porcelain with one sharp nail, her face wrinkled in distaste. "It's like drinking hot water."

Rasha's entire demeanor had transformed, her scowls replaced with soft smiles and her eyes focused solely on the empress's, though Evangeline was sure she was taking everything in. Two warriors guarded the entrance to the room, but that wouldn't stop Rasha's continued vigilance in securing the empress's safety.

Evangeline forced herself to sip the herbal tea, letting her eyes quickly flick to Jaden's. His expression didn't betray anything, but the hint of a threat shone in those green depths. If he was Empress Zelene's trusted advisor and longtime friend, did the empress already know his true identity? Not likely, considering his hand was still empty of any markings, markings Evangeline had been incriminated for.

What would he do when she told the empress who he really was?

"I have something—" Evangeline started.

"Do not speak unless asked to do so." Jaden's voice sliced through her, halting the words in her throat. "If you can't follow proper decorum, alternative arrangements can easily be made."

Evangeline kept her mouth closed but stared the false advisor down over the rim of her cup, hoping he could read what she was thinking.

What will you give me, Jaden, for my silence?

The empress's smile vanished, and Evangeline assumed pleasantries were over. "I am allowing you to live and reside here. Comfortably. But if you decide to lie to me or betray my hospitality, I won't hesitate to do what needs to be done."

Evangeline straightened before nodding.

Jaden didn't touch the food or drink in front of him, his eyes glued to hers since she had entered the room. "The empress wishes to ask you some questions, with myself, as first advisor, and Rasha, as first-warrior, to bear witness. Answer these questions honestly and with careful consideration. Perhaps then we can all get to the truth of this matter."

She matched his indifference by leaning back in her seat and twirling a strand of her hair between her fingers. She conveyed with her eyes, *I'll hold on to your secrets for now, so long as you tell me everything you know.*

The empress pushed her cup away from her altogether. "Were you behind the attack in the Summoning Grounds?"

Maybe it was the sun that insisted on beaming right into her eyes, the weight of everyone's gazes, or the fact that these Nytes had already declared her guilt before she could defend herself that led her to cock her head and cross her arms. "Am I allowed to speak now?"

Rasha stiffened next to her, slowly lowering her cup back to the table. She didn't have any weapons strapped to her as far as Evangeline could see, but most Rathans had their sharp claws for backup.

The empress placed a placating hand on Rasha's, and the warrior's shoulders dropped immediately. "Prince Ceven and I had managed to come to a peaceful arrangement. I hope the same for you as well, Evangeline. You may speak."

Air escaped her, her nails digging into the skin of her arms. Ceven had already spoken to the empress? Why didn't he tell her? She had her own secrets, but it still didn't hurt any less that he was keeping things from her too.

A faint smirk tugged at Jaden's mouth. The bastard.

"No, I was not behind the attack," she said. The attack . . . Jaden had left right before the Wretched emerged through the Shadow Doors. It could be coincidence, but something told her it wasn't. Still, if he was behind it, how was he controlling the Wretched, a species of Nyte that had lived peacefully isolated on the far east continent? Not to mention have the power to open that many Shadow Doors? Raiythlen had said the doors remained from a time long past, but to create a new rift in space required ancient knowledge and tremendous power from a Caster. Jaden was working with Avana, but was she powerful enough to create that many rifts?

"Were you working with that Caster to destroy my city?" Her words were sharp and precise.

Evangeline refused to glance at Jaden. "No, I didn't even know she was here." Her tongue suddenly felt heavy, and she shook her head, frowning.

The empress leaned forward, her chin propped on her hand. "Oh? So, you do know who this Caster is."

Evangeline opened her mouth when her gut screamed. She yelped and clutched her stomach. What was happening? "Her name is . . . Avana. She . . . used to work for Ryker," she bit out. Her eyes grazed the cup, still half full with dark liquid, and it dawned on her. "You poisoned me?" she spat.

Neither Rasha nor Jaden reacted. Rasha still sipped her drink—assumingly not poisoned—and Jaden, who had now propped one arm along the chair's armrest, titled his head enough for a curtain of black hair to fall across his eyes, partially covering his face.

The empress leaned back, a smile on her lips. "A necessity. To ensure that you answer correctly and obediently."

Evangeline grimaced as pain sliced her insides. This was what she had done to Ryker; maybe it was fitting she got a taste of how she had murdered her adopted father. "You don't need poison to do that . . . I—" She winced. "I'm telling the truth."

"I had to ensure your cooperation," said the empress, and the words sounded eerily familiar, dredging up memories of another Caster with an infuriating smirk and fondness for poison. "I want to be extra clear. Who is this Caster, and why was she here?"

Evangeline's grip hadn't left her stomach. She continued to bite out answers, saying she didn't know why Avana was here, managing only a nod when the empress pressed if the Caster knew about Evangeline's mark, what it meant. The empress's eyes narrowed as she snatched Evangeline's wrist across the table. Her marked hand. Her painted nail ran over the bold mark, across the encircled triangle and strange Castanian runes as Evangeline gritted her teeth when another bout of needles splintered her insides.

"Please, I'm telling the truth. Make this stop." Her gaze shifted to Jaden, who finally picked up his food, holding a slice of buttered bread between his fingers, his expression passive. No fangs flashed as he took a bite.

The empress didn't release her, nor did she give her an antidote, instead hammering more questions at her. Maybe she had planned on killing Evangeline all along.

Evangeline swallowed a scream. Gods, was this what Ryker felt? No, he had suffocated. He didn't look as if he had swallowed glass. Then again, she didn't really ask how he felt as he died. Her teeth slammed together, grounding out answers to the empress's questions, telling her that she was a part of Avana's family's history. That Anali, Avana's grandmother, had created the mark now branding Evangeline's hand. That Avana sought answers about the mysterious Caster mark, as much as the rest of them did.

The empress released her. "Hmm . . . interesting. Why did Avana save you?"

"Gods, I don't know!" She didn't care if she was yelling, that tears streamed down her face. This was so much worse than Vane's blades dancing across her skin. This was as if she had swallowed his blades and they were jarring around inside her.

And still, the empress stared at her. Almost bored. "Are you working with this Caster, Evangeline?"

"I already told you no!" she cried.

"Were you behind the attack on my city?"

"No, no, *no!*"

"Are you working with anyone?"

Evangeline fell to the floor, hunched over, her stomach shattering, her eyes feeling like they were rolling into the back of her head as the empress's words hammered at her skull. It felt as if something were trying to crawl out of her skin, over-taking her throat, her sight. The room cascaded between an unnatural vibrancy, as if a box of paints had dropped from the sky, splashing the world in rich color, before fading back to normal. Her tongue roved over sharpened teeth, her mind splintering. In her distant mind, she realized it was the beast fighting for control. Fighting to save itself.

The sound of a chair sliding back erupted in the room. "Zelene . . ." Jaden's voice rumbled from far away, matching the crashing waves in the distance.

A sigh, close enough that it had to have come from the empress. "You're too merciful, advisor. You may give her the antidote."

Mercy came in the shape of a pinky-sized vial, Jaden popping the cork and pouring the brown liquid into her mouth. She didn't care what it was or that it tasted foul, like soured apples, as long as it took this pain away. The glass in her gut disintegrated, allowing her to breath easily again. She blinked away the haziness, taking in Jaden's crouched form in front of her, blocking Rasha and Empress Zelene's view. His finger traced a single drop of the antidote that didn't make it to her mouth, sliding up her cheek and pushing the digit past her lips to feel the sharp fangs that had grown there.

His voice had lowered to where she could barely hear him. "You will not lose control here, Evangeline."

She stared up at him, temporarily dazed. "Tell me . . . everything . . ."

Shadows towered over them, blocking the rays of sun shining through the windows as Rasha and Empress Zelene stood over Jaden's shoulder. The empress beamed a smile down at Evangeline's crumpled form. She was too scared to move lest it call back the pain. "Thank you, Evangeline. Rest up, and we'll revisit this another day."

Evangeline decided the empress was no longer beautiful, nor charming. *Two-face puss-filled Nyte.* "Don't you ever poison me again," she snarled.

Rasha glared at her, but the empress's smile remained as she whispered something to Rasha before leaving the room. Evangeline flinched when Jaden leaned closer, his arm sliding around her waist to help her to her feet. She wanted to shove him away, but the poison had taken its toll on her. Rasha nodded at him and reached out to take his place when Evangeline leaned back, using the wall as leverage instead until she could trust herself to stand without help. Rasha scowled while Jaden rested a hand on the warrior's shoulder. He parted with a "good luck," serving to deepen her scowl.

"That attitude of yours is going to get you killed," Rasha sniped.

Evangeline shrugged, her legs still trembling. "I'm not dead yet."

Rasha sighed and beckoned her to follow. Evangeline stared at the Rathan's retreating back as her hand slid into her dress pants' pocket, her fingers brushing the folded edges of Jaden's hidden note.

CHAPTER 18

What is it you really want out of all this? The empress's words returned to the forefront of Ceven's mind as he walked from the palace grounds into the city, accompanied by Tarry, who he'd met with after his encounter with Eve. The former Royal Guard despised not being by his side, but after the attack, the empress had made arrangements to question them both separately until she could secure Ceven's trust—or at least a sliver of it. He hated leaving Evangeline behind in her care, but after his discussion with Empress Zelene, he knew she wouldn't make a move to harm Evangeline. It would go against her own plans and make an enemy out of Ceven.

But if she did, no one could stop him from seeking vengeance.

"An army," Ceven murmured, taking a few more drops of millow weed before sliding it back into the pocket of his gray trousers. He'd slept in later than usual, even with Evangeline's surprise visit this morning. Beads of sweat dotted his white cotton shirt due to the mid-day sun's heat, the crisp breeze against his exposed arms and chest the only reprieve. Bodies grazed past him, and the smells of spices and fried foods told him he stood near the capital's marketplace where all the stalls and shops sold a much wider variety than what Castle Peak's marketplace had in store. Ceven's favorite was their food—a dish called Fire Skewers where mixed meats were covered in flour and fried with a spicy fruit sauce poured on top. It didn't come close to what they served in the castle.

"An army," Ceven repeated. *He may actually have a chance to fight Sehn. He could make a difference in his country. But would it be worth it? Was* he *worth it?*

Tarry yanked him out of the way of a moving wagon. "Look alive, Your Highness."

"Stop calling me that," he retorted but shoved away those thoughts and focused on navigating the cobblestone streets. The healer at the palace had told him to return to his room and rest, but not only did he find it hard to leave Eve, but the information he gave her worried him. It would have been shocking to learn Zindelis was working with Avana, if Ceven hadn't personally confronted him at the stadium, sensing there was more than met the eye with the cold man. Whether or not Eve had told the empress yet, Ceven wanted to do some investigating of his own, knowing Empress Zelene would need proof before turning against her first advisor.

The tavern—the bronzed plate fixated to its smooth and circular siding reading 'The Sun's Bounty' in bold Atiacan—was busy even in the afternoon. Boisterous Nytes and humans shouted at one another, drinks in hand. Others, dressed in sheer, provocative clothes, flitted from patron to patron. A

Rathan, half the size of Ceven and no older than fourteen or fifteen, strummed a lute, humming a melody. Ceven and Tarry skated past until the humming molded into words. The song glued Ceven to the spot, several people behind him running into him and swearing oaths.

A marked criminal, she is
For the people of the empire, justice is needed
Trial of trials, we now got her
Trial of trials, what a slaughter

Cold shivers ran down his spine, the words haunting him. Ceven reassured himself that the empress wouldn't hurt Evangeline, and he trusted Barto's judgement as well. The empress needed them both alive and well for her own schemes, which served Ceven just fine as long as it granted both of them their freedom.

"What is it?" Tarry shifted closer to him, people rustling behind him.

Ceven shook his head. "I wish Barto was here. He's better at maneuvering the crowds. Knows all the shortcuts and the right people." And though the Rathan healed just as fast as Ceven, he was confined to his bed by concerned guards. Tarry had tried to do the same to Ceven, but Ceven knew how to get his way with the old Aerian—by stressing the importance of finding that Caster and finding out how the Wretched invaded, lest they try to attack them again.

"You should tell Empress Zelene about what happened here two nights ago," Tarry said when they finally made it to the stairwell leading to the second floor of the inn.

"I will, as soon as I'm done with my own snooping." Ceven pounded on the door. There was shuffling behind it, and a disgruntled torn-ear Rathan peeked his head out. He reeked of alcohol.

"What ye want?" he said gruffly in slurred Atiacan.

Ceven crossed his arms, and Tarry followed suit. "We need to borrow your room for a moment. Important business."

The half-ear man didn't look cowed. "Piss off." He went to slam the door, but Ceven shoved his boot in it, forcing the flimsy frame back. Two more people were inside, a square-jawed human male and a white-tailed female Rathan, both in states of undress. Ceven had certainly interrupted.

"We just need the room for a moment," Ceven said when the torn-ear Rathan took a swing at him. He ducked, gripping the man's wrist and using his own momentum to throw him out the door. The white-tailed woman wasn't far behind, aiming a high kick at Tarry's face while the human pulled out a knife. "Tarry," Ceven growled.

Tarry grunted and stabbed a needle into the woman's neck. She slumped to the floor as the square-jawed man leapt from the bed and stabbed at Ceven's wing. Ceven knocked the knife from his hand and pinned him down as Tarry pricked the back of the man's neck as well. The human stopped resisting. The Rathan Ceven had thrown out the hall was hunched on the floor, already passed out.

"Next time, we'll do it my way." Tarry gave him a pointed look.

"This worked."

Tarry raised one graying, thick brow, but Ceven turned away, not wanting to waste time arguing that they should have paid and reserved the room for themselves. Ceven had a limited amount of coin Barto had given them in exchange for the Peredian gold they carried on their persons over the border. Now that he was on his own, Ceven didn't have anything to his name except a useless title that only served to put a target on him.

They searched the room, trying to find any hidden panels or rune marks left over. Even blood, but any sign of Caster magic was non-existent. Ceven had mentioned to Tarry on their way here what Eve had told him. He suspected Avana had also been the Caster to attack them here, though there wasn't any definitive proof. Also, it didn't make sense that she would attack them if she wasn't working for Sehn, unless that wasn't her goal?

Ceven remembered feeling an immense pressure that night he woke from his drunken stupor. "That night, I felt like my chest was being crushed."

Tarry nodded. "I felt that too."

"Then again in the Summoning Grounds." Ceven ran a hand through his hair when something else clicked into place. "And now that I think about it, the west wing felt the same. This . . . bizarre tension in the air. What does it all mean?"

He crept farther into the room, taking in the expansive bed still left in an array of bundled sheets and blankets. The wall was the color of hardened clay and unremarkable. A couple cracks here or there, but nothing unusual. He took another step, wishing he had a Rathan's nose, when something caught his eye. At the space in front of the bed, when he focused on it, the wood floorboards moved in waves, the bronzed sconces against the wall shifting. He blinked and gazed around, the room remaining firmly fixed in one place, except for this instance.

Ceven crouched beside the bed. "Look at this."

Tarry turned as Ceven carefully outstretched his hand, brushing against the strange distortion. His hand passed through it, bumps raising along his arms, his heartbeat picking up as an uncomfortable sensation of light prickles cascaded across him, but otherwise it seemed harmless. Was this left-over Caster magic?

"Did the Caster first appear here?" Ceven asked. It was only a couple feet away from the foot of the bed. So close to where Ceven had been passed out drunk. If Tarry never let him live that down, he would hold himself accountable. Never again would he allow himself to be caught unaware.

Tarry nodded and frowned at what he was seeing. When Ceven had asked the guard outside Rasha's quarters for clues regarding the attack on the Summoning Grounds, he said the Wretched had infiltrated from the inside. All entrances to the stadium were guarded by a set of warriors, but none had seen any Wretched entering, nor recalled seeing the Caster enter either. Like the Caster here, the Wretched had seemingly appeared out of nowhere—both in the Summoning Grounds and back at the castle.

He glanced up at Tarry, his brows pinched. "I think everything is connected. The Wretched appearing in the west wing and here, Nytes and humans vanishing without a trace, the strange markings on both the prisoners and guards back at the castle . . . but Calais and Ryker are dead, and these occurrences are still happening, so who is pulling the strings? And what is their goal?"

"I've also found this." Tarry handed him a dark scrap of fabric. "It's a piece of their hood. Ripped off where my axe had pierced it."

The fabric was thick and dyed a dark brown, the same color as the cloak he'd seen the Caster—Avana—wearing at the Summoning Grounds. He could have dismissed it as coincidence if he didn't catch a whiff of its scent. Stagnant water and burnt paper. The same scent he'd caught in the arena when he'd encountered Zindelis. He said as much to Tarry.

The ex-merc rubbed his black and gray beard. Since they no longer lived in the castle, the old Aerian had allowed himself to grow it out, making him appear even older. "Avana and this advisor may be part of a larger sinister plan, but we'll need more evidence before presenting it to the empress."

Ceven nodded, and a rustle shifted behind them. Instead of their knocked-out guests waking up, it was a troop of guards in leather and steel with swords pointed their way—and one spear.

"Assaulting patrons is against Atiacan law, Ceven," Quan said, his face lacking the usual smile he'd once graced him. Gods above, this Rathan really was going to carry a grudge against him to his grave.

"They started it." Ceven shrugged, counting Quan and two other guards, with maybe two more in the hallway behind them. In such close quarters, Ceven and Tarry may be able to take down the bearded Rathans at Quan's side, but the bald Rathan himself would give them trouble. And with how good this millow weed worked, Ceven wouldn't feel any of their blows, not that he wanted this meeting to end in violence. Quite the opposite. "What does this smell like to you?"

Quan frowned but lowered his spear and took a step forward, the floorboards creaking beneath his boots. His companions kept their weapons trained on Ceven and Tarry, and the two of them were careful not to make any sudden movements as Quan took the scrap of fabric and inhaled.

His eyes narrowed. "Where did you find this?"

Ceven gestured to the room, also noting this was where the Caster had first attacked himself and Tarry. "I don't have a Rathan's keen sense of smell," he said, "but there were caves and ruins I used to explore near the castle as a kid. That distinct scent of being deep underground where water collected in still pools and the air grew thick is unmistakable."

Quan raised his hands to the rest of the guards, barking orders to tend to the unconscious citizens. Ceven knew the Rathan was strong and capable, but he hadn't been in a position of power upon Ceven's first arrival in the empire years ago. It seemed he had been promoted since.

Ceven met Quan's gaze. "I believe the individuals we're looking for are somewhere underground. If I were you, I'd mobilize a group to search every cave and ruin close to the capital that we can."

The warrior pinched the bridge of his nose before nodding. It was the first time since Ceven stepped foot in the capital that he and Quan were in complete agreement.

CHAPTER 19

Hurry up, the empress doesn't have all day. She is a very busy woman," Rasha barked at Evangeline from the entrance to her new "room." It was directly connected to Rasha's quarters and looked to have served as a large closet at one point before being remodeled into a bedroom—at least Evangeline had guessed due to the pointed lack of windows and flat opaque ceiling.

Evangeline didn't hide her scowl as she threw on another pantsuit she tore out from the armoire that had been brought into the remodeled space. It was the shade of lavender that bloomed along the sides of Lani's slave quarters when it wasn't covered in snow. She wished her old friend were the one standing here and yelling at her. Griping about sore muscles and how she needed to get out of bed and get to Ryker's. *Gods, I miss you, Lani.*

Two days had passed since the empress had poisoned her, Ceven's temporary treaty with Empress Zelene, and Jaden's cryptic note was the only thing keeping her leashed here and preventing her from snapping at Rasha and the empress.

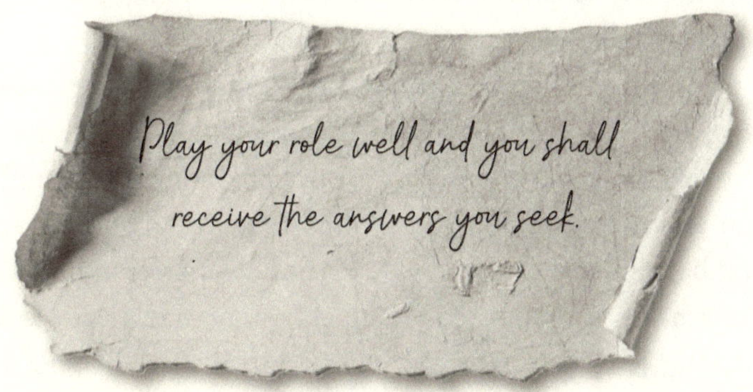

That was all Jaden had written to her, whatever the blazes that meant. She hadn't seen him since that day, and her patience would only last so long before she took matters into her own hands. It didn't help that Rasha and the other warriors had also separated her from Ceven, allowing only written correspondence between them.

Per his last letter, Ceven was far from pleased with the situation as well but was working on his end to find evidence. He didn't mention on what or who—in case their letters were being monitored—but Evangeline knew he meant Advisor Zindelis and Avana in relation to the attack. Evangeline neglected to mention she knew about Ceven's meeting with the empress, waiting, *hoping*, he would eventually tell her himself, but the longer he remained silent, the more hurt she became.

Maybe it's sensitive information he doesn't want others to see? she told herself. *You can't be upset when you have your own secrets from him.* And she was full of them.

"You're doing it wrong." Rasha snagged the ribbon at Evangeline's waist, yanking it tight, squeezing the air out of her while the ribbon on the warrior's own silk pantsuit hung loose and comfortable.

"The empress refused to meet with me the past two days. Why now?" She slapped Rasha's hands away, tying the rest of the pantsuit up herself. Ryker always had humans on staff to clean and dress her before his important meetings or events. She'd hated it then and still hated it now. "I'll dress myself."

Rasha's brows knotted but quickly smoothed as she set the matching jewelry on Evangeline's bed, smaller than Rasha's but much more comfortable than the one in the dungeons. "As the empress's personal prisoner, you are not in the position to make any demands. She will see you when she wants to."

The empress's personal prisoner. Was this the role Jaden expected her to play? To obey the whims of another Nyte master? Again? If that puss-filled advisor didn't show his face today, he would see just how disobedient she could be.

Evangeline made quick work of clasping the jewelry, finding it humorous that a "prisoner" should have to wear such finery. A platter of fruits, nuts, and dried vegetables sat on a glass cart nearby that a servant had rolled in not too long ago, and while she had mustered a few bites, the ache in her belly grew. The beast had been so spoiled between her nightly hunting trips prior to arriving at the capital and Jaden's blood that it thrashed impatiently inside her, demanding more. She did what she had been doing the past two days: ignored it.

"And what of Ceven?" she asked. Evangeline had written to him of her new "position," but either those letters had purposefully been misdelivered or the lines blotted out, since he never remarked on it. She wouldn't put it past Rasha and the other guards to hide that fact from him, keeping the prince as complacent as possible. Little did they know, they should be worried about keeping her complacent too.

Rasha ignored Evangeline's complaints as she sat her down at the vanity, tossing her hair into an up-do. Evangeline didn't know why she bothered, considering it would only be covered in a decorated hood. Only the empress, her advisors, and select warriors knew that Evangeline was still alive.

"Per their terms, he is acting in the empress's best interests and will be treated as an ally until proven otherwise." The Rathan was ruthless in twisting her gold strands into a crown braid, only to be shielded by a thin purple veil.

"And those terms are?"

As usual whenever Evangeline asked Rasha for the specifics, she dismissed her. Evangeline let it slide and fell into her role of obedient prisoner as she trailed Rasha to a new area of the palace. This time, instead of floor-to-ceiling windows overlooking the sea or beautiful tile work and painted walls, they walked down a set of innocuous stairs, the cooler air brushing at her bare arms, the stone smooth beneath her bare feet. The sunlight streaming from the overhead domed roof grew fainter the farther they descended, and for a moment Evangeline found it hard to take another step. Memories flooded back from her time in the Peredian dungeons, the fear, the hunger, and despair she had felt between Vane's visits. Then again when she had descended into the darkness of the west wing, the light of day refusing to touch any part of that forsaken place.

"Move it along." Rasha's voice cut through her thoughts, and Evangeline blinked down at her. The Rathan stopped a few steps below her, her expression softening a fraction when she took in Evangeline's frozen form.

"I promise I'm not taking you to the dungeons. You won't be thrown into another cell. We're just going to a more reserved part of the palace, away from visitors."

That didn't make Evangeline feel any better, but she swallowed down her momentary panic, leaning on the fact that she had a monster prowling inside her now. That she had faced worse and lived through it.

Thick stone bordered them on the both sides, the light from the sun now non-existent as the steps curled down into darkness. Light came in the form of blue and purple glowing rocks carved into geometric crevices along the sides of the walls, but on closer inspection they weren't rocks at all but . . . torn bits of fabric? With blood and runes marking the strips, thrown together to create a fire that burned with magic. Evangeline's mouth hung open as she turned to Rasha.

"While we dislike Caster magic, we'd be errant not to use it for our own gain here and there," was all the warrior said on the matter.

The stairs ended at a set of double doors made of steel and etched with a series of cogs and wheels—so at odds with the rest of the palace. Rasha stuck her hand into a hole within the door, and a beat later, they slid open with a groan, revealing a room seemingly from another world.

"This way," Rasha said, unaffected by the polished tiled floors, white walls filled with shelves of jars, organic material she couldn't place, and large machinery that eerily reminded her of the ruins where she was found in back in Peredia. Only two other people were here, engrossed in the giant machines in front of them as if the answers to life were going to spill from them. As far as Evangeline knew, maybe they would. The room was also blaringly bright, the Caster fire replaced with domes of white light fixated to the ceiling that emitted a low hum.

"What . . . is this place?" Evangeline's steps faltered, and she spun to take it all in. It looked like a room out of her memory, similar to the laboratory that she had seen Anali work in, fingers dancing across keys to control the pictures on the screens. The clicking, ringing, and beeping noises were lacking anywhere else in nature. She'd seen places like this back in the kingdom and now in the empire, either still in use or abandoned throughout the country and labeled as ruins. How different had the world been back then? And what had happened to change everything? *If I continue to chase my own memories, will I find out that truth?*

"Remnants of a time long passed, but revitalized to serve our purposes today," the empress said, emerging from behind a curtain and sliding it shut behind her before Evangeline could see. As if Evangeline had truly left Atiaca, Empress Zelene stood before her, looking nondescript in a plain black shirt and slacks, her dark brown curls pulled into two buns, her drooped ears, a shade lighter than her hair, even more prominent.

And what purpose is that? Evangeline wondered as she straightened, unable to hide the scowl and bite from her words. "Why have you brought me here?"

She felt his presence, like a flame that sprang too close at her back, singing her nerves. "We want to conduct several tests. To . . . rule out some theories."

Evangeline turned to Jaden. The black attire on him felt more natural, something her memory told her was more common than the false posh clothes he wore when roleplaying as advisor.

Her eyes narrowed, but Jaden's face remained expressionless.

Empress Zelene nodded at Jaden, an unspoken conversation taking place between the two, before she dismissed Rasha with the flick of a hand and disappeared behind a thick, black curtain. Rasha frowned but quickly recovered when Jaden raised a brow at her. Evangeline pretended not to notice the odd exchange as she followed the false advisor to the opposite end of the room, where another curtain awaited them.

"I've done my part. You better do yours," Evangeline whispered as soon as Jaden closed the curtain behind him, enclosing them in a space just large enough for a cart of vials, tubes, and needles alongside a metal table designed for non-Aerian patients. While they were shielded from view, the buzzing and humming of the room whirled around them, the blaring white lights overhead spilling down on her like a spotlight.

This time, she would get her answers. Find out who she was, if there were others like them still alive. And how she could control the beast before she hurt someone.

"Get on the table. We'll make this quick." Jaden turned, picking up one of the needles to test its sharpness.

Her gut churned, and her fingers curled into fists. "No. You'll tell me the truth. Starting with how the blazes you're here, *now*."

His eyes flicked to hers, pupils darkening the vast green when he blurred out of focus. She gasped when he closed the space between them, his hand cradling her cheek, the needle at the tip of her neck. "Patience, Eve. Now sit on the table."

She clenched her jaw, shifting her gaze to the curtain and then back to his. A silent threat.

He sighed. "I'll start at the beginning, what our original purpose was. What we were made for." He beckoned her to sit, and this time she listened. "We were designed by Anali and her team of scientists to be the weapons and shield of the Council, the original Council from our time. We were nothing more than tools to be used and discarded by those in charge. That is, until we fought back."

"Who is we?" The metal chilled her through the thin pantsuit, and she rubbed at the raised flesh on her arms, her feet not touching the floor.

This place felt lifeless, sterile, and she didn't know which was worse. Here or a dungeon cell.

Without warning, the pinch of the needle pierced her arm, blood swirling up into the clear tube. She jerked away, but he snatched her wrist, holding her steady.

"I need something to bring back to the empress. Be still, Eve." Jaden's tone was clipped, but he continued, "You and I . . . we started the rebellion against the Council. We led our people to freedom."

Evangeline stilled, but her nostrils flared, his words stirring up the memories she had recalled these past several weeks. "I remember bits and pieces. Us as kids with Anali, the constant fighting, and how they treated us like monsters . . . How you proposed to me in your study . . . Places like the ones in the castle I grew up in. We once lived together in that castle, didn't we?"

Jaden kept his focus on the tube, nearly filled now with her blood. "We didn't just live there, Eve. We ruled."

She swallowed. The truth of it, now that it was spoken aloud, seemed . . . like too much. Too surreal. And she wouldn't have believed it if her memories had never returned to her. The prospect of her being queen, once *ruling*, preposterous.

"The Old Council was from centuries ago. Have you . . . been alive this whole time?" Was that even possible? "Or did you enter that Shadow Door too? The one that transported me into the future?" It felt bizarre admitting that, the truth Avana had originally told Evangeline on the balcony of the glass ballroom not too long ago. Evangeline had laughed in her face, but now . . . it all felt too real to be fake. And Jaden, someone who she thought she'd never see again, now stood before her, proving she wasn't crazy, that this had all happened.

Evangeline flinched when he withdrew the needle none-to-gently. "When I found out about your and Anali's plan, I followed you as fast as I could, but you'd already entered that forsaken portal. I went in after you and had arrived here, decades before you would return to this world." He paused, as if debating his next words, before eventually saying, "I couldn't bear to lose you, but it didn't matter. I still did."

She shook her head, trying to corral the memories in her head into an organized timeline, to make some semblance of where it all went wrong. She remembered Anali, saying her final goodbyes before she entered the portal and emerged as someone new. What had they planned together? Her past self wouldn't hurt someone she loved for no reason, right?

Evangeline had so many questions: Was he behind the attack? Why was he working with Avana? The empress? Why was a twisted version of their mark now plaguing Nytes and humans? What had happened to the rest of their kind? How long had he wandered this world alone before she arrived? But something kept pulling her back to what she felt was the heart of it all. "Why did I betray you, Jaden?"

When he faced her again, the calm mask he usually wore completely eroded. Those multi-colored eyes with every speck of color, the eyes of the beast within, stared back at her. The pulse at his neck raced, his jaw clamped shut tightly. Despite all the signs that told her to run, that she was in danger, Evangeline didn't feel scared.

Without realizing it, her arm stretched toward him, as if to comfort him, before she yanked it back to her side.

He blinked, and the calm, indifferent mask fell back into place, even as his eyes fought to return to their usual green depths. "We'll follow up here in our next session. Continue to be on your best behavior, Eve, and I'll answer any question you have except that one. Because I don't even know the answer myself."

"There won't be another session." She hopped off the metal table, and he immediately blocked her path. He leaned closer, his arms framing either side of her against the table, the cold metal digging into her lower back. Her heart raced, the familiar tension of fear pulling at her spine, but she ignored it. "If you won't give me the answers I seek, I'll find them elsewhere."

He didn't say anything, staring at her with those strange, beautiful eyes and an unreadable expression, as if calling her bluff. The smell of him, his very presence so close, pressed against her senses, luring out the part of herself she'd lost.

Evangeline didn't even know where she would start to get more answers about herself and the beast, if that was even possible considering they could be the last of their kind. They both knew that. But blast it if she was forced to keep playing his game.

She swallowed. "Three days. I'll give you three days. If you don't answer every single question I have truthfully by then, I'll tell the empress everything." Even though she still planned to do exactly that, after she got what she wanted from him.

"A week."

She scowled. "Three days. I didn't escape Peredia to become a prisoner again. I'm already at my limit, Jaden." She wasn't only dealing with her own thinning patience, but that of the beast's.

He bent down, as if to kiss her, but his lips curled into a snarl. She caught a glimpse of fangs. Her own extended, her hands curling into fists before he reeled back giving her space to breathe again.

"Very well, Eve. I'm at your mercy," he said, looking anything but merciful.

She didn't move, fighting against herself, the monster struggling for dominance. When she felt she'd grappled back her control, she whispered, "I can't tell if you care for me or despise me."

The hint of a smile grazed his lips. "Why not both?"

His hand shot towards her neck. Her nails dug into his wrist, drawing blood, but the needle he gripped was already lodged in her neck.

"Three days, Eve. I'll tell you everything you want to know," he said as the room spun around her, narrowing down to Jaden's beautiful eyes, which still hadn't turned back to their usual green. It was such a shame he had to hide them. Were hers as beautiful?

As the world faded to darkness, Jaden's voice continued to echo around her. "Yes, yours are just as beautiful."

CHAPTER 20

So have you started a new rock collection, Ceven?" Barto relaxed in the worn threaded seat, tipping back the small glass with his left arm, the other currently resting in a sling. The vibrant green liquid disappeared in one gulp, and Ceven knew his friend's insides had to be burning, though Barto could drink a case of mumba and still be walking. Ceven, not so much.

The small alcove, nestled in the corners of thick insulated clay and orange-stained walls of the Sun's Bounty tavern, between the cloying smoke and sharp smell of alcohol was a rounded table packed with mumba and other spirits, alongside Ceven, Barto, and a motley crew of people.

Tarry hung close by Ceven's side, leaning on the battered wood post beside the worn chair Ceven propped himself in. Barto nestled in the middle, looking as if he'd never been injured at all, if you ignored the sling and bandages around his torso that peeked from underneath his shirt with the occasional shift. But Ceven wasn't amiss to how his eyes pinched every time he moved, with one hand around his medicine of choice, another around Lily's waist as she strummed her nails across his chest. Her smile was sensual, and though Barto entertained her with winks and riveting tales that ended with bouts of laughter, he treated her no different than Ceven or Quan—who glowered at them from the other side of the table. Everyone was armed, but all opted for the loose-fitting, breathable fabrics stained in a multitude of bold colors as was common within the empire.

Lily repeatedly tried to pull Barto in closer for more intimate whispers, but the Rathan leaned back, casually disengaging her weaving arms before pulling Ceven into whatever conversation he stirred up. This time it was about his "rock" collection.

Ceven sighed. Barto would never understand how priceless his collection really was; most people, aside from artisans in both capitals' bustling marketplaces, didn't. Not that any of it mattered now, with his prized collection locked away in his room back in Peredia, a country that wanted him dead. "If you're talking about the new sword the empress gave me, no." Ceven had met with Empress Zelene several more times to finalize the details of their shared plan. Navigating negotiations with her was a lesson in patience, but his frustration quickly dwindled when she pulled out the stunning blade he now always wore at his side. Atiacan steel embossed with the empress's insignia, the hilt encrusted with a large chunk of frostlite that would have cost a fortune back home. It was going to be needed in the upcoming battles he and the empress had discussed at length, planning for his takeover.

"It will instill fear into those you strike down. They'll be wary to take up their blade against you," the empress had said.

The steel was forged with Caster blood, the runes engraved on the inside of the hilt. At the mention of Caster magic, a deep buried malice for the craft stirred inside Ceven. He shouldn't be surprised the empress would use everything at her disposal, even something as volatile and unpredictable as Caster magic. Then again, maybe it was his own ignorance of the magic that made it seem unpredictable.

"I've never had trouble in intimidating my opponents. Even rarer that they live to tell the tale after." His response hadn't been born of arrogance, but fact. Despite Ceven's inability to fly, he made sure he excelled in every other aspect in battle, and his enemies always regretted underestimating him.

Ceven pulled himself from his thoughts, taking a swig of his own drink—a much smoother aftertaste than mumba. "Maybe if we didn't have mixed company, I could explain a bit more. No offense," Ceven added when Lily shot him a heated look.

Barto looked more than thrilled to have an excuse to remove himself from the beautiful Rathan female. "Lily, dear, if you'd be a friend and give us a bit of privacy."

Her lips puckered in a provocative way that would've stirred lust in most people if it'd been aimed at anyone else in this tavern outside this table—Quan perhaps being the exception, his eyes bouncing back to Lily's for most of the night.

"I'll miss you," she whispered, her fingers trailing along Barto's square jaw.

His returning smile didn't reach his eyes.

A hum of voices and clanking of glasses carried to every stone wall of the tavern, but Ceven still lowered his voice to avoid any eavesdroppers. Or assassins. Quan leaned in closer,

Barto closer still, the heat of his body grazing Ceven's shoulder, his breath a slap of mint and something much stronger.

"It was a gift from the empress. Or an advance, if you will, of what she can offer if I follow through on her plan." *One I'm still thinking about*, he added to himself. It'd be unwise to back out of said plan, but it'd be more unwise to decline the empress's offer as a wanted criminal with no major allies. Not that he was against it. With an army of the empress's best warriors behind him, he didn't fear making it past Peredia's borders and laying siege on Castle Peak, though it will be tough facing the soldiers he had once trained and fought alongside. What he feared was what he would do if he won. How he would rule a body of people who detested him.

Barto offered him a shot of mumba, but Ceven declined. He'd already had a few drops of millow weed and didn't want to mix the two. If he was being honest, he wasn't sure if he even needed the medicine anymore, having not stopped long enough to sense if his body was in pain anymore. Only the wicked red gash by his heart indicated how close to death he'd been.

"I'm sure she made it to where you couldn't refuse." Barto slung his arm back behind the chair, and the tips of his finger toyed with the feathers on Ceven's wings, a sign that Barto was feeling more than a little lightheaded from drink. "So, Goddess tell, what deal did you strike?"

A shiver ran up him when Barto's nail curved closer to the arch of his left wing, and he immediately tucked them in, shooting his friend a pointed look. He pouted, very similar to Lily's display.

"She offered me an army and sanctuary in exchange for me taking the throne from my brother." He kept his voice low but shifted his gaze around the tavern. Who knew who could be hiding in the midst.

Quan's shock was notable but vanished as quickly as Barto's newly filled glass of mumba. "You can't be serious."

"I am completely."

Tarry grunted, and Ceven knew the old Aerian was wary of the empress's true motives, as was he. It seemed their goals aligned; the empress wanted to keep her current treaty terms and the freedom of her people, while Ceven wanted . . . well, it seemed lately he wanted a lot of things. Respect, revenge, to prove to everyone that he could be a leader, that he could make a difference. But ultimately, he wanted to make sure he and Evangeline were safe and free from Sehn's clutches. With every breath they took, still alive and hidden within the dense city of Kazummar, the empress risked a full-blown war. It was the only reason he agreed to the empress separating them—for now. Ceven stood out too much as it was, and the more Eve could stay out of the public eye and away from him, the higher her chances of staying hidden within the empress's protection. Safe from harm.

Barto stretched for another glass, but Quan snatched it away. "Enough. You shouldn't mix your medicine with spirits."

A ferocious snarl erupted from Barto, and Ceven's head whipped to his friend, eyes narrowed. He knew Barto was neither possessive nor mean when he drank, meaning something more was going on. "Barto, what's wrong?"

As if realizing his reaction, he rubbed his fingers over his face and lay back in the seat. "Nothing." That was a lie, but he continued before Ceven could point that out. "Even if she gives you a troop of our best warriors, going against Sehn and the entire Peredian army. . . It'll be tough."

"I think the word you're looking for is impossible," Quan said, still glaring at the intoxicated Rathan.

Ceven propped his leg across his other, the brown cotton wrinkling against his black boots. At least he was grateful he could dress how he wanted, unlike the tight, flashy fabric the king had insisted he wear, who was now dead. *And I'm about to set off to kill his son, my own brother.* Because there was no possible way of dethroning Sehn unless Ceven killed him. "I received word from Taryn and Ed last night. They have recruited a few more soldiers to our side."

"Our side?" Barto grumbled. "I know you've been talking about this since we got here, but . . . you're seriously considering going back and killing your brother? Goddess, Ceven, Quan's right. It's impossible!"

Ceven's eyes flicked around, as did Tarry's. "Keep your voice down. And yes, it'll be difficult, but not impossible. Besides, I don't have much of a choice."

"And what of Evangeline's situation? Do you simply not care about her anymore?" Barto's gaze sharpened, as if the thought sobered him.

For his friend to even say that made Ceven want to reach across the rickety table and throttle him. "I know you're deep in your cups, so I'll let that comment slide. Evangeline will be safer at the empress's side, under Rasha's care, until I can take over the Peredian throne and secure a place for her by my side." Guilt pricked his chest, imagining Eve's anguished look when he broke the news to her. *I'm not leaving her behind; this is for a better future. For both of us.* He had been putting off telling her in his letters, knowing that leaving her again, especially now after losing Lani, would break her heart.

"I heard she and Rasha have been at each other's throats." Barto smiled. "Glad I'm not around to deal with that, am I right, Quan?" He cast a look of camaraderie at his friend, but Quan's stare remained on Ceven.

"We've been investigating all known caves and underground facilities in the area," the furless Rathan said, changing the topic. "Nothing of interest has come up so far, except some ruins, half a day's trek outside the city. They were marked and explored years ago, nothing but machinery and old relics already excavated and salvaged by the empire, but upon recent investigation, the ruins looked to have been . . . disturbed."

Laughter erupted to their left, causing Ceven to tense alongside Quan and Tarry. A group of boisterous Nytes hung onto each other, slurred words dripping from their mouths as they bounded between tables, earning ire from other nearby patrons. Ceven's grip loosened on his drink when he assessed no immediate threat. He was now currently under the empress's protection, and the locals knew to give him a wide berth, but that wouldn't stop any assassins sent by Sehn.

Barto sat up, his palm slamming down on his leg. "Why is everyone so serious? We're at a tavern, for Goddess's sake. We can talk business back at the palace." Behind him, Quan sighed, and Ceven was of mind to join him. With Barto still in recovery, Quan leading the investigation on the attack, and Ceven bouncing between discussions with the empress and his own investigation into Advisor Zindelis's background and Avana's whereabouts, it wasn't often they could all get together.

Ceven ignored his friend. "Disturbed how?"

Quan's face paled, as if recalling unpleasant memories. "I . . . I think it's better if you saw for yourself."

A suffocating gasp whipped Ceven's attention to Barto, whose mouth moved without sound as he clawed at his throat. Both Quan and Ceven reached for him as he retched all over the floor, splattering everyone's boots with splotches of vomit tinged in blood. Ceven and Quan held him up on either side and tilted his head back against the wall, the glow of the lanterns highlighting his face. Barto's pupils were dilated, his breathing shallow.

He wasn't drunk. He'd been poisoned.

"Tarry, get Barto to a healer now!" Ceven demanded, his eyes sifting the room. Barto had been drinking for a while; the bottle of mumba had been smuggled in by Barto himself. Nobody else had been close enough to . . .

Lily.

Quan came to the same conclusion, cursing the petite Rathan woman who was nowhere to be seen.

"I can't leave you, you're in danger." Tarry's eyes flashed, and Ceven was not in the mood to fight this. Not when his friend was dying.

"Tarry, so help me, you will fly him to a healer. He's *dying*!" Ceven placed a hand on his new sword. "You know I can handle myself. I'll find out who did this."

Tarry warred with himself, but when Quan thrust a panting Barto in his arms, bloodshot eyes and bloodstained vomit crusting around his mouth, Tarry gave a curt nod, slinging his arm around Barto.

Quan met Ceven's gaze. "They probably escaped into the alley behind the tavern." The three of them shoved through the crowd, elbowing and shouting until one warning that their friend may puke again had everyone scrambling out of their way.

The backdoor into the alley swung, slamming the building with enough force, the wood splintered. Chilled night air cleaned away the smell of hot bodies, alcohol, and thick perfume.

"I'll be back as soon as I can," Tarry said, a pinch in his face as he readjusted Barto in a better position to carry. Purple feathers spanned out, beating wildly a few times, before he sprang up and took off. Quan already had his spear drawn, his nose in the air.

Ceven unsheathed his new sword, the metal ringing in the soft thrums of the night. Where they stood, only a few people scurried down the narrow alley blocked on either side by cascading buildings stacked on top of each other, their eyes shifting to their weapons before quickly shuffling by.

Quan motioned to follow him. Their boots crunched against the gravel path, and droplets darkened his sleeves. It had started to rain.

If I could fly, this would be a lot easier. Ceven flicked his wings. The instinct was there, but the coordination between the two were off, his left side substantially weaker. He swore an oath but trailed after Quan, who darted left around a building with cracked windows and painted art along its clay-packed surface.

A shadow stepped in front of him.

Ceven's sword flashed, the frostlite swirling blue, lighting up the dark area. The soft glow reflected off green eyes with long black hair and the definite physique of a male. One who looked deadly familiar.

Advisor Zindelis.

The frostlite churned pitch black, and the shadow blurred. When Ceven blinked, a hooded figure stood in his place, charging at him. Ceven flicked his wrist, parrying the blade just in time, dodging the other aimed at his lower left beneath his ribs.

They were fast, incredibly fast. If it wasn't for the attacker's brief hesitation—whether it be from the magic inside Ceven's sword or blessed circumstance—he would be nursing another wound.

Ceven lashed out with his boot but met air when the figure jumped. Their clawed hands—so it was a Rathan—dug into his shoulder as they leapt over him. Grabbing their wrist, Ceven twisted, yanking the Rathan to the ground with an audible smack against the gravel. They didn't stay down long, a knife point on the tip of their boot whipping towards him, forcing Ceven to rear back.

In one frame, the Rathan went from lying on the ground to being back on their feet in a flurry of swings, a dagger in each hand. One struck Ceven's shoulder, hot sticky blood seeping down his arm the only indication he'd been hit. Any pain he may have felt was locked behind a haze of numbness still thrumming in his body, but it gave Ceven an opening.

He sliced the attacker's upper right torso and reeled back, aiming his next attack for their neck. Ceven wasn't fast enough, the attacker shoving off his chest and retreating paces away.

Sweat beaded Ceven's temples, his chest heaving while the hooded figure appeared unaffected. He hadn't been training as much since he'd fled Peredia, and it showed. With the attacker's unnatural speed and Ceven's lack of stamina in the current moment, if he didn't end this quickly he was going to be in trouble.

Purple and blue danced along the sharp edge of his blade, catching his attention. The brief distraction caused him to stumble back just as the attacker's dagger grazed his throat. Ceven swore. They had closed the distance between them in less time than it took for Ceven to raise his sword.

Blades clashed behind him, echoing farther and farther away as Ceven dodged and parried his pursuer's blows. The hilt of his sword warmed in his hands, the swirling hues of blue and purple growing in vibrancy, as if the tendrils of color themselves were attacking alongside the blade.

The attacker grew sluggish, as if fighting against themselves. Left. Right. Up. Up. Lower left. Ceven waited for the right moment before hammering the hilt of his blade into the crown of their head. The yelp came from a female.

Ceven whipped back their cowl. "Why'd you try to kill Barto?"

Lily's rounded face scrunched in pain, flecks of blood dotting her cheeks like freckles. She didn't move for several heartbeats. Ceven wondered if he had knocked her out cold when her feet slammed into his chest, shoving him back. A decent-sized gash marred Lily's right shoulder, the black shrouded garb torn, showing blood and a hint of pink silk underneath. Quan was still nowhere to be seen.

"Tell me and no one has to get hurt!" he shouted, beating

his wings in two powerful pumps to propel him towards Lily.

Swoosh. The Rathan was back to their previous speed. She zipped away, but Ceven forced his legs to match hers, cinching his wings and spiraling in their direction. She was too quick. Her figure vanished behind a building, her footsteps near silent against the paved pathway, collecting puddles of water. The rain came down in heavier streams, the droplets clattering around him. His blade glowed but softened as the figure got farther. Ceven had no intention of letting them leave.

His wings flicked out and flapped every eight to nine paces to gain momentum. His heart raced, his eyes and ears open, listening to every movement, every whisper and chatter in the dark night. His eyes caught on every shadow, every face and hunched Nyte and human that passed, their faces equally plastered in alarm.

He concentrated on a moving shadow ahead of him, failing to notice Lily on a roof above him until his sword flashed bright once more. She leapt, and he stepped out of the path, her dagger ripping down his left wing, close to the weak muscle. The blue and gold feathers morphed into a crimson, clotted mess, but Ceven felt nothing. He whipped around, purple and blue waves reverberating off the blade. The woman had almost succeeded in stabbing him in the back, but like before, she'd lost her speed, her movements lacking confidence. The empress hadn't lied about the sword's powers, and he was bloody grateful for it tonight.

Ceven grasped the dagger, yanking it from her grip, and thrust a fist into her gut. Lily bellowed and collapsed to the ground.

He bent over her, his hand gripping her throat. "Why'd you try to kill Barto?"

Her brown eyes blinked up at him, but they looked distant. Any sign of the flirtatious, bubbly Rathan gone. "It was supposed to be you," she said, almost mechanically as she squirmed beneath his grip. She froze when Ceven tapped the edge of his blade over her heart, life returning to her eyes in a flash of fear. It didn't matter that Lily had been a familiar and friendly face these past two years. Ceven had killed before and would do it again if she forced his hand.

He curled his lips into a smile that was as cold as the rain pelting them. Barto had almost died, may possibly be dead, because of this slip of a girl. One who had fooled all of them. "I've never been the biggest fan of mumba." His blade edged deeper into her chest, and her expression changed into one of panic.

She blinked, as if coming out of a daze. "Please don't kill me, I-I swear I didn't mean to hurt him!" Tears brimmed her lashes. "I-I couldn't control it."

The callous smile still played at his lips, even as he felt his stomach hollow at the words. "We'll see what the empress has to say about you harming her captain."

Her eyes bulged at the same time Ceven slammed the hilt of his blade into her temple, this time making sure she was knocked unconscious. The purple hue that coated his blade faded, but the frostlite chunk at its hilt still swirled in maddening colors of blue. Strong magic was still present.

He frowned, remembering how Tarry's ring went black when confronting Advisor Zindelis. He'd never seen that color arise before in the sensitive rock, nor did he know what it meant, but it couldn't be good.

The sound of the rain shifted, and Ceven peered over his shoulder. Quan's shirt was soaked from the rain, blood leeching out from the rips in the fabric. A bruise was forming beneath his left eye.

"What happened?" Ceven asked.

"The other attacker was human."

Ceven's brows shot up. "A human managed to strike a blow on you?"

Quan ignored the question and hunched beside him. "Did you kill her?"

"She's knocked out. We'll take her in for questioning."

It was Quan's turn to cock his brow. "Your wing and shoulder . . . they look pretty bad."

Ceven shrugged, knowing he would feel the pain later tonight when the plant's sedative properties wore off. "She was fast."

Quan's eyes darkened. "So was the human assassin. It's why your blade is glowing; they're both afflicted with the same cursed power plaguing Peredia." Quan's thick hands traced Lily's slender cheekbone. His thumb rubbed down it, and interweaving lines and markings popped up in its place. Ceven pursed his lips, a sense of dread and unease uncoiling in him as Quan continued to smear her skin, rubbing away the makeup with the help of the rain. Quan turned her over, the faint trail of familiar runes continuing down her underarms, the length of her sides, the rest hidden by soft fabric. Just like the soldiers he encountered in the west wing, like the humans that had been marked and deemed missing. Like the marking on Evangeline's hand.

"Whoever sent these assassins, they were both after you."

Quan's brows furrowed as he brought his fingers to his nose. "And both have the same scent. Stale water and burnt paper." He took out a flask and poured some of the contents into Lily's mouth. At Ceven's frown, he said, "It's saliver. It's probably far too late to help counteract the magic in her system, but worth a shot."

All Ceven smelled was the rain-soaked ground and the faint remnants of Lily's perfume, but he knew better than to doubt a Rathan's excellent sense of smell.

Advisor Zindelis's green eyes flashed in his mind. Twice now the mysterious advisor had appeared before he was attacked. Not to mention he, Avana, and now these assassins all bore the same scent. Ceven wasn't a fool. Advisor Zindelis wanted him dead, but why? Ceven hadn't known the advisor was working with Avana when he first encountered him in the Summoning Grounds, nor would Zindelis have any knowledge that Ceven now knew the truth about his duplicity. Ceven had kept his thoughts on the advisor private, knowing it would risk Zindelis fleeing before he could prove his treachery to the empress.

The advisor could be working with Sehn, but something told him there was more going on here.

Quan met his gaze. "Those ruins I mentioned . . . the magical corruption that tainted Peredia, it's already infected Atiaca too." He swallowed. "And I fear we're too late to stop it."

CHAPTER 21

❦ EVANGELINE ❦

More memories came flooding back over the next several days as Evangeline was thrust into dresses, decorated veils, and masks to meet with the empress for questioning (who thankfully refrained from poisoning her again) in the oval room overlooking the sea, as well as continue her "sessions" with Jaden down below in that cold, sterile room. Evangeline stayed in touch with Ceven through their letters, but whenever she insisted on seeing him in person, Rasha refused. Ceven was still searching for evidence, which led to him and a team of warriors exploring a nearby cave. He still never mentioned his meeting with the empress, or what terms they had agreed to, but she also hadn't told him about Jaden. Partially out of guilt for how she felt about the man, even if it was from a time long ago, but mostly because it would open the door to more questions. Questions she didn't want to answer.

As much as she didn't trust her turbulent feelings where Advisor Zindelis—Jaden—was concerned, he remained earnest in giving her answers while he withdrew her blood, inspected her teeth and eyes, and tested her reflexes. She felt this was more for his benefit than the empress's, and he confirmed as much when he asked her questions about her cravings, fighting abilities, and if she remembered anything else.

A drop of blood welled from the tip of Jaden's finger as he stood in front of her routine perch on the metal table, the curtain drawn around them and the overhead light banishing every shadow in the intimate space. Evangeline stiffened, the alluring smell of spiced wine drawing her closer, but she stopped herself. "I don't want it."

Jaden didn't move, hovering his bleeding wound closer to her flaring nostrils. "Don't be stubborn, Eve. You haven't eaten in a while, and I can't have you losing control and ruining everything."

Rasha still insisted on dressing Evangeline in full regality while Jaden, the empress, and several other advisors she stumbled upon in the strange underground room dressed entirely in black. She now knew it was to hide the blood and byproduct of the experiments concocted down here. While Evangeline didn't know the specifics, she learned through stealing stray research notes in passing and subtle glances around the otherworldly room on her repeated trips here that it involved creating weapons with Caster magic. Ironic how they condemned her for her Caster mark, yet willingly used Caster magic for their own gain.

Evangeline met his eyes over the slash of blood that trailed down his hand, which still showed no signs of markings. "You still haven't told me why you're working with the empress, or Avana for that matter." He'd also neglected to elaborate on the

Wretched attack, or why a twisted version of their shared mark was plaguing humans and Nytes, placating her instead with tidbits of their shared past. How Anali had tried to protect them as kids, before the Old Council had ripped them away to be trained as soldiers, controlled and forced to serve using magic that Anali and her team had created. As he spoke, Evangeline recalled the flashes of war, fire, and blood. The pain searing her as the mark on her hand flooded with light, forcing her to kill unarmed people. Humans and Nytes both.

It wasn't fair. To be used in such a way, simply because of her birth.

"You agreed to answer all of my questions," she spat.

Impatience flashed across his face. "You will learn the truth in due time. When you're ready."

She smothered an indignant laugh. "That's not what we agreed to, Jaden. Today is your last day. If you don't answer my questions, I can't promise you what I will or won't do."

He arched a brow before shoving the bleeding digit past her lips. She went to jerk away, but the beast had latched onto it, taking in his life essence as if it were its last meal. Power surged through her limbs, the lights shining even brighter overhead, the room's noises heightening from a low thrum to a cacophony of voices, rustling paper, and whirling machinery as blood rushed past her teeth and down her throat. Time passed, but she couldn't be sure how long, lost in the bloodlust, the taste, the feel of him.

It was everything.

The spell broke when he jerked his hand away, and Evangeline caught a glimpse of those beautiful, colorful eyes before he spun away, wiping his hand with a rag.

"You visited me. Back at the castle," she said. "I would sometimes wake up with the taste of blood in my mouth. The taste . . . it's the same."

He remained silent, scribbling something she couldn't see from over his shoulder.

"Why didn't you show yourself then? Why even bother at all, if you were only going to try to get me killed here?"

He rolled his neck and sighed, as if he were dealing with a nosy, ignorant child. "You had lost all your memories. You were a completely different person. I had to . . . handle the situation very delicately."

"By leaving me there alone and confused?" She thought of Ryker and Avana, all the tests they had performed, how she constantly questioned if she had parents or if she had just been abandoned. "If I had known . . . if you could have helped me, I wouldn't have had to deal with Ryker, or Vane, or—"

Jaden spun around and snarled. "I wanted you to remember who you really are, Evangeline. Not the weak-willed woman who had betrayed me, but the powerful, unstoppable one I had fallen in love with. I did what I had to do for your sake."

She sat, frozen, her heart pounding in her ears. A quiet overtook them, bringing the sounds of hushed conversation, paper shuffling, and machinery buzzing to the forefront.

Eventually she whispered, "For my sake, or yours?"

His face shuttered, the calm mask eclipsing his features once more. "That's it for today's session. We'll continue this discussion next time."

Evangeline hopped down from the metal table, her hand slipping into her pants pocket, brushing against Ceven's most recent letter as if to bolster her confidence. "No, we're done here." She had hoped Jaden would tell her more, but she would follow through on her threat, especially when continuing to keep this a secret risked the lives of others, of Ceven, who Jaden had attacked, even though he had remained silent when she accused him.

Ceven didn't know Evangeline was being held captive; she was sure of it. Regardless of what terms he agreed to with the empress, he wouldn't let this happen. Tonight, after Rasha left, she would escape using the balcony, relying on the beast's speed and agility, which she'd perfected on her hunts, to flee into the city.

Her hands tightened around the one-page letter, the paper crinkling beneath her fingers. The Sun's Bounty, the tavern Ceven had written to her about, she'd find him there one way or another. Then, together, they would confront the empress with the truth about her advisor. The empress couldn't out-right deny Evangeline's claims against Advisor Zindelis if she was with the former prince of Peredia and the empire's new-found ally.

She was done playing the subservient human to Jaden and these Nytes. She was done being a prisoner.

Something in her expression made Jaden smile. The first genuine smile she had seen from him in this lifetime. It was unsettling.

"Maybe you are ready." He closed the gap between them, but Evangeline didn't step back, raising her chin to meet his eyes as he grazed her cheek with his thumb. "Meet me tonight on Rasha's balcony when she leaves to meet with the empress.

I'll tell you what I've been working on for all these years, what my plan is. I'll tell you everything, Eve." He lowered his head, his words barely a whisper in her ear. "Then you can decide whether you want to stand by my side again. Or betray me a second time."

CHAPTER 22

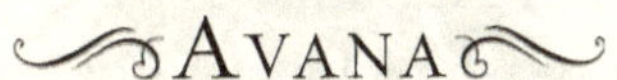

The cavern room was silent except the dripping of water far off, reverberating from the attached rock tunnels like whispers. Jaden was absent again this evening, telling Avana nothing of what he was doing, leaving her with empty promises and no closer to finding the truth than she had enduring the royal snobbery back in Peredia.

The marked body was still warm beneath her palm, the familiar ancient Caster language having already strangled the life from this Rathan, whose thick tail was covered in dried blood, her blonde hair still in its previous ponytail matted with dirt. Avana had discovered the marked bodies shortly after Jaden had brought her here. Albeit by accident, as she had been searching the cave for him when she stumbled upon a room reeking with decaying flesh. She'd seen Nytes and humans alike, angry before, but it had never scared her as much as Jaden's silent rage as he dragged her far from that room, forbidding her to ever leave the heart of the cavern and her personal bedroom. Since then, she hadn't figured out what the purpose of those bodies were, or why he was keeping it a secret, and for the first time in a long time, she was too terrified to find out.

Until tonight.

"He's taking the original meaning of the Caster symbol but changing it . . ." Avana muttered to herself, her sharpened nail tracing her grandmother's mark, which also graced Jaden and Evangeline's right hands. "But why?" When Jaden left, Avana wasn't sure how long she had before he returned. She followed the smell of rotten flesh, leading her back to the room she'd first stumbled upon, this time with far fewer bodies, a single desk, and a table used to strap patients in for medical reasons, like in the hospitals back home for those mentally unwell, or to torture like the ones in the Council's interrogation rooms.

It had taken her some time to find this place, the cave being larger than she'd originally thought and filled with more twists and turns than the man she temporarily shared them with. This Rathan's body lay on the metal table, her hands and legs still cuffed at her sides, her wrists and ankles bruised and bloody from fighting her restraints, like the nine bodies that were piled in the far corner of the room. Avana had attended, even participated in multiple interrogations sanctioned on the Council's behalf, pulling whatever information needed, no matter the cost. But this . . . this resembled the workings of a madman, with blood marking the ground in differing dark shapes and sizes, pages upon pages nailed to the wall and covering the desk's surface. Knives and carving tools lay scattered about as if their owner had left in the middle of their project.

A thought crossed her mind: would she one day turn into this? Someone possessed with finding the truth, using their blind determination as a shield against the obvious utter cruelty of it all?

The unsettling part: she didn't have an answer to that yet.

Her gaze focused back on the black marking curling and slithering as if it were trying to leave to find a new host. "These words, their meaning . . . he's using their lives to fuel something, but what? And how?" She shook her head, unable to piece things together just yet. "The only way he would be able to bring out the magic in these runes is to have Caster blood . . . but not just any Caster blood. He would need the blood from its original creator, or similar enough to it." Ice trailed down her spine. Like her blood.

But the bodies she'd seen that day looked to have been decaying for some time, well before she had arrived. If not her blood, than whose? Who else had blood ties to Anali strong enough to revive the magic in her original marking, in its original meaning?

Her eyes widened. No, it wasn't possible . . . She bit her lip, sniffing the blood-etched rune. She didn't have the sense of smell like a Rathan, but it was a useful tool in her work, smelling to identify different herbs and plants. To smell when two alchemic compounds stirred a reaction that wasn't visible to the eye. Her nostrils flared as the smell of damp cloth, decay, and minerals assaulted her, but beneath all that, she caught the familiar scent of blood. But not just any blood—it smelled like her own.

Whispers grew louder, echoing around her, sounding more sentient than distant running water. She reeled back, her muscles stiffening against her internal commands. Despite this new piece of evidence, she needed to do what she had set out to do in the first place.

The contents of the glass vial tasted like charcoal and dirt as they slid down her throat; her black hair remained unchanged, except it now hung in a low ponytail like that of Advisor Zindelis, and if she glanced at a mirror, green orbs would peer back at her. It wouldn't last long, having thrown this potion together last minute, but Avana didn't have much time to work out the finer details of this specific glamour. She unclasped the dead Rathan from the table, pale blue light tracing the tattoos along Avana's arms beneath her disguise as she lifted the marked body and stepped through the Shadow Door hovering nearby.

CHAPTER 23

~ EVANGELINE ~

Rasha escorted Evangeline back to their connected quarters after a long, grueling day of meeting with Jaden and then Empress Zelene and two other advisors she hadn't seen before, listening to them prattle about her as if she wasn't there while contemplating Evangeline's involvement in the disappearances and whether she was the key to unraveling the mystery. Evangeline had bit back her snort. If they only knew the truth about the empress's precious first advisor, how he knew far more than she did.

After Jaden's promise to meet with her tonight, Evangeline's racing heart hadn't had a moment of peace, her skin prickling with anticipation as she stifled it behind irritation at being under the empress's thumb and Rasha's incessant demands. Did his plan involve the missing persons? The attack on the Summoning Grounds? The thought of all those innocent people dying in the attack, even if they had sat and vied for her death, didn't sit right with her. If Jaden was behind it, why? And would there be anything he could say to her tonight to convince her to join a cold-blooded murderer?

Absolutely not.

And yet, a thread of doubt squirmed in her gut, the beast shoving images of Jaden's glowing eyes filled with tenderness while locked in his embrace, the way he had always looked at her as if she were the only thing that mattered in this world, no matter if they were in the thick of war or strolling the castle halls. She remembered his prowess on the battlefield, envious of his fighting skills but also how he drew others to him with his magnetic confidence. How he drew her in and protected her when no one else would.

It would be easier if she completely hated the man. But then she would be lying to herself.

Moonlight streamed through the wide windows and the translucent domed roof, illuminating the tiled floor in a cascade of blues and grays of Rasha's quarters. It slithered through the open door connecting to Evangeline's room, illuminating the barren stone walls and enclosed ceiling, the only other light emitting from the lanterns hung on makeshift hooks on either side of Evangeline's bed—her plain blankets and pillows strewn about from fitful nights of sleep, unlike Rasha's.

Standing behind her by the vanity, Rasha helped Evangeline remove the multiple beads in her hair, though it was more so her yanking them out, when Evangeline snapped, "What is your problem?" Evangeline snatched her precious hair away from Rasha's clutches and whirled around to meet her eyes. She also made sure to put a few steps between them.

Rasha's slitted pupils expanded, swallowing her brown irises. A muscle in her neck popped, and her spine lifted as if someone had woven a string through it and pulled it taut. Despite the flowing satin dress that draped her skin, Rasha's posture screamed as if she were ready for war. "My problems are none of your concern."

She started for her hair again, but Evangeline took another step back, her hip bumping into the corner of the vanity. "They are when it involves you ripping my hair out." She barely knew Rasha, an obvious distance built between them, one cemented with mutual distrust and dislike. Who knew when the warrior would decide Evangeline was no longer worth the trouble and decided to kill her and ask for forgiveness later? As if Evangeline wouldn't fight back, but then she would risk ruining Ceven's temporary alliance with the empress and her planned visit with Jaden tonight. She wasn't expecting her and the Rathan warrior to become friends overnight, but it would be nice to have someone on her side for once.

Rasha's burgundy-painted lip curled, revealing sharp teeth. "Come here, Evangeline. I don't have all night." She gestured for her to sit down on the white chaise, but Evangeline remained on her feet.

"No, thanks, I like my hair the way it is." Evangeline made a point of smoothing it back—and wincing when she came across a knotted bead. "I know you're not my biggest fan." *It seems no one ever is,* Evangeline sniped to herself. "But can we at least pretend to be civil? I've been a good little prisoner; the least you can do is give me some grace."

Rasha's fingers rolled into a fist, the muscles moving beneath her dark skin. "It isn't easy, going from a respected warrior and one of the empress's closest confidants to a captain's bodyguard and now some glorified servant to our enemy."

"And here I thought we were the *closest* of friends?" she spat, her temper getting the best of her.

Rasha closed her eyes. An inhale and an exhale later, she said, "I want to know what you and the empress have been discussing behind closed doors."

Evangeline's other brow joined, both raising. Rasha had only attended that first meeting where Evangeline was poisoned, having been dismissed the last several discussions Evangeline had been forced to have with the empress and, sometimes, her advisors. "And why should I tell you?"

"Forget I asked," Rasha snapped and then looked away. For a moment, her mask slipped, and hurt sliced across her features before she regained her steady fortitude. "It's not my place to intrude on the empress's business anyways . . ."

It was the first time she'd seen Rasha so vulnerable, and Evangeline wasn't completely naïve to not assume something more was going on here between her and Zelene. Maybe if Evangeline were honest with Rasha, the warrior would return the favor. Maybe it would help bridge the distance between them.

Evangeline conceded in sitting down, angling the vanity mirror so she could get a better glimpse of herself and the angry Nyte in her room. "She's only asked me the same questions everyone has been asking me since the day I was found. How I got this mark, If I've always had it, its meaning, if I've discovered any side effects . . ." *Like having a bloodthirsty beast co-exist with you,* Evangeline didn't say as she pulled out the rest of the beads, placing the ornaments in the mosaic boxes on top of the impeccably clean vanity, as if she were the first one to use it.

Rasha frowned, skepticism etched into her expression.

Evangeline attempted to brush out the knots in her hair, making eye contact with the Rathan in the mirror. "If you're not going to believe a word I say, why bother asking me in the first place?" She sighed. "Let me repeat myself. Again. I'm not behind these attacks. I have no idea why Nytes and humans are showing up with my marking. I'm just as confused as everyone else."

Rasha cocked her head, standing by the door as if Evangeline would try to run. "You say that, but as soon as you were captured, the disappearances stopped. Quite a coincidence."

Evangeline paused mid-stroke. No one had mentioned that to her, and she didn't know what to make of it. Then she shrugged. "Or the real culprit knew I had taken the blame for their actions and is taking a hiatus." She locked eyes with her again. "I'm not going to harm the empress—with the constant surveillance, when would I even have the opportunity to strike?" When Rasha remained silent, Evangeline tried another angle. "And no, I have no romantic interest in Empress Zelene, nor she in me." Evangeline would think that was obvious after the empress had poisoned her and watched her writhe in pain on the floor, but given Rasha's reaction, maybe there was more going on than met the eye.

The warrior—though Rasha hadn't looked much like one since arriving in the palace—stiffened, her eyes narrowing to slits. Evangeline hid her smirk by bending over to undo the ties of her dress. She'd hit the sore spot.

Footsteps stamped across the tile, and Evangeline jerked back up to meet Rasha's furious gaze, her palm smashing down on the vanity beside her, rattling the beads and knocking off a tube of lip stain. Despite her best efforts, Evangeline flinched.

"If you thought I was angry before, if you mention any of this to the empress, you'll discover the true meaning of being on my bad side," she spat.

Evangeline kept her gaze, even as her heartrate spiked, her toes curling against the cold tile in preparation to fight if she had to. There was nothing of value to use as a weapon in Evangeline's room, with only a bed, armoire, and vanity now filled with hair beads and knocked-over tubes of face paint. Still, Evangeline wanted to avoid violence if she could.

"I simply want to make it through the day, Rasha, let alone involve myself in your relationship. Though I've been more courteous in that regard then you have." How many days has it been since she'd seen Ceven? She thought her heart had been crushed when the prince first left for the empire and stayed for two years, but now that Lani was gone, the threat of losing Ceven again was too much to bear. He was the last thing keeping her from losing her sanity altogether.

She hated to admit it, but Evangeline was lonely. Maybe she had been naive in thinking she could make a friend in this foreign place.

Rasha reeled back, brushing her braids behind one shoulder. Tension still weighed on her shoulders, but her expression relaxed into indifference. "I apologize. You have been obedient thus far and do not deserve my ire."

Without another word, she left the room as Evangeline pulled out a thin cotton shirt and shorts cut off at the thigh from the armoire. Even with the windows cracked, and the breeze from the sea soaking up Rasha's bedroom, it didn't make it into Evangeline's makeshift space, the air hot and stifling at night. Still, she'd prefer that over leaving the door open with Rasha sleeping only a few feet away.

As much as the Rathan infuriated her, Evangeline did understand some of Rasha's anger. If she believed the warrior's words, it was odd that the empress had regarded her so highly but saddled her with Evangeline, a supposed criminal wanted for heinous crimes. It could be because she trusted Rasha to keep an eye on Evangeline, but another part wondered if it was to punish her. Test her.

Before turning down the bedding and shutting the door for the night—at least until Rasha left, when Evangeline would then sneak out onto the balcony to wait for Jaden—she hovered at the entrance. Rasha hadn't changed out of her satin dress, instead standing by the window, the moonlight outlining her figure. Her face revealed a level of vulnerability Evangeline was sure Rasha didn't want her seeing.

If she was wise, Evangeline would go back to her room, but a small part of her, the hopeful part she thought had died alongside Lani, wanted to make amends somehow. To try to unravel the tension tied between the two of them, loosen it to where they could at least be somewhat open with each other. After all, they were temporarily living together.

Evangeline stepped out of her room into the expansive space, and Rasha peered over her shoulder, the glimpse of emotion gone. "What?"

The turquoise blanket and silk sheets stayed neatly tucked into the corners of the large bed, as it was every morning. Untouched throughout the night, much like it would be tonight. These past several days, Evangeline had witnessed Rasha's gaze lingering on the empress, while Zelene pretended she didn't exist. Rasha visited the empress most nights, but was always back before Evangeline rose, helping her get ready for another day of meetings and "testing" despite the bags under the warrior's eyes. "It's not any of my business, but . . . obviously you care for the empress. Does she feel the same about you?"

Rasha turned away. "You're right. It isn't any of your business."

Evangeline opened her mouth, then closed it before leaving the Rathan to sulk alone in the moonlight. That sliver of hope curdled in the pit of her stomach.

The click of Rasha's door stirred Evangeline from her bed. She tossed a silk robe on top of her nightclothes, her steps careful as she exited her temporary room and stepped into the empty quarters.

As expected, the bed was still neatly made, no sign of disturbance as Evangeline padded across the cool tile to the large glass window Rasha had stood at earlier. Wind howled at the glass, whistling through the cracks where it was pried ajar for air flow. The glass door leading to the balcony sat nestled within the wall of windows and would have been entirely missable if Evangeline hadn't snuck glimpses of Rasha slipping outside some nights, cross-legged and chanting on the balcony floor covered in rugs the colors of a sunset and framed with beaded pillows and candles encased in stained glass. Evangeline had asked about the strange chanting, since it didn't involve Caster magic and wasn't something she'd seen anyone do back at the castle, but the Rathan wasn't forthcoming when asked questions not pertaining to Evangeline's role.

The spray of salt crashed into her, her hair whipping into tangled knots around her face as she stepped onto the balcony. She pulled the strands away from her eyes and stepped close to the stone railing stretching only about five paces lengthwise, giving the balcony a more intimate feel. The moon hung low and bright tonight, tinged with a yellow glow, its light dancing across the ocean's rippling body, outshining the dots of civilization speckling the cliffside and the soft illumination emitting from the palace, where Evangeline heard the rumblings of laughter and conversation even at this hour. The scene was breathtaking and far superior to the gardens Ryker's suite had overlooked. Until she glanced down, her heart plummeting to the pit of her stomach.

Rasha's quarters sat above a bluff, rising high enough that if she wanted to try to escape, she would have to shimmy along the curved ledges of the palace's walls before either the wind or lack of grip had her falling to her death. If the sheer height didn't do it, the jagged rocks at the bottom would finish the job. She gripped the railing a bit tighter.

The crashing waves eventually lulled her heart into a comforting rhythm, her thoughts pivoting to Jaden and his parting words. What was he planning and why? Her past and present self felt like two separate beings, divided by a vast sea of different life experiences. Did Jaden feel the same? Was he a different person now than he had been back then? Or did the past still cling to him, guiding his decisions in the present?

A roar of birds stole her attention, the flock swarming the darkened sky as thunder urged them to take shelter before the storm hit. A few separated from the pack and landed on the railing an arm's length away. They were an odd mix of blue, green, and gray with elongated heads.

"You two want to trade places?" Evangeline stared at them, leaning against the railing. "I'd love to fly to wherever I wanted. To do as I please without any Nytes to lord over me. To truly be free." *You realize you're talking to birds, Eve?* She shook her head.

The bird's black eyes turned to her, and she couldn't tear her gaze away. The beast hummed inside her, still sated by Jaden's blood, but for how long? If tonight ended poorly with Jaden's proposal, when could she slake her bloodlust again? Away from prying eyes?

One step at a time, Evangeline slid closer to the birds. They ruffled their feathers, cleaning their pudgy bodies, plump and easy to squeeze. Evangeline's stomach tightened in anticipation, but she felt more in control than when snow had gathered at her ankles, bare branches wrapping around her instead of expansive water. When a terrible cold, a numbness worse than the Peredian winter hollowed out her insides, and she couldn't remember who she was or why she was holding back anymore. When nothing mattered except the blood that rushed into her mouth, past elongated teeth to where it coated her throat, her insides, sparking her to life.

To stay in control, to stay alive, Evangeline needed to keep the beast fed.

When she slunk closer, both birds propped their heads up, their black eyes once more staring at hers. Evangeline's mouth opened, her fingers twitching. Closer and closer. . .

Squawk!

Evangeline snatched the closest bird, sinking her teeth into its wiggling body. Its blood rushed into her mouth, and the fire in her belly surged in delight, unfurling through her veins as the world exploded in a whirl of vivid color and nuanced sound. Then, as if she couldn't help it, she reared her head back and laughed. It was joyous, unanimous, liberating.

She felt alive again. In control.

But when her eyes landed on the bird, crimson blood staining its once beautiful feathers, its body limp in her fingers, feelings of shame, guilt, and fear quickly chased away any lingering euphoria. Ceven skirted past her thoughts, his lip curled in disgust as he peered down at her bloodstained mouth and iridescent eyes. His sword drawn and at her throat, ready to cut down the monster that she was.

More bird calls rang overhead, the shadowy mass swarming around her, as if accusing her.

She released the limp bird and watched it sink into the waves below. She wiped her mouth, scarlet staining her shaking hand. The bird's companions came closer, their squawks like a cacophony of screams. Closer and closer they gathered until she jerked her chin up, her eyes glaring at the morphing cluster. They instantly dispersed with a shriek, and Evangeline would be lying to herself if she didn't feel a thrill from it.

Gods, what's wrong with me?

The night stretched on. She counted more and more stars in the inky sky, her impatience surging like the waves the longer Jaden failed to arrive. Eventually, it reached its peak, and she turned on her heel, ready to call it a night, when the palace roared to life.

It started with a low thread of voices, rising in volume, and meeting its crescendo with a scream. Evangeline darted from the balcony, fleeing Rasha's quarters. The sharp end of a spear immediately met her throat when she slammed open the door, her chest heaving and flicking across the palace hall still covered in night except for a few lanterns casting shadows across the speckled tile and a yellowish glow tinging the dome above.

"What's going on?" she barked at the warrior eyeing her as if she was the reason for all the screaming. Two warriors always guarded the entrance to Rasha's rooms, but not tonight. Something serious must be happening.

The warrior dismissed her question, demanding that she go back to her room. Evangeline hesitated, knowing the actions she made here would decide her future. Should she turn back and continue being the obedient prisoner, bowing to the empress's every whim? To continue waiting for Jaden to tell her his plans? Or hope another letter came from Ceven in the morning with evidence against him?

Evangeline's answer came with the quick turn of her foot, hooking around the warrior's ankle as her elbow smashed into their throat. They let out a surprised yelp—the one advantage to appearing human was that they always underestimated her— but kept a firm grip on their blade, lashing out as they stumbled back. She ducked, the tip nicking off a sliver of hair, and sped down the hall after the eruption of voices. The warrior's boots clattered behind her, but with fresh blood invigorating the beast within, she felt she could outrun anything and everyone. Her body was moving with her instead of against her.

A figure crashed into her chest, knocking her backwards. Evangeline quickly regained her balance, staying on the balls of her feet in time to face Asmen. She stood in her nightclothes, clenching an unsheathed scimitar in one hand. The bronzed collar and armbands appeared more prominent without her usual armor, her short black hair not yet brushed back in its usual slicked rigidness.

Evangeline was weaponless, but that didn't stop her from crouching low, arms raised and prepared for a fight, when the Sun Warrior said, "Empress Zelene wishes to speak with you immediately. Tonight, we believe we found the true culprit behind the missing people."

CHAPTER 24

Asmen escorted Evangeline through the halls alive with warriors reassuring masses of Nytes that had emerged from the crevices of the palace to investigate the screams. Asmen hung close enough to shield Evangeline from their view—Evangeline hadn't thought to grab a veil as she left Rasha's quarters in a hurry—but few gave her a passing glance, focused on the warriors shuffling them back to their rooms.

Evangeline met the entrance to a familiar stairwell descending into the palace's depths, where blue Caster fire replaced the moonlit dome overhead. What she didn't expect to find, as they entered through the strange mechanical doors to the white, sterile space she had grown to consider her second bedroom, was a pair of beautiful blue and gold wings framing a face she'd been yearning to see for what felt like an eternity.

A smile lit Ceven's face when he locked eyes with her, both meeting each other halfway, arms folding around one another as if they would disappear at any moment. Gods, it felt good to be back in his arms. To feel the brush of his feathers against her bare skin as they enclosed them, to breathe in the heady scent of a lush forest sprinkled with spice that wholly belonged to Ceven. It chased away all the dark thoughts that had been looming over her, the haunting memories that strived to confuse her, make her doubt who she really was in this present moment. She didn't ever want to let go again.

Asmen cleared their throat. For a brief instance, Evangeline debated telling the Sun Warrior where to shove it when she noticed they had an audience.

Thin, sheer fabric draped the empress's form in shades of lavender, highlighting the gold of her bracelets and choker where she stood across from them. Barto and Quan shouldered her on either side, equipped in fighting leathers like Tarry, who stood a few paces away, eyes scanning the room with his usual stoic expression, and Ceven, whose arms haven't left her sides. Evangeline knew Barto had been injured in the attack, but aside from the dark circles ringing his eyes, the Rathan looked fully healed. She also hadn't smelled any old blood or felt bandages beneath Ceven's leathers when she embraced him. Relief ebbed away some of the stress weighing on her shoulders, grateful everyone was alive and well.

The empress always appeared relaxed, but tonight told a different story. Lines bracketed narrowed eyes, her jaw tight. Rasha wore a similar expression, still in her satin dress from when she'd left her quarters tonight to see the empress. Though anyone else would be none the wiser given the distance between them, with Rasha standing closer to Tarry than her comrades. Despite the blinding overhead lights glinting off white tile and miscellaneous sharp tools, the atmosphere felt bleak. Even if the earlier screaming and commotion hadn't alerted Evangeline to the fact that something was seriously wrong, the tension in this room alone would have.

The room was also absent of any of the empress's advisors.

"I have brought all of you here tonight to discuss something of the utmost importance." The empress's voice carried easily here in the white room, flights below the main halls of the palace and where the shuffling of feet and panicked voices were replaced by the low whirrs of machinery. "It concerns the future safety of the Atiacan empire." She nodded at Ceven. "And the Peredian kingdom."

Evangeline leaned in closer to Ceven's warmth, the strange room colder than the rest of the palace, and his arms tightened around her waist. Everyone's expressions were pulled taut, a rigidness in them that told her she was the only one left in the dark about what had truly happened tonight.

The empress's eyes fell on her, and Evangeline stiffened. "You were the last person to speak to Advisor Zindelis. What did the two of you discuss, Evangeline?"

It felt like the air had been sucked from her lungs. Did the empress find out? Did Jaden do something tonight? The room spun, her mind buzzing, and she dug her nails into her palm to draw her back to the present. "Nothing of interest, Empress. He's not one for small talk."

No one moved, but Evangeline didn't miss the subtle flick of Barto's gaze, quickly meeting hers before swerving back to the empress. Needles of ice formed in the pits of her stomach and her throat. Flashes of being hunted down on horseback, the mix of adrenaline and bloodlust as she leaned in for her kill, emerged in her head. The stricken look on the captain's face when he caught up to her, sensing something more prowling under her skin. She assumed the uncertainty of what he saw had sealed his lips shut. Until now. The only thing she cared about: Did Ceven know?

The empress's gaze remained fixated on her. "He seemed to have a lot to say when you two were alone together in my dungeons."

Bile rose in her throat. Ceven's arms, which had felt reassuring, were now caging her in. The feeling of betrayal rose unbidden, pricking her eyes, but she told herself that Ceven had no way of knowing. He had no way of knowing that what she told him in confidence, she now wanted kept away from the empress. Not when he thought the advisor was dangerous, when he believed Evangeline was fighting for the same goal. It was she who had tried to play both sides, to selfishly seek out answers from someone who may have hurt Ceven, hurt all those people without any remorse. "I . . . Yes, he did meet with me in my cell, after the attack."

Evangeline didn't think it was possible for the room to grow even more quiet. What few shadows were cast about from the shifting curtains and metal tables stretched as if the space around them were slowly sinking into darkness.

"He didn't meet with you. He attacked you and then tried to cover his tracks." Ceven rose to her defense. Although she couldn't see his face from where she stood in his arms, she imagined him staring down everyone whose eyes shifted accusingly to hers.

Evangeline swallowed and nodded, regaining her confidence. "I was waiting until we had solid evidence against him before telling you, since, as you all know, people here don't tend to believe the words of a branded criminal."

In meetings past, when Evangeline's temper got the best of her, the empress would wave her off with a condescending smile or ignore her jabs altogether, continuing the conversation as if they were old friends and not prisoner and empress. Tonight, Empress Zelene did neither, her eyes boring holes into her skin as if she knew every secret Evangeline was desperately trying to hide. And maybe she did.

"Well, we now have that evidence you've been seeking." Her gaze finally left Evangeline's, shifting around the room. "Everyone, follow me."

Evangeline had always wondered what was lurking behind the curtains throughout the room. Empress Zelene crossed the space to the far wall, away from the entrance, and pushed a set of thick white curtains aside. Rather than it leading to a space filled with nothing but a metal bed and sharp tools, much like her encounters with Jaden down here, it revealed another metal door. After the empress inserted her arm into the crevice of the silver frame, the doors slid back with ease—and the foul smell of decay assaulted her senses. Evangeline bit back a gag, covering her mouth and nose. Everyone else had a similar reaction before pulling out masks to cover their faces. Ceven offered her one, and she took it without hesitation.

The white walls and tiled floors ended abruptly when they stepped through the doors, replaced with un-sculpted rock slashed through with veins of blue and green gems, as if they were entering an unrenovated part of the palace or an underground cave that had been here centuries before civilization built itself atop it. Evangeline's mouth and nose were now covered by a thick, breathable fabric, but the horrid smell was still overwhelming, and she took slower breaths to keep from gagging. At least she wasn't the only one suffering; everyone's faces scrunched in discomfort except for Rasha and the empress. As if they both had been here a hundred times.

The space was illuminated by more Caster fire, revealing a hallway that branched out into different rooms not hindered by any doors. Beds made of copper and thin sheets occupied the rooms, some empty, some filled with dark figures that resembled Nytes or humans. None of them moved or made a sound, and the longer they traversed the eerie hallway, the more Evangeline tensed, her muscles tightening. Her senses instinctually expanded beyond the stench, gauging if there were others down here with them and how far they were from the surface. Something akin to drums beat to the rhythm of everyone's steps, and the dimly lit hallway brightened a fraction, not by any artificial light or otherwise, but through her eyes adjusting.

The drums became louder, and Evangeline jerked when she realized where the noises were coming from. It was everyone's beating hearts, pumping life through their veins, and Evangeline had subconsciously narrowed in on it. Ceven sensed her panic, his fingers twining with hers. She quickly glanced away, fearing her eyes had changed to the beast's.

Yes, yours are just as beautiful.

Jaden . . . What the blazes did he do tonight?

No danger greeted them at the end of the hallway, but Evangeline recognized the two advisors who occasionally accompanied the empress to their meetings—Advisor Lynne with silver-streaked hair, and Advisor Janton, whose rounded spectacles hung too big on the tip of his large nose—both wearing masks that covered half their faces and dark robes.

The empress spread her hand to the series of bodies that lay on metal beds in the center of the rectangular room lit in blue and purple fire and lined by shelves and tables of sharp tools, bottles of various shapes and colors, like the tools in the sterile room they had come from. "It's not made public yet, but Quan, with the prince's help, discovered ruins not far from here housing several missing persons. All marked, and now all deceased."

Evangeline reassessed the room, making out the same markings that had scarred Lani, Shani, and the other humans and Peredian soldiers. All were in various states of decay, which explained the smell. Still, everyone looked expectant, as if this was old news. This was all for Evangeline's sake, but why?

"Now? Are you implying they weren't before?" she asked.

Ceven squeezed her hand, reminding her their fingers were still intertwined. "When Quan and the other warriors first discovered the ruins, they had all been alive but unresponsive."

Quan nodded, his brows furrowing as his eyes swept over the marked bodies before latching onto Evangeline's hand with the same runes. "Comatose. Alive and breathing, seemingly healthy too, but unresponsive to sound and touch." He winced, as if recalling an unpleasant memory. "Until we tried to physically move them. We lost two good warriors when they attacked out of nowhere."

The sinking feeling in Evangeline's stomach grew as she re-examined the bodies. Upon second glance, they didn't look drained of life like Lani had before she died, or the other humans she'd seen in the depths of the west wing. Fatal gashes marred their throats and chests.

Barto placed a hand on Quan's shoulder in silent camaraderie as he continued, "We were forced to fight back. The ones we managed to avoid killing in the fight slit their own throats."

Ceven inhaled as if he hadn't known that fact, his grip tightening on hers. It didn't make sense. From what she had seen in Peredia, all the humans that were marked looked to have already been dead, in no shape to fight back, while the marked soldiers still had their full facilities, stronger and faster than before. She thought of Vane, with his runes snaking up his neck, covering his shaved head. The way he had morphed into something beyond any normal Rathan she'd seen, but a beast that matched her own.

The empress, at first glance, still looked aloof, but on closer inspection, a potent anger gripped her eyes, creasing the corners, the barest furrow of an eyebrow betraying the façade. Then, as if thinking, "What was the point?", the empress's lip curled back, and a throaty snarl escaped her, showing how deep the anger ran, that it had resided there for a while now, growing and festering. "If only I had looked harder at what was in front of me."

"Empress," Advisor Janton, who had remained silent since they all entered the room, started when Advisor Lynne stopped him.

"I understand your pain," the other advisor said, stepping forward slowly as if consoling a child, "but let's think things through here, before we act rashly."

Rasha was the one to step in front of Lynne, cutting her off and meeting the empress's gaze for the first time since they'd all gathered tonight. "Your compassion and trust in others are not to be blamed. We both know it's inevitable in this line of work, but don't lose sight of who is really at fault here."

Barto's eyes flicked to Evangeline's again, and this time she met his stare, as if daring him to say what was truly on his mind.

Before he could, however, she snapped, "It's clear everyone knows what is going on, but I'd appreciate it if someone could enlighten me."

Ceven stiffened beside her, and she sensed a silent reprimand from him, but her patience had evaporated. She was tired, annoyed that Jaden hadn't arrived tonight, and frightened by what the empress possibly knew about her. If blame was about to be laid at Evangeline's feet—yet again—she wanted it said and over with. The pressure of not knowing had formed a headache that pulsed at her temples.

Empress Zelene's bare feet whispered against the floor as she stood next to one of the metal beds. She pulled back the covering, and Evangeline's mouth peeled open in recognition. "Tonight, Advisor Zindelis was found next to our latest victim, Serah Helkan, before fleeing the scene."

Her mouth hinged open before snapping shut. This was why Jaden hadn't shown up. Was this what he planned to reveal tonight? His involvement in the missing persons, starting this . . . this magical corruption, not only here, but in Peredia? She wished she could be shocked. Shaken to her core at the truth, but deep down? She had known. Her gut telling her what her mind didn't want to process as it was still tangled up in memories of a different man she had fallen in love with in the past. Jaden remembered who he was, who they were. His knowledge was vaster than any Nyte she knew, with powers that seemed unrivaled. Aside from Raiythlen and Avana, no one else could have known the truth about their marking, what it could do.

Her teeth sank into her lip as she recalled Lani's final moments, the suffering she'd endured along with all those other humans, all started by someone she had once called husband. But . . . why? And how did he manage to get caught tonight, after years of secrecy? Right before he had planned to tell her everything? Something didn't add up.

Evangeline glanced away from Serah's body to find Empress Zelene watching her, scrutinizing every feature on her face. "Zindelis is clearly a master at deception, having deceived us all, but you are not, Evangeline. I've seen the way you look at him, the familiarity you've tried to shield when you believe no one else is watching."

Pain licked up her arm from where Ceven crushed her fingers in a death grip. At her gasp, his hold loosened, but he didn't release her when she tugged. His gaze wasn't accusatory, unlike everyone else's in the room—perhaps aside from Tarry, who replicated a statue behind Ceven—but she knew him well enough to see the flash of hurt. The doubt forming between the greens and browns of his eyes, dark in the dim light, eclipsing the flecks of gold that always shone vibrantly when the sun hit them.

Evangeline had been right to be terrified of what the empress knew. Now she was forced to tell the truth—in front of Ceven—and she wasn't ready. She didn't think she'd ever be ready.

"You're right." She had planned to tell the empress anyway. "I'll tell you everything I know, but . . . in private." She refused to meet Ceven's gaze.

But the prince had other plans. He jerked her around to face him, his thumb propping her chin up so his eyes could stare down into hers. Any remnants of hurt and doubt were obliterated by the angry heat that rose in his gaze. "Sea watery hells you will. What's going on, Eve?"

She shoved at his chest—not that it mattered, as his massive frame didn't budge—and yanked her chin out of his grip. "Why don't you tell me, Ceven? What terms did you and the empress agree on?" The heat in his eyes dampened but didn't vanish entirely as she continued, "Did you agree to leave me here as a prisoner while you went gallivanting around the capital and exploring caves?"

He frowned, glancing at the empress. "What do you mean?"

She waved a hand at herself, drawing his attention back to her. "I haven't had quite the warm welcome here in the capital, unlike you. If you had even bothered to try to see me, you'd know." She knew that was unfair of her, given they were up against the empress's orders and her entire army. Evangeline had asked Rasha relentlessly to let her see Ceven, even a glimpse, but she had been denied. Ceven had written about his displeasure with the situation, but had he even tried to see her?

He scowled, his eyes darkening. "Don't you dare give me that, Eve. You don't know anything."

"And that's the problem!" She stepped back as his fingers twitched, either to hold her close or thrash her, she didn't know. "I haven't been the only one keeping secrets, so don't you dare act like I owe you anything." She was painfully aware of everyone's eyes on them, witnessing her at one of her most vulnerable moments, but she didn't care. Anger, hurt, and fear festered in an ugly trio, bringing out the worst in her.

He straightened, as if suddenly aware of their rapt audience as well. Like slipping on a mask, his expression morphed into indifference with a hint of haughty arrogance. Distant and unreachable. An expression she hadn't seen on him since his and Sehn's welcoming ball at the castle. "Have it your way, Eve."

She opened her mouth as Empress Zelene stepped forward, not close enough to touch, but close enough to interrupt whatever was about to explode from her. "Another ruin was discovered hosting more marked victims. Given the proximity to the city and what we witnessed tonight, I believe Zindelis may choose to hide out there, if he hasn't already."

She froze. Judging by the narrowed eyes and whipped heads of everyone else, this was recent news.

"Not only did I bring you all here tonight to bear witness to the treachery that is occurring in both of our countries, but to make plans to thwart it. Tomorrow we will prepare to leave for these ruins and devise a strategy moving forward, given tonight's turn of events." The empress faced Evangeline. "And on our travels, you will tell me everything you know. You have been branded a criminal, but I am granting you the opportunity to make yourself into a hero. We will see what path you choose."

CHAPTER 25

~ EVANGELINE ~

The distance to the ruins from the capital took several days to cross, with towns sprinkled between over vast stretches of grassy plains, sandy beaches, and a sweltering heat made worse by the dark cloak and mask she wore. At least she wasn't the only one; the rest of their entourage—Empress Zelene, Rasha, Asmen, Ceven, Tarry, and Quan—wore something similar to disguise their identities. Well, as much as they could, given Ceven's wings. Even the mud that'd been caked on the beautiful blue and gold feathers to shield his identity started to slip away, flecks of gold sprinkling through to catch the afternoon sun.

They traveled on horseback in two separate groups to avoid attention. Ceven, Tarry, and Quan followed a good distance behind them, their figures specks in the distance but never farther than a short sprint away. Evangeline rode with empress, Rasha and Asmen framing them on both sides, with

Rasha shooting none-too-subtle glances at her and Zelene. Only a few warriors accompanied both groups when they left the palace in the dead of night.

As much Evangeline hated to be on horseback again—with the empress no less—she was grateful for the distance between herself and Ceven. After their confrontation, neither had spoken a word to the other, even when the group would come together to set up camp at night. Honestly, she didn't know what to say, not when she couldn't figure out her own feelings. And talking with the empress about it the last several days had only made it worse.

As she told Empress Zelene how she knew Zindelis by another name—Jaden—and how he shared her mark, that she had lost her memories as a child while Jaden remembered everything, how he was working with Avana and had a plan he never got around to telling her, the more guilt festered to the surface. Evangeline still hadn't forgiven Zelene for poisoning her, or almost condemning her to a public execution, but keeping this information that could have helped or saved innocent people didn't sit right with Evangeline. She had willingly waltzed with a murderer, selfishly seeking answers for herself instead of thinking about the greater good. Based on Asmen's increasingly rigid posture throughout their journey and Rasha's grimace, she wasn't alone in feeling this way.

Lavender and crimson slashed the sky, melting into a velvet night of stars and a sickle moon. The rhythmic beat of hooves pounding into the land rumbled alongside leisurely cascades of wind from the sea a few hundred paces to their left. Not too far back, Evangeline had glanced longingly at the faint glow of civilization, craving a soft bed and a cold shower at an inn like they had the first night, but the empress wanted to cover as much ground as they could, fearing Jaden may have already left.

"I've known Zindelis from a time before I became empress. Did you know that?" the empress said after moments of quiet with nothing but snorts of their horses and crickets chirping in the sparse foliage lining the dirt-trodden path around them.

Evangeline sat in front of the empress, careful to keep her back straight and as far away from Zelene as possible lest Rasha pluck out her eyes, so the empress didn't miss the shake of her head.

"He had been the one to pull me out of my chains, placed on me merely for defending my honor, my body when I had been only a child." She let the sounds of encroaching night take over for several moments before continuing. "He'd seen the anger in me, at the injustice done to my people, my family, by someone who had called himself a leader, by someone who had demanded respect rather than earned it. He helped me bring together my army, helped me prove Atiaca was worth more than a cluster of useless leaders who hid behind egos and took from the weak in a show of strength."

Asmen gave a slight nod, and Rasha's grip tightened on the reins.

"Zindelis had proven his loyalty ten times over throughout the years, helping me claw through the empire and steal its throne out from those that didn't deserve it. Aiding me in eliminating the rebels and remaining loyalists to bring about the era of peace. But it was only in the aftermath of war that I saw all the qualities that had made him a remarkable general, strategist, and warrior on the field had turned him into a callous, cutthroat, and exacting advisor of the people. The hardships we had endured together, the bond we had formed, blinded me to his true nature, which had always been creeping underneath the surface."

The grassy hills slowly swallowed the sun whole as the silence stretched longer and longer, eventually pulling a response from Evangeline. "Being raised as a human in Peredia, you get used to being surrounded by those that held all the power, leaving you scraps of it to fight amongst your peers."

Evangeline remembered surviving with Lani, sharing a mutual understanding with the other human slaves within the castle—until Ryker adopted her. She was still powerless, but held more power than the peers she had once worked alongside, and while Evangeline loathed to admit it, she had changed. She'd become colder and colder to the humans around her. Their hatred towards the larger scrap of power she had been given drove the knife deeper and deeper until the only way she could live was to shut everything out except herself and those she cared about. It was why she was so terrified of the growing power inside her now. How much more would she change? Would she turn into a power-hungry monster like those soldiers in the west wing, empowering themselves off human lives? Or like Vane, who thrived off the never-ending suffering of those beneath him?

Or would she become like Jaden? Someone who had changed completely from a respected king, husband, and close confidant into a murderer consumed by the past and driven by . . . Well, she didn't have the answer to that yet.

Evangeline drew in a shaky breath. "Those with power will always want more, because power itself corrupts, ruining even the kindest of souls." Evangeline neglected to say she believed the empress was no exception to the rule. She didn't think anyone was. Including herself.

Asmen glanced at her, her gaze thoughtful, before focusing on the road ahead. Now that the Sun Warrior knew it hadn't been Evangeline but Jaden who had attacked her in the dungeons, she had been far more amiable. Evangeline had also learned Asmen had once been a criminal herself, accidentally killing the wrong Nyte when she'd set off to avenge her mother, who had been kidnapped and murdered. The real culprit had been her father—who later had been sentenced to death. Asmen had laid blame at another's feet and unknowingly killed an innocent by meting out justice with her own hands. The story wrought more sympathy and understanding for the Rathan, and compassion for the empress's mercy, though Evangeline still wouldn't want to be left alone with either Nyte.

The empress hummed in contemplation. "Interesting. So, do you believe Zindelis was truly innocent at one point? A kind soul, as you put it?"

She answered without thinking. "Absolutely. I had loved him."

Those words fired like a shot into the still night. It was the first time Evangeline had said it aloud. The utter truth of it slipped from her tongue before she could reel it back.

"I had loved him too." Zelene's words were a soft whisper at her back, so soft Evangeline almost mistook it for the wind.

"But loving someone doesn't make them kind, it only makes you more forgiving of their flaws."

The following morning, they arrived at the mouth of the ruins, a benign opening between two large shoulders of rock lodged into the hillside with the closest towns a day's travel on either side. Evangeline kept her eyes trained away from Ceven, even as she felt his pressing stares as they all unpacked the horses, preparing themselves for whatever awaited them inside the cave.

Thank the Gods they'd camped near a river last night, allowing Evangeline to wash off the grime from traveling. She didn't even care about the lack of privacy as their entourage unabashedly joined in the stream together under the moonlight, her only saving grace being that the males at least washed farther downstream. It didn't stop Evangeline from thinking about Ceven, naked and dripping wet, like he'd been during their moment together by the spring, before remembering his face, mottled with rage as she accused him of keeping secrets. Only because she was too scared to reveal her own.

Asmen handed Evangeline a sword, which she took with a raised brow, but no one batted an eye at them, busy slipping their own blades into sheathes at their arms, thighs, and boots. Evangeline wasn't sure if it was the fact that they now knew Jaden was behind the missing persons, or if her vulnerable honesty with the empress the past few days had finally bridged some of the gap between them. Either way, Evangeline didn't complain, sliding the sword into the sheath at her hip. While Barto had stayed behind to guard the palace, he was sure to

have told the empress of Evangeline's prowess on the battlefield. Though she preferred daggers, she'd take any line of defense against whatever monsters lurked in the cave.

Despite ignoring the prince—at least to the best of her abilities—Ceven kept close to her back as they delved into the ruins, leaving their horses tied outside under the protection of several fallen trees, creating a hidden canopy paces away from the mouth of the cave. Inside it was blessedly cooler, shielding them from the rising sun, the smell of limestone brushing her senses along with . . . blood. She wasn't the only one. Everyone tensed, their grips flying to the handles of their weapons.

Rasha brought up the front, a lantern filled with blue Caster fire attached to her hip as well as the empress's and Asmen's, illuminating the jagged rock closing them on either side. No one said a word, cueing into the sounds over the soft patter of their feet and bated breaths. The path dipped, a slight decline pitching into complete darkness. Rasha's blade was already out in front of her, Empress Zelene at her back, with her own sword and matching leathers, a glimpse at the warrior empress before she had stolen her throne.

Evangeline adjusted her own leathers, the protective torso supple enough to form to her body but hardened in the right areas to give some protection if a fight were to break out. Ceven had frowned when he'd first seen her in the fighting gear this morning at camp, and she knew he'd prefer her far from the battlefield. When she had caught his gaze, she purposefully tightened the straps on her thighs and boots, a silent rejoinder that she wasn't the helpless human he always seemed to think she was. As if she would allow anyone, Ceven or the empress herself, to prevent her from joining them. A part of her was scared to see Jaden again, while another, much smaller part of her that she tried to ignore, was excited.

The jagged rock narrowed on either side, forcing them to follow single-file until the walls disappeared altogether, their footsteps echoing off what sounded like a cavernous pocket within the ruins. Rasha froze mid-step, her lantern flickering across beady eyes and the outlines of faces, all different shapes and sizes.

The cavern was filled with marked people, all standing in rows, utterly still. Their gazes not even flinching when everyone withdrew their weapons, tension thickening the cool air.

Before Evangeline could wrangle the beast back, her nostrils flared, breathing in the smell of blood, fire, and sweat linking the marked figures together, a hint of their unique scent nearly covered beneath the dark magic wrapping their skin. The sound of boots sliding against rock, the steady breathing, the pulsing hearts of everyone in the room grew tenfold, creating an orchestra of sound. The vibrant blue and green of the Caster fire slowly bleached into a whiteness that slipped off an arching ceiling spanning several lengths above them to the cavern walls stretching even farther on all sides, down to the crowd of humans and Nytes in a myriad of clothes as if they had been plucked from their daily lives without warning. Warriors, mothers, merchants, children, courtiers . . . no one had been spared.

"By the Goddess . . ." Asmen stood on her right, her knuckles bleeding white against the hilt of her blade. "This is . . . this is madness."

The Rathan's voice reeled Evangeline back to herself, mentally chaining the beast back to the crevices of her mind.

She was grateful for the darkness, hoping no one noticed the change in her, if her eyes reflected an iridescent array of colors. The ease at which she slipped into something more than . . . human was becoming instinctual. Too accessible.

Ceven stuck close to her side, his arm brushing hers. Intentional or not, it helped ground her, an unsettling feeling curdling in her stomach as she stared back at the lifeless crowd. The others had identified several familiar faces—people who had been missing for months—as well as those they had seen only days prior with no signs they had been declared missing yet.

Ceven and Quan shared a look. Evangeline decided to break her silence with the prince in favor of her curiosity. "What is it?" she whispered, scared her voice would trigger the still figures to come to life.

He grimaced before reluctantly saying, "Lily, a tavern worker who we had known for years, attacked us recently. She had the same markings, was abnormally fast and strong, but when questioned it kept coming back to the same thing: she had no control over her actions." His eyes shifted to the empress. "She'd been moved to the dungeons, but before we could get more information from her, she had clawed out her own throat."

Evangeline covered her mouth in horror. Her eyes fell back on the mannequin-like Nytes and humans who Rasha, Zelene, and several other warriors observed from a careful distance as they explored the cavern further. Were they doomed to the same fate? Controlled like puppets to serve their master and massacred when no longer needed? Did they even know they were puppets? Was there any life left in them?

"Another thing you forgot to mention," Evangeline said, turning away from him, even as she immediately missed the feel of his arm against hers. "Anything else you'd like to share?"

His voice lowered, pricking the back of her neck. "Don't start, Eve. Not when you've been keeping things from me too."

He was right, but she still couldn't help the temper that flared at her insides. So, she ignored him, trailing behind Asmen to the far side of the cavern, where an opening to another part of the ruins lay behind the eerie breathing wall of flesh. It led to a room a third the size of the cavernous one they came from, the walls smooth and lined with wires and lanterns fixated every few paces farther in. Aside from the marked individuals, there were no other signs of life, nor any pressure indicating any active Shadow Doors nearby. If Jaden and Avana were here, they were doing a great job at staying concealed, but Evangeline didn't think that was the case.

She'd been mulling over this thought for a while, as it just didn't make sense. "You had witnessed Zindelis that night, next to the marked body . . ."

"Serah," Asmen said, standing next to what Evangeline now could see were metal cages stacking the perimeter of the room, barely large enough for one person. "I witnessed him holding Serah when passing the western halls during my night watch. I didn't even recognize her at first, someone whom I had personally trained for years. The dark magic had twisted her face into something beyond comprehension."

Evangeline stood in quiet solidarity for several beats. She recalled Lani in her final moments, how her skin had hung from her bones, the life dripping away from the woman she had considered a mother. She understood too well the effect of this magical plague, how it took your loved ones in the worst way.

"Was there anything . . . off about the advisor that night? When you saw him?"

Asmen crouched beside the cages, opening the doors and peering inside despite all of them being empty. "He stood there holding her so blatantly, so self-assuredly, that I didn't even suspect him. He'd been . . . a highly respected advisor for longer than I've been a Sun Warrior. His betrayal didn't even cross my mind until he dropped Serah, as if she meant nothing, and fled. No matter how much I called out, how fast I chased him down, he disappeared into the night, screaming his guilt."

Evangeline stood beside Asmen, but she refused to get any closer to the cages that looked black in the dim light of Asmen's lantern. It could be because they reminded her of the hundreds of humans trapped in cells within the west wing, but something else tugged at her mind. A memory past. Herself and Jaden trapped in cages just like these, awaiting their next orders. The next battle they would be forced to fight in.

She shook away the uneasiness skittering across her skin, focusing on the details of that night. Rasha and the empress had also seen Jaden fleeing when the screaming lured them from her quarters. And they hadn't been the only ones. It was as if Jaden had purposefully drawn as much attention to himself as possible before vanishing completely.

"Why, after all these years of secrecy, reveal himself now?" She refused to think it had all been a mistake. Not when Jaden had been so careful, meticulously curating this persona for decades. Not when he planned to meet with her that same night. "I . . . I don't think it was him you saw that night." Asmen stiffened, her eyes narrowing, but before she could speak, Evangeline continued, "Not that what you saw is wrong, or that Zindelis isn't a part of all this, but I think . . . I think it was Avana wearing a glamour." She knew the two of them were working together and that the Quincara siblings had a fondness for glamour magic. It would make more sense if Avana had purposefully sabotaged Jaden, but then that begged the question: Why? And did that mean they were no longer working together?

Asmen's mouth peeled open, and fighting broke out behind them.

The Sun Warrior beat her to the cavernous room, the marked figures having come to life in a whirl of limbs. Evangeline held out her blade when a marked Aerian with pastel wings and a torn sundress landed in front of her. She was too slow to dodge the Aerian's strike to her stomach. Air escaped her lungs, and she lashed out, steel slicing ribbons across the Aerian's marred skin. Before the Nyte could deal another blow, Evangeline aimed her sword for the pulsing beat at their throat, ready to strike when she caught their gaze.

They were crying.

These people . . . they're innocent. Evangeline's grip faltered, and the brief distraction landed another kick to her side, pain radiating up her bones and locking her jaw tight. The rest of the group were engaged in battle, all of them severely outnumbered. They had skill and pure strength on their side, but they were up against innocent civilians. Would they be forced to cut them down?

Evangeline rolled to the side as a chunk of stone slammed down next to her, shaking the floor. The Aerian had pulled the slab of rock free from the cave wall and lifted the massive slab again, prepared to crush Evangeline's skull in one swing. She dodged, watching the Aerian's feet, while dancing around other figures that had come alive. Thankfully they passed her, and on second glance—after side-swiping another swing from the Aerian—most of the marked individuals weren't fighting. They were running.

Empress Zelene had noticed as well, barking orders to several warriors who sped after them. Evangeline met Ceven's eyes over the clash of swords, his shout lost in the calamity as the Aerian's arm snaked around Evangeline's throat, taking her to the floor. The beast clawed to the surface, but Evangeline fought back, snarling, "You are *not* in control here." She knocked her head back, a crunch echoing behind her as air seeped back into her lungs, the Aerian's hold loosening.

Evangeline whipped around. She held her blade at the Aerian's throat when they yanked the steel tip, impaling themselves on the blade. Evangeline cried out, covering the fatal wound with her hands as crimson blood poured from their neck, down their torso, staining their faded sundress. It was too late. Evangeline watched the light fade from the Aerian's eyes, her fingers soaked with their blood as she hurled a curse.

"Jaden." Evangeline spat with as much venom as she could, staring at the dead Aerian. Her gaze shifted to the other Nytes and humans that had been cut down in self-defense, their bodies lying still across the cavern floor. How could Evangeline have loved someone who massacred innocents? Was he truly this cruel? "I will put an end to this," Evangeline said to no one, her gaze retuning to the innocent Aerian slumped before her. "One way or another, I *will* stop you, Jaden."

CHAPTER 26

Exhaustion hugged Evangeline's bones, pulling down the lids of her eyes as she slumped forward in the saddle. This time she rode with Asmen, grateful to be away from Zelene and Rasha's glares, which she didn't conceal as well as she thought she did. The aftermath of the ruins stole most of the conversation from them, leaving the trip back to the palace quiet with more breaks than on the way to the ruins.

Quan and a few other warriors had given chase to the marked Nytes and humans that fled the cave, leaving their group slightly smaller. The empress had already gathered the others to discuss their plans moving forward, sending troops out to search as many caves and ruins as possible within the empire, as well as creating checkpoints to survey citizens for any markings that may be hidden on their body. While most warriors were required to take daily doses of saliver, as Evangeline did since Quan gave his saliver-filled flask to her in Peredia, the empress wanted to increase the dosage and extend the mandatory practice to the general public. It wasn't confirmed it would help prevent the magical disease, but at this point the empress was willing to try. The possibility that anyone could be marked and controlled by Jaden to attack at any moment left a weight on everyone's shoulders that hadn't dissolved with a bit of sleep and full bellies.

Thankfully they stopped at the same town they'd strode passed when first traveling to the ruins, with low pitched roofs and flatter, more elongated structures than the piled houses that climbed the hills of Kazuumar. Street lanterns illuminated the paved path towards the inn where they would stay for the night before returning to the capital at sunrise. Rasha paid for their rooms as the rest of them slipped through the back, their thick cloaks still in place to hide them from plain sight.

Evangeline stopped in front of a non-descript door, eager to scrape off the thick coat and plunge into an ice bath, when Ceven brushed up behind her.

"You're with me tonight." His tone left no room for negotiation.

She straightened, glancing at the others, who had all already dispersed into their own rooms. She'd missed seeing if Rasha shared a room with Zelene. Not that it was any of her business, but given their earlier conversation, Evangeline wondered if the distance the empress gave Rasha was intentional because of her feelings towards Jaden. And if Rasha knew, but was still hopeful things would change.

Shaking away those thoughts, she shoved open the door, stripping the sweat-soaked clothes from her skin. Secretly she craved feeling Ceven close to her again, his arms wrapping around her and squeezing her tight even for a moment. But would he feel the same if she told him the truth about Jaden?

The door clicked shut behind Ceven, his expression shadowed in the dim light of the lanterns. The room was simple, with a bed large enough to fit two humans or two Nytes that weren't Aerians. With Ceven's size and wings, they'd be forced to sleep nearly on top of one another. Her heart fluttered at the thought.

A basin of cool water sat behind a half wall designed out of bits of clouded glass that Evangeline quickly made use of. It wasn't large enough to sink herself in like the baths in Rasha's quarters or the suites back in Peredia, but she was grateful to wipe off the dirt and the sweat from the day. There was a clang of buckles unclasping, followed by the whisper of clothing falling to the floor, before Ceven appeared behind her. As bare as the day he was born.

She swallowed, her gaze immediately darting away. Oh, he was definitely not playing fair tonight.

Heat sizzled where his chest grazed her naked back, reaching for the cloth beside her. "Are you okay?" he whispered, as if scared he'll startle her.

She nodded, though those words somersaulted in her stomach. The Aerian's blood had dried underneath her nails, which she had desperately tried to clean the past few days with no luck. A part of her recalled with horror the blade slipping into the Aerian's throat with ease, the tears in their eyes as the Nyte had been forced to kill themselves. Another part of her fixated on the blood, the warmth, the smell, and the power it would grant her. The beast had roared in defiance when Evangeline denied it what it really wanted.

"Are you?" she whispered back, still not daring to turn around. The lanterns by the front door wavered through the clouded glass, casting a soft glow across the tiled floor and highlighting her dirt-streaked arms and legs, making the moment feel more intimate.

She flinched when the cool cloth touched her back. Ceven was gentle and slow as he rubbed circles along her spine, a part of her relaxing despite herself. "I'll have to be. There's too much weighing on my shoulders to give in now."

"And what's weighing on you?"

The cloth paused along her lower back, his sigh raising bumps along her arms where it teased her neck. "I'll tell you . . . if you tell me what's weighing on yours first."

The flare of anger uncoiled in her gut, and she squirmed away from him. "I don't want to talk about it right now." He slipped an arm around her waist, pulling her full body against his, stealing the breath from her lungs.

"Please, Eve . . ." His lips touched her ear, and the tenderness in his voice broke something in her. She was expecting his anger, his demands, not this.

He was *so* not playing fair tonight.

She ran her hand across his arm, still caked with dirt from traveling. Her fingers traced the firm muscle, caressing his sun-kissed skin down to his fingers, where they paused on the gold band crusted with a multitude of jewels she knew gleamed a cascade of different colors in the sunlight. It was the same ring he'd wore back in Peredia, and the same ring Jaden had given to her when he asked her to be his queen all that time ago. The same ring she twisted nervously as she contemplated her betrayal with Anali. Even now, Evangeline didn't have the courage to tell Ceven the truth, but she had to start somewhere.

Soaking in the moment, knowing her words would soon divide them, she said, "I . . . I knew Zindelis by another name—Jaden—long ago. I had forgotten about him, but he still remembered me."

Ceven's arm tightened. "Jaden . . . you whispered that name back at the castle. When I rescued you from the dungeons. When you were . . . not yourself."

Her eyes widened. She hadn't known that, nor remembered much from that time, only that she had tasted blood and lost her mind—now she knew it'd been the beginnings of the beast waking up, taking control.

He remained quiet, patiently letting her find the words to continue. She took solace in the low hum of insects right outside their room, the warmth of Ceven at her back as the smell of him, a heady mix of woods and spice, surrounded her, making her feel safe for the first time in a while.

She sighed, knowing she couldn't delay it any longer. "Those hallucinations I had . . ." Ceven had figured out that much when they'd been together in Xilo's son's house, before he left for the castle, before things had all taken a turn for the worse. "They're memories. They're a part of me, of another woman from a period when the Old Council ruled." It sounded delusional, crazy, when said so matter-of-factly, but she knew, without a doubt, it was the truth.

"That . . . you know how that sounds, Eve."

Even though she'd expected his disbelief, it still stung. She stepped out of his hold, and he let her as she scrubbed down her arms and legs, the basin water turning murky where she dunked the rough cloth and rinsed the remnants of the day's travels. "And that's why I didn't want to tell you." He hadn't believed her when she told him the truth about Sehn, how he was really Council member Aimee in disguise, either.

Another sigh, but he resumed washing her back, sweeping her matted blonde hair over her shoulder. "Did you tell the empress this?"

Evangeline had told her about their shared past, the memories she had of Jaden, but skimmed over the tampered Shadow Door that had funneled her possibly centuries into the future. The empress had taken it in stride—more so than Ceven had—oddly enough, but she had been more focused on Jaden's betrayal, his motives. Whether or not the empress believed her wasn't Evangeline's concern. Jaden was still guilty for capturing and killing hundreds, possibly more, of innocents. He still harbored sinister intentions that had infected both countries. She told Ceven that much.

He poured cool water down her back, rinsing away the suds and the remaining drudge of sweat and mud that had clambered beneath her leathers. She turned, keeping her eyes pointedly on his toned chest as she gave him the same treatment, sliding the cloth gently across scars of battles passed and his new one. The one when he'd encountered Jaden in the Summoning Grounds.

"If . . . if what you're saying is true, how did you two know each other?" He stood still, letting her wash him, his eyes delving past her hands and trailing down her body. Her skin prickled where his gaze lingered.

She swallowed. That was the part she didn't want to admit, had accidentally said aloud to the empress and the others. It was easier to bare her soul to near strangers than those she cared about the most. "Your turn," she said instead.

He grunted and pushed back several strands of chestnut hair that had grown down to his chin, brushing against the faint growth of a beard. The prince was always so well-groomed back at the castle; she liked getting to see this other side of him.

"Please don't be upset. Before you say anything, I'm doing this for us, but also because it's the right thing to do."

All the warmth froze in her veins, and she stilled. Her blood coagulated, her heart pounding faster to force the thick clumps through her system. "You're leaving. Aren't you?"

His mouth peeled open, his eyes dark and glistening with so many different emotions. Then, he molded himself to her, stealing her breath in a heated kiss. She dropped the cloth, her hands weaving through his hair as he pulled at her waist. Fury at him for not telling her warred with simply wanting him close, embracing this time together while they had it.

"Please don't go," she murmured breathlessly when they pulled apart, her face still inches away from his. "Please . . ."

His fingers trailed down her temple to her cheeks, his arm still hooked around her waist, as if she were the one leaving him. "I wish it didn't mean leaving you, but I must return to Peredia."

She reared back. "Is this what you discussed with the empress? For you to return to a country that will kill you the moment you set foot in it?" Ceven had announced he'd return to the few loyal soldiers that had helped them flee Peredia, but when it hadn't been brought up since, she foolishly believed they'd been empty words.

Ceven's eyes glittered dangerously, a side she rarely saw. She'd experienced it firsthand when he'd mistaken her for a spy when she'd been glamoured at his and Sehn's ball. "I agreed to take back *my* country, with the help of her army."

The admission shocked them both. She never knew Ceven felt that strongly about the throne. She assumed he had given it up years ago when he was first branded as a bastard.

Her hands curled into fists as she shoved at his chest, her foot knocking into the filled basin. Water sloshed over the sides to pool between the tiles' grooves. "Blast it, Ceven, you were going to keep *this* from me? Why? Why do this?" *Why do this to me*, she didn't say.

His lips thinned. "I was going to tell you eventually. I don't want to live as a traitor the rest of my days. You deserve a life better than this, one I can give you as king. You could be a queen, Eve."

Will you be my queen?

Evangeline glanced again at the gold band resting upon Ceven's index finger. She knew those words would be etched inside it, and she couldn't resist a shudder, the revulsion she instantly felt in her stomach. She'd been down this path before with Jaden, even if she didn't remember all the details. It didn't end well. Was history doomed to repeat itself?

Ceven mistook her revulsion for rejection, and he spun around, yanking the towel from the hanging rack beside the half glass separating the bedroom from the bathing room. "Regardless, I deserve the throne as much as Sehn. In fact, I deserve it more than him."

Evangeline followed him into the bedroom, ignoring how the droplets of water collected at her feet, making a mess of the wood floorboards. She couldn't breathe. As if she was climbing the steep, treacherous path up the mountain to the castle again like she had for years, but this time while carrying a boulder on her back. "You said you didn't care about the throne. That you never wanted it—"

He none-too-gently patted himself dry before pulling on a pair of loose-fitting trousers from his bags on the floor. "It wasn't because I never wanted it, it was because I thought I didn't *deserve* it."

No, no, no . . . she couldn't lose Ceven. Lani's death was still fresh in her mind, and if she lost another friend . . . "You can't go. I can't lose you too."

He sighed and pulled his towel around her dripping form, gently drying off her arms and legs as she stood blankly, not wanting to process what he was saying. "I won't be gone forever, Eve. Trust me, I have good people watching my back. We'll win this. I'm sure of it. And together we'll put an end to this magical plague, to . . . to Jaden."

She wasn't listening. All she could think of was Ceven, cold to the touch like Lani had been, his eyes staring out blankly like Ryker's had when she killed him, like the marked Aerian who had died in her arms. "But what if you don't? I just don't understand . . . Why do you have to do this? Have someone else fight. This isn't your battle, you don't owe them anything." She didn't even remember pulling on the thin nightclothes, only registering the cool air no longer kissed her bare skin.

His fingers mussed his hair again, tangling the thick locks. "But it *is* my battle, Eve. If I want to be king, I have to be the one to take the risk, to fight for my country. To fight for what's right. Who knows what things Sehn will drive Peredia to do?"

She pointedly met his gaze. "You mean Council member Aimee?"

Ceven continued, ignoring her question. "Besides, they've already brought the battle here with their assassins. It's better to fight away from where innocent people could get hurt."

As if the Wretched and this magical disease weren't enough. As if escaping a kingdom set on killing both of them wasn't enough. It seemed everything was working together to finish the job. She just wanted that cottage with the garden Ceven had promised her, in the woods far away from all this. Far away from everyone and everything.

Absorbing her heated cheeks and balled fists, Ceven said, "We've survived this far because we had good friends who looked out for us. The same ones that will be by my side when I'm in Peredia."

She crossed her arms, focusing on the painted wall behind him, the blue and yellow starlike patterns across the clay-packed wall blurring as she fought back frustrated tears. "Are these the same friends who would have condemned me to die? To let me be held prisoner?"

"We wouldn't have let that happen. You're safe at the palace."

Her lips peeled open, taken aback. "And did you even stop to ask me how I felt about all this, Ceven?" She stormed past him, cursing when her foot knocked into one of the bedpost's legs. Half of her wanted to say blast it all, steal a horse, and run far away from here. The other wanted to curl up in bed and wake up to find this was all a dream.

Lines formed between his brows. "You're a wanted criminal, Eve. With the Wretched, the assassins, and now . . ." His jaw tightened. "And now with Jaden targeting you, you need allies. You need more help than I can currently give."

Her gaze lingered between Ceven and the door. "I don't need anyone's help. I just need you with me."

Noticing her attention elsewhere, he stepped directly in front of the room's only exit, crossing his arms. "I've already made up my mind on this, Eve."

It wasn't fair. She didn't want to lose him. Why did that blasted kingdom even matter? Why did any of it matter? She threw up her hands. "You don't owe that kingdom a single thing. All it's done is belittle you. They don't even recognize you as their prince, all because you have a different father."

Hurt flashed across his face before it hardened into anger. "Not all of them. And once I become king, I'll earn their respect."

"And what if that doesn't work out?"

"It will."

Her face was surely as mottled red as Ceven's now. "How stubborn and naïve can you be to think that?"

"I'm not naïve. I simply won't accept any other option," he growled.

"You're going to die!"

"I'm not going to die."

"Who cares about that puss-filled kingdom, that whole country—"

"*I* do."

"It can burn to the ground for all I care!" Rage burned so hot that the edges of her vision faded to black, tunneling around Ceven's strewn hair and fired cheeks. "This whole blasted world can just *burn*!"

Ceven stared at her, his jaw slack, and in the silence, embarrassment flooded her. She covered her mouth and slanted away from his judging gaze. Dismantling everything he'd once thought about her.

You're the kindest, most selfless person I have ever met, he once told her.

She'd never been kind, no matter how many times she'd try to tell him that. He only saw what he wanted to see, and now, he caught a glimpse of the truth.

That she was a monster.

The fight left her at the thought, and she sank into the bed, her hands shaking, her vision blurry. Maybe that was why Jaden was still drawn to her after all this time. Maybe she was more like him than she thought, and that idea terrified her.

Bugs roared beyond the window, a chorus of staggered chirping disrupting the quiet night. Ceven turned off the lanterns, and Evangeline was happy to plunge into the darkness, to not feel the full weight of Ceven's accusing eyes. He didn't crawl into bed, but sat in the empty space beside her. A few beats of silence passed between them before he said, "When we return to the palace, I'll be preparing to leave for the border in a week's time."

She didn't say anything. Her eyes traced the wood beams separating the ceiling coated in silver moonlight that slithered through the cracked curtains. She didn't bother to get under the covers.

"Eve . . . please," he whispered, and it made her feel even more guilty. It wasn't that she didn't love him, or even that she was still mad at him. It was the stark realization that she wasn't good enough for him. Here Ceven was, fighting against his own fate, to make Peredia a better place, with people who were willing to risk their lives for him, with friends who cared. He was honorable, respectable, and charming . . .

And she was none of those things.

She'd torn and drank the blood of a harmless bird and other small prey, relishing in the taste like she had in those woods, murdering Aimee's allies, or in the tall grasses beyond Barto's village. She had murdered Vane and her own father and didn't feel a drop of remorse. She'd selfishly withheld information from the empress, information that could have saved people, in favor of seeking answers from Jaden—and she still didn't truly know what she was, or how she had betrayed Jaden and her people in the past. What Jaden was planning and why.

She wanted—no, she *needed*—to know why. Once she found out, she could put a stop to him, to all this. Maybe that would make her feel honorable and respectable . . . instead of like a villain.

But right now, she wanted to sink into a deep sleep for the next few months.

"Goodnight—" Her voice cracked.

His arms curled around her, his hair brushing her neck and smelling of soap and spice. For one selfish moment she pretended she was his equal, that she too had the respect of those around her. That she wanted what was best for both countries and to help everyone affected by this magical plague, to save humans from another tyrant's reign in Peredia. That she wasn't conflicted by the kind savior she wanted to be and the monster she really was—and what that meant for her in the future.

"I love you, Evangeline." His arms squeezed tighter, even as she didn't return his embrace.

I love you, too, she couldn't say.

He sighed and pulled away, muttering that he needed some air. His warmth, his scent, and everything that could be drifted away.

Evangeline knew deep in her core things would never be the same between them again.

The door opened and shut behind Ceven with a finality that shattered her. She rolled over and sobbed into the pillow.

PART 3

WHEN THE PAST AND
THE PRESENT COLLIDE

CHAPTER 27

The passing days were a blur for Evangeline. Once they had returned to the palace, Empress Zelene was a force to be reckoned with, barking commands and organizing her people, the city, and beyond for the possibility of war. Whether it was in retaliation to Jaden's marked soldiers or in preparation for Ceven's clandestine attack into Peredia, Evangeline didn't know. Probably both. And while Quan and the others had returned to the palace, claiming they'd lost track of the escaped marked individuals, they did manage to find several more locations of Jaden's hidden soldiers with plans to sedate the marked individuals until they could find a way to reverse the magic.

While it was unclear if Evangeline was still the empress's prisoner (since her presence was still a secret, she remained in Rasha's quarters for now), Ceven's words from the inn stuck with her. She needed allies, especially now that Ceven was leaving—they had gotten into several more arguments upon their return, with her insisting she would fight beside him, since he refused to stay in Atiaca, and his insisting she'd be safer behind the palace walls. Evangeline didn't know Jaden's whereabouts, nor did she have the resources to track him down like the empress did. She needed to play nice and work together if she was to help put an end to Jaden's schemes. A part of her also hoped her aggressive stance to aid the empress in her search for Jaden would make Ceven think twice about leaving, as selfish as that was.

While Evangeline was far from defenseless, she hadn't trained properly since leaving Peredia, nor had she much practice fighting alongside the beast without it taking complete control of her. Rasha, surprisingly, humored her with daily training regimens. At night, Evangeline curbed the beast's appetite by resorting to birds unlucky enough to land on Rasha's balcony when the Rathan was preoccupied with the empress, and during the day the two of them sparred in the palace's walled courtyard filled with sand and rocks, the sun pelting down on them overhead. The heat was near unbearable, far hotter than what she was used to in Peredia no matter the time of day, and it wasn't even summer yet.

Rasha had finished correcting Evangeline's form—for the sixteenth time—when she snapped, "Sooner or later you're going to have to get over it. Just because Ceven is leaving doesn't mean you're any less of a person."

Before their training sessions, Rasha would berate Evangeline to sit with her under the shade of the trees repeating the same mantra: *I am strong, I am fast, I am capable. To think otherwise is to forfeit before the fight has even begun.* It took several sessions of their quiet chanting and rigorous training before Evangeline's mind calmed—no, not her mind, but the beast itself. The constant pull for power, the dull ache of bloodlust she'd grown to live with, all faded into the background, and Evangeline found herself able to focus more on dodging Rasha's attacks, feel the rush of adrenaline without the beast wresting for control.

However, the excitement at learning to control the beast better and the joy it gave her to fight in the open with Rasha—whose attitude grew on Evangeline more and more—waned as each day grew closer and closer to Ceven's departure. She felt more sluggish and exhausted. Not even the weight of a sword, a spear, or a dagger in her hand had the same rush it used to.

Evangeline readjusted her grip on the hilt of her spear—again—only for her fingers to slip back into the wrong placement when she arched the dulled blade at Rasha. She missed, of course, not that she cared.

Rasha's dark eyes morphed into narrowed slits. "You're sloppy, as usual. Your form is wrong again, and there's no effort in your offense or defense." She sighed, the sounds lost in the strengthening winds. It was cloudy today, storms rolling off in the distance, lightning flashing every few minutes, but Rasha insisted they continue training until Evangeline was able to break through Rasha's defense.

"I told you, I don't want to do this." Evangeline scowled, but her fingers shifted, a bit of space between her digits, a lax but more controlled grip near the base and the tip. She bent her knees, becoming more fluid and ready to move at a moment's notice.

"Your body says otherwise." She propped her practice sword against the packed clay and stone wall, not as high as the walls that enclosed Castle Peak, but tall enough to shield them from the prying eyes of any passersby, the training grounds located towards the side of the expansive palace. "You just won't let your mind believe it. I'm not being mean, I'm trying to make you understand."

"Because you pity me." Self-conscious of her body now, Evangeline dropped the spear, crossing her arms. "I don't want or need it." She knew she was acting ridiculous, being stubborn for no reason, but she couldn't help it. Lani was dead, her death hanging more starkly over Evangeline's head now that Ceven, her closest friend, was leaving, potentially never to return. She felt so utterly alone.

"It's called empathy. I understand what you're feeling." Rasha's lips thinned like the slits of her eyes. "I . . . when the empress asked me to accompany Barto to Peredia, I didn't want to go. It both physically and mentally pained me to be separated from her, even if it was only for a few weeks."

"It's not the same at all. You left her. You accepted her decision and left of your own accord. I don't want to Ceven to leave, and I certainly wouldn't have left if our circumstances were switched." A bite of anger grew into a small flame, warming her stomach.

Rasha's voice was calm but had the weight of a string pulled taut before an arrow is released. "I respected her enough to accept her decision. Because I trusted her. That's what true loyalty and trust is. To be a part of another's life wholly, untethered by space or time, or judgement."

The flickering candle inside her gut grew brighter. Evangeline hated how Rasha always fought her in everything, even when it came to Evangeline's own emotions. The Rathan would disregard them in favor of her perspective. "If the empress told you to take that sword and run it through your heart, you would do it?"

"Without hesitation."

Evangeline raised a brow. "And if she asked you to run the blade through her own heart?"

Silence.

Satisfaction hitched the corner of Evangeline's mouth, even as she felt guilty for taking out her temper on Rasha. As much as she found the Rathan to be annoyingly good at everything, argumentative, and unbearably persistent, she had been willing to take time out of her day to train her. To try to help her, in her own way. Even if Evangeline didn't agree with it.

"We're done for the day." Rasha's tone was tight. The string was still pulled back, and Evangeline sensed she badly wanted to let loose what was really on her mind, but the warrior's cool demeanor didn't crack.

For an instant, Evangeline debated apologizing, for what she didn't know, when two warriors approached them. The empress requested Rasha's presence. It was urgent.

Evangeline ignored Rasha's demand to stay behind, glaring down the warriors who reached for their weapons. Rasha sighed, waving off the threat of violence, as Evangeline accompanied her.

They both didn't bother changing out of their leather breeches, dirt-trodden boots, and sweat-soaked tops, though Evangeline did draw her cloak in closer around her. She pulled down her hood, despite the stifling heat, to shield her face.

The empress awaited them on a terrace, several floors above where they had trained in the enclosed courtyard, facing the sea and cliffside. It was the first time Evangeline had been this high within the palace—aside from Rasha's quarters—and she wondered if this was a part of the empress's private rooms.

Zelene waited for them on a chaise piled with blankets and pillows, her form covered in a fitted emerald dress with a triangle slit around her navel. The gold cuffs on her wrists shimmered in the afternoon light, matching the gold hoops in her ears. Long gone was the glimpse of the warrior empress Evangeline had witnessed during their travels, whose shimmering dark skin had been covered by leathers, her curls pulled and braided tightly back beneath the heavy cowl of her hood. Her jewelry was replaced with silver blades at her sides. At first Evangeline wondered which side was the façade the empress performed, but realized both suited her too well for either to be faked.

Rasha and Evangeline paused at the threshold onto the terrace, a series of glass doors separating the adjacent sitting room from the balcony, red and pink speckled vines pouring from the terrace, as if it too sought shelter from the unyielding sun.

The empress arched a brow at Evangeline before turning to Rasha. "You two seem to be practically joined at the hip these days." Evangeline crossed her arms; the last thing she wanted was to be caught up in whatever odd dynamic the two of them had, but before either of them could reply, Zelene continued, "He's returned. He'll be joining us shortly."

Rasha had moved to the neighboring chaise beside the empress when she stiffened, her gaze shifting to meet Evangeline's before she cast it about the terrace. "Should she leave?"

Evangeline narrowed her eyes on them as she pulled back her hood, billowing out her cloak to let the salty breeze cool the sweat slickening her skin. This high up and in the privacy of the empress's rooms, she figured she didn't need to worry about hiding her identity—also it was too spitting hot to keep her hood up. "Too late, I'm already here. Who is this 'he'? Does he know where Jaden is?"

The two Nytes shared a look before the empress smiled. "Not quite, but he will be an invaluable asset to our search. As well as stopping this magical onslaught of my people."

Evangeline sensed there was more to it than what the empress was saying, but since this mystery man would arrive soon enough, she focused on other matters. "Any whereabouts on Jaden's accomplice, Avana?"

Zelene picked up a goblet that had been sitting beside her, the sharp smell of alcohol stinging Evangeline's nostrils when the breeze wafted her way. "She has been just as elusive, for now."

Shadows danced across everyone's faces as a flock of birds soared overhead. Evangeline's stomach hollowed at the collective cawing, shame heating her cheeks even as her mouth watered. If either Nyte knew about Evangeline's nightly hunts on Rasha's balcony, the current fragile truce they all shared would crumble instantly.

"I have a plan," Evangeline said, shoving down those dark thoughts, "to capture Avana."

Rasha's brows rose while the empress filled her gold goblet and another, almost as if she hadn't heard her. Zelene outstretched the glass, past Rasha, offering it to Evangeline instead. While it was a bit too early to drink, when the flock of birds swooped back around to land on the balcony paces away,

Evangeline snatched the glass, gulping down any thoughts of blood, sharp teeth, or the monster sleeping within her. She didn't miss Rasha's frown and the way her gaze lingered a bit too long on Zelene, as if waiting to be offered her own goblet.

The empress remained aloof to Rasha's stare, twirling a curl around one slender digit. "Interesting. What are the details of said plan?"

Gods, Evangeline almost preferred it when the two Rathans hated her guts rather than pulling her into this game of . . . whatever the blazes they were playing. "As I've shared with Asmen before, I think Avana betrayed Jaden, glamouring herself as the advisor that night to draw attention to him. Why, I'm still not sure, but I don't believe they're working together anymore." She took a sip from her goblet, the alcohol sweet with an aftertaste of berries, when she wasn't gulping it down.

"If she's working alone, and still hunting down answers around this mark"—Evangeline lifted her branded hand, the dark lines hidden beneath her glove—"she'll try to get to me somehow. We already have the location of a Shadow Door she's used before, where Jaden was initially spotted with Serah, and using myself as bait, sooner or later I don't doubt she'll make an appearance to capture me—or at the very least convince me to leave with her."

Zelene looked to be pondering her words when footsteps echoed behind her. "Oh, I'm sure Avana is still waiting to get her hands on you."

Evangeline froze, the goblet nearly falling from her hands. *No . . . it can't be him. There's no way,* she thought turning around—

Gods, drag her to the fiery pits, it *was* him.

Raiythlen Quincara bowed, a smirk to his lips. "Good afternoon, ladies."

The Caster was covered head to toe in various dark shades of fabric, paired with a heavy cloak on top, but, unlike Evangeline, sweat didn't bead his brow, and his black hair curling around his temples looked bereft of any perspiration. His blue eyes paused on her for a beat before glancing away.

He waltzed past them—Evangeline was sure her mouth was still agape—snagging the bottle of wine at the empress's feet and a glass before hopping on the terrace railing, one leg dangling precariously over the edge as if the drop wasn't a straight plummet to his death. He rolled up the sleeves of his shirt, sunlight glinting off metal on his left arm—a mechanical arm, Evangeline realized with a jolt.

"Lovely for you to finally join us, Agent Quincara," Zelene said, avoiding the icy glare Evangeline shot her and Rasha. While she wasn't disappointed to see Raiythlen—okay, if she was being honest, she was more than happy to see the infuriating Caster alive—the fact the empress was collaboratively working with said Caster who knew more about Evangeline's mark than she did, while she had condemned Evangeline to a life or death trial for simply bearing the same mark, filled her with rage. She said as much.

Rasha curled her lip. "Watch your tongue. You forget you're talking to an *empress*."

Zelene waved off Rasha's retort, and her mouth thinned. "I'm reaping the consequences of my earlier ignorance. I apologize, Evangeline, for the trials and tribulations you've experienced thus far in my empire simply because we lacked full understanding of what was happening and still do." She turned to Raiythlen. "Agent Quincara and I have connected relatively recently, finding we both have a lot of valuable information to share."

Raiythlen poured himself a glass, and Evangeline watched in fascination at the metal arm gripping the bottle, the individual digits moving with a fluidity that defied the fact they were made up of bolts and screws.

Evangeline shook her head as Raiytheln knocked back his glass, shooting her a wink as if his very presence hadn't rattled her to her core. "The last time I saw you, you were bleeding out on the throne room floor . . ."

"Nasty business that was."

"How—"

"I agree with your plan to lure out Avana," he cut her off. "Knowing my sister, she won't give up on you that easily, and it may be the quickest way to get intel on Zindelis."

Evangeline frowned but nodded. She had a feeling she and Raiythlen would have their own private meeting later—she'd make sure of it.

Raiythlen pulled a small satchel from within his cloak, tossing it towards Rasha, who unfurled pages from it bound in string. "With the treaty between Sundise Mouche and Peredia, especially given Peredia's change in leadership, things don't bode well for the empire here. No matter what terms the new King of Peredia disclosed to you, war is on the horizon."

"What treaty? Sundise Mouche betrayed Peredia. Those were Mouchian Caster assassins in that throne room," Rasha murmured, skimming the documents before passing them to Zelene.

Raiythlen waved his hand, this one fully made of flesh still. "The majority of the kingdom doesn't know that, not to mention Sundise Mouche got what they wanted—one of their own Council members on the throne. The treaty is still very much in place."

"It's a shame Calais died before he had gotten the chance to break it." Empress Zelene swirled the contents of her glass, her eyes perusing the documents with careful scrutiny. "Per the prince and I's debrief, the former king had also planned to betray Sundise Mouche from the beginning, naively thinking they could harness the power of this dark magic that is corrupting both countries." She sighed, her gaze unfocusing. "He'd been a respectable king when he'd aided me in fighting the rebels over half a century ago, solidifying the peace treaty we formed between both countries. He died as a tyrant, corrupted by greed and revenge."

Evangeline knew about the king's history with the empire from her tutoring sessions with Ryker. She'd also been told of the king's planned betrayal with Sundise Mouche, but Ceven had never told her why. When she asked the empress, Zelene cocked her brow, a look that said: *he didn't tell you?*

"Queen Beatrix's lover, Ceven's true father, is Mouchian. The king was ready to destroy his country over a broken heart," the empress shared and Evangeline gaped at her.

Another secret Ceven hadn't shared with her. Was it because he was ashamed? Or was it because he wanted to forget everything that had happened, much like she did?

Raiythlen let out a whistle at the admission. "Well, we can only hope our prince will save the day and unite both countries once more."

Evangeline stiffened at the reminder Ceven was charging off to face his own execution. "And if he doesn't?" she dared ask.

Zelene's eyes swiveled to Evangeline's, narrowing a fraction in contemplation. "You lack quite a bit of faith in your lover. I'm sure the prince finds that disheartening as well."

She crossed her arms, dodging everyone's glances her way. "You don't know anything about our relationship."

While Evangeline kept her eyes firmly on her goblet and the tiled terrace, in her peripheral, Rasha's lips twitched as she met the empress's eyes, and Evangeline's grip tightened on the stem of her glass.

Zelene continued, "Regardless, I will not bow to the whims of another tyrant king, nor what another country says I should do with my own. If war is inevitable, then let us prepare for the worst of it. I'm no stranger to violence."

"But now there's another player in our midst." Raiythlen met Evangeline's gaze, brimming with questions. "A friend from the past?"

Evangeline bristled, but at least she wasn't the only one. The empress snapped the pages back at Rasha, irritation marring her features. "Former Advisor Zindelis will be dealt with swiftly." Her eyes darted to Evangeline's hand. "And we will put an end to this magical attack."

Raiythlen hopped off the railing and rolled his neck. "Easier said than done."

Evangeline peeked over Rasha's shoulder to get a better glimpse at the documents, but the Rathan had already resealed them back in the satchel. She sighed. "First, we'll track down

Avana using myself as bait." For the first time in days, Evangeline grinned. "And if she doesn't come along willingly, I'll happily knock her out cold."

CHAPTER 28

⧼ EVANGELINE ⧽

Evangeline's plan to capture Avana had sounded great when she'd proposed it, but after several nights of hovering near the alcove, where Asmen had first spotted "Jaden," she had nothing to show for it except a lack of sleep and rising frustration. Asmen, Rasha, or another warrior would always accompany her, keeping their distance so Evangeline could lure Avana into a false sense of security before attempting capture. The lingering distortion of the Shadow Door was visible even in the soft silver light of the illuminated dome and flickering lanterns, like a piece of reality had been slashed, the tear a blur against the backdrop of mosaic tiles, cresting waves, and speckled floors.

Tonight, Evangeline hadn't yet left Rasha's quarters, sitting on the warrior's neatly made bed and gazing out at the raging sea painted in the moon's light. Tomorrow Ceven, Tarry, Barto, and a crew of warriors would depart for the

Barto's village before veering towards Peredia's borders. There had been nothing stopping Evangeline from joining Ceven's bed, or he in hers, since they'd all returned from the ruins together, but with their recent fighting, neither had left their own bedrooms. Each night as she lay alone in Rasha's quarters, after unsuccessfully tracking down Avana, the deeper the knife dug at her heart. And like every night since then, she was restless.

A part of her wanted to cave, to crawl into bed with Ceven and hold him close, as it could be their last time together. The other part of her still lived in denial. As if seeing him now would make everything feel even more real. She was scared it would break her entirely.

She didn't bother undoing her braid or changing out of her fighting leathers from earlier as she lay across Rasha's bed. A drum of thunder, followed by lightning, illuminated the dark corners of the sparse room. Evangeline told herself she'd get up soon. That she'd find Avana one way or another even if this plan failed. But for now, she allowed her eyes to drift close, letting the waves cleanse the clambering thoughts inside her skull. Whatever happened tonight, tomorrow, years from now, she'd figure it out. She was a survivor, even when sometimes she felt this life wasn't worth surviving.

"Lost." Evangeline stared at the gold band on her finger, the ring encrusted with priceless gems, the inside carved with Jaden's proposal: "Will you be my queen?" It was funny how at times the beautiful piece of jewelry melded with her fingers, light as air, and other times it weighed heavier than any load, tugging down her hand. Her heart. Her soul. "I just feel so lost. Am I truly doing the right thing?"

The nights were getting warmer. The windows to Evangeline's bedroom were wide open, allowing the remains of the cool spring breeze to stroll through her chambers. It stirred up the outdated beige curtains and potted roses she had on display, rather than the gold-framed paintings and carved statues around the rest of the castle. While Jaden adored all the king and queen's former works of art, Evangeline chose to leave her part of the castle bare aside from her necessities and the bits of nature she could bring in. Without it, she felt trapped, like she was back in her cell, surrounded by stone walls. Day after day.

Oh, she understood why her husband obsessed over the bedazzling, gleaming collector pieces. She understood too well that neither of them had ever fully owned anything. Had the right to. And now that they were free, he wanted only the best for himself. After all, they both deserved it. Their people deserved it.

Yet Evangeline didn't want any of it. Not anymore.

"I can't do this, Anali. I love him." Evangeline slipped off the ring, setting it on the windowsill she sat beside. She couldn't bear the weight of it right now.

The small, slender figure propped on the simple, single-sized bed (Evangeline only ever slept here when Jaden was away) cocked her head, her thick black bangs dancing across tightly curled horns. "Who do you love more? Him? Or your people?"

Evangeline whipped her head around to pin her friend with a scathing look. "You're cruel for saying that."

"I'm not trying to be." Her blue eyes were calm. Always so calm, so unaffected by anything. "I'm putting it into perspective."

A stampede of horses snapped Evangeline's attention back to the window, but it wasn't Jaden with an army of soldiers. Just farmers, bustling their crops from the nearby land to trade in the main hall, the sun beaming down on their wide hats and plain clothes.

Once her heart settled, Evangeline said, "It's not that simple." Her knuckles turned bloodless from how hard she clasped them. "You're not the one being asked to kill the man you thought you'd spend the rest of your life with."

"No," Anali whispered, "but now that you know the truth, like I do, can you continue to let this happen?"

The blood rushed back into her hands as she relaxed her grip, her shoulders drooping. Anali's heels clicked against the marble floor, cracked with holes from the castle's recent battle, as she stood by Evangeline. Her touch was gentle and warm on her back.

"Peace was never going to be an option for him," Evangeline said. "I thought my love could save him. I thought it would be enough."

Anali's hand rubbed in circles, trying to ease her fears, like the wheels in Evangeline's mind, constantly spinning, churning. Neverending cycle of worries and uncertainties.

"No matter what happens to me, Anali, Jaden can never know the truth," Evangeline whispered, her husband's presence always casting a dark shadow over her even in his absence. "I won't let history repeat itself."

Static crackled across Evangeline's skin, and her eyes snapped open. Pressure swarmed and built in the room, swelling to the echo of the thunder, radiating with intensity with the lightning. Evangeline blinked away images of Anali and the lingering feeling of doom that pulled at the deepest parts of her innards as confusion rumbled down her spine. She knew what this pressure was, but she hadn't noticed a Shadow Door hidden within Rasha's quarters, not that she should be surprised. Before Raiythlen had left their meeting with the empress to Gods knows where, he mentioned that Avana or Jaden or both weren't utilizing old Shadow Doors but creating new rifts. Like the doors created during the Summoning Grounds and back at the west wing. As if things couldn't get worse.

Evangeline leapt from Rasha's bed, her eyes still groggy from sleep, the blue sheets now the messiest Evangeline had seen them since staying in these quarters. Her eyes darted around the room, flashes of lightning catching on every dark shadow as she searched for the distortion of a Shadow Door. Her hands itched to unsheathe the strapped daggers at her sides from her earlier sparring with Rasha, but Evangeline needed Avana to lower her guard if she wanted to capture her. Charging the Caster with a pair of blades, like she wanted, would have the opposite effect.

And then there was the possibility it wouldn't be Avana at all.

The crackling expanded, tickling Evangeline's skin as she sucked in a breath, anticipation skittering down her bones and rousing the beast from its slumber. The pressure grew and grew before popping as a figure emerged from the other side of the room.

CHAPTER 29

~ EVANGELINE ~

Evangeline didn't want to dwell on the disappointment she felt at seeing the familiar Caster emerge from the Shadow Door instead of a man with haunting green eyes.

Avana hadn't noticed Evangeline yet, who crouched in the shadows beside the armoire and the entrance to her makeshift bedroom. The Caster came equipped in a dark cloak and slacks, a pair of tightly curled horns merging through her loose black hair, curving around blue eyes and a face that eerily resembled Anali's. Evangeline knew Anali was Avana's grandmother, but with the memory fresh in her mind, it was as if she was seeing her friend again even though Anali was long gone.

Avana whispered something beneath her breath. Evangeline thought it was a spell, but when nothing happened, she dismissed it as crazy ramblings. This Caster, Evangeline learned, was not entirely of this world all the time.

"You better have a blasted good reason why you're here," Evangeline said, emerging from the shadows, her bare feet whispering across the floor—an ability she mastered, or maybe always had within her, during her hunts back in Barto's village and her nighttime visits on Rasha's balcony.

Avana spun around, shock expanding the whites of her eyes before narrowing. It was clear Evangeline had startled her, irritating the Caster, who believed she would have the upper hand here tonight. Flashes of lightning reflected off buckles clasping the Caster's waist, showcasing a set of knives and glass vials. Avana matched Evangeline's scrutiny, taking in her own fighting leathers and twin daggers attached to both legs.

"Make any sudden movements and I'll call for the guards." Let Avana think Evangeline was helpless, that the Caster hadn't fallen for her trap. That she didn't stand before a beast hiding in sheep's clothing, ready to spring forward at any moment. If Avana decided to take Evangeline anywhere by force again, she would find out soon enough anyways.

Avana slowly raised her hands in surrender. "Of course," she whispered. "Please, just hear me out." Another strike of lightning, highlighting her silhouette standing in front of the expansive windows, the sea raging and pounding like the thud of Evangeline's heart.

"Why are you here? Why now?" Not that Evangeline expected Avana to tell her the truth. Nothing good ever came from this Caster. She had tricked her into escaping Castle Peak's walls and getting her in trouble with Ryker . . . even if Ryker had already known. Then she had tried to take Evangeline by force after the massacre in the throne room and nearly got her killed during the attack in the Summoning Grounds.

"You're in danger." Avana took another step forward, and Evangeline mimicked it in the opposite direction, giving the illusion she was scared, despite the fury building in her gut. "I came here to warn you."

Avana was powerful and unpredictable—and a good liar. "Or maybe it's you who's in danger. I'm sure Jaden didn't appreciate you foiling his plans and making him enemy number one within the empire."

Her expression betrayed nothing, but Evangeline swore unease crept into her blue gaze. "I can tell you everything, but not here. Not when anyone can walk in at a moment's notice. Come with me to a safe place."

We're not going anywhere. Evangeline inched closer, her fingers brushing past the hilt of her dagger into the pocket sewed into the side of her leathers. "How did you meet Jaden? Did you already know of his plans to kill, capture, and mark hundreds of innocents before working with him? Or did that not matter to you?" After Evangeline had murdered Ryker, Avana's previous employer, it made sense she would seek out another powerful ally. It was possible she had already been working with Jaden during her time in Peredia, but her genuine surprise over Evangeline's mark—the same mark Jaden had—and bewilderment told Evangeline it was the first time the Caster had witnessed the ancient magic in person.

Avana's lip curled before smoothing into a firm line. "I . . . I wasn't aware of what his true plans were, but now I am."

Evangeline swallowed. While Jaden was the clear culprit in marking Nytes and humans, stealing both their lives and will, Evangeline still had a sliver of hope he wasn't behind this. That the man who had cared for her, protected her, and loved her in the past wasn't guilty of such heinous crimes. But it wouldn't be the first time.

Her dream came flooding back to her. Jaden had been down a similar path like this before, she was sure of it. He claimed she betrayed him, their people, but what if she had been trying to save them?

"Did Anali ever tell you the 'truth' about me? Our people?" Her fingers brushed the top of the small pouch, hidden within her slacks. If she could just get close enough . . .

Her heart plummeted when Avana's gaze caught her searching hands, suspicion shadowing her features. "I don't know what you're talking about."

Evangeline stilled. "Don't know, or won't tell me?"

A knowing smile toyed with the corners of her lips, irking Evangeline. "I'm willing to sit down and have a long overdue discussion, Evangeline, but not here. Those are my terms."

"No, your terms are for me to just blindly follow you through that Shadow Door to Gods know where."

"It's safe, I promise."

Evangeline raised a brow at her, gauging how quick the Caster's reflexes would be if Evangeline lunged at her from this distance. She'd seen Avana take on a horde of Casters by herself back in Peredia. Evangeline wasn't stalking rabbits or birds here; she was stalking a former top agent of the Council. "And where does it lead?" She risked a step forward, leaving only a few strides between them, and while Avana didn't move, she logged Evangeline's movement with calculating eyes.

"A place in Ostin Lon, far away from here and Peredia. You'd be free. You wouldn't be anyone's prisoner."

Evangeline blinked. Ostin Lon? But that was a wasteland. An empty desert, permanently destroyed from the war hundreds of years ago. A war she and Jaden had participated in, she now realized. "Just yours?"

A tick in Avana's jaw pulsed, and Evangeline grinned internally at the blatant impatience. Good, at least she was irritating this Caster as much as she irritated Evangeline.

"All I want is to find out the truth, just like you." Avana's cool smile returned. "Whatever that truth may be, it's tied to Anali, my family's legacy. We can help each other, Evangeline." Then, as if sensing that wasn't enough, she said, "I know where Jaden is."

At his name, Evangeline's heart skipped. "Where is he?" She risked another step forward.

Avana's eyes darted to the door. "It's not safe here. Please come with me."

"You mean you're outnumbered here. You want me alone." Evangeline narrowed her eyes, a hint of a smile tugging the corners of her mouth. Avana wouldn't be returning to Ostin Lon tonight.

Evangeline lunged.

The pouch of sleeping powder was in her hand, inches from the Caster's face, when Avana blurred. Evangeline yelped when her arm snapped back in pain, the powder flying from its sachet in the opposite direction as Avana ducked, landing a kick to her wrist. Evangeline leapt back, letting the beast's power climb up her veins. She channeled Rasha's mantra, finding that moment of stillness she had under the trees, letting the beast's instincts seep through without allowing it take hold. Her focus narrowed on Avana. She charged her again, this time grasping the Caster in a headlock.

"Guards!" Evangeline screamed as Avana knocked her head back, fire splintering in Evangeline's jaw.

The Caster broke from her hold as Evangeline fell back, her mouth filling with blood from where her teeth had bit into her skin. "It's pointless. I sound-proofed the room. Nobody is going to hear you." Avana rubbed her neck, her eyes bloodshot and brimming with a fury that matched Evangeline's.

Blast it, she hadn't expected this. Neither Evangeline nor Rasha had noticed any symbols or smelled any blood, meaning Avana must have placed them well in advance, possibly weeks ago. The fact Avana had been planning to abduct her since then spurred Evangeline to want to throw another punch at the Caster's face. Her nose looked straight, and uninjured unlike their last encounter at the castle, but Evangeline would rectify that.

"I don't want things to be like this between us. I just want help you." But the bare flesh around where Avana's dark boots met her pants lit up along with the dark symbols creeping up at the collar of her shirt, activating the Caster magic she had placed on her body beforehand. Readying herself for a fight.

Evangeline wiped the blood from her mouth, spitting it on the floor, where red speckles mixed with blue and beige. "You don't want to help me. You've never wanted to help me. Don't act like you are when it's all for selfish reasons." If she did, she wouldn't have watched Ryker beat her and lock her in a cage like an animal. She wouldn't have continued to draw her blood and test her mark with her potions, knowing she would be sending Evangeline back into a dark hole. She wouldn't have stood by and let Vane torture her.

No, Avana couldn't care less if Evangeline was *well* or not. She just needed her *alive*.

Avana darted left, and Evangeline pedaled after her. Glass shattered at her feet, a blinding light flashing before her eyes. Evangeline's vision blurred, white dots blocking her sight. Avana shuffled behind her. Evangeline had to act now before the Caster got the upper hand.

Running blind, she expanded her senses, angling away from where Avana scrambled, whispering incantations. But Avana didn't give her a chance to catch her bearings, launching another bottle her way. Evangeline reached to catch it, but something shot out and shattered it mid-air—a knife—and another wave of blinding light burst right before her eyes. A third bottle crashed beside her, a high-pitched ringing clouding her hearing.

Nails bit into Evangeline's arm, one tracing something onto her left forearm, but she knew Avana's magic wouldn't work, not with the saliver in Evangeline's system.

Avana cursed when nothing happened. Evangeline wrenched her arm from the Caster's grasp, lashing out a kick. It landed when her foot met flesh.

The ringing hadn't stopped, and white light still danced in her vision as she grappled for her senses, fire now licking the inside of her skull. The calmness in her mind cracked, her control on the beast slipping. Dizzy, Evangeline threw a punch. Her fist connected with something, and Avana hurled a curse, retorting with a boot to Evangeline's stomach that she was too slow to avoid.

Air was knocked from her lungs, and she tumbled backwards, slamming into the tile. When she scrambled back up,

Avana was smearing her blood on the floor with her index finger, and Evangeline didn't wait to find out what spell she would hurl next. Her vision cleared and focused in on the Caster in front of her, framing her concentrated and frantic gaze, the pulse pounding in her neck in a fiery glow in her mind.

Balancing on the balls of her feet, Evangeline launched herself at Avana.

Avana's head jerked up in time as Evangeline shoved her to the floor in a fit of snarls. Evangeline had her neck gripped in one hand, the other ensnaring her wrist with her bloodied index finger. The blue irises in Avana's eyes took over, her black pupils like small islands. Fear pounded beneath her pale skin, and without realizing it, Evangeline's mouth had opened, her stomach tightening. The threads of control were unwinding, the beast's roar becoming louder and louder.

Take it. Take it. Take it all and leave nothing.

Snapping her teeth, Evangeline lunged for her neck when Avana's knee connected below her ribs. Her breath came out in a hiss as Avana rolled away, patting down her black garment. Searching.

The fire hardened around Evangeline's chest, and any pain vanished before it swirled again, lifting her to her feet. She felt so light, flexible. Like she could do anything. It was . . . intoxicating. *No, no, I need to get control back.* The beast railed against Evangeline's protest as she sucked in a deep breath, seeking that stillness again.

A small sound escaped Avana as Evangeline jerked her attention away from her inner struggle. A small silver coin glimmered in the little light of the room, pulled from Avana's pocket. Her index finger coated the top of it and—

She vanished.

No! Evangeline whipped her head around. Right. Left. Behind her. Nothing.

Pain shattered in Evangeline's kneecap, and she crumpled. Another blow knocked into her skull, escalating the fire. She roared out loud with it, the pain diminishing in comparison as she jumped back to her feet. But she couldn't see where the Caster was.

You don't need to see to find her, the beast whispered. Reminded her.

In a rush of unsettling clarity, the room sharpened, and even in the dark Evangeline could make out every detail. From the fine cracked lines in the tile to the small figures in pictures on the vanity across the room. The waves were now thunderous against her ears, but she could still make out the slow and steady breaths of her two guards right outside the door. The hush of footsteps farther down and whispers. And with it came the overwhelming smell of salt water, bird feces, and a mix of perfumes that coagulated together in an unpleasant boggle. But underneath all that was the scent of burnt paper, stale water, fresh and old blood.

And the sour stench of fear.

A subtle breeze moved, and Evangeline moved with it as something whizzed by her face. The whirling smells of Avana exploded next to her, and Evangeline struck. Her fist landed with a crunching blow as Avana swore another oath. The room was deceptively empty, but blood dripped to the ground where the air shimmered unnaturally. Evangeline honed in on the scarlet droplets, the smell luring her closer.

"Stay away, Evangeline," the empty space in front of her said.

Evangeline stunned herself when a laugh rumbled deep from her chest. It sounded like the one on the balcony when she had devoured that bird. Confident. Dangerous. As if a stranger had taken over. "I've been telling *you* to stay away from *me*."

The Caster's scent moved, but she was slow. *No match for me,* Evangeline realized with stunning clarity. A whip of wind and Evangeline ducked, then twirled when another blast of movement tried to hit her thigh. The high slice of air around steel alerted Evangeline to the use of a weapon. Then the invisible blows retreated, and Evangeline circled the room. Waiting. When she couldn't hear movement, she expanded her senses, searching for the Caster's scent.

There.

The fresh blood was a dead giveaway and led Evangeline straight to the right side of the bed, closest to the balcony door. Red symbols were etched into the ground, and before Evangeline could pounce on the invisible Caster in front of her, Avana shouted, "Trap, bind, stay!" in Castanian.

Blue and white flared up from the ground. Evangeline jumped back, but it surrounded her. Encircled her. The magical tendrils lurched up and around, all connecting at the top. *No!* Evangeline threw a kick, but the bright blue tendrils were like steel. Another kick, and a punch, then her whole body, but the magical lines didn't budge. She was trapped in a magical cage.

The fire inside her reached its extreme, but it had nowhere to go. No target.

"*Let me out,*" Evangeline growled.

Avana's invisibility dissipated, revealing the bruising be-neath her left eye and smeared blood from her nose, which looked broken. Evangeline took pride in having done that twice now. Her breathing was haggard, and gone was the cool and collected Caster.

The Caster slid closer to the cage, hovering around the blue and white bars. Their eyes locked on one another, but Avana's betrayed the fear in hers, something Evangeline thought she'd never see when facing a Nyte. Seeing the same fear they had in-stilled in her. In Lani. In all humans. She couldn't help another slow smile that spread. *You shouldn't have underestimated me.*

Electricity crackled, and the pressure of a Shadow Door became prevalent. Avana was leaving. *Fleeing*, Evangeline re-alized.

The air behind Avana's shrinking figure coalesced, blurring and disrupting the wall. "We could have helped each other, but you've turned out to be just like *him*."

Avana faced the Shadow Door and instantly dropped to her feet.

The magical bars came down the instant she fell, and Evan-geline darted to the Caster, holding her to the floor, though it wasn't needed. A dart the size of her pinkie protruded out of her neck.

Rasha emerged from the balcony, its door still ajar. She wore her training gear from earlier, but it looked as if it had been put back on haphazardly as if she had just woken up else-where. Like in the empress's rooms.

Evangeline opened her mouth and then closed it. "How'd you get on the balcony?"

Rasha took a couple more steps but kept a visible distance between them. "I returned early tonight, and when I found you sleeping in *my* bed, I stepped outside for some air."

She gritted her teeth. "You've been here the whole time? Some help would have been nice."

"It didn't look like you needed my help at all." A flash of light gleamed off the side of Rasha's unsheathed sword as she pointed the blade at Evangeline's throat. "What in all the Goddess's lands are you, Evangeline?"

Evangeline's shoulders sagged. Eventually she would be found out, like Barto had after her and Ceven's attempted assassination, or Xilo when she lost control beyond the castle walls. Maybe it was for the best Ceven was leaving. She was now the furthest thing from the girl he fell in love with.

"I don't know." Evangeline stared down at Avana's closed eyes. "But she might."

CHAPTER 30

The humid air slapped at Ceven's flushed cheeks. Sweat built beneath the threaded mask covering his mouth and nose and gathered in uncomfortable pools down the back of his neck as well that was enshrouded in a brown hood matching the dye hiding the rich blue and gold feathers of his wings. His only reprieve from the stifling heat was the breathable fighting leathers that protected him in all the right places but allowed air to circulate so he wouldn't die from a heat stroke.

The empress, in a similar disguise, stood a couple paces away, surrounded by Sun Warriors, the afternoon sun glinting off their metal bracelets and neck pieces. The wind kicked up wisps of air and loose fabric, filling the cream and blue stained sails above them, marking them as a trader ship, and it was small enough to not warrant any unwanted attention.

Zelene hadn't left the railing since the ship had departed the docks, hidden in the crook of rocky cliffside below the palace where an entire cavern resided under the protection of rock and hanging plant life. Like their trip to the ruins, their mission required secrecy, everyone's identity concealed. Including the Caster currently kept in frostlite chains below deck who had been cooperative thus far in helping them locate Zindelis, but Ceven didn't believe Avana was telling them everything.

"We'll find him and put an end to all this," Ceven said, feeling the need to fill the space between them. He and his army had been prepared to set off for Peredia days ago when news of Zindelis's whereabouts changed everyone's plans. When Barto heard of the former advisor's location, it took everything to reel the Rathan back before he stormed off on his own, Ceven not far behind him.

If they were to believe Avana, Zindelis was currently hiding in Laba Estonos near Barto's family's village.

"Oh, I'm certain of that," Zelene said, gazing into the open sea. Despite her advisors' protests, the empress refused to stay behind, wanting to witness Zindelis's death personally. A hardness had set into her jaw and eyes ever since his betrayal, no matter how hard she tried to hide it.

Rasha approached them, the skin between her brows pinched. "Empress Zelene, Avana hasn't omitted anything else."

The empress didn't look concerned. "Perhaps she will be more forthcoming with Evangeline." Ceven's stomach churned when the empress's eyes fell on him.

They'd been on the water at least a day, land bordering them on either side as they took the river west, but Ceven still hadn't spoken a word to Evangeline, who had spent most of her time below decks in her shared cabin with Rasha and Asmen. It was obvious she was avoiding him too. He couldn't leave things as they were, especially not before he left for his kingdom, but he didn't know where to start. He didn't know how to fix this.

He also wasn't blind to the new tension that had emerged around Evangeline after the night Avana was captured—a plan pioneered by Eve herself, much to his fury. She shouldn't have put herself in danger like that, another argument they've hashed out this past week. While Zelene had given Evangeline the choice to accompany them, Ceven wasn't entirely sure she had an option. While she had the freedom to roam about the ship, every time she stepped foot on deck, it was as if a string connected every warrior in vicinity, pulling their hands to their swords, even if subconsciously, all keenly aware of her presence.

"What aren't you telling me?" Ceven had asked Barto last night, the lanterns swaying back and forth from the chains attached to the ceiling of the cabin. Flames flickered back and forth across the groaning wood, and the spools of hammocks tied to the corners of the intimate space. Quan occupied one, his snores drifting to a pause, indicating he was no longer asleep but eavesdropping. Tarry sat beside him on the floor, a book in hand.

Barto lay wrapped up in his own hammock, his black tail spilling out the side and twitching ever so slightly. "Do you really want to know?"

Ceven stood by the door, not ready to retire for the night. His muscles were rigid, his mind spinning in circles over everything that has happened. "I wouldn't be asking if I didn't."

His friend sighed. "How well do you know Evangeline?"

"Not this again—"

The Rathan's head jerked up, his yellow eyes snapping to his. "I've told you before, Ceven, people change. The girl you described, before we all left for Peredia together, is very different from the one I met. You're the only one who doesn't see it, and I'm starting to think you don't want to."

He balled his hands into fists at his side. "See what? You all accused her of being an accessory to these missing people, to the innocents being marked and drained of their lives. I was the only one who truly believed her innocence. I think it's all of you who need to reassess who their real enemy is."

Tarry's eyes didn't leave his book, but he hadn't turned a page in some time. Quan had given up the pretense of sleep, his head propped up, ears tilted towards them.

Barto squeezed the bridge of his nose. "I never said I believed she was behind the attacks, just that she wasn't as innocent as you made her out to be." Before Ceven could reply, he said, "In our religious texts, there were those that walked these lands before us—before Rathans, before all Nytes. The name changes depending on the book and period it was written, but all describe them as people of many-colored eyes. I didn't believe the stories, most are exaggerated anyways, but . . ."

Ceven snorted, struggling to comprehend what his friend was saying. "Don't tell me you believe she's some mythical creature, Barto. That's stretching it, even for you." His friend was a masterful storyteller and lover of the dramatics, but this was pushing it too far. He glanced at Quan, expecting his comrade to laugh and claim it was all some twisted joke, but he remained quiet. Not even Tarry, whose gaze now strayed beyond the book to the creaking floorboards, contradicted his words.

Barto closed his eyes, as if recalling a memory. "Evangeline's eyes, I'd seen them first-hand shift to what could only be described as glass being filtered by the sun. They were beautiful. And terrifying. I thought I had imagined it, but Rasha witnessed it as well the night Avana was captured . . . among other things." When his eyes flicked back open, they settled on Ceven's once more. "I don't know how else to say this, Ceven. Evangeline isn't human."

Something tugged at his memory, a moment back in the castle when he'd thought he had glimpsed a change in Evangeline's eyes. When he had carried her from the dungeons Ryker had thrown her in and she had called him by another name . . . Jaden.

His nostrils flared as he shut down that train of thought. Ceven trusted Barto to have his back, trusted his knowledge on the battlefield, how to command a group of soldiers, but this was one thing he couldn't agree with him on. He had told Barto that much, the two devolving into a tense silence before sleep eventually took hold, but that tension never dissipated. Tugging and pulling on his consciousness like the wind lapping at the sails and kicking up everyone's coats on deck, who preferred the breeze to the stagnant heat down below. It wouldn't be long until they arrived at the closest port towards Barto's village. He couldn't put it off any longer—he needed to talk with Evangeline.

Turning on his heel, he headed towards the stairs leading to the depths of the ship. Zelene and Rasha didn't move, but he swore he felt their eyes tailing him. He descended into the humid pit branching out into a relatively sparse storage area, several private cabins, and more spacious ones for the remaining crew that had joined them. He bypassed warriors and workers in various states of leisure. Some slept while others played a round of cards, smoke drifting through the haze of heat, lingering before dispersing out the cracked portholes.

His boots paused at a nondescript door towards the mast of the ship, a matching one beside it—another room reserved specifically for the empress. He raised his hand to knock when it swung open.

Raiythlen emerged, opting for rolled-up sleeves and fitted trousers rather than the fighting leathers most currently wore on the ship. When Ceven had first discovered Raiythlen's presence after docking, it took all his willpower not to throttle the Caster. He still hadn't forgiven him for wrapping Evangeline up in his insidious plans, his attitude a constant test of patience.

The Caster bobbed his head in a mockery of a bow. "Your Highness—or should I start calling you Your Majesty? We were just discussing you."

Ceven's jaw tightened, his gaze shooting to Evangeline, who peered behind him, her cheeks flushed from the heat—or maybe something else.

She shoved at Raiythlen's shoulder, a familiar gesture that wasn't lost on Ceven. "Don't sound so blasted cryptic. Ceven, we were just discussing some plans—"

"Plans that didn't involve me?" he snapped, before he could help himself. Jealousy flared in his gut. Ceven had worked so hard to regain Evangeline's trust since he returned to Peredia, had promised to protect her, yet she had chosen to work with this Caster behind his back, instead of him. Why was she still choosing Raiythlen over him?

"Told you he'd get upset." Raiythlen smirked, and Ceven was moments away from wiping it from his face permanently.

Evangeline thrust her hands on her hips, shooting the Caster a glare. "Stop talking. You're not helping." She turned to Ceven. "And no, they don't involve you, because I already know what your answer would be."

"You didn't even give me a chance!" His voice had risen, his control slipping. "Sea watery hells, Eve, has nothing changed between us? I thought you trusted me . . ." *Am I not good enough?* An echo of doubts plagued him, as taunts and insults swam over him from memories past. The king and Sehn belittling him, telling him he would never be fit to rule, that he wasn't strong enough, that he was defective. A bastard child no one wanted.

"This has nothing to do with trust—Ceven!"

He'd already spun around, his boots pounding into the squeaky floorboards. He wasn't sure he had ever felt this angry before, and a part of him, the one that turned off his emotions and played the level-headed prince when engaging with other royals, court politics, and strategic battle-planning, said he was being ridiculous. To turn around and talk this out. But he didn't stop, not even when Evangeline continued to call after him.

He found himself walking past the stairs towards his own cabin on the opposite end of the ship. Tarry shadowed not far behind him, but Ceven made sure to firmly shut the cabin door, a warning he wanted to be left alone.

While Ceven wasn't sure what he would do or say if Evangeline had followed him, he needn't bother. She never came knocking, and he felt that distance that had been growing between them turn into a chasm. He remained alone in the cabin, his head in his hands and his heart broken.

CHAPTER 31

After spending a few days on the water and fighting the blights of motion sickness that hadn't abated fully, Evangeline was thrilled to be back on land. They had traveled with several mounts, some of the crew taking to foot while the rest paired up on the horses. Evangeline had purposefully avoided Ceven's gaze atop his own mount, though she felt his eyes bore holes in her back as she climbed behind Rasha on hers. The Rathan shot her an arched look but didn't argue the matter. Raiythlen—who chose to travel by foot—glanced curiously at the two of them, a smirk grazing his features until Ceven swiveled his glare on him. The Caster raised his hands in surrender, his smirk still in place, before blending in with the rest of the group.

They trekked a lot farther than Evangeline would have liked under the blazing sun, and she almost wished to be back on the ship if only for the steady breeze. At least their travel time on land would be cut, having taken the river for most of the way here, unlike her first trip, when she had left Barto's village for Kazuumar. It had only been a couple weeks since then, and while she was no longer facing a death sentence cast by the Atiacan people, she was facing a whole new one. Jaden wouldn't go down without a fight. He had displayed powers that rivaled most Nytes she'd seen and more. But maybe, just maybe, they would be able to defeat him and put an end to his reign of marked puppets.

She didn't want to think of the alternative.

They traveled across expansive, unpopulated land filled with patches of tall grasses and hovering insects that buzzed around them between intervals of trees with fronds stretching out to cover them only partially from the ray's heat. She and Rasha rode in the middle of the pack, lining the empress's side, with Asmen bordering the other. Thankfully both Ceven and Raiythlen were far behind her, hopefully not dueling to the death. Both Nytes had given her a pounding headache the past few days, made worse by her nausea from the rocking ship. She'd spent the remaining time in her cabin blessedly alone—or as much as she could be until Rasha and Asmen retired for the night, only sharing a few words with her. It was a kinder greeting then the one she'd received from the rest of the warriors, who acted like she would pounce and tear out their throats every time she got too close. She wasn't that hungry. Yet.

"You two haven't talked it out already?" asked Rasha after a particularly long, grueling silence that reminded Evangeline of the beads of sweat, damp clothes, and sweltering sun without any distraction. Since the night they'd captured Avana, when Rasha watched Evangeline turn into . . . something more . . . the tentative mutual understanding they had shared crumbled, morphing into something Evangeline didn't know how to navigate yet. Sometimes Rasha acted as if nothing had changed; other times her hand would reach for her swords, her eyes narrowing as if recalling that night.

Evangeline, too exhausted from her recent fight with Ceven, would gladly take the former. Pretending nothing had happened and that Rasha still thought her a troublesome human. "I'd love to, except there would be little talking and a lot of yelling."

Asmen snorted, though her eyes kept forward to the path ahead of them. Empress Zelene appeared less amused, but ever since they departed the palace, her face had become shadowed with deadly intent. Evangeline was sure her thoughts only revolved around Jaden and how she'd best like to slice him open.

Rasha sighed. "The tension between you two is thick enough to cut. You'd be doing us all a service if you just apologized."

Evangeline sat behind Rasha, who was oblivious to the daggers she was aiming at the warrior's back. "You expect *me* to apologize? What makes you think this is my fault?" Ceven had promised to protect her, to always be by her side, yet he was the one leaving her behind. Again. Like he had years ago when he first left for the empire, except this time by his own doing. Then he had the audacity to say she didn't trust him, when he had been the one to keep it a secret from her. When he didn't trust she was powerful enough to fight by his side for the throne.

Against her best efforts, she tossed a look behind her and found Ceven in the crowd of cantering hooves and stampeding feet. No matter how hard he tried to disguise himself with his hooded cloak covering his strewn brown hair, his wings plastered in mud and dye, she'd always know it was him. She didn't see Raiythlen but wasn't surprised, knowing the Caster had a fondness for disappearing acts.

"Never said it was, but sometimes you need to bend in order to reshape things into something new."

This time Evangeline snorted, her words pitched low. "Is that why you're always 'bending' to the empress's will? You're hoping things will change into something new?"

Rasha squared her shoulders. She didn't reply.

When the silence between them returned with a vengeance, Evangeline's thoughts turned to Avana, who had been left on the ship in chains, watched over by several warriors who stayed behind. When Rasha had asked her to speak with the Caster a few days prior, Evangeline jumped at the opportunity.

Rasha had introduced Evangeline to a door on the lower levels of the ship, a small rectangle decked in iron bars cut out in the center, revealing Avana sitting on the ground with her hands cuffed behind her back and her head bowed against her chest.

Evangeline had entered the intimate room framed by wood and metal while Rasha and another warrior eavesdropped outside. Between the constant sway and the suffocating room, Evangeline had been tempted to pound at the door that clicked shut behind her, but she swallowed and took a deep breath.

Avana hadn't look up when she entered. No markings or bruises marred her skin, but that didn't mean Rasha hadn't thoroughly interrogated her, just that she chose less violent methods. For now.

"Evangeline, nice of you to come and visit," the Caster had said, her tone like honey-coated knives.

Evangeline leaned against the wall across from where Avana sat. She still hadn't raised her head, and a part of Evangeline, albeit a very small part, felt pity at the sight. "I have questions."

"I may have answers."

Evangeline scowled but took a breath. Rasha had given her instructions on what to ask, but she ignored those. "Why are you being so cooperative?"

Avana shrugged. "I have no reason not to be."

Because you think you still have me within your grasp? That you're safe here from Jaden? she had thought. "Why did you betray Jaden?" Evangeline didn't believe the Caster would simply give up on her life-long quest to discover Evangeline and Jaden's heritage because Jaden's methods were violent and extreme. Avana had proven she was just as cutthroat and equally determined.

"He had planned to betray me from the start. We were never working together, at least, it wasn't a true partnership." Frustration bled into her voice, and Evangeline had reason to believe she was telling the truth.

"Like Ryker?" The name still evoked fear and a hint of guilt, her adopted father's dying expression searing her brain with an uncomfortable clarity.

Avana finally looked up, her black hair matted and sticking to the sides of her pale face, her painted eyes smeared from sweat. "Both had their secrets, but at least Ryker was more accommodating. Before you killed him."

Evangeline bit her lip and mentally cursed, but she shouldn't be surprised that Avana knew the truth. If people like Kel and others among the rebel forces in Castle Peak knew about Evangeline's act of treason, it was no surprise that Avana came to the same conclusion as well.

The Caster cocked her head, observing her carefully. "Then again, Ryker had been working for Jaden. So in the end I guess it really didn't matter."

That got a rise from Evangeline, even as dread curdled in her stomach. "What do you mean?"

An unpleasant smile stretched across her face, making her look like a ghastly spirit haunting this ship rather than a captive. "I will admit it took me awhile before I figured it out. I suspected Ryker had been working with someone else, even before I arrived in Peredia. The wealth of knowledge he had seemed out of place for an Aerian royal with no background in Caster magic research or development. Not to mention the times he would seemingly disappear where not even my familiar could find him."

At the mention of her familiar, Evangeline's gaze shifted to the cracked porthole above Avana's head, streaming in sunlight and a slight breeze that didn't do much to break up the trapped heat.

She didn't see any slick black birds flying nearby like the one Avana had used on their trip to the ruins back in Peredia. She didn't know if it was still alive or if Avana was using it to eavesdrop and collect information on them as well. Evangeline would have to mention that to the empress, if she didn't already know.

Avana's eyes met hers, her gaze steady. "It wasn't until I met Jaden and saw his research that I recognized notes scattered about with a familiar penmanship I'd seen before. The same knowledge, the same goals. Looking at it now, of course Ryker had been working with Jaden. Or more accurately: Ryker Ardonis served as Jaden's puppet."

Evangeline frowned. Ryker's knowledge of her mark, how he had known about Anali and Jaden . . . how he knew about seemingly everything. It was painfully obvious now *how* Ryker knew all those things. *We are only tools. Pawns in a game bigger and far grander than you or even I can imagine,* Ryker had said to her the night before he died. Evangeline had thought he meant the king's schemes, but now she wondered if he meant Jaden's this whole time. The fact Jaden had been working with Ryker—*controlling* him—felt like a stab through her heart. Which was ridiculous. Jaden was committing atrocities, might as well have killed Lani with his own hands, yet this betrayal left an equal mark on her soul. The woman she had been before, married to Jaden, felt as if her heart were breaking. Again.

The ship groaned, and the subtle heartbeats, the bated breath trickled beyond the metal-enforced door behind Evangeline. As much as she was learning all of this, so was Rasha and the rest of the crew. She didn't care; she wanted answers.

"But . . . why? Why would Ryker work for someone like Jaden? As far as I remember he didn't have any markings on him and, as the queen's cousin, he didn't need power or prestige; he already had it."

"I don't know. Truly," she amended, taking in Evangeline's pressed lips. "I'm sure Jaden had leverage over Ryker, something to sway or threaten his cooperation. There were rumors the

Peredian military had killed his wife and daughter when they were mistakenly taken as rebel forces. Perhaps Jaden promised revenge of sorts." Evangeline had also heard those rumors, amongst others that had whispered about her resemblance to Ryker's deceased daughter before Ryker himself confirmed it.

Avana plopped her head back against the wall, the chains wrapped around her limbs rattling in an offbeat rhythm with the groaning floorboards. "Still, I can't figure out why Jaden had Ryker adopt you, care for you, and punish you as he did, instead of meeting with you personally. Helping you understand who you are. It's almost as if he hates you, but can't let you go." Despite her hunched form on the floor, she managed a haughty look. "You care to explain why?"

Evangeline had wondered the same thing, when she discovered Jaden's blood was the same taste that would linger in her mouth some mornings. Why he didn't show himself then.

I wanted you to remember who you really are, Evangeline. Not the weak-willed woman who had betrayed me, but the powerful, unstoppable one I had fallen in love with. I did what I had to do for your sake.

She answered her question with one of her own. "You said Jaden planned to betray you from the start. What do you mean by that?"

Avana's eyes narrowed, as if she knew Evangeline was keeping something from her, but said, "When I agreed to aid Jaden in his work, I thought it would be a mutually beneficial arrangement. It turned out I was only his next subject to be used at his disposal, rather than someone whose intelligence and research could have helped us both. As you would say, I got what I deserved."

"No, you didn't. You didn't nearly hurt enough." Evangeline's nostrils flared, her clenched fists shaking as she remembered Avana standing by and doing nothing as Evangeline was dragged back down to the dungeons. Vane's knife cutting into her skin, the choking terror that gripped her, not knowing how much pain she would have to endure before she and Ryker would return. If Raiythlen hadn't been there, if a Caster she once sworn she'd kill herself for poisoning Lani, hadn't been there to give her strength and hope . . . "And that answer doesn't tell me anything."

Avana stayed quiet long enough Evangeline almost left, pounding on the door for Rasha and the other warriors who hovered near the barred window, peering into the ship's hallway, to let her out. After everything Avana had revealed, Evangeline needed time alone in the cabin, away from prying eyes and more questions that Rasha and the empress would surely bombard her with.

Eventually Avana whispered, "He wanted to drain me of my blood. To use the magic of my bloodline to continue making his cursed soldiers. Like he had my mother."

Evangeline's mouth dropped open. Then shut. Then opened again, but no words came out.

"I wondered how Jaden had been able to manipulate Anali's mark, a one-of-a-kind magical brand infused through her will and blood." Her blue eyes, a lighter hue than Raiythlen's, appeared darker. Like a swirling abyss that pulled Evangeline in, wanting to swallow her whole. "Magic manifests differently from family to family, harnessed within a Caster's bloodline and controlled by the relative's will. Jaden was able to replicate and manipulate Anali's magic from centuries ago using her daughter's blood, my mother, and Anali's will left behind in her journals."

Sweat trickled down Evangeline's back, and she licked her chapped lips, an unbidden dark thought entering her mind.

The blue depths of Avana's eyes hardened like ice skittering across a lake. "I know what you're thinking, but killing me to prevent Jaden from taking my blood won't stop him. Whether my mother is alive or dead . . ." She paused, and Evangeline caught a glimpse of how exhausted Avana really was. "Jaden hadn't taken anything from me prior to my . . . escape. Meaning he has access to my family's blood to make more soldiers without needing me. For now."

A queasiness settled in Evangeline's stomach. She wanted to resurface, take a deep breath of fresh air, and escape the stagnant warmth that crawled across her skin and down her back, but more questions pressed her. She asked about Avana's mother, how Jaden managed to capture her, pointedly avoiding Raiythlen's name, the fact he was still alive—and now a target too. She asked about Anali. If her will, these journals, like the one they found in those ruins in Peredia, contained a "truth" that would change everything. Or whatever Anali had insinuated when speaking to Evangeline from a memory past.

Avana, however, had stopped responding. Her chin sagged forward once more, a curtain of hair slipping down her shoulders and sticking to her pallid skin. Evangeline hated the pang of pity she felt at the sight, but she reminded herself Avana had once turned her back on Evangeline in an even worse position. "As expected, talking to you always gets me more questions, but we'll continue this another time." Without knocking or asking, Rasha opened the door appearing pensive.

Avana lifted her head enough for Evangeline to catch a glimpse of a smile. The same smile she had worn the day she attempted to execute her own brother. "I hope he gets what's coming to him." Evangeline didn't have to ask who. Only time would tell whether they'd be able to bring Jaden to justice.

Evangeline slammed into Rasha's back, abruptly pulling her back to the present. Her horse had reared up suddenly, the group around them slowing to a crawl.

Familiar dome-shaped houses dotted the land in the near distance, the dirt-trodden path they traveled winding through arching trees with dangling fruit and bushes brimming with berries. At the head of the path, roughly thirty paces ahead of them, stood a group of figures too far for Evangeline to clearly make out, smoke billowing behind their forms—coming from the village.

Evangeline's heart sank, fear coiling down her spine. They were too late.

CHAPTER 32

The empress whipped out orders, the pack separating into pre-planned groups, the warriors ahead of them charging directly forward. Evangeline tightened her grip around Rasha as they jerked forward behind Zelene, Asmen, and two other warriors. Their hooves collided into the dirt-packed ground, fronds slashing at their leathers as they veered right, mirroring another group of warriors, in a loop towards the village.

Wind whizzed past Evangeline's ears, her cowl straining at where it was clasped at her neck, as the village crawled into view. Plumes of smoke snaked out past the domed houses, shadows writhing in its fog.

Then the momentum of pounding hooves and weapons unsheathing cut to a halt.

Emerging from the smoke weren't tattooed soldiers but smiling faces with hands spanned out on cheeks, both young and old. All Nytes—Grace wasn't in their midst.

"Welcome, welcome!" Evangeline immediately recognized the rounded face and pale brown eyes of Barto's youngest sister, Hanna, who emerged from the crowd. A crowd that had gathered around the strange—and armed—guests. "How may we assist you fine travelers?"

A notable change swept through Zelene and her troops, furrowed brows swapped for softened eyes. Hands shifted away from their weapons to wave at the encroaching swarm. Zelene dismounted her house. Asmen and Rasha shared a look and went to dismount as well when Zelene raised a hand, freezing their movements, her focus never leaving the child. She bent down, a genuine smile breaking out across her face. "I'm looking for your father. May we see him?"

Hanna cocked her head, eyes scrunched, probably thinking why these strangers wanted to speak to her father. Before she could say anything, Tor himself came up beside his daughter. He placed a hand on her shoulder, subtly moving her behind his frame.

"May I ask why you're in need of my services, traveler?" Tor said, his voice friendly but his eyes carefully trained on their group, then past them to where the remainder of their crew had splintered, pausing at the edge of the village and awaiting orders from the empress.

Zelene stood just under Tor's full height. She met his gaze while his eyes widened. Not a single word passed between them. The crowd around them hadn't dispersed but instead continued to peer at them with open curiosity; only a few, older Rathans with gray hair looked wary.

Tor cleared his throat. "Ah yes, please, right this way—traveler."

The cluster of people fanned out only slightly as they traveled past. The smoke that had polluted the village came in streams from burning piles of wood and dried herbs—a ritual this time of year to keep the insects away, Tor explained. Evangeline wanted to laugh, more so in crippling relief that no one was hurt, but also at the expressions the rest of their crew wore, embarrassed they had all assumed the worst.

The empress signaled for the remaining troops to hold their posts outside the village, and only a handful of them—Zelene, Asmen, Rasha, Barto, Tarry, Ceven, and Raiythlen—tied their mounts to the trees lining the perimeter and followed Tor to his dome nestled toward the center of the village. Bundles of wildflowers tickled their ankles as they crossed its threshold, all remaining sisters sitting round-eyed at the table, platters of fruit and meat sitting in half-eaten piles in front of them. Grace and Sasha were nowhere to be seen.

"I'll be busy entertaining our guests if you girls can please play outside for now. Oh, and if you see your mother, let her know there's no need to return home early tonight. I'll take care of things." The girls collectively shuffled to the front door, staring as they passed. Evangeline resisted the urge to smile and wave, deciding it was safer to keep her presence a secret for now.

When the house was cleared and after Tor had closed the curtains, he flipped over the rug in front of the fireplace, revealing a hidden hatch. He ushered them all inside as they squeezed downstairs into a moderately sized underground room. There was ample space for the nine of them to spread out, but Ceven chose to hover at her back, her spine tingling at his presence. The room held a desk and neat piles of papers, the exception of several sheets posted against the clay-packed wall, lighting coming from built-out pockets where Caster fire illuminated maps and writing in harsh Atiacan that Evangeline couldn't read.

Tor shut the hatch behind him and took a breath. "Empress Zelene, what in all the goddess's lands are you doing here?" He wrung his hands, as if he couldn't believe the empress now stood in his village. In his very home.

Zelene flipped back her hood, but the rest of them kept their masks and hoods in place, though Evangeline desired nothing more than to rip the sweat-soaked cloak and tunic off her.

"Former advisor Tor Nu'yuen, I apologize for arriving without any proper notice, but this mission required the utmost secrecy. I fear your village may be in danger."

Tor rubbed the bridge of his nose. "Not what I was hoping to hear, though I had already feared the worst. Alright, what's the damage?"

To Evangeline's surprise, Zelene didn't omit any details in relaying the entire situation to Tor, despite his title as former advisor. It was clear she still held her former advisor's trust and loyalty, despite Jaden's betrayal. Asmen and Rasha stood at rapt attention, lingering close to their empress, while Tarry held his usual rigid posture by the hatch. Barto hung behind his father, who sank into the worn seat at his desk. The captain hadn't revealed his presence, keeping quiet—like he had for most of this trip—Evangeline now realized with suspicious clarity, his eyes far too focused on her and Ceven.

Raiythlen leaned against the opposite wall from her, toying the tip of his dagger with a finger, and she imagined him smirking beneath the mask he now wore. Evangeline hadn't forgotten Avana's words about her mother, how she and Raiythlen were now targets. Rasha had told the empress what she'd overheard, but how much of that traveled back to Raiythlen? When Evangeline found the time, and the right words, she'd drop that truth on the Caster—if he didn't already know.

Tor frowned, then peered at the hooded figures in the room. Zelene nodded at them, and they all lowered their hoods and masks. Evangeline practically ripped hers off, her sigh embarrassingly loud in the quiet room. Tor didn't seem surprised by the show of faces, except when his gaze landed on Raiythlen with barely veiled unease before settling on Evangeline.

"Evangeline? You're here too? I thought . . ." He blew out a sigh in blatant relief. He thought she had died in the Summoning Grounds, like the rest of Kazuumar's citizens, Evangeline realized. Not even Barto had betrayed the empress's secrecy in this.

"Yes, I'm here. I'm . . . fine." It was an utter lie, but better than being dead, she supposed.

"We don't know when Zindelis will make an appearance," Zelene continued, "if he will at all, but this is the only lead we have." Zelene turned to her. "And if Evangeline is truthful in this, unlike other matters, then she may be the key to luring him out."

Evangeline ignored the jab. If she had it her way, she'd keep the beast a dark secret for the rest of her life. "Well, you haven't called for my execution yet, so you still trust me somewhat." She chanced a look at Ceven, but his face remained expressionless. If he knew about the beast, listened to the news of her non-human glowing eyes that had spread like wildfire amongst the group, he didn't show it. However, the slight feathering in his jaw told her he still hadn't forgotten their last encounter, when he'd found her and Raiythlen together. Even if she had let Ceven in on what she planned to do, he wouldn't have approved of it. Worse, would probably have had her tied up and left guarded on the ship.

Tor's eyes narrowed in confusion, but no one dared to elaborate on what passed between all of them, tension creeping into the air like a tentative lover. Evangeline's undefined presence, uncertain power, hung over their heads like an axe.

"The warriors stationed around the village are ready to protect the village from a potential ambush," Rasha said. "But since we don't know if or when Zindelis will appear, we'll need to lay low until then. We have several people exploring the surrounding area for any suspicious activity."

Tor rubbed his black and gray beard, thicker than when Evangeline had last seen him. "Understood, I'll figure out what to say to the villagers. In the meantime, I'll have my family stay with our neighbors. You can use this room and the upper bedrooms if needed, but you'll get more privacy and fewer eavesdroppers down here."

"Thank you, Tor." Zelene gently placed a hand on his arm. "I know this is a risk for your people here, but we'll ensure their safety. If it looks to be too dangerous, we'll evacuate everyone immediately."

There were no windows in the underground room to tell Evangeline what time of day it was, but she knew night had to have fallen by now when Tor brought down extra food, blankets, and pillows for the remainder that had stayed below. Barto, Ceven, and Asmen had claimed rooms upstairs, Ceven not even gracing her a passing glance as he left. Evangeline ignored how it made her heart wrench, tears threatening to spill over as she laid out her makeshift bed of blankets and pillows, farthest from Zelene and Rasha, who, for the first time since Evangeline arrived in Atiaca, didn't hide the fact they were sleeping together.

"Not sleeping with the prince?" Raiythlen wasn't close, his own temporary bed between her and the Rathan couple, but still too close for her comfort. While the Caster wasn't entirely to blame for her and Ceven's current hostility towards each other, his antagonistic comments certainly didn't help.

"Shut up, Rai."

He arched a brow at the nickname.

"I'm not in the mood." Despite being stuck in her sweat-soaked leathers, the room was cool, the floors nice against the palms of her hands and feet, which she had stripped bare.

"The others have set up around the village, with signals prepared if any movement is spotted," Zelene said to Tor, who passed out bowls of stew from earlier to everyone. "With the sun gone, we should be able to see their fire signal from here. If Zindelis or his soldiers are here, we'll make sure to strike first."

"What if Avana is lying?" Evangeline asked, the bowl hot in her hands. While it tasted delicious, spices dancing on her tongue, it didn't satisfy the beast that had been growing hungrier by the day. She hadn't been able to hunt, lest the others catch a glimpse of the monster Rasha had witnessed hiding underneath her human skin. It was dangerous to keep denying the beast, but how could she indulge when Ceven lingered in her shadow? Hearing she was a monster and seeing it were two different things.

"She could be, but I don't think she is." Zelene mirrored Evangeline's position, looking the epitome of relaxed, but the fierceness in her eyes said otherwise. While they had all debated on it, ultimately it was best they had left Avana on the ship heavily guarded, deeming it safer than bringing her along lest she try to escape and risk Jaden capturing her. Evangeline didn't know if the same suggestion had been made to Avana's brother, but obviously either Raiythlen was in the dark about his situation or he refused to stay behind. She'd like to think it was more the latter, but the Caster was hard to read behind the mask of casual nonchalance he always wore.

"How can you be so sure?" Evangeline, for once, also believed Avana didn't plan on betraying them this time, but that didn't mean she didn't have a plan up her sleeve or an ulterior motive for everything.

"Zindelis had played us both. The Caster has no incentive to protect him now, not if she values her own life." Zelene's gaze flickered to Raiythlen's, but the former Council agent stared intently into his bowl of soup, lost in thought. Or carefully formulating a plan in his head.

Evangeline turned to Rasha, who had placed her soup beside her on the desk, instead roving over strategic battle maps, licking her thumb before placing down a pinpoint on the parchment. "When you interrogated Avana, did she say why here? Why Jaden would take interest in a remote village in the middle of Atiaca?"

"No, she didn't say." Rasha sighed, surely just as frustrated as Evangeline by the lack of answers. "But it could be related to Tor's former advisor position; maybe he had planned to glean additional information from him."

"Or it could be tied to you." Raiythlen finished his bowl, stretching out one leg and propping his chin on the other, his eyes finding hers. "This was the first place you stayed within the empire, formed bonds with, prior to your trial in Kazuumar, so I've gathered. If Zindelis—Jaden—is truly fixated on you, it would only make sense the two are related somehow." He tapped his lip with one mechanical digit. "Maybe this less of a lead, and more of a trap."

Ice skated down her insides, its jagged edges stealing her breath. She envisioned Grace and Tor's face. Barto's sisters, even Sasha. The kindness they had shown her even though she was a stranger, a criminal in these lands. The thought of Jaden hurting them, using them because of her . . .

"We'll stop him before he hurts anyone. If he even shows up," said Rasha, her patience thinning as she reviewed the paper in front of her for the hundredth time. "Empress, you should have stayed in the palace. Who knows how long it'll be before Zindelis shows his face, how dangerous—"

"Rasha." Empress Zelene's voice was quiet, gentle. "To even suggest that . . . I'd hoped you know me better than that."

Rasha met her gaze before casting her own back down at the stacks of organized papers, biting her lower lip. "You know it's not that, it's just—"

"I did not unite this country on flowery speeches and pretty words, though it may seem that way in recent years. Zindelis has personally betrayed my trust, and I will make sure to show others the consequences of those who wish to do the same. For those who wish to hurt the land I vowed to protect." The gentleness evaporated, replaced by guttural loathing that bled into Zelene's narrowed eyes, her peeled lips.

Rasha didn't say anything, but Evangeline could read the worry creasing her brows and flattening of her lips, the same worry Evangeline had at the thought of Ceven facing Council member Aimee and the Peredian army. She squeezed her hands into fists.

"We'll find him and make sure he answers to everything," Evangeline said with sudden conviction. Not just for the empress, but for herself, for Lani, for all the innocent people he'd kidnapped, killed, and forced to fight. For the magical blight he'd wrought across both countries.

At some point everyone had fallen asleep, or at least quieted for the night, drifting into a lull of rustling sheets and soft snores. Evangeline stirred when a gentle touch grazed her back, sleep still tugging at her. The hand slid over the curve of her hip before resting on her cheek, calloused fingers caressing her skin, pushing back slumber's call. Her eyes opened to Ceven. He crouched over her, wings pressed to his sides, still in his leathers. His face hung shadowed in the dim light cast by the single lantern hanging on a hook next to the hatch.

"Come to bed with me," he whispered.

Sleep completely escaped her, replaced by the steady thrum of her heart and the ache in her arms to hold him close. To be done with all this fighting.

She nodded. He scooped her up in his arms, smothering her protest into his chest. She couldn't see if the others were awake, if they watched Ceven carry her from the room, but she didn't care. She missed her prince. She missed being this close again.

The dome was quiet except the symphony of insects that echoed far louder upstairs than below. Warm air pricked her exposed hands and feet, the breeze a nice reprieve on the back of her neck, her braid dangling over Ceven's arm. He carried her all the way to his bedroom, the same one they had shared when first arriving in the empire, the makeshift door still in place. He shut it behind them and carefully laid her down, pulling the covers around her as he slid in behind her. He slung one arm around her waist, pulling her back against the hard planes of his body, his lips nuzzling her neck.

"I missed you," he murmured in her ear.

She twined her fingers through his, relishing the weight of him at her back. "Me too."

They didn't say anything for several moments, their breaths climbing into rhythm with one another, the night's chorus filling the calm silence.

Wanting to be closer, she rolled within his grasp, pressing her forehead to his. His eyes, like the leaves of summer fading into autumn, blazed with a heat that made her shiver, and when he joined his lips to hers, she melted. Limbs tangled with one another, mouths moving in sync as they both clawed at the straps and buckles of their leathers. It was everything she had been secretly wishing for this past week. Elated and completely consumed by him, his need for her, she reached a height she didn't want to leap from just yet.

But when she came crashing down, her chest heaving, sweat decorating her skin, reality set in once more. "This is goodbye." It wasn't a question.

One hand stroked her belly, the other propping up his head to gaze at her. "It doesn't have to be . . ."

They both knew she wasn't referring to him leaving for Peredia, or if they'd survive an attack from Jaden and his marked army, though both weighed on her equally. "Did . . . did Barto say anything?"

"You'll always be you, Eve."

She closed her eyes, the tips of his fingers tracing patterns from her naval up to the tips of her breasts. *Will I? Am I still Eve, the girl you fell in love with years ago? Or am I someone else? Someone who's grown teeth and a craving for the blood pulsing at your neck. Someone who still remembers the touch of another. How he, too, had once held me close, clinging tightly, as if letting me go was never an option.*

She stayed quiet for too long, finding Ceven's lids had closed. Soft breaths rocking him off to a land that was hopefully more peaceful than hers. Inching closer, she wove her arms between his, holding him to her heart, knowing it might be the last time she'd be able to.

Her cheeks wet, she whispered, "Goodbye," and closed her eyes.

CHAPTER 33

An urgent knock pulled Evangeline into an upright position, sleep morphing into something else as her skin prickled, her heart ratcheting up a notch from its calm pace moments before.

"We have movement," was all Asmen said behind the closed door before her footsteps padded away.

Ceven was already awake and fastening up his leathers as she climbed out of bed to do the same. Last night still clung to their skins, proof the love was not lost between them. He caught her gaze, tugging her into a tight embrace and crushing his lips to hers before reeling back.

"Stick to the plan, and then you get out of there, Eve. Retreat to Tor and the others and stay hidden. We'll handle this."

She frowned, an echo of an old argument leaving her lips. "I told you, Ceven, I can fight. I can handle myself." But he was already holstering his sword and moving out of the room.

Evangeline slid two daggers into the sheaths on either thigh, a sword strapped to her back. She looked around for her cloak—to hide her presence in case Jaden was here—but realized she'd left it downstairs.

"Signal from the east, but it also looks like Wretched are approaching the village's perimeter from the west," Asmen said, tightening her own swords at her sides as everyone gathered in the center of the dome, the lack of sleep clinging to their faces. An unspoken truce tied them all together by the events that were about to unfold. Evangeline met Raiythlen's eyes quickly enough to go unnoticed by the others but signaled their plan was still on.

"It's true then, Jaden must be controlling them somehow," she said, taking a colored stick, a signal flare, from Tor. They had speculated earlier Jaden was controlling the usually docile Nytes. It made sense, given what happened at the Summoning Grounds combined with the use of the Shadow Doors.

"Only one way to find out." Zelene shifted, showing the dyed, hardened leather and onyx underneath that melded to her body. Her armed bracelets gleamed like the scimitar that rested at her hip as she leapt toward the door. "Protect the villagers at all costs, and we'll bring the fight as far as we can." The empress had already fled out the door by the time Rasha could utter a protest.

Rasha shook her head, muttering a swear. "She's going to start giving me gray hairs. Asmen—"

"Understood," came the warrior's reply as she tailed Zelene out the door. Rasha nodded at the others, Barto clasping a firm hand on his father's shoulder before leaving, followed by Raiythlen, who tossed Evangeline her cloak on his way out. She threw it on as Ceven clasped her cheek in his, giving her a quick peck on the forehead before trailing behind Tarry, leaving only Evangeline, Rasha, and Tor in the unlit dome.

"I've already warned the others, they're all hiding in their own bunkers," Tor said, and Rasha gave the former advisor a respectful nod.

"Thank you, Tor. Go be with your heart-mate and kids."

The old Rathan's eyes shifted between the two of them, worry creasing the edges of them. Evangeline wondered what it would have been like to have a real father, someone like Tor who loved without expecting anything in return. Whose touch, as he placed a hand on each of their shoulders, was one of warmth and not pain. She murmured her own reassurances to the old Rathan before he left.

Rasha and Evangeline stood in the dark, a stillness creeping in from the windows, rustling the curtains and wrapping around Evangeline's throat. Not even the insects were singing, as if also sensing the danger encroaching upon them.

The warrior broke the silence. "I don't know who you are, or what happened back with Avana—"

"Rasha, I don't plan on betraying you all. I have as many questions as you do, trust me."

She pressed her lips together before releasing a breath. "The terrifying part is that I believe you. Don't let me down." Then she was out the door.

Per the plan they had discussed at length earlier, Evangeline waited several tense beats before making her own move. The muggy air made the cloak feel like multiple layers of clothing instead of just one as she left through the back window, looping around behind the village. Rasha was headed to the flare's signal while Zelene and Asmen spread out on either side of the signal's location, flanking them. Evangeline's goal was to run north, where traps had been set for Jaden's capture, and hopefully he would follow the bait and come after Evangeline there where she would light her own signal, one that produced a heady scent only notable to most Rathans. That would silently draw in the others to surround Jaden on all sides before he realized it was a trap.

Zelene wanted him alive for questioning, but Evangeline had a feeling the only way to defeat Jaden would be to kill him. Evangeline swallowed that train of thought, taking a sharp left. She'd ask him her questions after he's been subdued, and this time she'd make sure she had the upper hand.

An opening where the makeshift dirt road spread out large enough for two carriages to roll through greeted her, leading to the heart of the village. She would need to cross the main expanse to reach the marked tree Zelene's warriors had left to signal the direction where the traps had been laid. Her feet pounded against the dirt as she skated through the village, everyone told to remain indoors, with plans for an emergency evacuation to the empress's ship, but they didn't plan to let the enemy that close, and Zelene was confident their numbers and determination would be enough against Jaden.

Evangeline wasn't so sure.

The night was quiet and dark, not a single light peeping through the open windows of the surrounding domes. Evangeline carefully let the beast seep through, enough to enhance her senses, her speed and strength, but not enough to be consumed. As always, the shift was a punch of shock. Rain-soaked dirt, the village's leftovers from dinner, spiced meats and cooked vegetables and the occasional draft of fruit that had started to turn overwhelmed her. The pungent smell of a smoke signal still drifted on the slight breeze as she squeezed passed the opening between two domes on her right. Evangeline didn't hear any signs of fighting yet, but she clenched the forearm-length stick beneath her coat—that would ignite with a twist and emanate the distinct smell for the others to pick up on—her heart thundering.

Raiythlen's words lingered in her head. Did Jaden truly target this place because of her? What was his purpose? If it was to capture her, he could have easily done it at any point over these past several years. She shook her head. They should've evacuated everyone as soon as they arrived. Evangeline knew this was their home, that the path back to the empress's boat could be just as dangerous, leaving everyone out in the open for an attack, but it was more dangerous here. If Jaden showed up—

Sudden pain erupted in her lower stomach, knocking her backwards. Her head slammed against something hard, her world dancing.

"We finally meet again, Eve. I've been waiting for you."

Evangeline blinked, piecing together the figure towering over her. Jaden reminded her of a shadow with dark boots, pants, and a simple coat with his long black hair tied back. The only color was his green eyes, which looked down at her with something she could only describe as contempt.

"Same here," she rasped out, her stomach still clenched in pain. She mentally reached out to the beast that had stirred at Jaden's approach, its presence oddly comforting right now as her insides screamed. He was here. Jaden was actually *here*.

And he was too close to the village, with her nowhere near the marked tree. "Granted, I hadn't expected to be greeted with a fist to the stomach."

Jaden shrugged, making no move to help her up. The sound of something wet and bulky echoed to her left, then right, and Evangeline knew with sinking clarity she was surrounded by Wretched. *I need to get up. I can't let him take the advantage. I can't let him attack this close.* With the help of her beast and Rasha's training, she surged to her feet at a speed that had taken Avana off guard, her signal ready to be ignited in her right hand, but Jaden had already disappeared. Without waiting, Evangeline spun and launched herself toward the edges of the village, where she could make out the diagonal, Rathan-made slash on the giant truck still paces away.

A blur, and then suddenly her legs were kicked out beneath her, her signal stick flying behind her and landing with a thud several feet away. Evangeline called on her beast again, letting it surge through her veins, her muscles, urging her to rebound even faster.

Jaden's eyes narrowed, as if his beast sensed hers. She blocked one of his fists aimed again at her stomach, but she missed the blow to her shoulder, catching her off balance. She landed back on her feet, her balance a product of training and the help of her monster racing through her blood. She could now track his movements better if her eyes remained fixated on him. *The signal, I must let the others know.* But she was nowhere near where she was supposed to fire it, and it was still too close to the village. *I don't have a choice. If I don't try, Jaden will kill me or could hurt the others.*

Jaden's smile didn't reach his eyes, which hadn't left hers for a single moment. "I see you're not as useless as you used to be, but you're still in denial about who you are. It's holding you back, but don't worry. I can help with that." The sound of metal unsheathing rang in her ears before the sleek, curved sword appeared at his side. The Wretched hummed around her in one gathered chorus like mud shoving through man-made grooves, seeping closer to the domes. "Either way, we both know I'll win. I always win, Eve. One day you'll learn to accept that."

No, no, no, he's going to attack the village. He's going to attack the village! She unsheathed her own sword, shorter than his and limiting her reach. She had to get to that blasted signal; she couldn't take on Jaden and all the Wretched by herself. "We both know that's not true. We wouldn't be here, in a time that doesn't belong to us, if you had gotten what you wanted."

He snarled and lunged. It took all her might to counter before his blade could hit her chest. It was too late when she realized he gripped his sword with only one hand, the other aimed for her ribs. She dodged at the last second, his knuckles grazing her side. *He's too spitting fast!* Too fast to lure him away, let alone defend herself.

Her sword matched his with a series of clangs, the humid air rushing into her lungs, her eyes widening to catch Jaden's movements, the uncanny clarity that came with the power of the beast. His blood, rich and familiar, called to her and nearly eclipsed her train of thought. *Focus! Get to the signal!* But every time she made to move, Jaden was there, his sword glinting with a sharpness aimed to take her head off.

You're on the defensive. He hasn't expected a counterstrike yet, she told herself, sweat building beneath her coat and stinging her eyes and nose. *But it's only because I can't get in a blasted counterstrike!* But with his attacks keeping her on the defensive, he wasn't expecting her to attack back, and with her current speed and skill—beast or no beast—she was no match for him. She would have to fight dirty.

Jaden spun, an unnatural grace to his steps. His sword knocked hers from her grasp, a hiss rushing out through her clenched teeth as the smell of her own blood hit her nose. In her temporary daze, Jaden snagged her jaw in his hands and squeezed until she thought it would pop. "Why do you keep betraying me, Evangeline?"

He brought her closer. Almost as if to kiss her before she snapped out her leg, shoving her foot into his gut. He growled, his eyes shifting to a blinding white, an array of colors gleaming at her. The moon was covered in a clot of clouds, but the beautiful irises reflected back at her all the same, not needing light to showcase their ethereal nature.

"I'm not her anymore, Jaden," she panted, withdrawing the daggers at her side.

His eyes softened briefly. "No, but you're so close, Eve. The anger, the hate we used to share together. You're getting closer to your true self."

Evangeline dodged at the last instance, yelping as the blade found purchase along her upper left arm, leaving a gash, but it allowed her to feint a lunge for Jaden's neck. He blocked it with ease, but that wasn't her goal. She spun on her heel and leapt for the innocuous-looking stick, a deep green, nearly blending with the foliage. She twisted the signal, activating it at the same time screams pierced the quiet village.

Evangeline's blood ran cold. She was too late.

A dark, sinuous tentacle wrapped around Evangeline's arm, yanking her off-balance. With the beast roaring in her skull, she whipped around to the disgusting, massive shape of Wretched writhing in the shadows and alleys of the domes and trees. There were far more than she had originally seen, far more than she or any of them could manage. The stench reminded her of an animal that had been decaying for several days, but if she cut one open, she knew its blood would call to her like a starved man sitting before a feast.

"Eve!"

Her head whipped around to find Ceven, Barto, and a cluster of warriors barreling behind him. Blood—both black and crimson—speckled his form, and his wings shook the trees, bushes, and grasses around him as he propelled towards her.

"Cev—" She crumpled to her feet, pain vibrating up her spine. She sucked in air between her teeth, the smell of blood, *her* blood, flooding her senses.

"You should know better than to take your eyes off me, Evangeline. Surely you remember that much." Jaden loomed over her, sword aimed at her throat. It reminded her of all the scenes in her books she'd read over the years, when the villains appeared to have the upper hand, when all hope seemed to be lost for the good guys, the crew would come in to save the day. But she wasn't sitting in the castle's library, curled up on her favorite armchair with an exciting novel pressed between her legs. She was piled in front of Jaden, her life spilling from her and pain radiating throughout her body. The smell of blood and fire tainted the air, screams and ringing metal playing the melody of war, one she'd heard for most of her old life. Ceven and the others sprinted to save her, but they wouldn't make it in time. She was on her own.

I am strong, I am fast, I am capable. To think otherwise is to forfeit before the fight has even begun. Evangeline had been admitting defeat to herself far before this fight even began, but it wasn't over yet. Not until she couldn't move, or Jaden's head was on the floor.

Or my teeth were in his neck.

Evangeline blinked, an uncanny calm settling over her as her gaze fixated on the blood thrumming through his veins. His blood called to her, belonged to *her.*

Jaden smiled. "I know what you want, Eve. Are you ready to remember everything? Have the anger and hate had time to fester?" The tip of his sword dug into her throat, the warmth of her blood trailing down the sides of her neck, and his gaze trailed it, the whites of his eyes glowing brighter. "Release yourself and feed from me. I want you to remember what they did to us. What this world did to us, before you turned your back on me. On us and our kind. I want you to remember *everything.*"

Evangeline snarled and lurched to her feet, knocking the blade away and gripping his neck beneath her nails. Her eyes locked with his, faces inches apart. Hunger, rage, hatred, and a longing so deep it hurt to think about warred in her chest. The beast crept up her veins, reaching for him while engulfing herself.

A knowing smile played at the edges of Jaden's lips, his eyes reflecting her own sparkling orbs back at her. "You've denied the beast's hunger for far too long, Eve."

The pounding of feet and shouting reached her ears over the siren call of Jaden's blood. The pulse beating at his neck. She vaguely felt the shot of fear, her own internal screaming to pull back, to hide herself as Ceven and the others gathered closer, but it was too late. Jaden was right; she had denied the beast for far too long, and she was helpless to stop it.

Dredging up the remaining ounce of control she had left, she whispered into Jaden's neck, her elongated teeth brushing his skin. "You said you'd tell me what your plans are. I'm ready." She lifted her eyes as Ceven ran, arm outstretched for her. So close. Too close. Their gazes clashed, his widening when he caught her unnatural eyes, her lips peeling back to show sharp fangs. His outstretched hand faltered, his steps slowing as his expression betrayed Evangeline's worst fear.

Goodbye, Ceven. Then she sank her teeth into Jaden's throat.

CHAPTER 34

⸎ EVANGELINE ⸎

Roses wafted in on the summer breeze, the sun illuminating the clear blue skies and beaming through the window of Jaden and Evangeline's bedroom. The rays brushed the tips of Evangeline's slippers, warming the side of her face where she no longer sat at the windowsill. Instead, she shot to her feet as the peaceful, beautiful world turned dark. As if reality were an illusion and the harsh truths existed within its cracks, waiting to emerge like weeds in a flowerbed.

"You can't be serious, Jaden." Evangeline's arms had dropped to her side, the tips of her fingers rubbing her silk gown, seeking any type of comfort from this situation.

Jaden had entered their shared bedroom, dressed in gold and black finery. The edges of his collar were trimmed in glossed patterns, the cuffs folded and lined with ornate buttons tucked into form-fitting slacks. His hair was brushed back, his chiseled face appearing as if it had been carved from granite.

Always put together, ever since they had won the war. He was the biggest illusion of all.

He looked as if he hadn't heard her, fixing the collar of his shirt in their standing mirror, which was encased in gold and lined with false metal flowers. Gaudy and excessive like most things in this castle. "I will begin the preparations. Organize our people." He turned to her, a smile stretching his lips, though it didn't reach his eyes. "Don't worry, I always come back alive."

Her fingers curled into fists. "I'm more concerned for the citizens you wish to slaughter. You can't just kill them because they were born different, Jaden. Doing this . . . we'd be the same as those who enslaved us."

"The *rebel* forces will be taken care of swiftly," he stressed, his lips flattening in disapproval, and she hated herself for wanting to concede, to bring a smile back to his face once more. But conceding, letting Jaden do this . . . this would prove that they were the monsters everyone believed them to be.

"I won't have anyone threatening our safety, the new lives we have built for one another. For our people." He walked towards her as Evangeline stepped back, bumping into the wall. Not even the sun's touch could warm the ice prickling her skin. Invading her heart.

She stiffened as he cradled her cheek in his hand, a matching gold band resting on his finger. His eyes flicked to her neck, to the healed gash where a rebel soldier had attacked her during an outing into town. The cut had been deep, almost taking her life. She had dealt with the attacker swiftly, his blood healing the wound he created. No one else had gotten hurt, and she had made a full recovery. She had the situation handled, but Jaden . . . Jaden had lost it.

His green irises darkened before shrinking, overtaken by a cascading wave of color. "I'll eliminate them all," he murmured. "I'll make sure *no one* ever hurts you again."

The room vibrated in a low hum of machinery and buzzing lights, a sound that simultaneously calmed her and terrified her. It was her birthplace, the sounds of what she would consider to be her mother's womb. It also was the same place that separated her from everyone else in the world. Made her irrevocably different.

Evangeline walked past the glass tubes spanning the wall of the lab, her hand tapping the life-sized cylinders. They were now empty, no longer active, but it had been where she and her kind spawned from. Where it all began, before she and Jaden had participated in the Council's wars, before they started their own rebellion. Before they took over and subjugated the very Nytes that had enslaved them.

The doors of the lab slid open to a Caster in a white robe with her black hair plastered to her sides and bunched in tangles around her horns. Dread crawled down Evangeline's throat to curdle in her gut as she met Anali in two strides, gripping her sweat-slicked hands. The scientist's eyes rounded, the usual calm blue that had always reassured Evangeline completely vanished.

"Anali, what is it?" She gripped their hands tighter, her mind pacing through all possible scenarios. There was an attack on the castle, Jaden was hurt, or worse—he had hurt others. She cursed herself for leaving the castle, for traveling north with Anali in search of answers. In search of solutions.

Anali's mouth opened and closed like a fish out of water. So unlike the intelligent Caster who had a hand in raising her and Jaden, always confronting problems with a level head and a clear mind.

"I didn't plan on telling you, but the others have pushed my hand . . ." Then, as if remembering herself, she took a deep breath. "There's something I never told you. About you and Jaden, your kind. If I had it my way, we'd all take this secret to our graves, but the other scientists want to release this news to the public and . . ." She swallowed. "And if this gets out, we will witness a war the likes of which these lands haven't seen in millennia."

Evangeline scrunched her brows. "Anali, what are you talking about?"

She rolled her shoulders back, the swift change morphing the terror into indifference. "It's better if I show you."

CHAPTER 35

Raiythlen sat crouched between two domes, panting and shoving down a stick of dried meat between breaths to stave off the lightheadedness creeping in. His finger throbbed from the number of blood runes he'd placed around the village's perimeter. The ones he'd placed earlier in the day had already been consumed, the horde of Wretched slamming into the invisible walls, disintegrating them in blue fire like moths to a flame. Only problem was he hadn't anticipated this many would come out and attack, shedding his barriers quicker than he could put them back up.

Tor, a few villagers, and Zelene's warriors stood in the village center, equipped with crossbows and swords, plucking off the Wretched that managed to slither past his magic. Zelene, Ceven, and the others he'd left behind in order to protect the village had been holding off a troop of Wretched and marked soldiers. Seeing his grandmother's magic twisted in such a way was like a stab to his gut every time he encountered its destruction first-hand. This time was no different. The cursed soldiers were innocents, victims to the swarming black symbols wrapping their bodies, but Jaden had left them no choice. Raiythlen's Caster fire still streaked the ground and trees paces to the east where he'd set aflame a group of them. The rest had met the empire's blades.

Sucking in a gulp of air, he surged to his feet, gripping the side of a dome for support, his head throbbing. Sliding to his belt, he withdrew a vial, tipping back the contents in one swallow. It wouldn't replenish what his body really needed, rest and mineral-rich food, but it would act as a temporary bandage for now. He needed to find Evangeline.

His blurred vision managed to snag back into focus enough for him to follow the clash of blades closer to the village than the other bouts of fighting throughout the surrounding woods. Leaning against a tree, sliding his body between its base and adjacent shrubbery, he spotted Jaden and Evangeline locked in battle. The first thing that stole his attention was their eyes. Something he'd never seen before but had read about in Anali's journals before he burned the ones he managed to get his hands on. It'd sounded impossible—unbelievable—but he couldn't deny what he was seeing. The eerie glow of coalescing colors in the place where the iris and pupil should be, the speed at which they clashed and withdrew in an ebb and flow of metal and blood.

Ceven's shout stole Evangeline's attention, and Raiythlen cursed the prince as Jaden used it as an opening to disarm her. Despite their pre-planned arrangement, Raiythlen's daggers

were already in hand, ready to join the fight, when Jaden paused, something passing between them he couldn't hear from this distance.

Then she sank her teeth into his neck.

Raiythlen froze, enraptured by the scene unfolding before him. The red fluids dripping down the side of Jaden's neck as he cradled her close. As if they were embracing for the first time in years and not ripping out each other's throats.

A wave of pressure snapped his arrested gaze, sweeping over him like a blanket made of needles. He'd never seen another traverse a Shadow Door besides him or his sister, the portals a hidden part of history after their collapse centuries ago when traversing them became too unstable. Jaden made it look effortless, a slash of arm movement, his skin—his mark—illuminating before he entered the portal, cradling Eve in his arms, her teeth still clasped to his neck as if she would die without him.

Then they were gone.

He immediately climbed out of his hiding spot, running toward the shimmering distortion in the midst of splatters of blood and pockets of dug dirt where their violent dance had been. Jabbing his finger with the sharp point of his serpent ring, he rolled up his sleeves and got to work, drawing the Castanian runes for "protect" and "sacrifice" along his arms, muttering their incantations under his breath. The Shadow Door wouldn't take anything more than the magic he was willing to give it.

He added the final touch to his forehead, "locate," the same symbol he had etched into the nape of Evangeline's neck. It was a risk for her to stop taking the anti-magic concoction, saliver, in the meantime, but it was the most efficient path for Raiythlen to track her down.

"Bring her back." Ceven came up behind him. His friend and bodyguard had halted a distance behind him, as if uncertain about the scene they had all just experienced. Proof that something not quite human, but not quite Nyte either, existed. That something else lurked among them, making them question everything they'd been taught to believe. Or maybe Raiythlen was projecting his own thoughts onto their blank stares.

Ceven clenched his sword, whose jeweled hilt blazed a vibrant blue, his eyes shot through with pink veins. Black and red blood stained his leathers and the right side of his wing, matting the blue and gold feathers together in clotted heaves. It was a feat those were his only injuries; Raiythlen had witnessed him take on a horde of Wretched led by two marked soldiers alone. Maybe he'd survive long enough to become king after all.

He waved his hand, as if the situation were far less grave than it was. And it appeared so, as more of Zelene's soldiers emerged from their surroundings unscathed, the call of fighting dwindling. "I plan on it. Besides, she asked me to ahead of time." Though ripping out her ex-lover's throat wasn't something they had anticipated, Evangeline got what she wanted all the same—to find Jaden's true hiding place. Now as long as the crazed advisor didn't find the Caster mark, Raiythlen should be able to track Evangeline down and leave breadcrumbs for the others to pick up Jaden's real location.

Raiythlen grinned at the prince's confused expression, not feeling an ounce of pity. He hadn't seen Evangeline's true potential, but Raiythlen certainly did.

Ceven hurled a curse at him, but Raiythlen was already sinking into the portal, the distortion growing and wrapping around his being like an invisible hug that squeezed too tightly. He concentrated on Evangeline, brushing the symbol on his forehead and homing in on her presence, pulling on the thread that appeared in his mind's eye. Other threads dangled before him, linked to different locations. He felt them, rather than saw them, an innate knowing telling him where each would lead, but he only cared about one.

The world spun, magic pulling at his limbs in attempt to rip him apart, but the magical coat kept him intact as everything grew brighter and brighter before suddenly depositing him in the dark.

The smell of decay, trapped moisture, and lingering smoke assaulted him. Scrunching his nose, he thumbed the onyx coin in his pocket, another layer of magic enveloping him once more. He blended in with the muted rock and creeping darkness that clung to the myriad tunnels and passageways, barely lit with the occasional lantern fixated every twenty paces or so. He hoped Jaden hadn't sensed his arrival, that this Shadow Door was nestled far enough away. Time would tell, his hand never straying too far from his arsenal belt.

However, the more he trekked, the more of a chore it was to keep himself moving, the amount of magic he'd used today weighing on him like he'd been sitting in an ice bath for far too long. If it wasn't for the Caster mark he'd placed on Evangeline, her string of energy, a magenta swirl visible only to his eye, leading him through the twists and turns of the underground caves, he'd be hopelessly lost. Still, every few intersections, as he crept and waited for any signs of movement, he'd slip a thumb-sized cartridge into the groove of a rock. He'd shown the empress prior how the tracking devices worked, his location now marked on her end within the palace. Whether or not the empress will be able to infiltrate this maze of underground tunnels was another story. Especially since it was in Ostin Lon, protected by the treacherous Araji Sea from passing boats and turbulent winds from flying airships.

Lanterns morphed into ornate candelabras and vintage lamps—absurdly out of place given the rest of the barren, dark cave—as crimson rugs trimmed in gold frills padded his steps, covering the uneven rock prodding underneath.

Murmurs had him freezing in his tracks, one hand on his dagger, the other on his belt of potions. He'd seen Jaden fight—Evangeline fight—and he didn't even know if he could go up against something like that on his best day, let alone now, depleted and worn as he was.

Get in, get out, he muttered in his head.

The tunnel he traveled swerved into a makeshift room complete with a canopy bed, navy blue rugs and a vanity that looked to have been stolen from a noble's estate. Why the crazed man even bothered dressing up a cave, he had no clue. As an esteemed advisor, Jaden had his own quarters within the palace, but it seemed he preferred his opulent isolation in the middle of a barren wasteland of a country.

The invisibility magic still clung to his skin, disguising him with the jagged stone in various shades of blues, grays, and greens as the lights grew brighter in this section of the caves. He didn't know enough about Evangeline and Jaden—aside from their unnatural speed and taste for blood—to know if their sense of smell was heightened like a Rathan's or if their hearing was as elite as the Wretcheds'. Erring on the cautious side, Raiythlen crouched roughly thirty paces away. Close enough to glimpse Jaden looming over Evangeline, who was lying atop the sea of blue blankets and pillows from across the hall, but far enough to avoid drawing attention.

Jaden whispered something to her, red still slashing his neck, but it was no longer bleeding. Or at least, he paid it no mind, his fingers tracing Eve's closed eyes. Raiythlen wished he could hear; in other circumstances he would down the blue corked vial at his belt to listen in to even the softest of murmurs, but the layers of magic he'd already piled on himself sank into his bones like lead, his eyes dangerously craving to close. And he still needed enough magic to protect himself and Eve when they escaped back through the Shadow Door. Or fend for his life.

A few more whispers and then Jaden left Eve's side, Raiythlen carving himself into the side of the tunnel wall as much as he could, willing his body to relax, his heartbeat to slow as he managed his breaths in a pattern that matched the combined atmospheric sounds of water dripping alongside the hum of lighting.

Once the former advisor was out of sight, Raiythlen glided on silent feet to Eve's bed, checking for traps or anything to warrant a quick escape. When nothing probed his internal alarm bells, he turned to Eve, her chest moving to the steady rhythm of sleep. Despite the dirt and blood caking her sides, shoulder, and face, something about her was . . . different now. Almost ethereal.

She didn't stir when he drew the runes "protect" and "sacrifice" along her neck, the only parts of skin that were currently bare. He retraced his own, gritting his teeth as the magic pulled at his being, like he sat in the desert and the sun was soaking up the rest of the water in his skin. Pinching himself to keep awake, he gently prodded Eve, but she didn't move, not even when it progressed to an urgent shake. He cursed under his breath.

Sliding his hands beneath her, he gritted his teeth and lifted. He didn't have time to care that her head lolled backwards or that his grip was far from firm. Not to mention his invisibility magic didn't envelope her as it should've, a testament to his body no longer cooperating with his magic. *You owe me big time, Eve.*

It took every ounce of his willpower to keep his breathing steady and Evangeline from tumbling out of his hold as he navigated the tunnels, looking for the tracking devices to indicate he was on the right path. However, none of that mattered when he stumbled upon Jaden halfway back to the Shadow Door, leaning against the wall with his arms crossed as if waiting for him. *Expecting* him.

Raiythlen was royally screwed.

"I sincerely hope you're not taking my wife away, just as soon as I found her." Piercing emerald eyes pinned him in place. Raiythlen rarely felt a healthy dose of fear anymore, his years of doing the Council's dirty work—about which the citizens would riot if they ever knew the truth—evicting the emotion that had once ruled his life in his earlier years. But Raiythlen would be a fool not to feel it in this man's presence.

Raiythlen's usual mask slipped into place—not that Jaden could see it with his invisibility magic around him, or perhaps he did given how little Raiythlen knew of him—more for his sake. To ease back into the role of the carefully controlled and untouchable agent, disguising the exhausted and frightened Caster underneath. "I'm just following orders. Don't kill the messenger, so to speak."

"And whose orders are those?" Jaden's smirk rivaled his own, shoving off the wall and striding toward them with all the grace of a predator stalking its prey. "That way I can be sure to kill you both."

Raiythlen's arms wobbled from the strain, his breathing more labored. His mind whirled through a series of different plans, all of which didn't bode well for him. He'd have no choice but to activate a flash grenade this close, double that with a smoke bomb—

Jaden blurred out of focus before appearing in front him, his hand slamming into his throat as Raiythlen's invisibility fell away. Jaden's mouth unhinged, fangs extending from its depths. Evangeline slipped from Raiythlen's grip as he reached for his tool belt.

Evangeline hit the ground, her eyes snapping open to an iridescent white. "They were *my* orders," she growled.

Jaden turned his head in time for her to slam two fingers into his eye sockets.

Air squeezed back into Raiythlen's lungs as Jaden released a howl that would haunt his dreams for weeks to come. Raiythlen coughed, stumbling on his feet as he felt fingers firmly wrap around his bicep, yanking him forward. His body followed, like a puppet on strings. It took several more inhales, blinking the dizziness from his head, before he caught Evangeline, pulling him in the opposite direction of the Shadow Door he'd entered.

"*Evangeline!*"

Another scream, full of rage, pounded off the sharp rock biting the heels of their feet. The space ahead of them flowed differently. A rip in reality.

Raiythlen closed his hand over Evangeline's. He whispered the incantation to activate the magic on them, nodding that it was safe to leap into the rift as pressure burst from behind them. Not a Shadow Door, but something malevolent, something dark. Raiythlen swore he felt the tips of fingers brush the nape of his neck as they dove into the rippling portal.

This time was far different than any other trip before, his fingers tangling Evangeline's in a death grip as the rift yanked and pulled at his magical shield, trying to take more than he was willing to give. Landscapes of trees, waters, towns, cities, all buzzed in his mind too fast for him to grasp, his mind on the precipice of collapse. It was only instinct and years of traversing these Doors that allowed him to pick a location that hopefully wouldn't deposit them miles underwater or in the pit of a volcano.

Unlike the last time they'd traversed a Shadow Door together, Raiythlen emerged stumbling to his knees while Evangeline landed on her feet, a feverish glow to her eyes. Not white like before, but heavy with an emotion he couldn't quite place. The portal had deposited them in a field, buzzing with insects that pummeled his exposed neck and face, tall grasses bleached of color stretching up to Evangeline's thighs and his shoulders as he hunched over. The sun split the sky in pinks and purples, arching through the trees, glinting off the dew that darkened his trousers where he collapsed. If he had to guess, they were still somewhere in the empire. Beyond that he had no clue, only that they needed to put as much distance between themselves and the Shadow Door as possible before Jaden figured out where they went.

Sucking in a pocket of air, he pushed to his feet. He reached for Evangeline's hand, ready to sprint, but she was already charging off at an envious speed.

"Show off," he mumbled, reaching for a flask at his hip. *One final push, then you can rest,* he bargained with himself as he swallowed the concoction whole. It would take a couple minutes before the potion would work through his system. If it did at all. He'd never pushed himself past this limit before, his magic becoming less potent as it fed off his own energy. Which was damned near empty at this point.

Evangeline paused, waiting for him at the edge of the trees lining the patch of open field. The damnable woman wasn't even out of breath.

A smirk teased her lips. "Do you need me to carry you?"

With the rising sunlight streaming behind her, highlighting the strangeness, the newfound grace that followed her movements, it was obvious the girl he'd first met in Peredia no longer existed. Something wholly different stood in her place now.

He raked in a shaky breath that humbled him. "At this point I'll let anyone carry me. Even my bloody sister if she offered." But then the magic hit his veins, expanding his muscles, his lungs. It wouldn't last long. He took off without waiting for her reply.

Endless terrain of grass, trees, and shrubbery chased them as the sun crept higher and higher. The rift grew farther and farther. They shared a look, pausing beneath the canopy of a tree that appeared to have been untouched by humans or Nytes for its entire lifespan, its trunk massive, the limbs branching out farther than the size of an average airship.

"I don't think he followed us," she said, her eyes still alight, a clash of blue and green like the reflection of the sea at midday. Raiythlen hated to admit it, but he was fascinated by them. By her. He knew she would be something else, but this . . . this far exceeded his expectations.

He leaned back against the tree, feeling as if his heart would climb out of his chest, sweat dotting his forehead. It was a crime to be running this exhausted, let alone in this heat with clothes that soaked up the sun like a fire consuming oxygen. "Well," he said once he caught his breath, "considering you jammed two fingers into his eye holes, it *may* be a tad hard for him to find us."

"He did seem a little upset by that." She smiled before her eyes, those captivating eyes, moved away from him. Staring off into the distance as if she were seeing beyond into another time. "But he will find me. Eventually. He won't stop until he has me, or I'm dead." She met his gaze once more. "The others . . ."

He clenched and unclenched the fingers of his mechanical arm, testing its movement post-fight and the rough treatment he'd put it through today. It needed another tune up, as much as he dreaded seeing his former companion again. "When I left, the tides of battle were in our favor. There were casualties, but as far as I'm aware, the villagers were still safe inside their homes. Thanks to me, of course."

She bit her lip, and Raiythlen knew what she wanted to ask. A part of him wanted to wait to see if she would, to assess what emotion would win. The inquisitive side that sometimes looked at others as if they were unidentified artifacts, a curiosity to be unraveled and dissected for a specific value, wanted to watch her struggle for the words. The other side, the much smaller one he usually kept hidden, relented, "Your prince is fine. A little distraught over seeing you taken by the enemy, sure, but alive."

A sigh, then another distant look. "I can't go back."

He cocked his head. "I didn't think you would."

Still needing to explain herself, she said, "As long as Jaden is alive, I'm a danger to whoever I'm around." She gave him a pointed look.

He shrugged. "If you haven't noticed, I'm not exactly the epitome of safety myself, with the Council still gunning for my death, among others," he added with a smirk.

Pushing off the tree, she shielded her eyes, scanning the vast plains around them. A soft breeze shimmered through the tall grasses like waves. No civilization in sight. "That may be so, but I don't think you'll be as agreeable for the next thing I'm about to say."

He stayed in the shade, the tree the only thing supporting him at this given moment. "If you say you've decided to join your prince in the fight for the throne, you may be right."

She shook her head. "As much as the thought pains me, I can't think about Ceven right now. I need to focus on stopping Jaden. I know what he's planning, but first . . . " She cast him a hesitant look. "I need to go to Sundise Mouche."

This time he sighed. "Well, I'm sure it's not to go sightseeing. So please, don't keep me in suspense."

Those heavy eyes fully turned to him. He knew why he couldn't place the emotion in them; it was because a chasm of them existed in unison, as if they all tangled together and couldn't be separated. "I need to go to the place I was born. Created. I need to find what your grandmother showed me centuries ago. It may be the key to preventing more bloodshed. To stopping Jaden."

Once her gaze caught his, he was unable to look away. Unable to muster up the humor that often shielded him from reality. This woman was dangerous in more ways than one.

"Raiythlen?"

He blinked and managed a nod. "I flew here on a private airship. I just have to figure out our location." Seeing her expression, he said, "Shadow Doors aren't the only way to get around. Besides, I don't think I can manage another trip anytime soon. I'm going to need to sleep for a week after this." He paused. "Are you sure you don't want to return to the others first? Even if it's to say goodbye?"

Evangeline stayed silent a moment before whispering, "I said my goodbyes." Rustling leaves and the melody of birds chirping filled the space for several beats before she continued, "Besides, if I return, Zelene won't let me leave. Not while I could be used as bait to lure Jaden to her. Not that she now knows what I am."

Raiythlen wasn't even fully sure he knew what Evangeline was.

They trekked off in a direction he hoped would get them to the coordinates of his ship, his thoughts curtailing to the mysterious woman traveling beside him. Evangeline would surely end up being the death of him, yet he couldn't wait to see what the future had in store for her. He had a feeling it lay on the precipice of altering the world as they knew it.

His lips curled into a grin. He couldn't *wait*.

GLOSSARY

Aerian(s)- A humanoid winged creature with extraordinary strength.

Atiacan(s)- Primary language spoke in Atiaca. Also refers to a citizen of Atiaca, or anything of Atiacan decent.

Castanian- Primary language spoke in Sundise Mouche and by most Casters.

Caster(s)- A humanoid creature with horns and the ability to perform magic through their blood.

Frostlite- A mineral found in the Frostsnare mountains. Reacts to Caster magic.

Halfling(s)- A creature born from two different species.

Millow Weed- A plant found throughout Atiaca. It has multiple medicinal properties but is predominantly used for pain relief.

Nyte(s)- Umbrella term for all superhuman species: Aerians, Rathans, Casters, and Wretched.

Peredian(s)- Primary language spoke in Peredia. Also refers to a citizen of Peredia, or anything of Peredian decent.

Rathan(s)- A humanoid creature that shares a likeness with a specific type of animal. Possess a greater agility and sense of smell.

Saliver- A plant found near riverbeds in the warmer parts of Atiaca. It's ingested to counteract Caster magic.

LEARN MORE ABOUT THE AUTHOR

www.AlexandriaCainlocke.com

Twitter: @WriterAlexLC

Facebook: @AlexandriaCainlockeBooks

Patreon: Patreon.com/AlexandriaCainlocke

ACKNOWLEDGEMENTS

While this book took a lot longer to write than expected, I'm super excited to finally share this with everyone. There were several times I thought this book would go in a different direction, the characters taking on a life of their own, but ultimately, I'm happy with how things turned out.

Thanks again to my amazing editor, Alexandra Ott, who has been monumental in shaping this series and helping turn earlier drafts into fully developed—and much more readable—novels.

To everyone at Enchanted Ink Publishing who always does a fantastic job with their cover designs and beautiful formatting. This series has turned out to be absolutely gorgeous.

To my family, whose support and love has been constant throughout this whole process.

To my friends who've stuck by me through all of my crazy shenanigans and continue to be my sounding board for all of my crazy ideas, it means a lot.

And to my readers who've proven that this story was worth sharing with the world, thank you so much!

ALEXANDRIA CAINLOCKE is a toss-up between artist, musician, writer, and avid gamer. Coffee is her number one life source and second love to her amazing friends and family. The sunshine state of Florida is where she was born and still resides.

www.ingramcontent.com/pod-product-compliance
Lightning Source LLC
Chambersburg PA
CBHW020348220726
48290CB00014B/1314